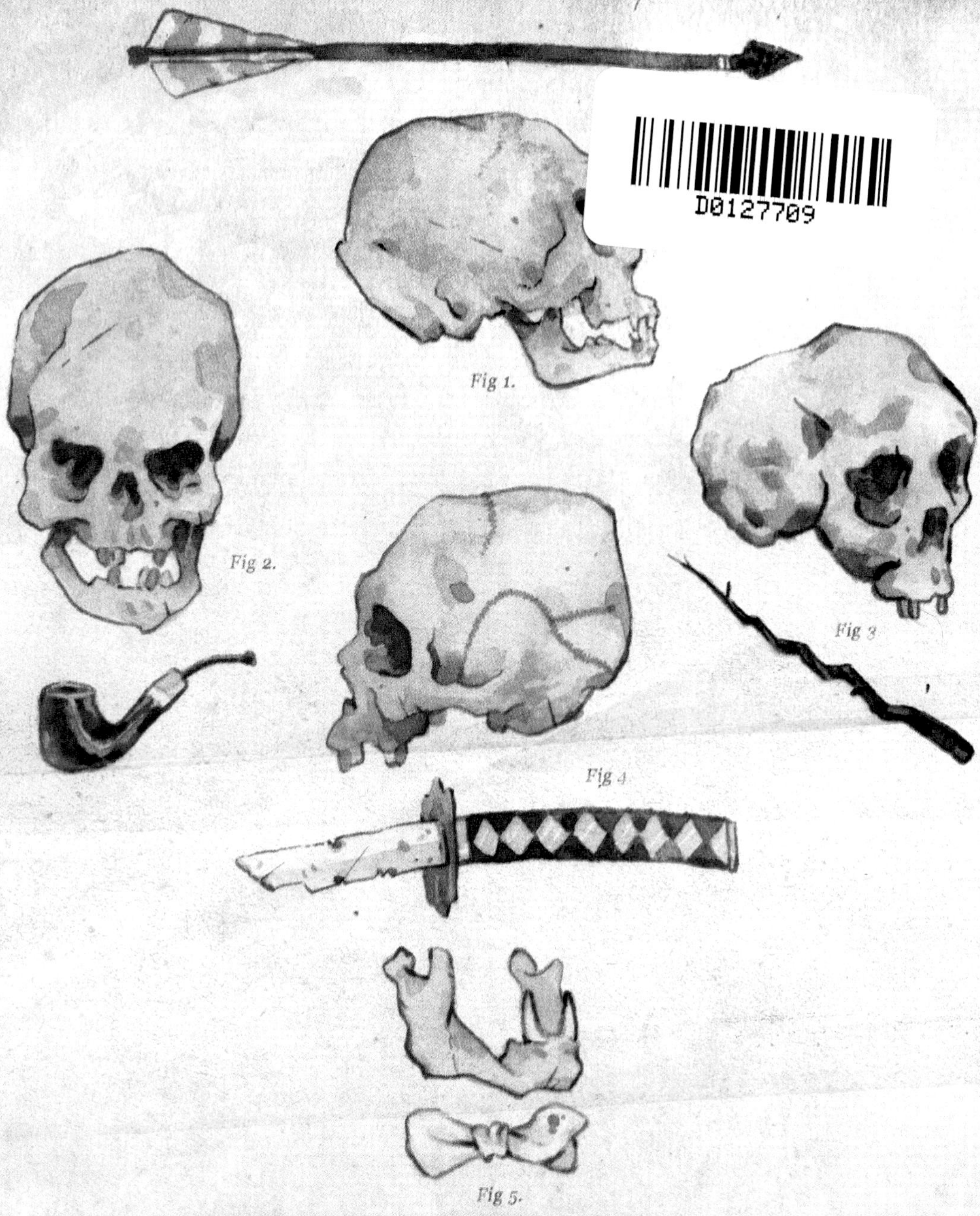
Fig 1.
Fig 2.
Fig 3
Fig 4
Fig 5.

METAMORPHOSES

NATURELLES

ou

HISTOIRE

de

FABIAN GRAY

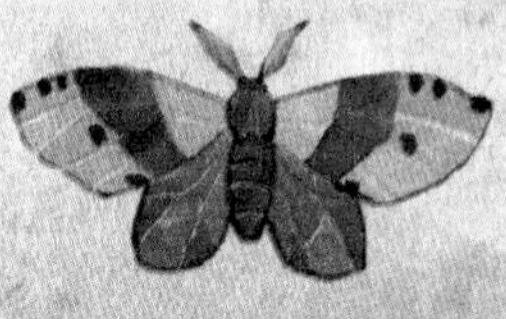

S.M. VIDAURRI

For Mom & Dad
— FJB

For my mother
— CTM

VARIANT COVERS BY **BEN TEMPLESMITH**
BOOK PRODUCTION BY **JANA COOK**

IMAGE COMICS, INC.
Robert Kirkman - chief operating officer
Erik Larsen - chief financial officer
Todd McFarlane - president
Marc Silvestri - chief executive officer
Jim Valentino - vice-president

Eric Stephenson - publisher
Ron Richards - director of business development
Jennifer de Guzman - pr & marketing director
Branwyn Bigglestone - accounts manager
Emily Miller - accounting assistant
Jamie Parreno - marketing assistant
Emilio Bautista - sales assistant
Kevin Yuen - digital rights coordinator
Tyler Shainline - events coordinator
David Brothers - content manager
Jonathan Chan - production manager
Drew Gill - art director
Jana Cook - print manager
Monica Garcia - senior production artist
Vincent Kukua - production artist
Jenna Savage - production artist
Addison Duke - production artist
www.imagecomics.com

FIVE GHOSTS, VOLUME 1: THE HAUNTING OF FABIAN GRAY.
ISBN: 978-1-60706-790-0. First Printing. September 2013.
Published by Image Comics, Inc. Office of publication: 2001 Center Street, 6th Floor, Berkeley, CA 94704.
Copyright © 2013 Frank Barbiere and Chris Mooneyham. Originally published in single magzine form as FIVE
GHOSTS #1-5. All rights reserved. FIVE GHOSTS™ (including all prominent characters featured herein), its
logo and all character likenesses are trademarks of Frank Barbiere and Chris Mooneyham, unless otherwise
noted. Image Comics® and its logos are registered trademarks of Image Comics, Inc. No part of this
publication may be reproduced or transmitted, in any form or by any means (except for short excerpts for
review purposes) without the express written permission of Image Comics, Inc. All names, characters, events
and locales in this publication are entirely fictional. Any resemblance to actual persons (living or dead), events
or places, without satiric intent, is coincidental. Printed in the USA. For information regarding the CPSIA on
this printed material call: 203-595-3636 and provide reference # RICH – 511613.
For international rights, contact: foreignlicensing@imagecomics.com

FIVE GHOSTS

THE HAUNTING OF FABIAN GRAY

WRITTEN BY **FRANK J. BARBIERE**

ART BY **CHRIS MOONEYHAM**

COLORS BY **LAUREN AFFE**

S.M. VIDAURRI

LOGO AND GRAPHIC DESIGN BY **DYLAN TODD**

1 THE WIZARD   2 THE ARCHER   3 THE DETECTIVE   4 THE SAMURAI   5 THE VAMPIRE

"Once meek, and in a perilous path,
The just man kept his course along
The vale of death.
Roses are planted where thorns grow,
And on the barren heath
Sing the honey bees."

--WILLIAM BLAKE

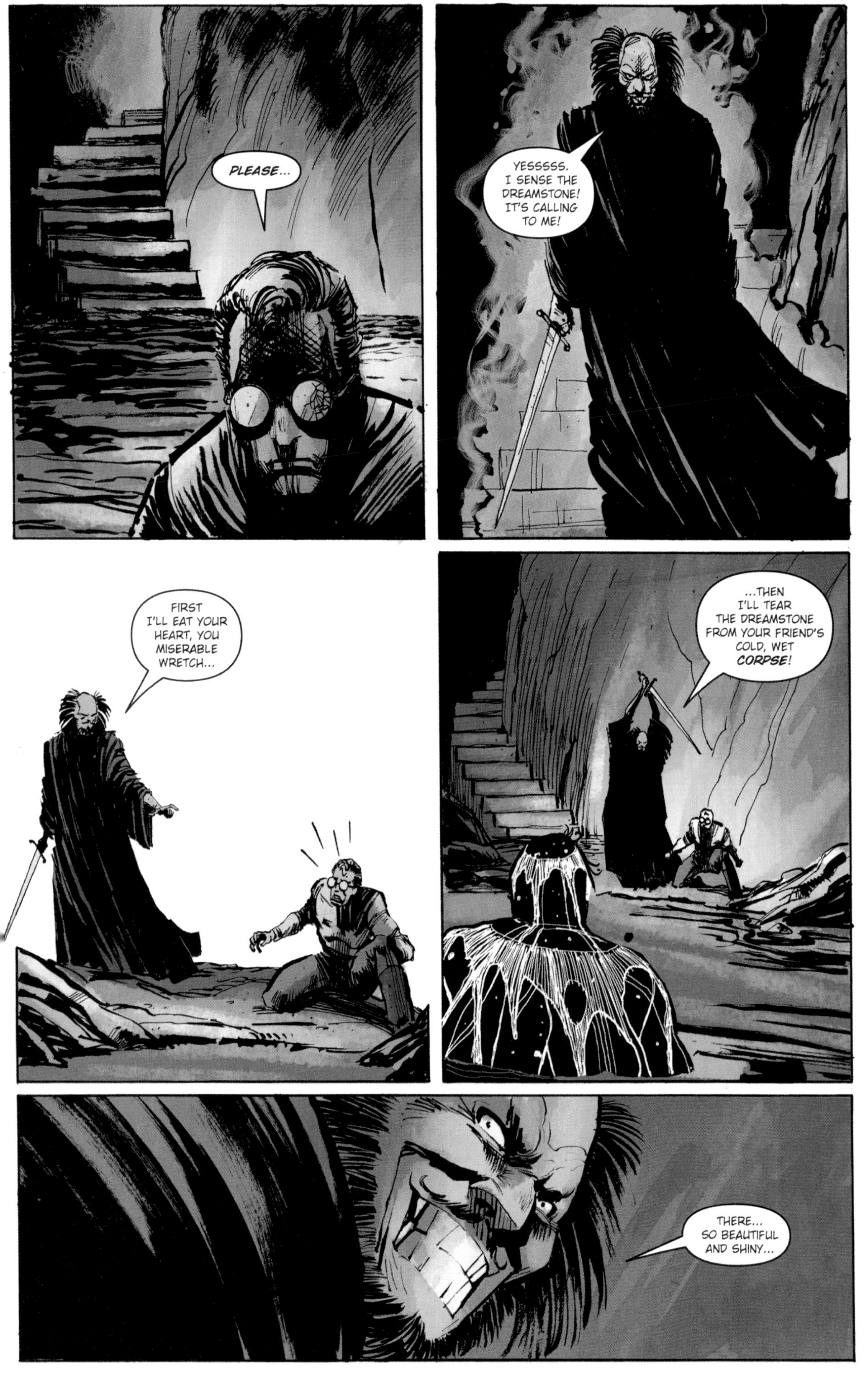
PLEASE...
YESSSSS. I SENSE THE DREAMSTONE! IT'S CALLING TO ME!
FIRST I'LL EAT YOUR HEART, YOU MISERABLE WRETCH...
...THEN I'LL TEAR THE DREAMSTONE FROM YOUR FRIEND'S COLD, WET CORPSE!
THERE... SO BEAUTIFUL AND SHINY...

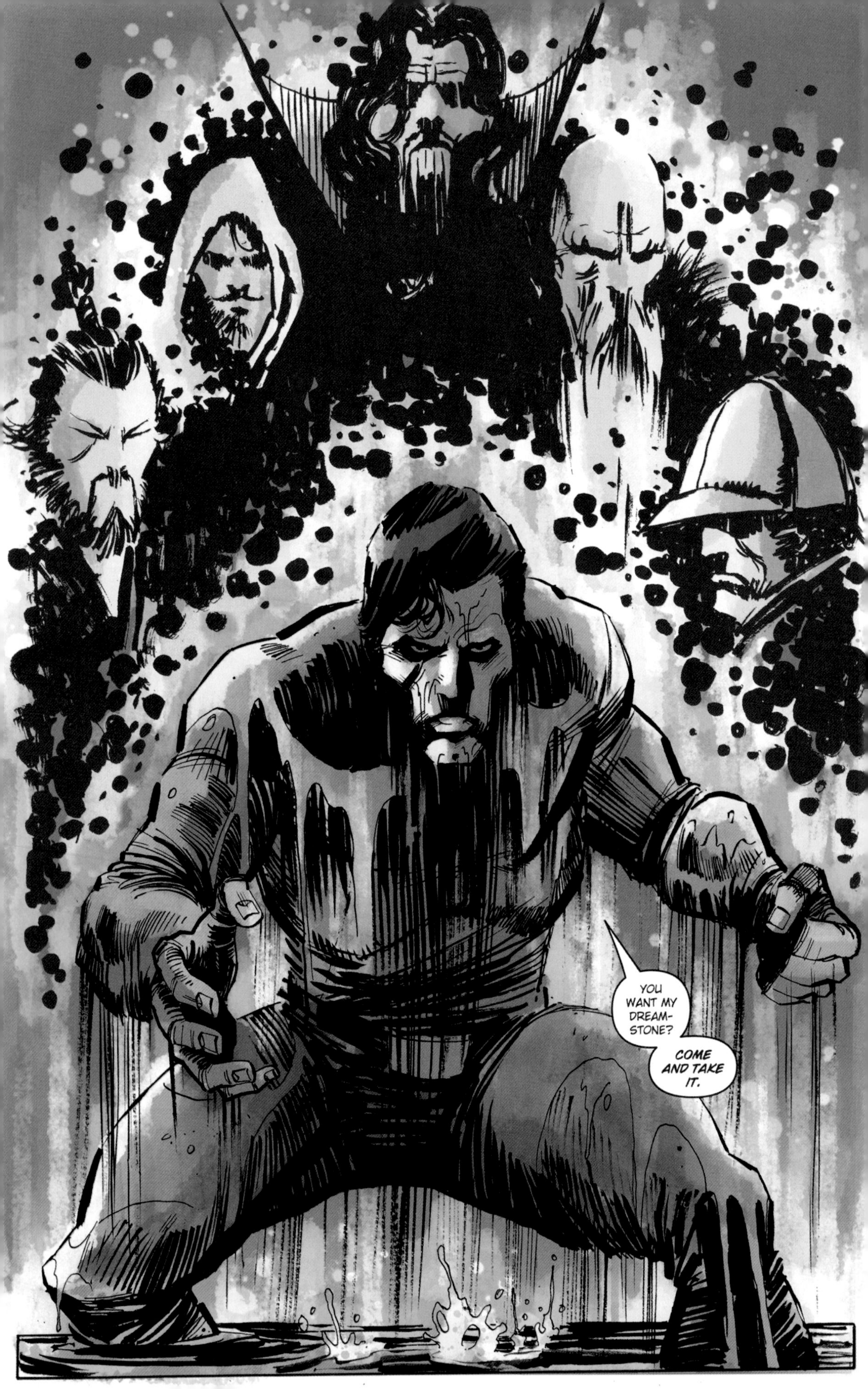
YOU WANT MY DREAM-STONE?
COME AND TAKE IT.

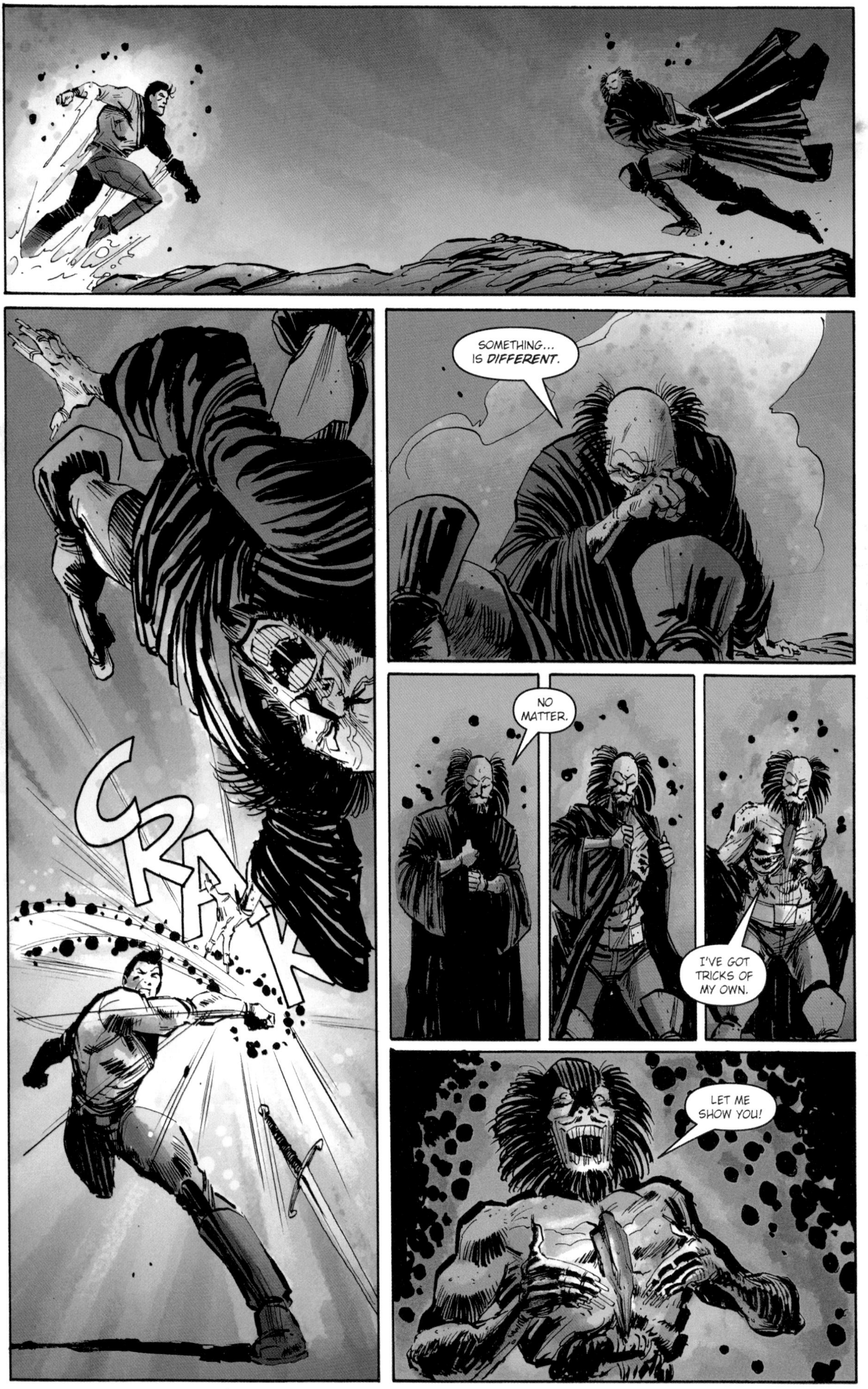
CRAK
SOMETHING... IS DIFFERENT.
NO MATTER.
I'VE GOT TRICKS OF MY OWN.
LET ME SHOW YOU!

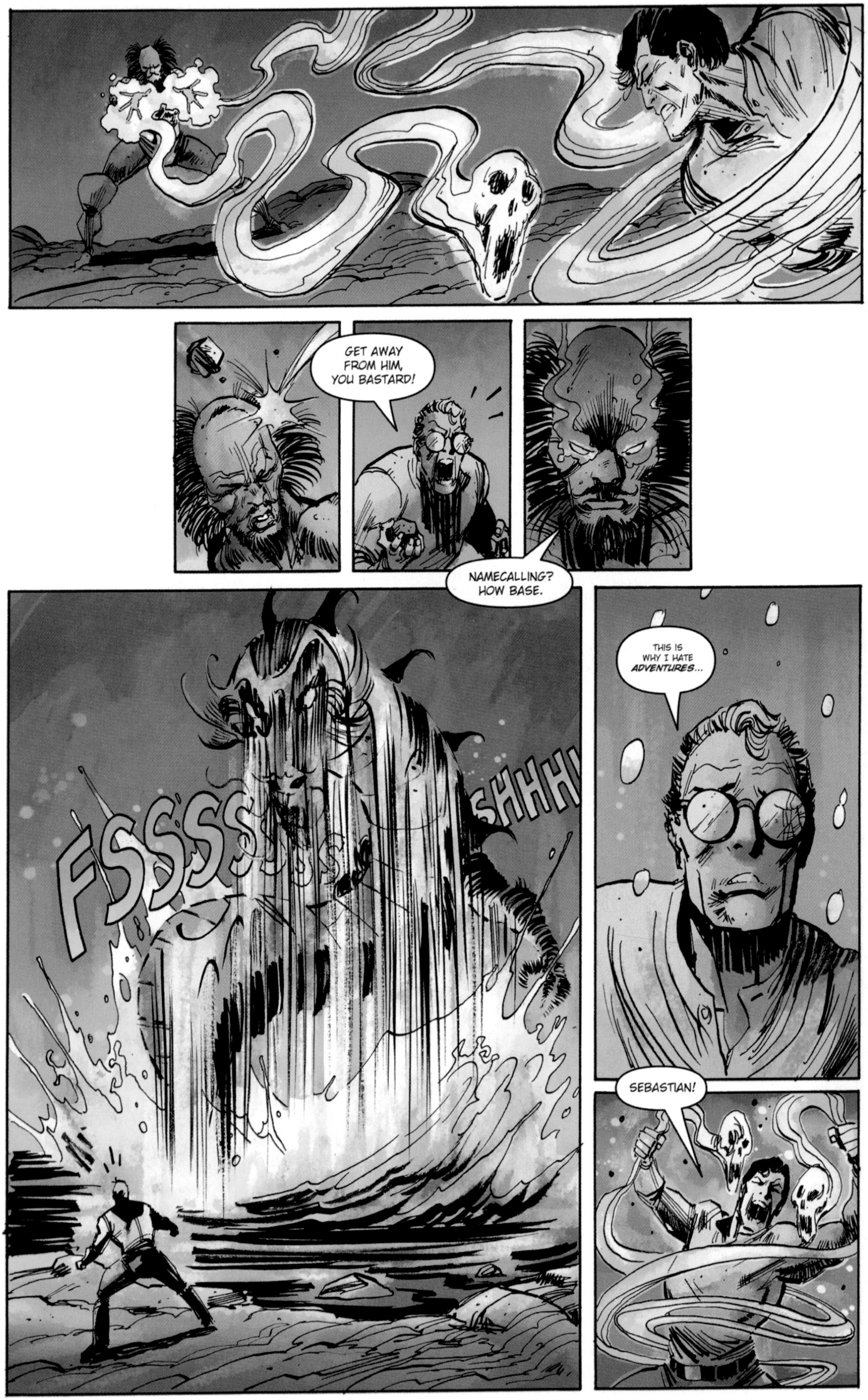

GET AWAY FROM HIM, YOU BASTARD!
NAMECALLING? HOW BASE.
FSSSSSHHH
THIS IS WHY I HATE *ADVENTURES*...
SEBASTIAN!

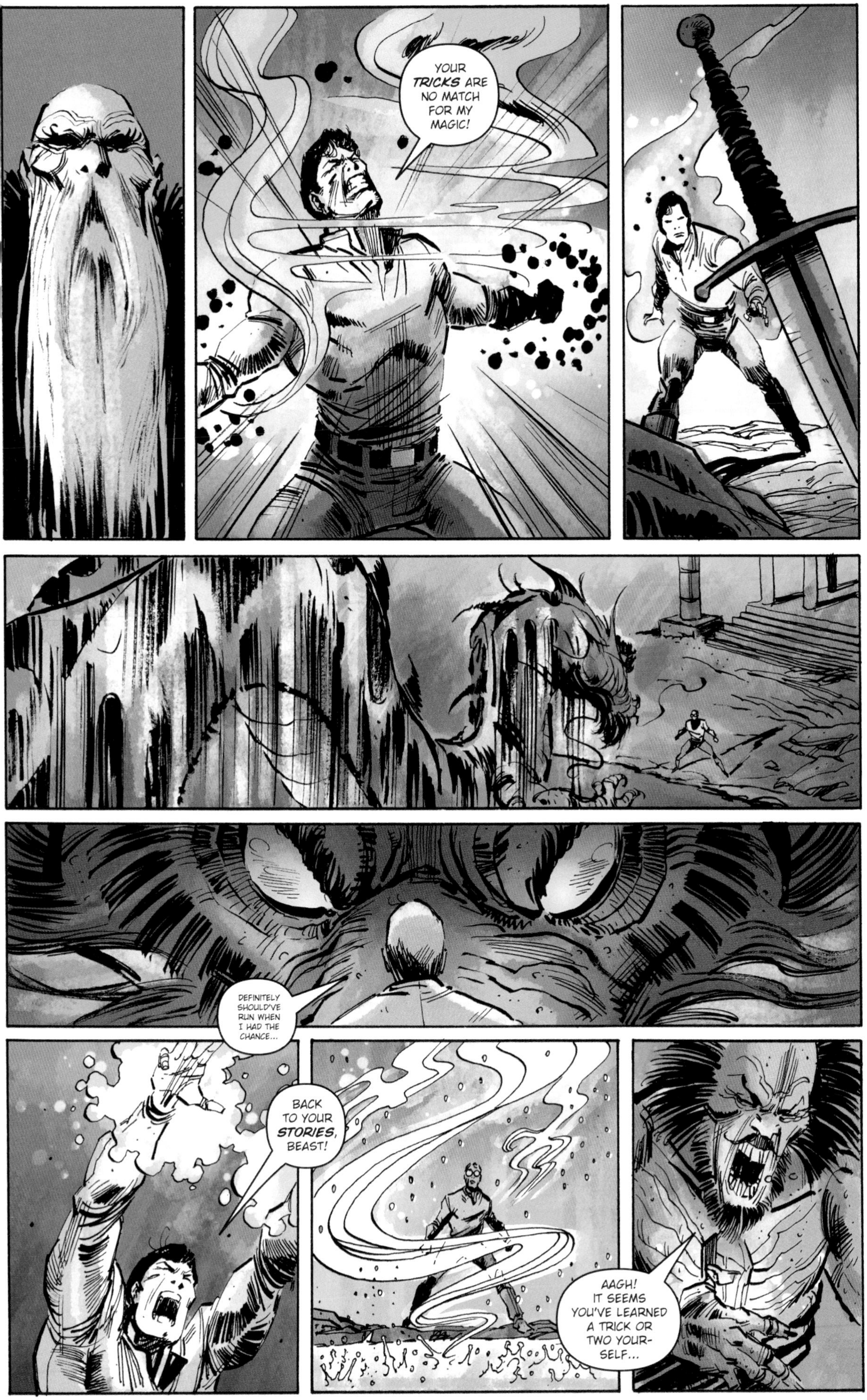

YOUR TRICKS ARE NO MATCH FOR MY MAGIC!
DEFINITELY SHOULD'VE RUN WHEN I HAD THE CHANCE...
BACK TO YOUR STORIES, BEAST!
AAGH! IT SEEMS YOU'VE LEARNED A TRICK OR TWO YOUR-SELF...

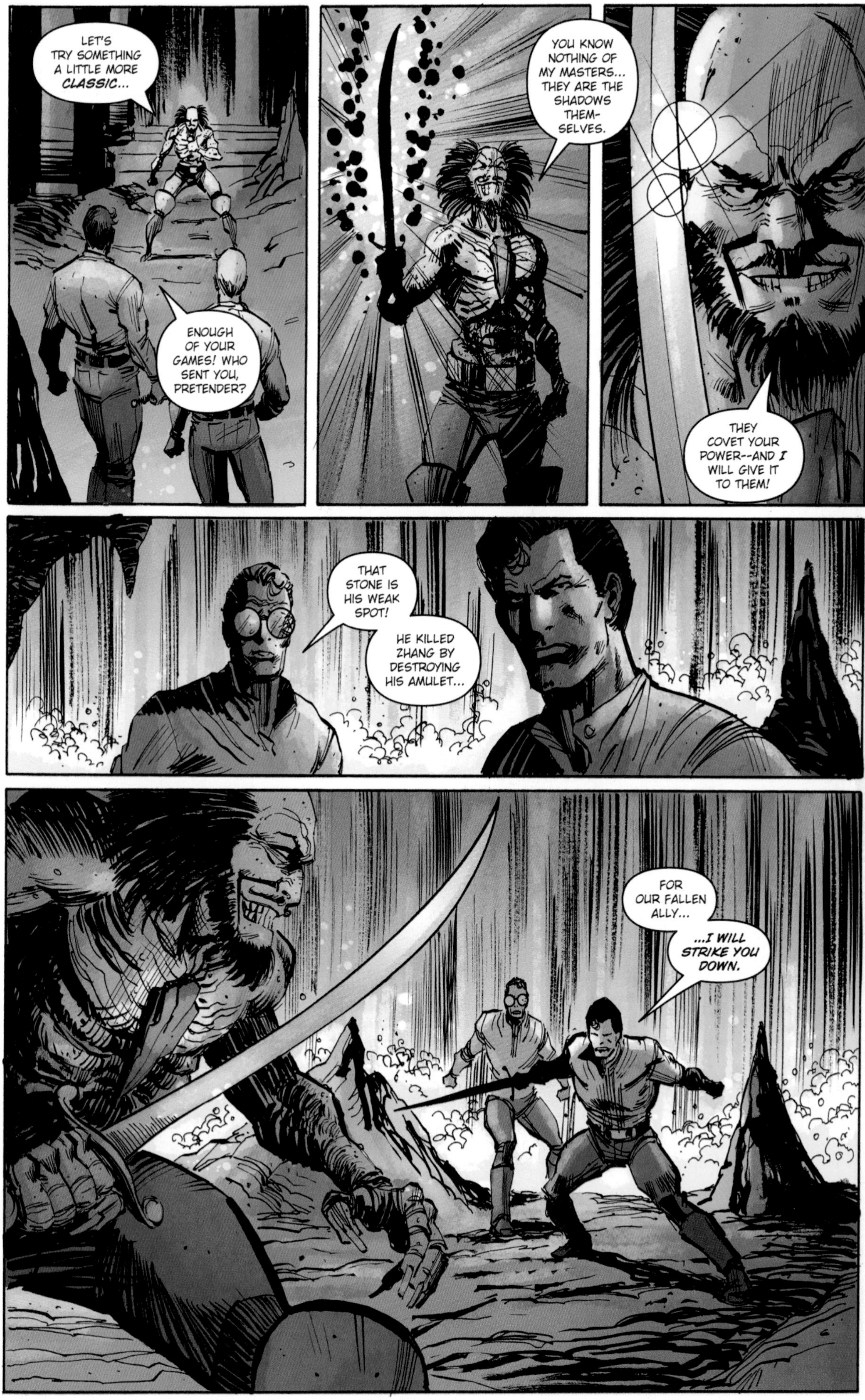

LET'S TRY SOMETHING A LITTLE MORE *CLASSIC*...
ENOUGH OF YOUR GAMES! WHO SENT YOU, PRETENDER?
YOU KNOW NOTHING OF MY MASTERS... THEY ARE THE SHADOWS THEM-SELVES.
THEY COVET YOUR POWER--AND *I* WILL GIVE IT TO THEM!
THAT STONE IS HIS WEAK SPOT!
HE KILLED ZHANG BY DESTROYING HIS AMULET...
FOR OUR FALLEN ALLY...
...I WILL STRIKE YOU DOWN.

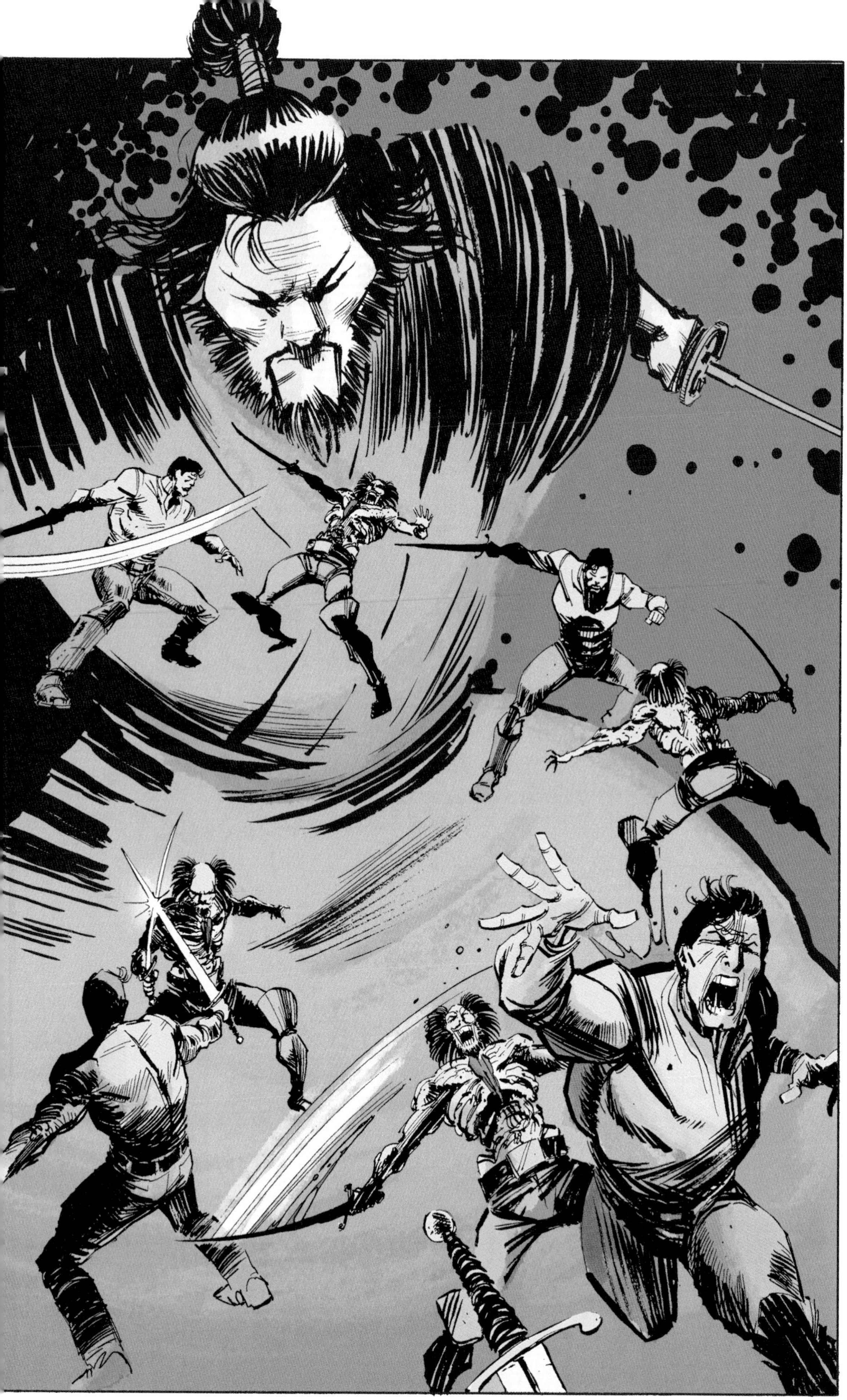

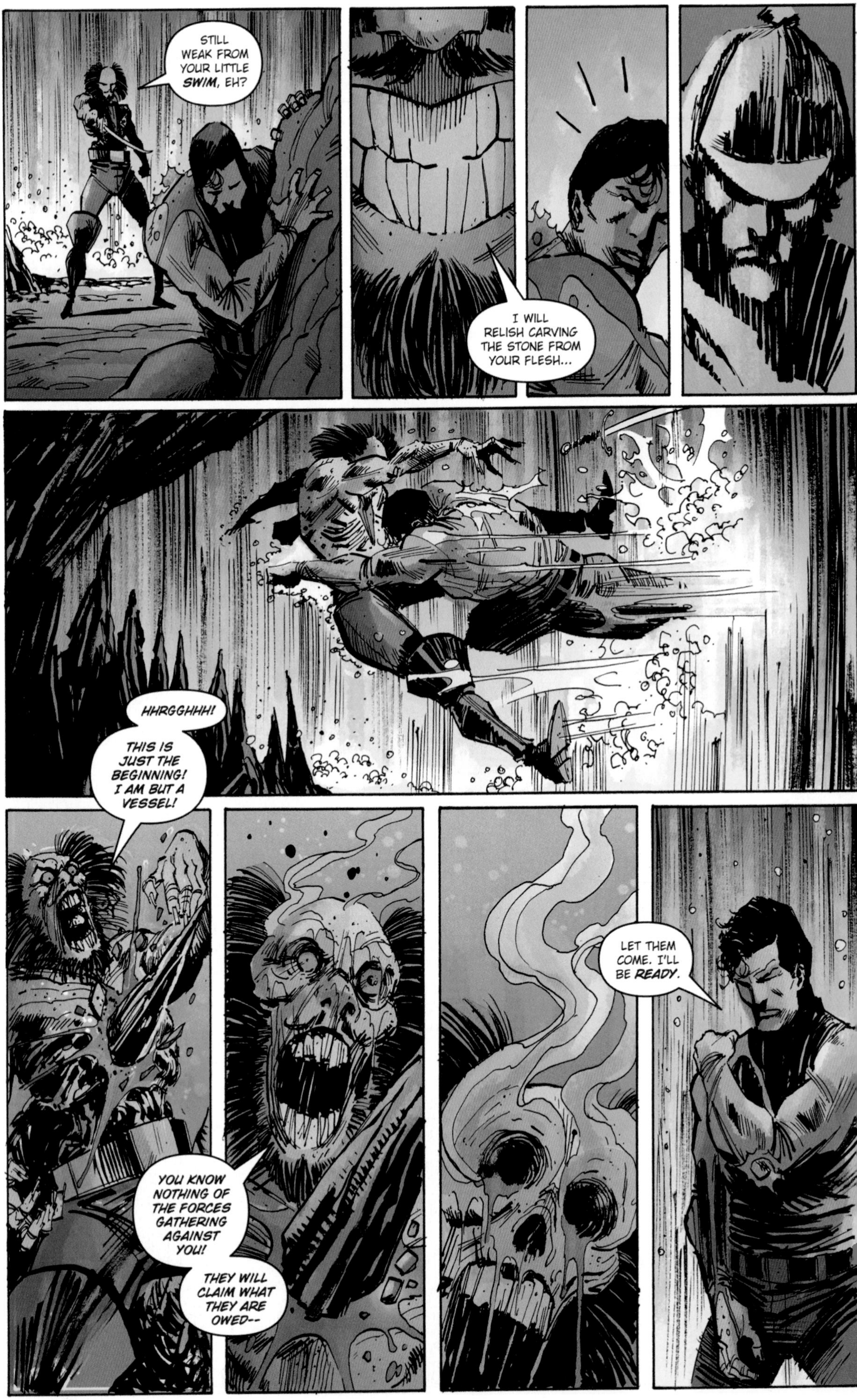
STILL WEAK FROM YOUR LITTLE SWIM, EH?
I WILL RELISH CARVING THE STONE FROM YOUR FLESH...
HHRGGHHH!
THIS IS JUST THE BEGINNING! I AM BUT A VESSEL!
YOU KNOW NOTHING OF THE FORCES GATHERING AGAINST YOU!
THEY WILL CLAIM WHAT THEY ARE OWED--
LET THEM COME. I'LL BE READY.

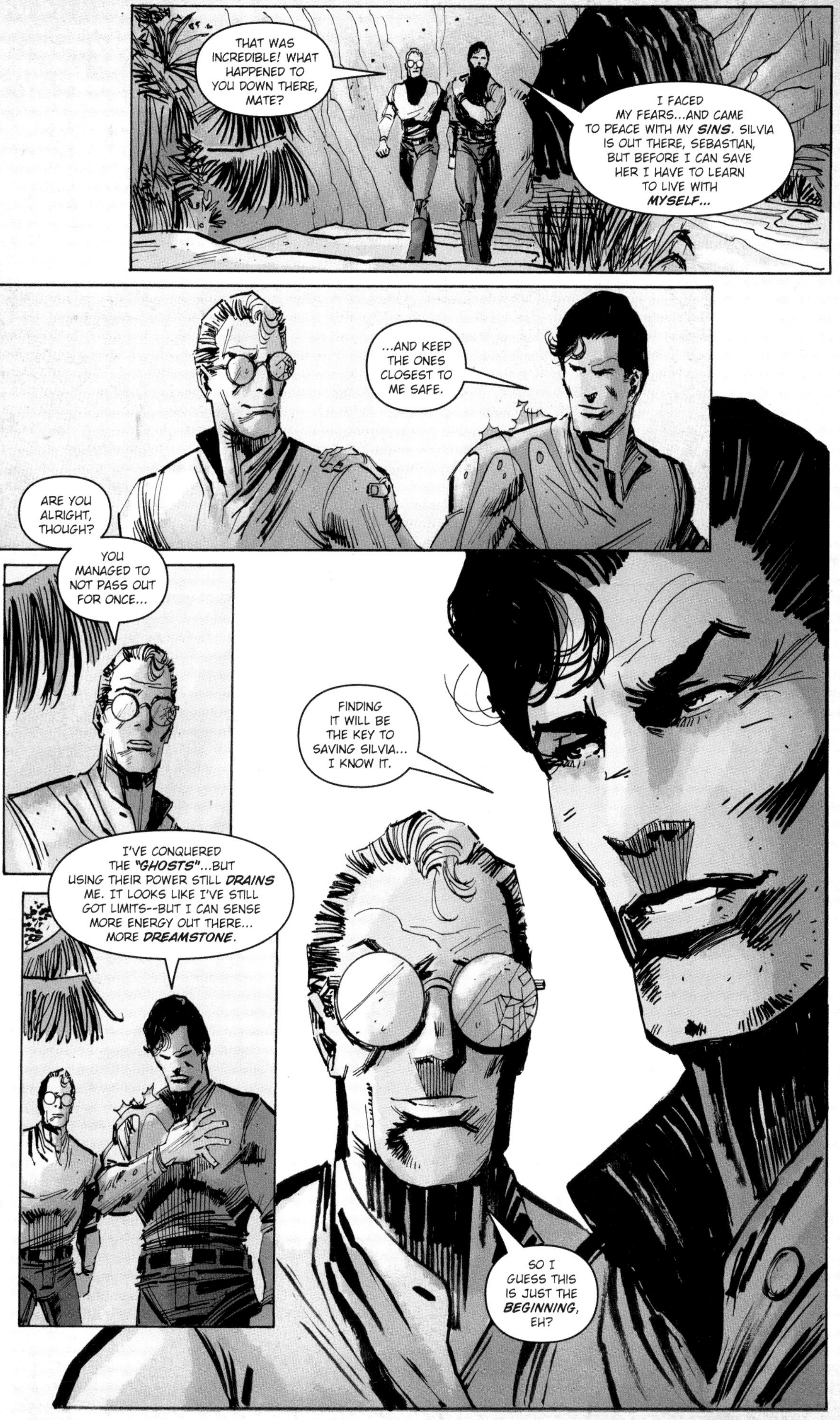
THAT WAS INCREDIBLE! WHAT HAPPENED TO YOU DOWN THERE, MATE?
I FACED MY FEARS...AND CAME TO PEACE WITH MY SINS. SILVIA IS OUT THERE, SEBASTIAN, BUT BEFORE I CAN SAVE HER I HAVE TO LEARN TO LIVE WITH MYSELF...
...AND KEEP THE ONES CLOSEST TO ME SAFE.
ARE YOU ALRIGHT, THOUGH?
YOU MANAGED TO NOT PASS OUT FOR ONCE...
I'VE CONQUERED THE "GHOSTS"...BUT USING THEIR POWER STILL DRAINS ME. IT LOOKS LIKE I'VE STILL GOT LIMITS--BUT I CAN SENSE MORE ENERGY OUT THERE... MORE DREAMSTONE.
FINDING IT WILL BE THE KEY TO SAVING SILVIA... I KNOW IT.
SO I GUESS THIS IS JUST THE BEGINNING, EH?

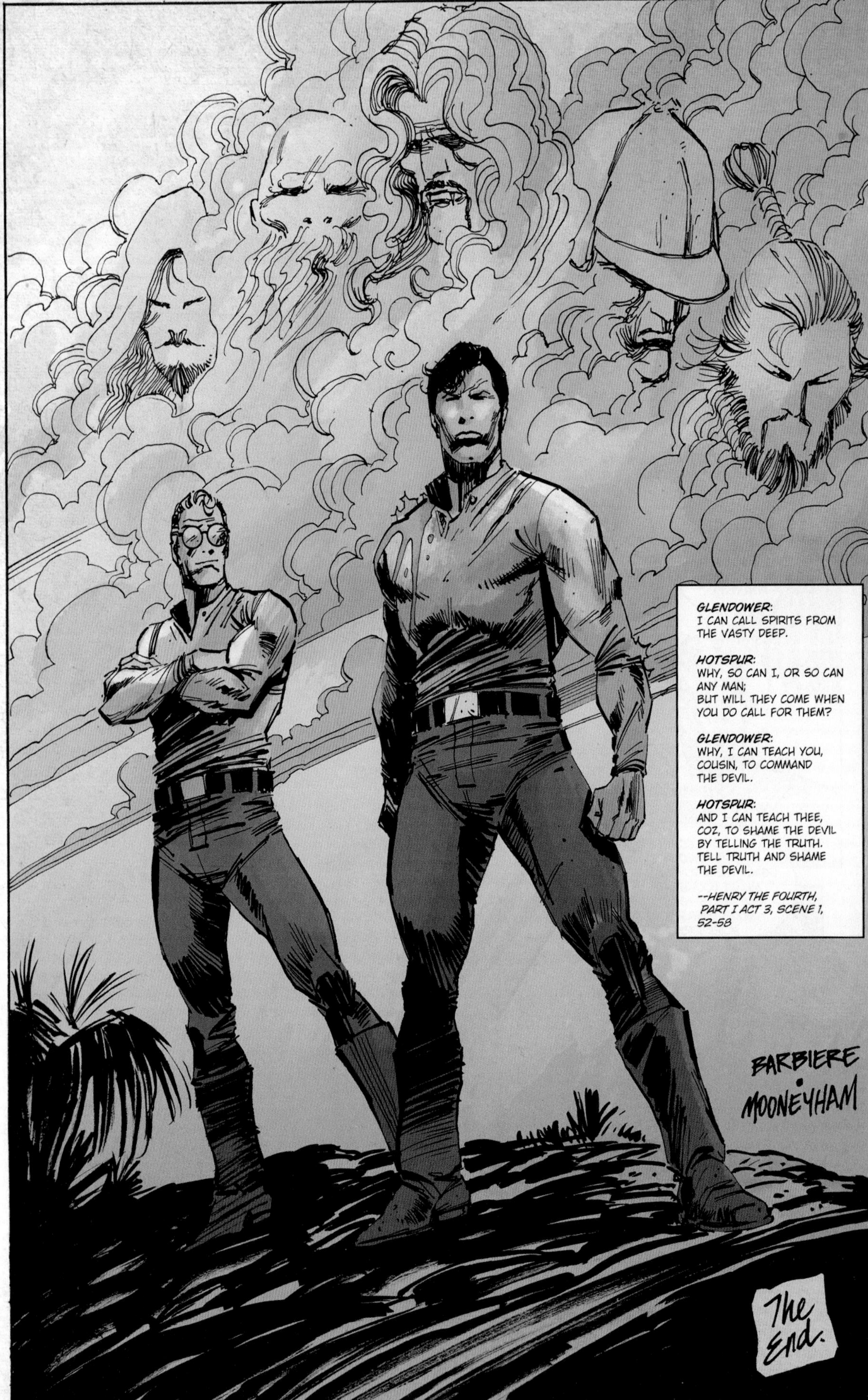
GLENDOWER:
I CAN CALL SPIRITS FROM THE VASTY DEEP.
HOTSPUR:
WHY, SO CAN I, OR SO CAN ANY MAN;
BUT WILL THEY COME WHEN YOU DO CALL FOR THEM?
GLENDOWER:
WHY, I CAN TEACH YOU, COUSIN, TO COMMAND THE DEVIL.
HOTSPUR:
AND I CAN TEACH THEE, COZ, TO SHAME THE DEVIL BY TELLING THE TRUTH. TELL TRUTH AND SHAME THE DEVIL.
--HENRY THE FOURTH, PART I ACT 3, SCENE 1, 52-58
BARBIERE • MOONEYHAM
The End.

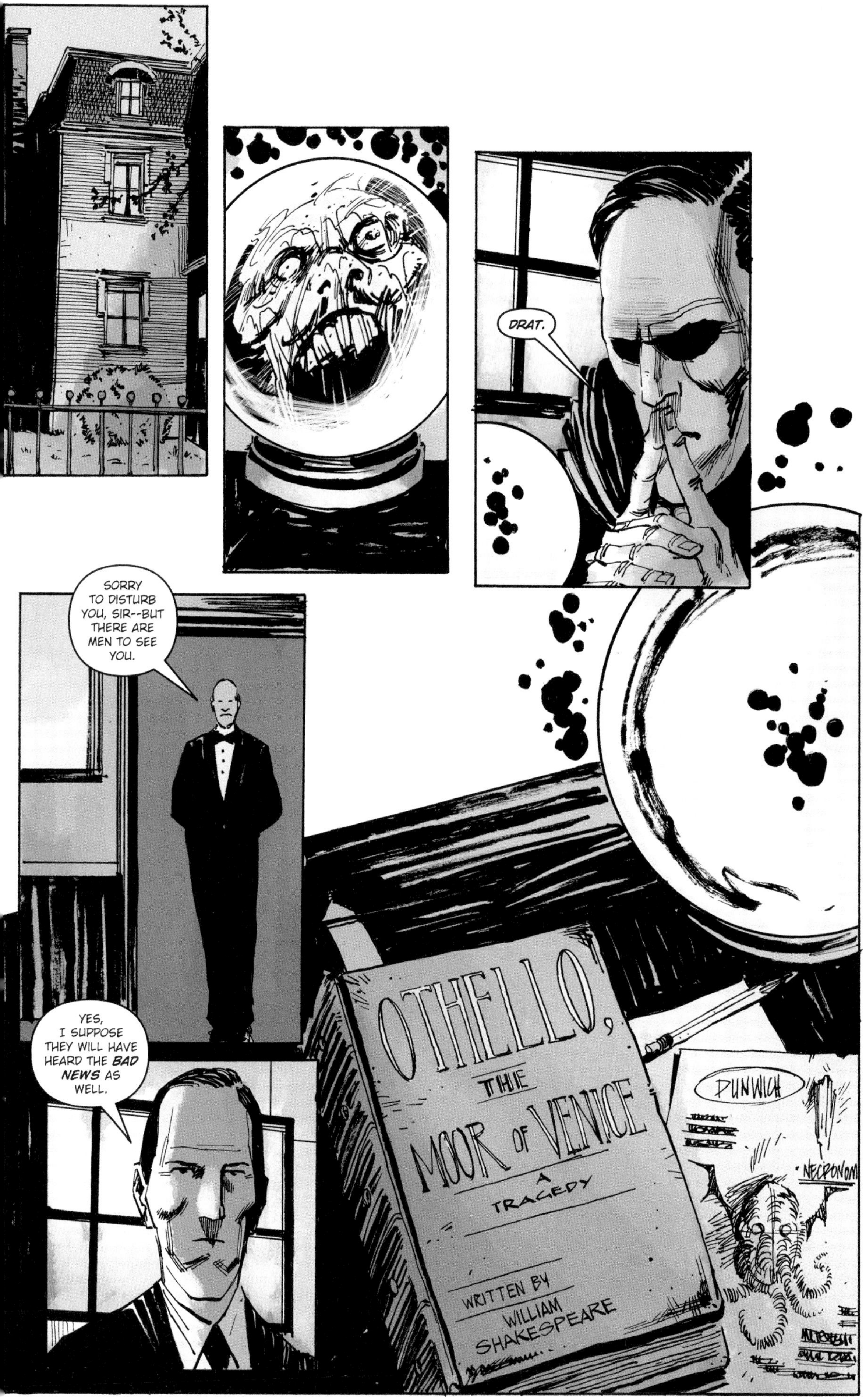
DRAT.
SORRY TO DISTURB YOU, SIR--BUT THERE ARE MEN TO SEE YOU.
YES, I SUPPOSE THEY WILL HAVE HEARD THE BAD NEWS AS WELL.
OTHELLO, THE MOOR OF VENICE
A TRAGEDY
WRITTEN BY WILLIAM SHAKESPEARE
DUNWICH
NECRONOM

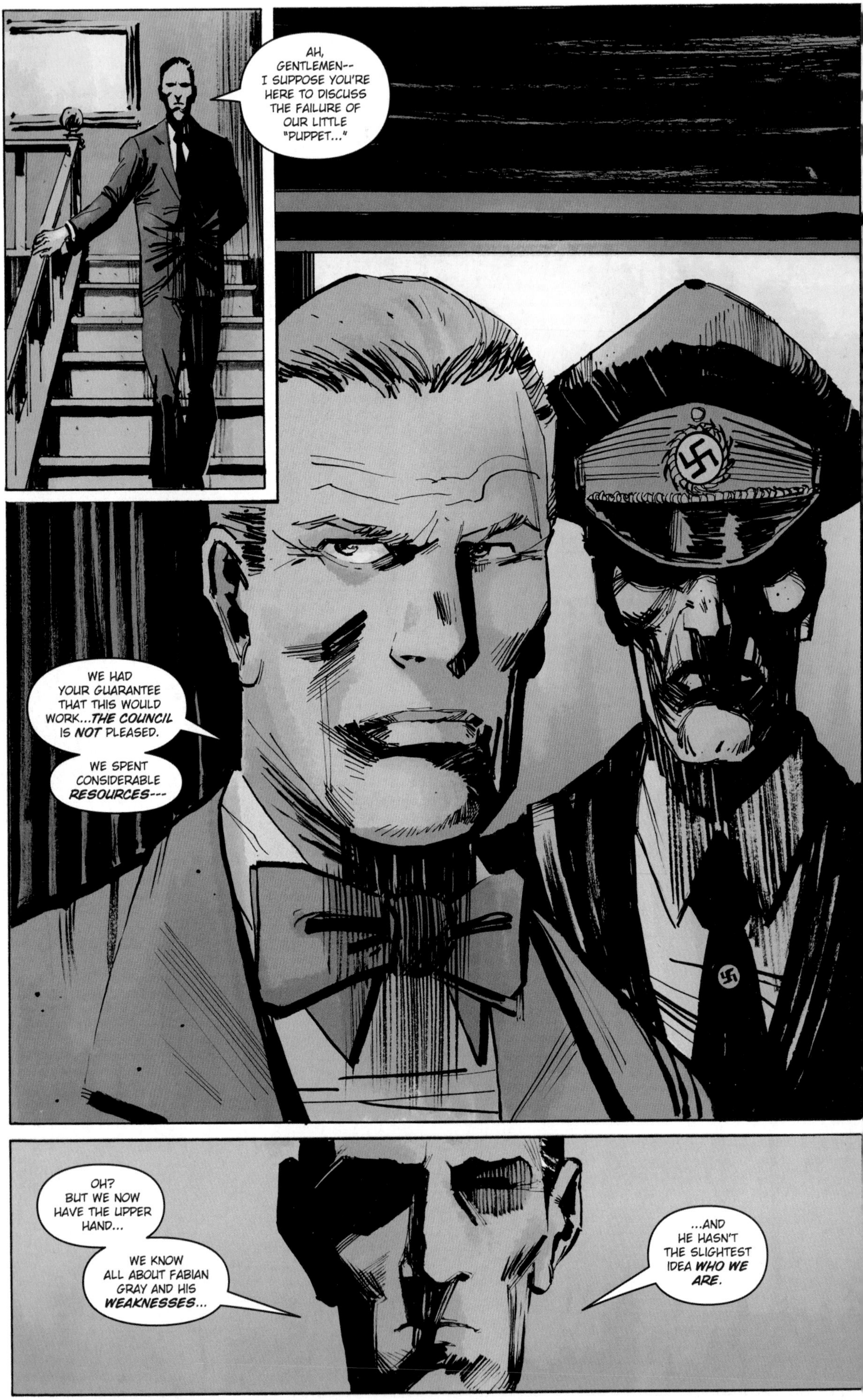
AH, GENTLEMEN-- I SUPPOSE YOU'RE HERE TO DISCUSS THE FAILURE OF OUR LITTLE "PUPPET..."
WE HAD YOUR GUARANTEE THAT THIS WOULD WORK...THE COUNCIL IS NOT PLEASED.
WE SPENT CONSIDERABLE RESOURCES---
OH? BUT WE NOW HAVE THE UPPER HAND...
WE KNOW ALL ABOUT FABIAN GRAY AND HIS WEAKNESSES...
...AND HE HASN'T THE SLIGHTEST IDEA WHO WE ARE.

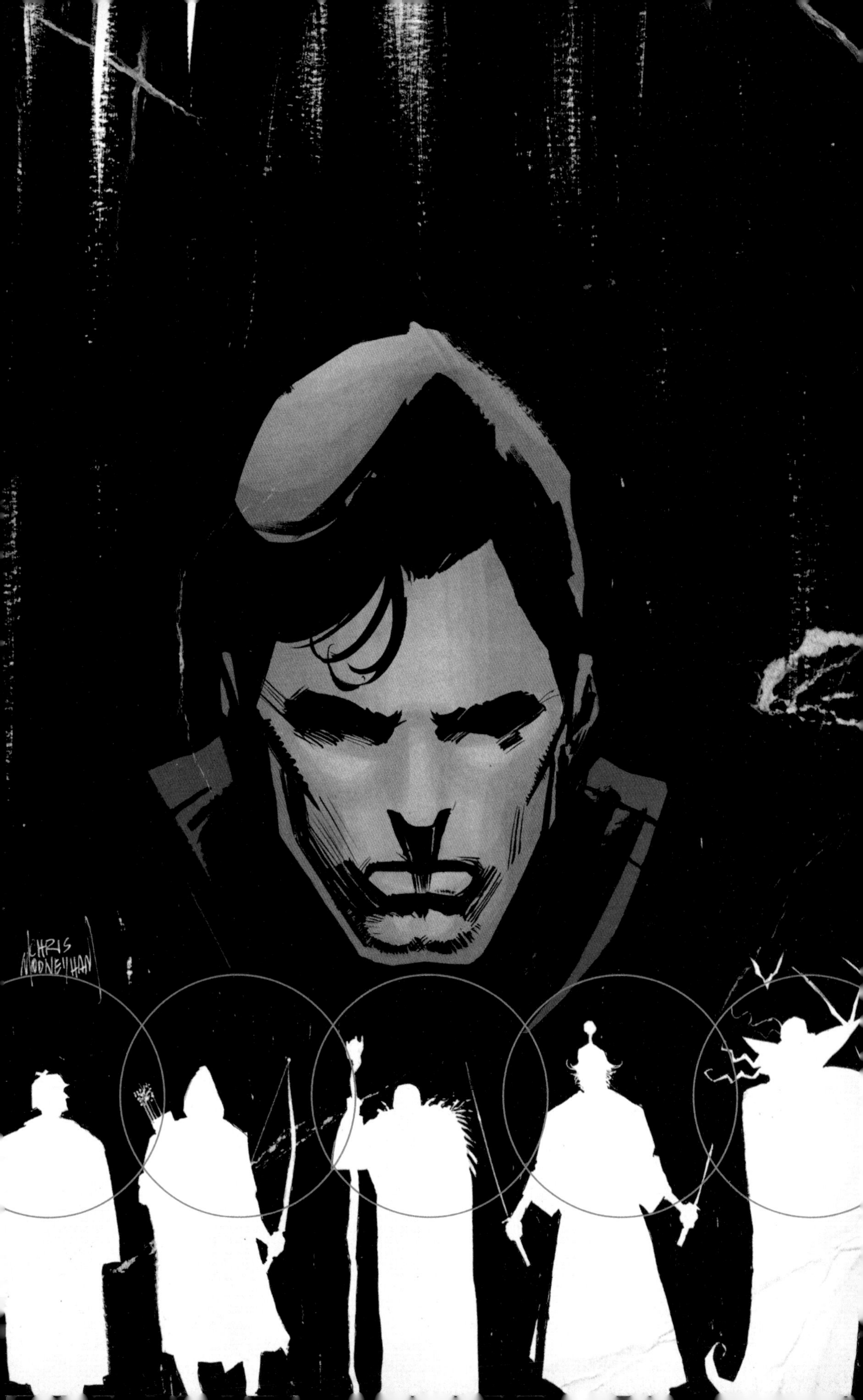
CHRIS
MOONEYHAN

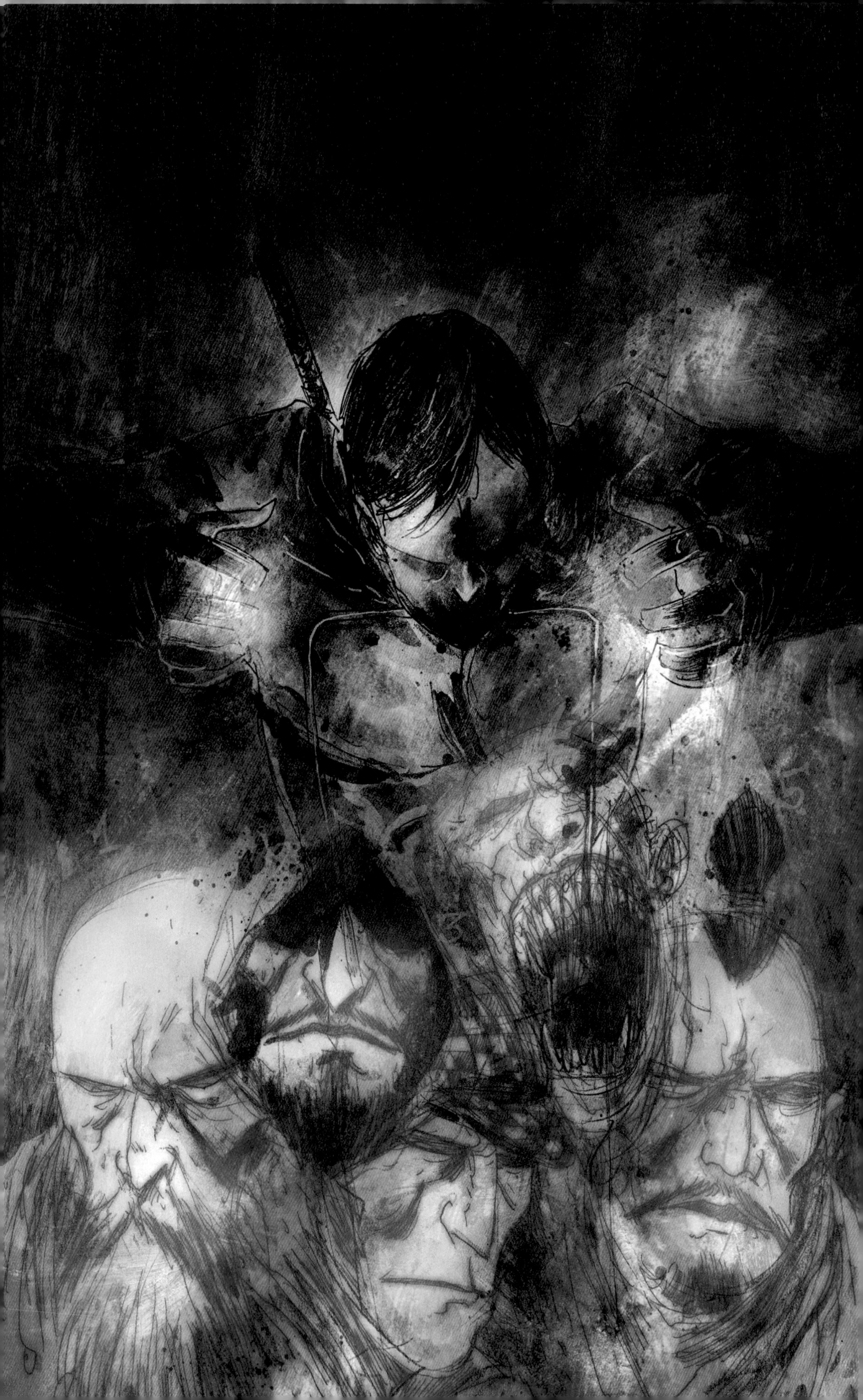

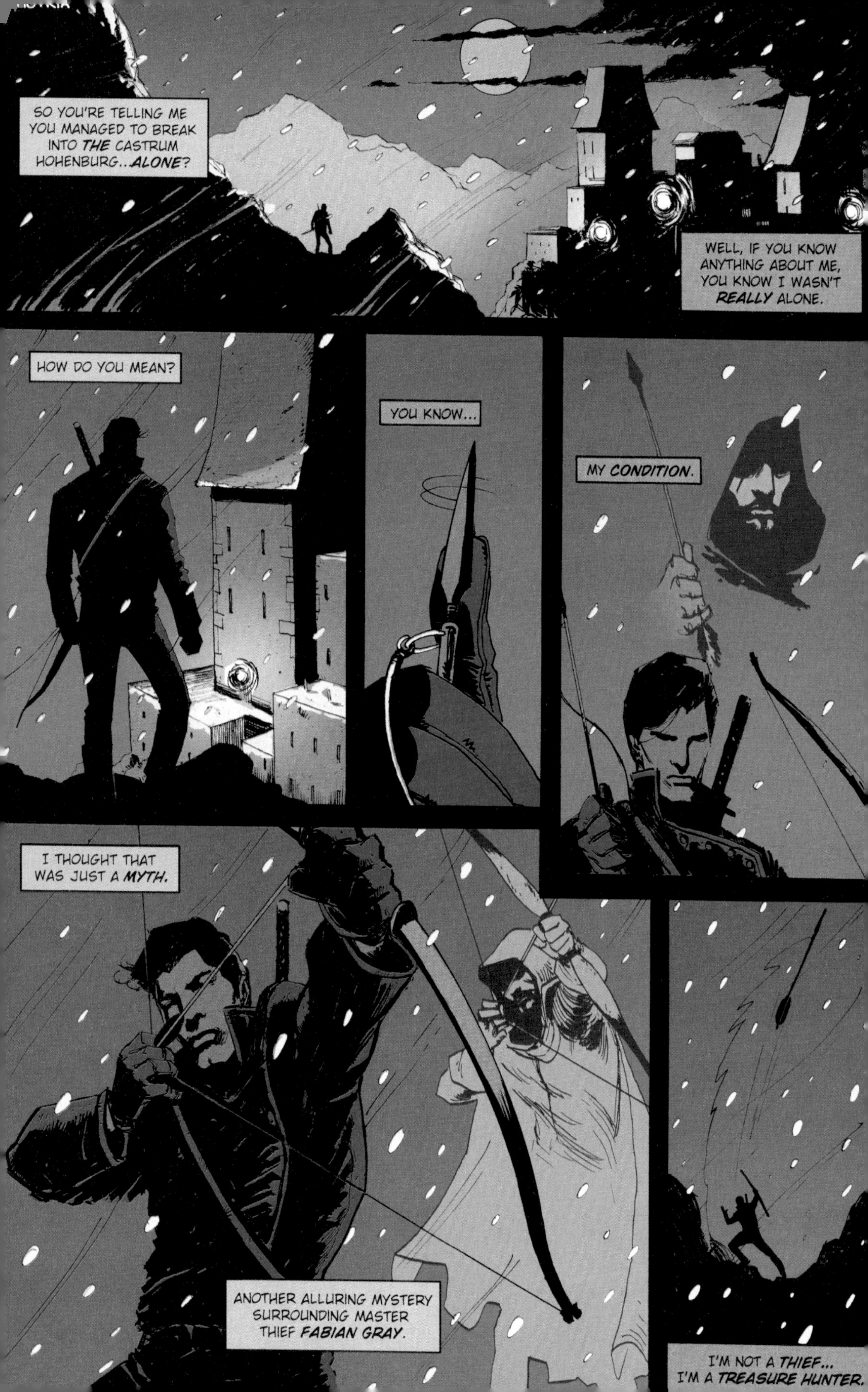
SO YOU'RE TELLING ME YOU MANAGED TO BREAK INTO THE CASTRUM HOHENBURG...ALONE?
WELL, IF YOU KNOW ANYTHING ABOUT ME, YOU KNOW I WASN'T REALLY ALONE.
HOW DO YOU MEAN?
YOU KNOW...
MY CONDITION.
I THOUGHT THAT WAS JUST A MYTH.
ANOTHER ALLURING MYSTERY SURROUNDING MASTER THIEF FABIAN GRAY.
I'M NOT A THIEF... I'M A TREASURE HUNTER.

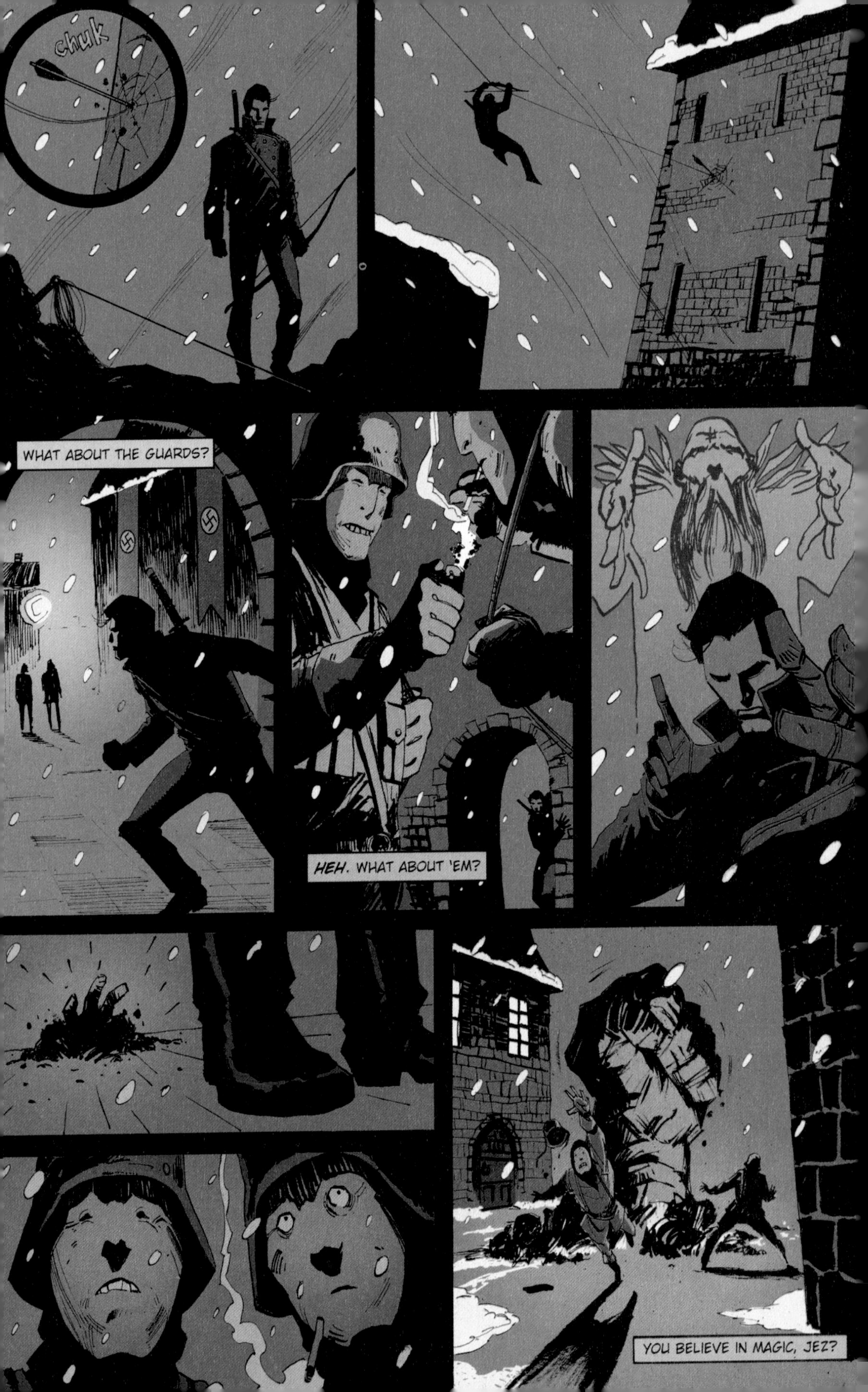
chuk
WHAT ABOUT THE GUARDS?
HEH. WHAT ABOUT 'EM?
YOU BELIEVE IN MAGIC, JEZ?

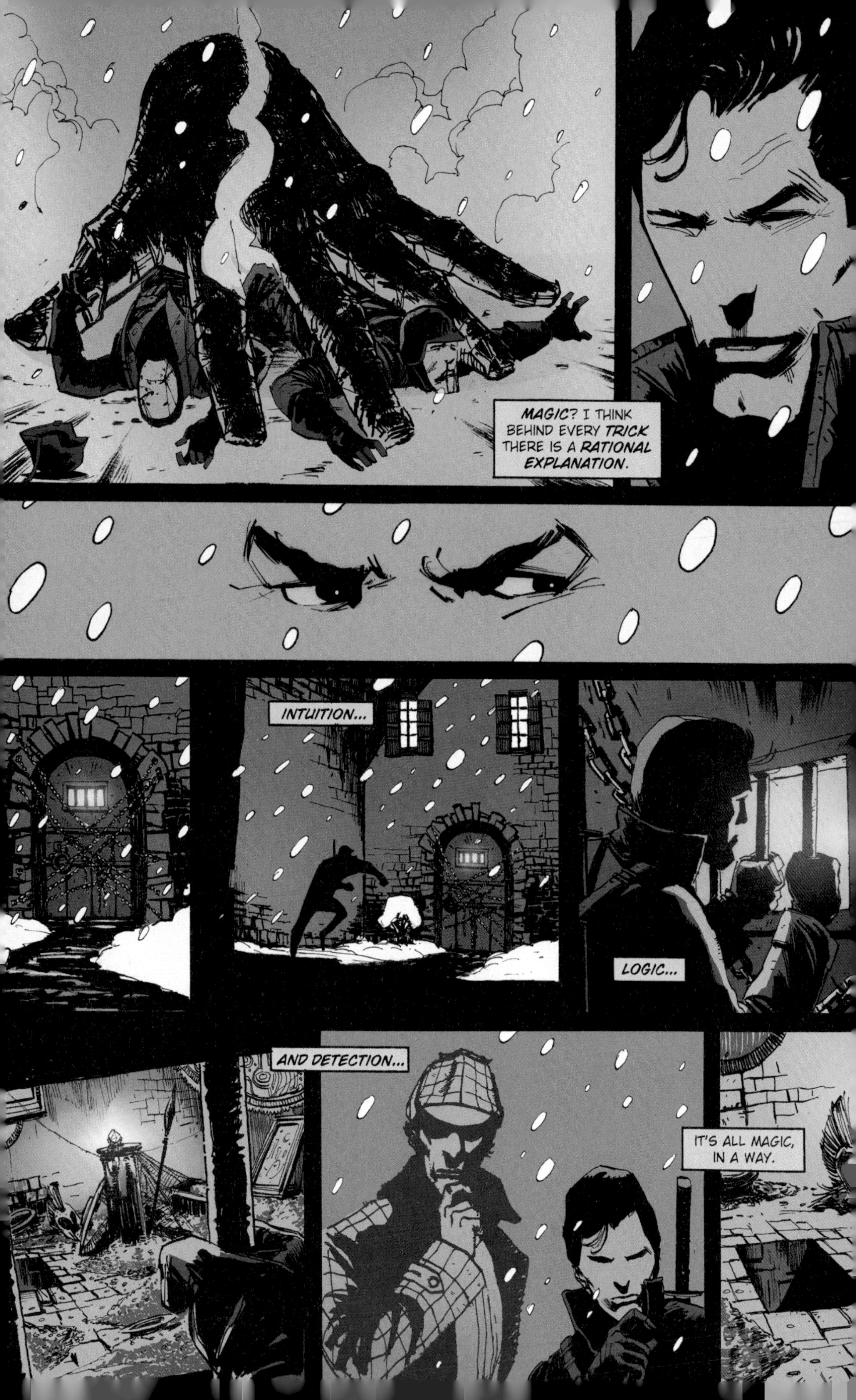
MAGIC? I THINK BEHIND EVERY TRICK THERE IS A RATIONAL EXPLANATION.
INTUITION...
LOGIC...
AND DETECTION...
IT'S ALL MAGIC, IN A WAY.

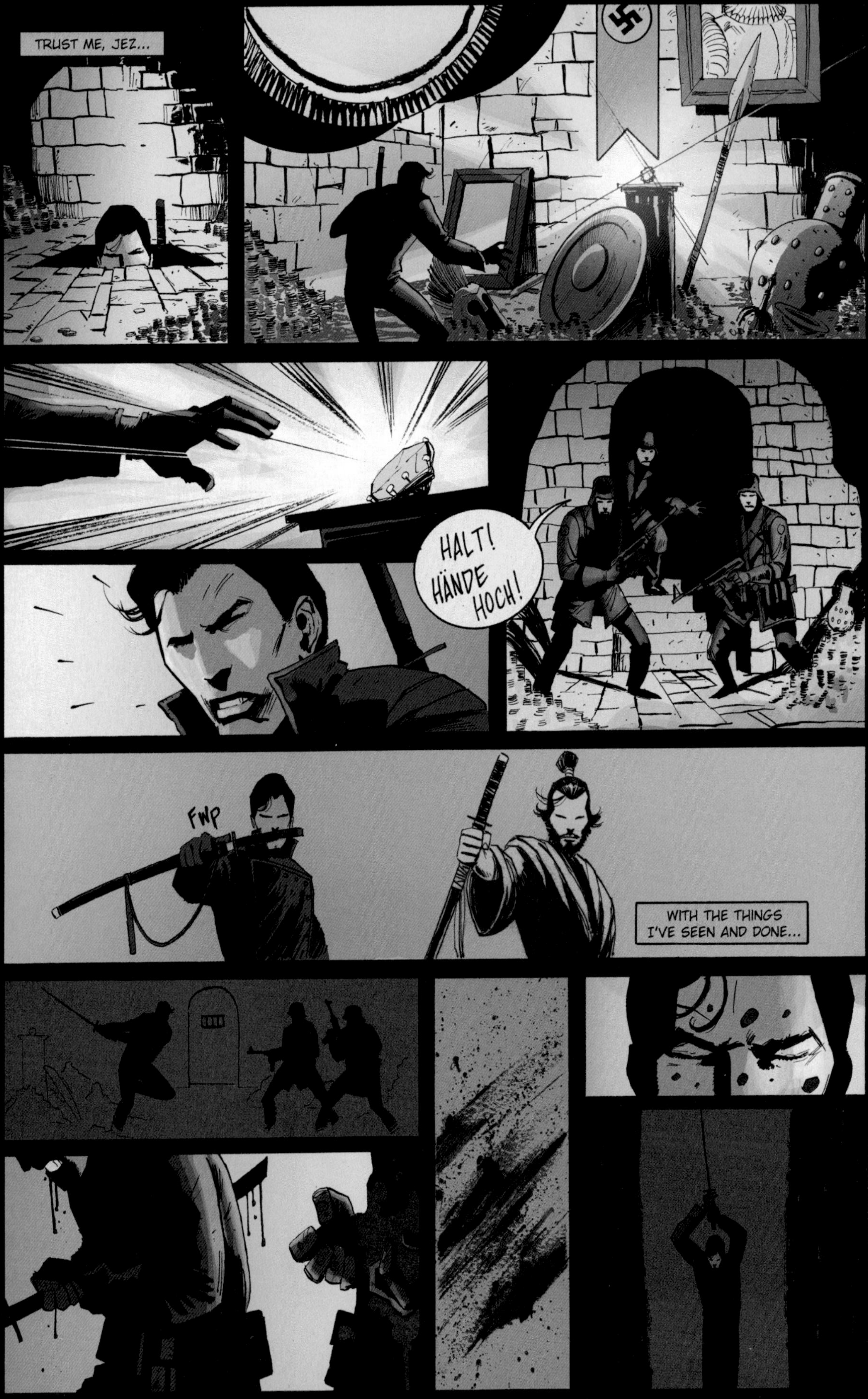
TRUST ME, JEZ...
HALT! HÄNDE HOCH!
FWP
WITH THE THINGS I'VE SEEN AND DONE...

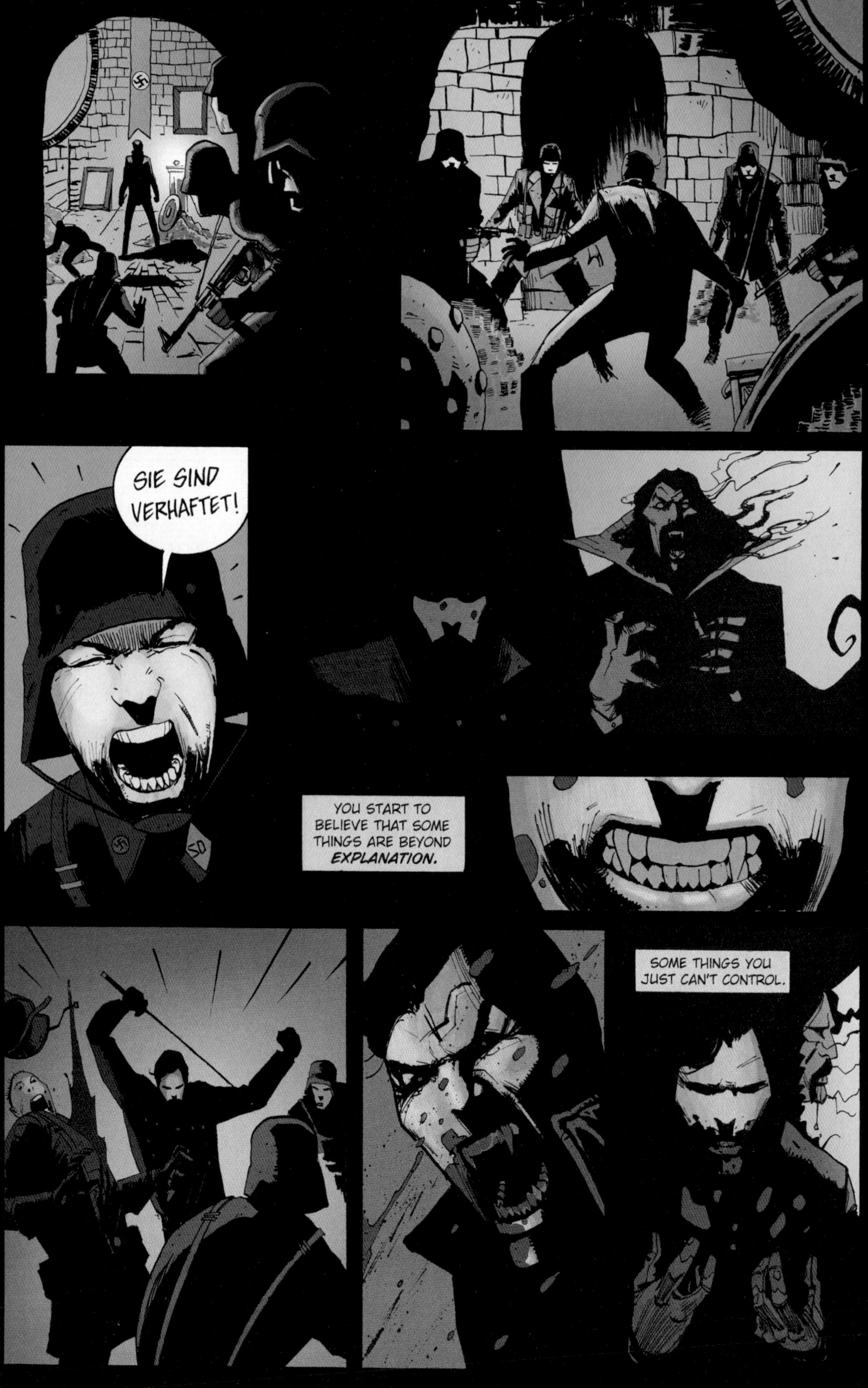
SIE SIND VERHAFTET!
YOU START TO BELIEVE THAT SOME THINGS ARE BEYOND *EXPLANATION.*
SOME THINGS YOU JUST CAN'T CONTROL.

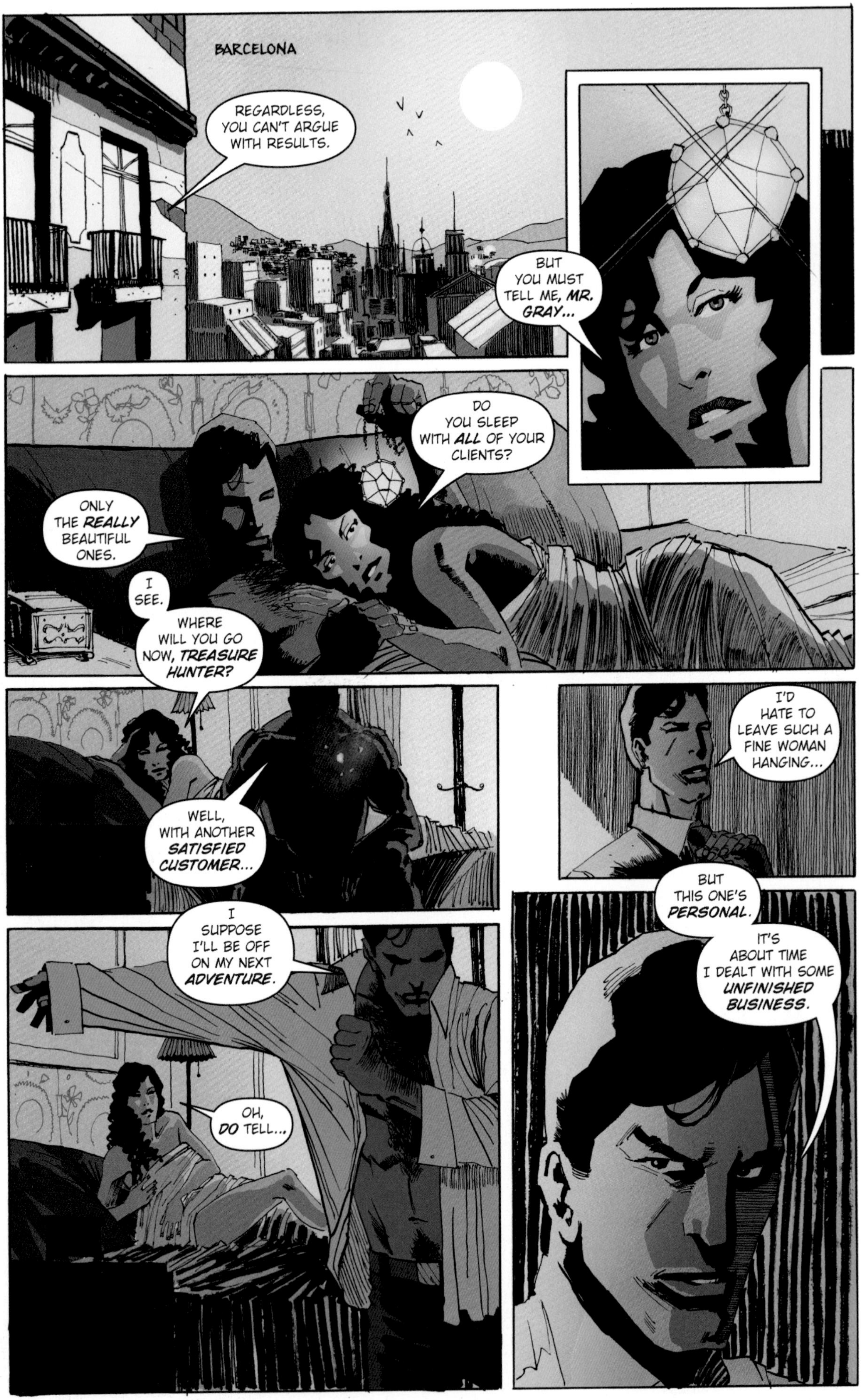
BARCELONA
REGARDLESS, YOU CAN'T ARGUE WITH RESULTS.
BUT YOU MUST TELL ME, MR. GRAY...
DO YOU SLEEP WITH ALL OF YOUR CLIENTS?
ONLY THE REALLY BEAUTIFUL ONES.
I SEE.
WHERE WILL YOU GO NOW, TREASURE HUNTER?
WELL, WITH ANOTHER SATISFIED CUSTOMER...
I'D HATE TO LEAVE SUCH A FINE WOMAN HANGING...
I SUPPOSE I'LL BE OFF ON MY NEXT ADVENTURE.
OH, DO TELL...
BUT THIS ONE'S PERSONAL.
IT'S ABOUT TIME I DEALT WITH SOME UNFINISHED BUSINESS.

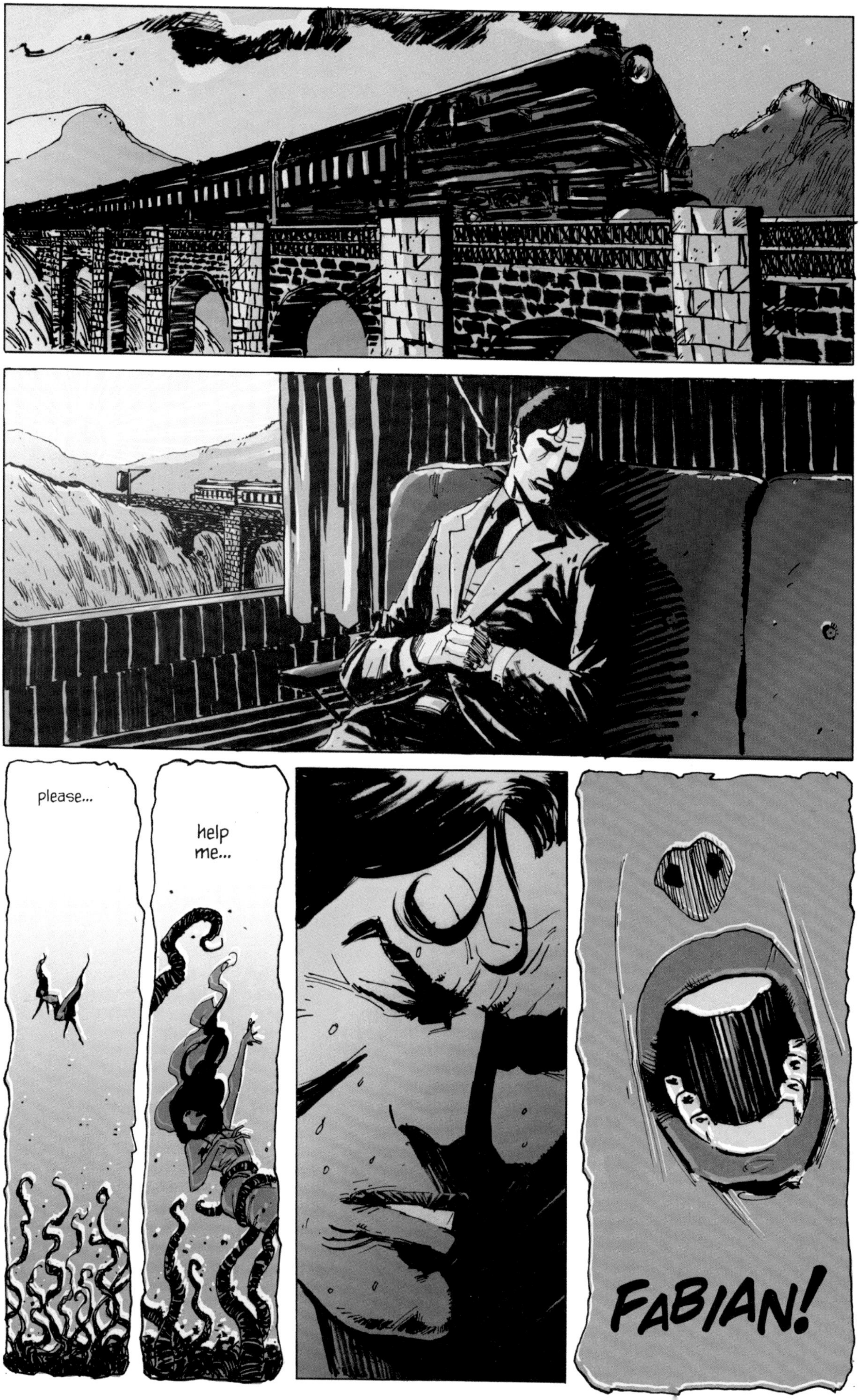
please...
help me...
FABIAN!

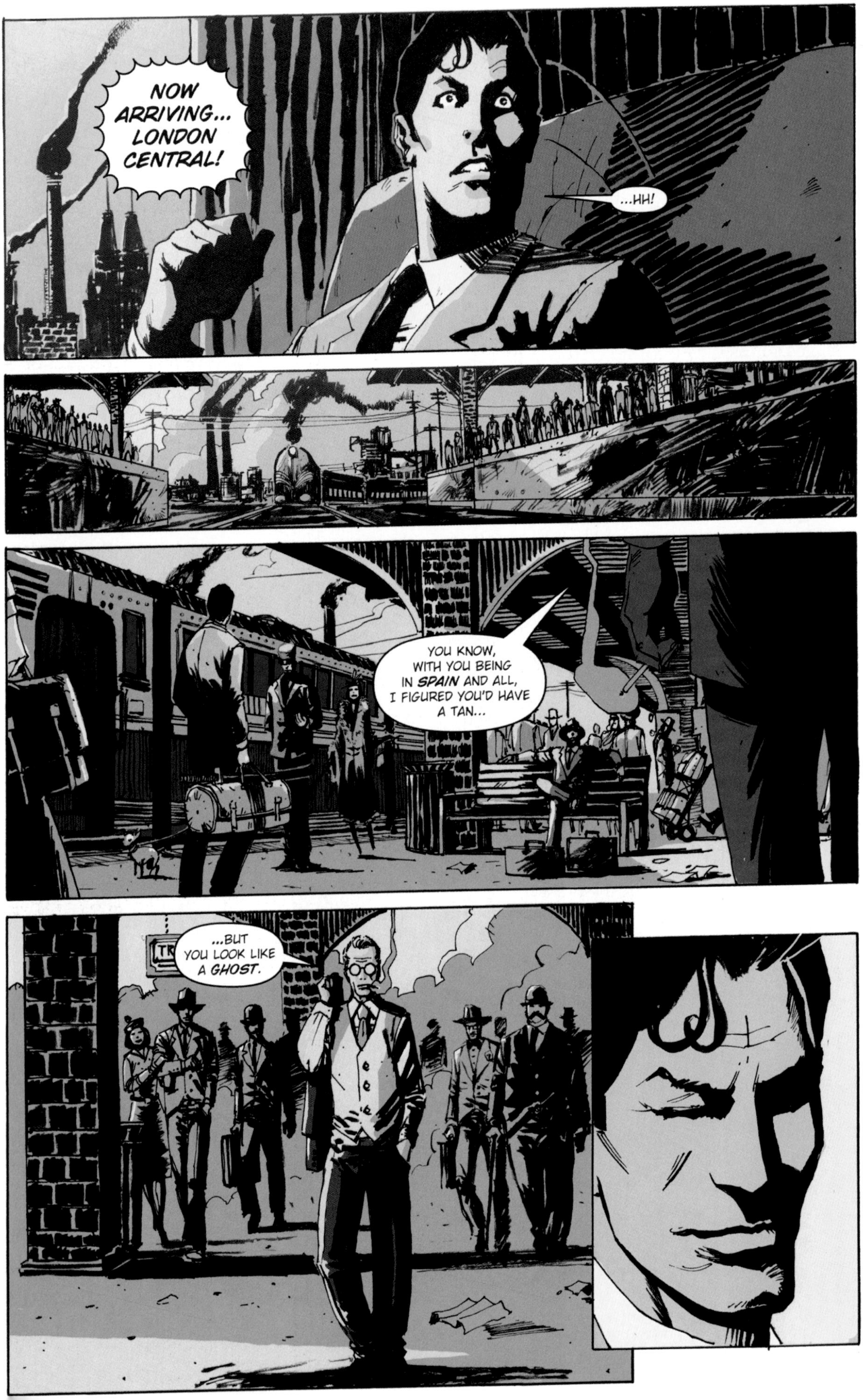
NOW ARRIVING... LONDON CENTRAL!
...HH!
YOU KNOW, WITH YOU BEING IN SPAIN AND ALL, I FIGURED YOU'D HAVE A TAN...
...BUT YOU LOOK LIKE A GHOST.

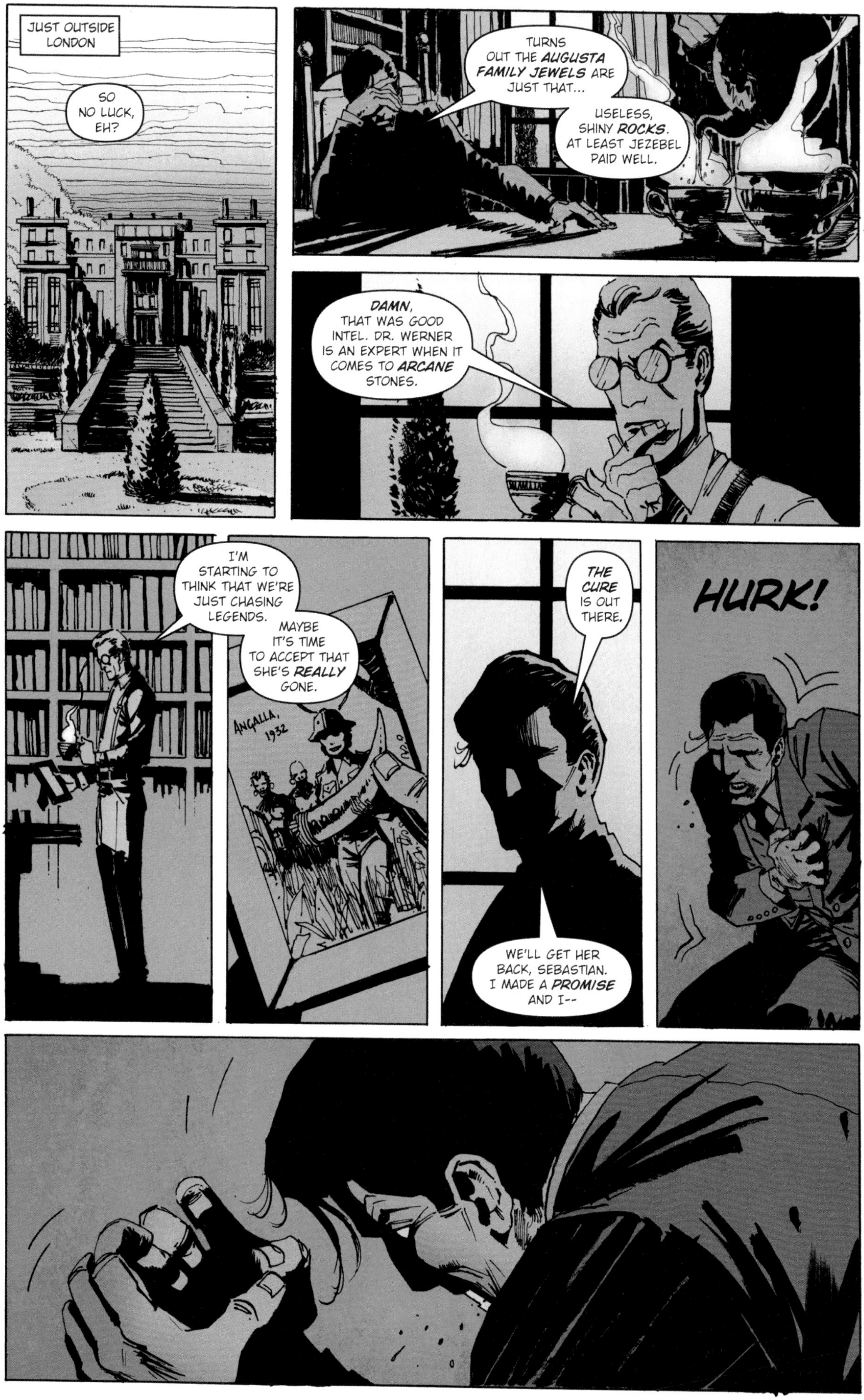
JUST OUTSIDE LONDON
SO NO LUCK, EH?
TURNS OUT THE AUGUSTA FAMILY JEWELS ARE JUST THAT...
USELESS, SHINY ROCKS. AT LEAST JEZEBEL PAID WELL.
DAMN, THAT WAS GOOD INTEL. DR. WERNER IS AN EXPERT WHEN IT COMES TO ARCANE STONES.
I'M STARTING TO THINK THAT WE'RE JUST CHASING LEGENDS.
MAYBE IT'S TIME TO ACCEPT THAT SHE'S REALLY GONE.
ANGALLA, 1932
THE CURE IS OUT THERE.
WE'LL GET HER BACK, SEBASTIAN. I MADE A PROMISE AND I--
HURK!

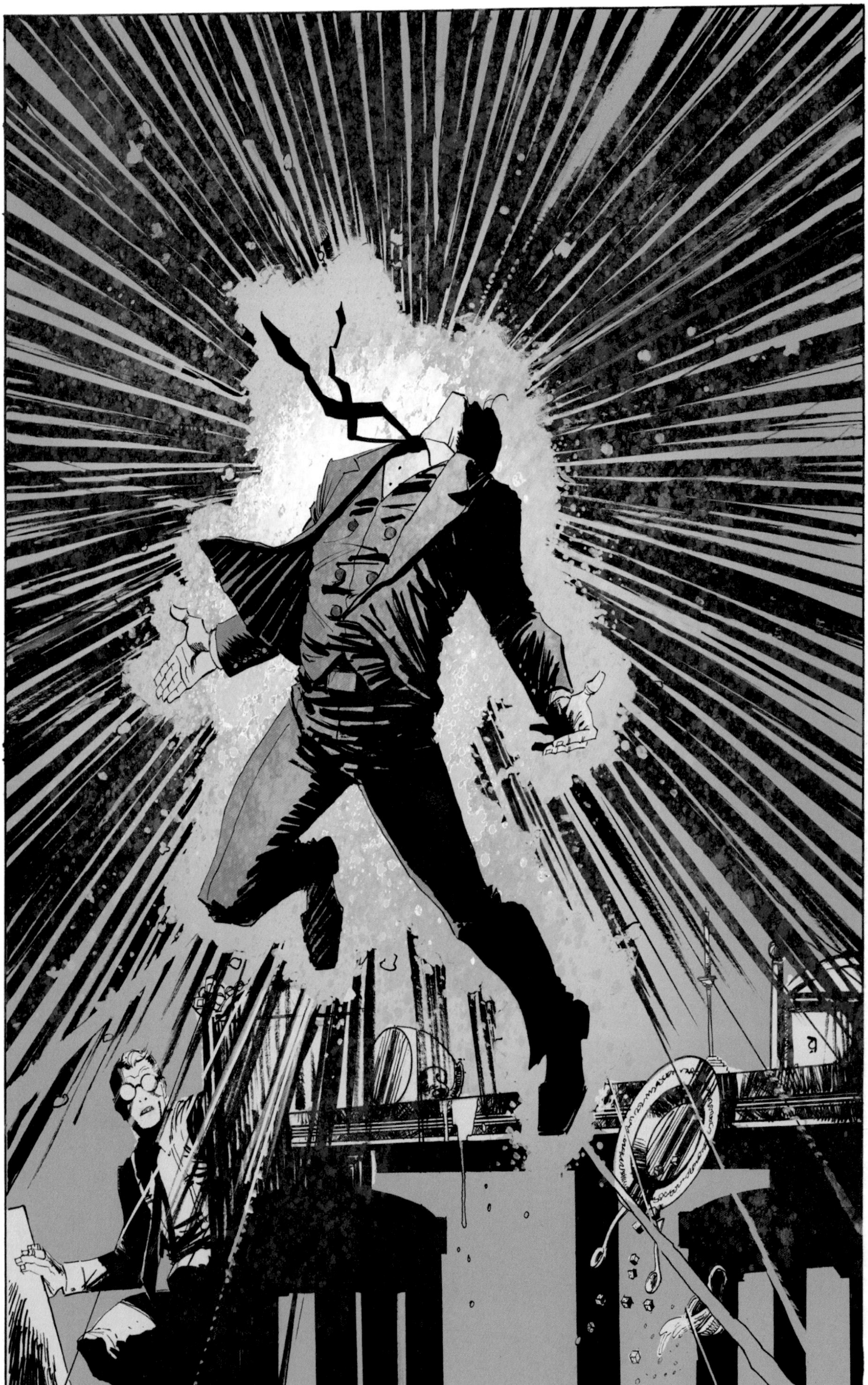

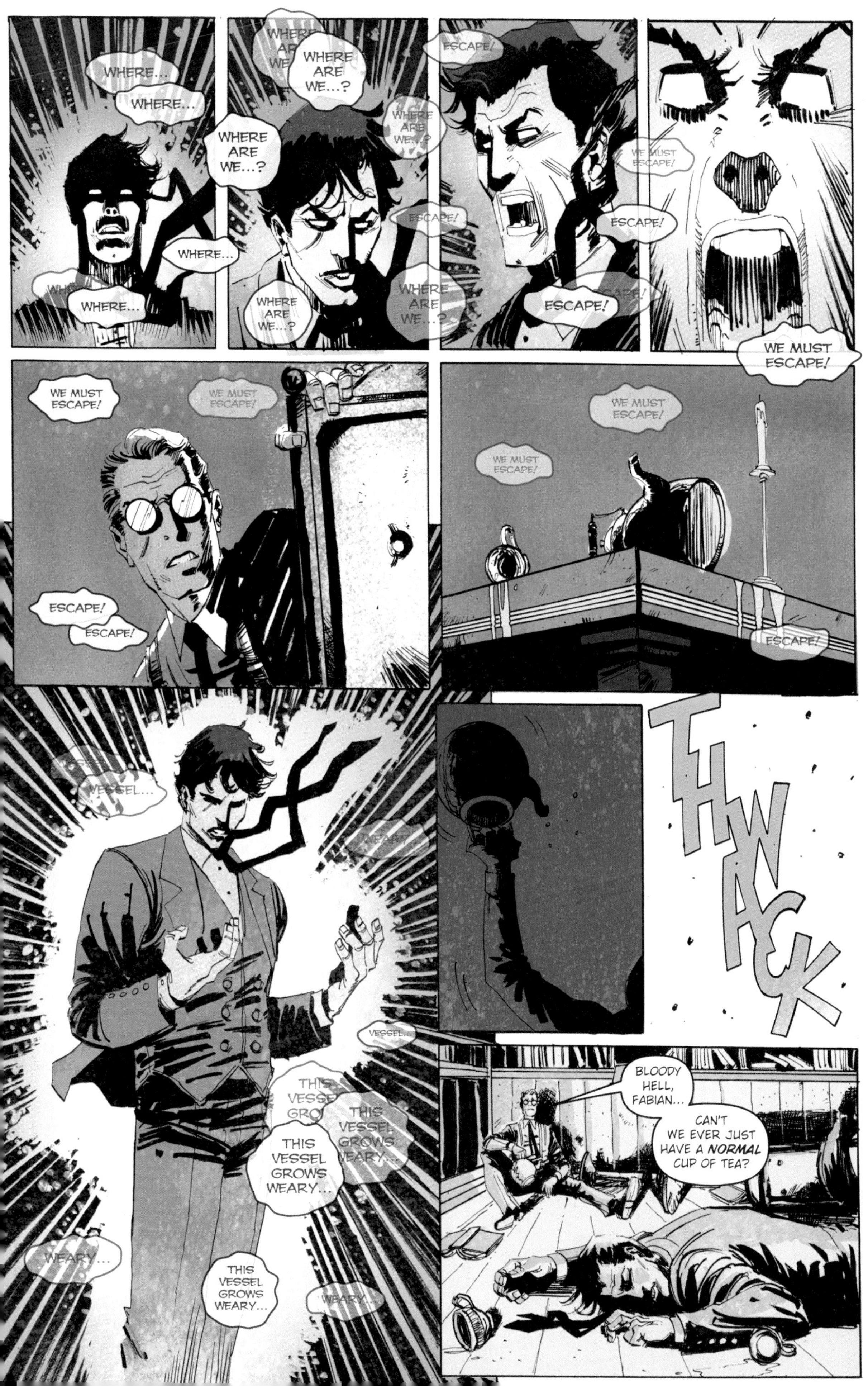
WHERE...
WHERE...
WHERE ARE WE...?
WHERE...
WHERE...
WHERE ARE WE...?
WHERE ARE WE...?
WHERE ARE WE...?
ESCAPE!
WHERE ARE WE...?
WHERE ARE WE...?
ESCAPE!
ESCAPE!
ESCAPE!
WE MUST ESCAPE!
WE MUST ESCAPE!
WE MUST ESCAPE!
WE MUST ESCAPE!
ESCAPE!
ESCAPE!
WE MUST ESCAPE!
WE MUST ESCAPE!
ESCAPE!
VESSEL...
WEARY...
VESSEL...
THIS VESSEL GROWS WEARY...
THIS VESSEL GROWS WEARY...
WEARY...
THIS VESSEL GROWS WEARY...
WEARY...
THWACK
BLOODY HELL, FABIAN...
CAN'T WE EVER JUST HAVE A **NORMAL** CUP OF TEA?

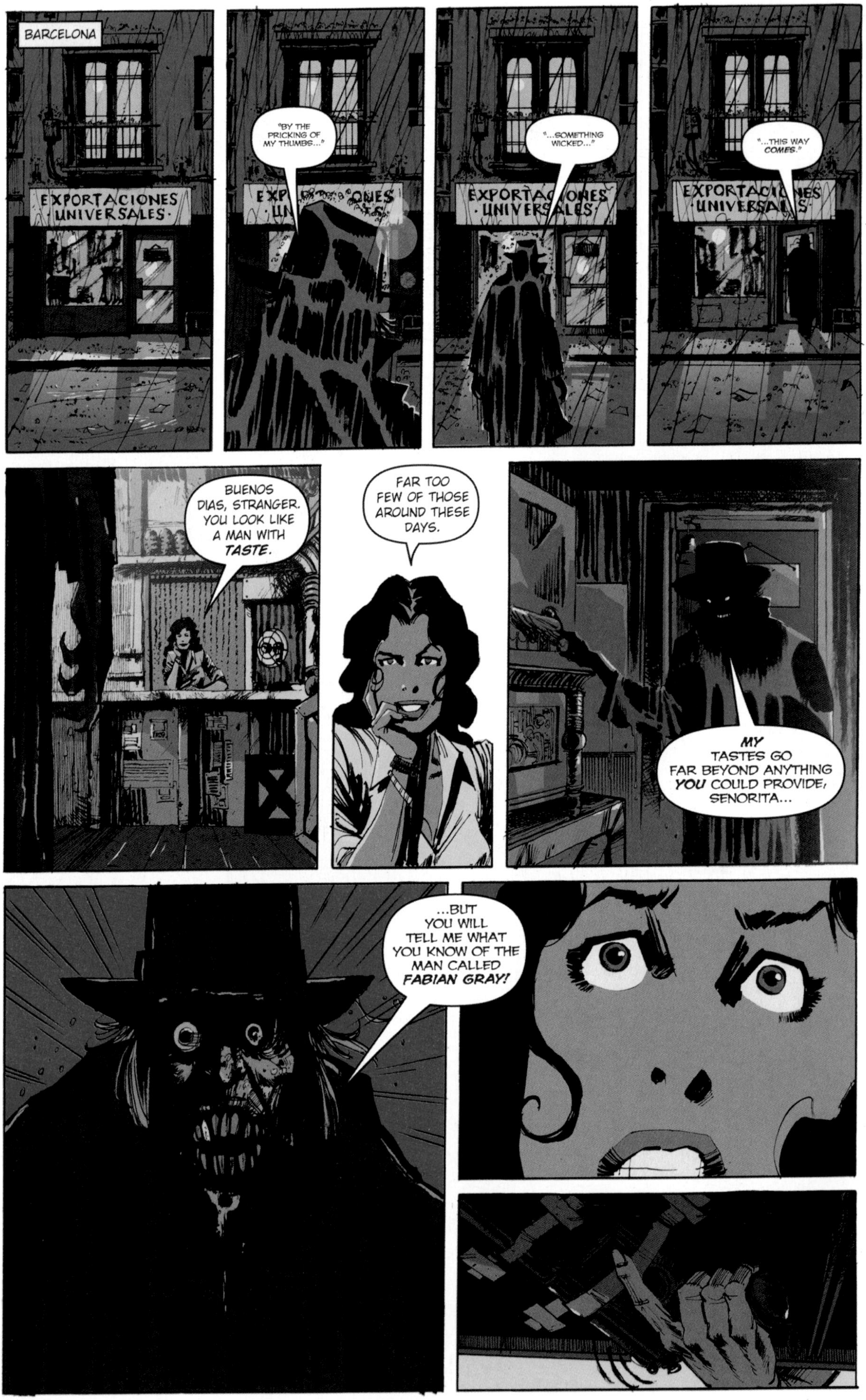
BARCELONA
EXPORTACIONES UNIVERSALES
"BY THE PRICKING OF MY THUMBS..."
"...SOMETHING WICKED..."
"...THIS WAY COMES."
BUENOS DIAS, STRANGER. YOU LOOK LIKE A MAN WITH TASTE.
FAR TOO FEW OF THOSE AROUND THESE DAYS.
MY TASTES GO FAR BEYOND ANYTHING YOU COULD PROVIDE, SENORITA...
...BUT YOU WILL TELL ME WHAT YOU KNOW OF THE MAN CALLED FABIAN GRAY!

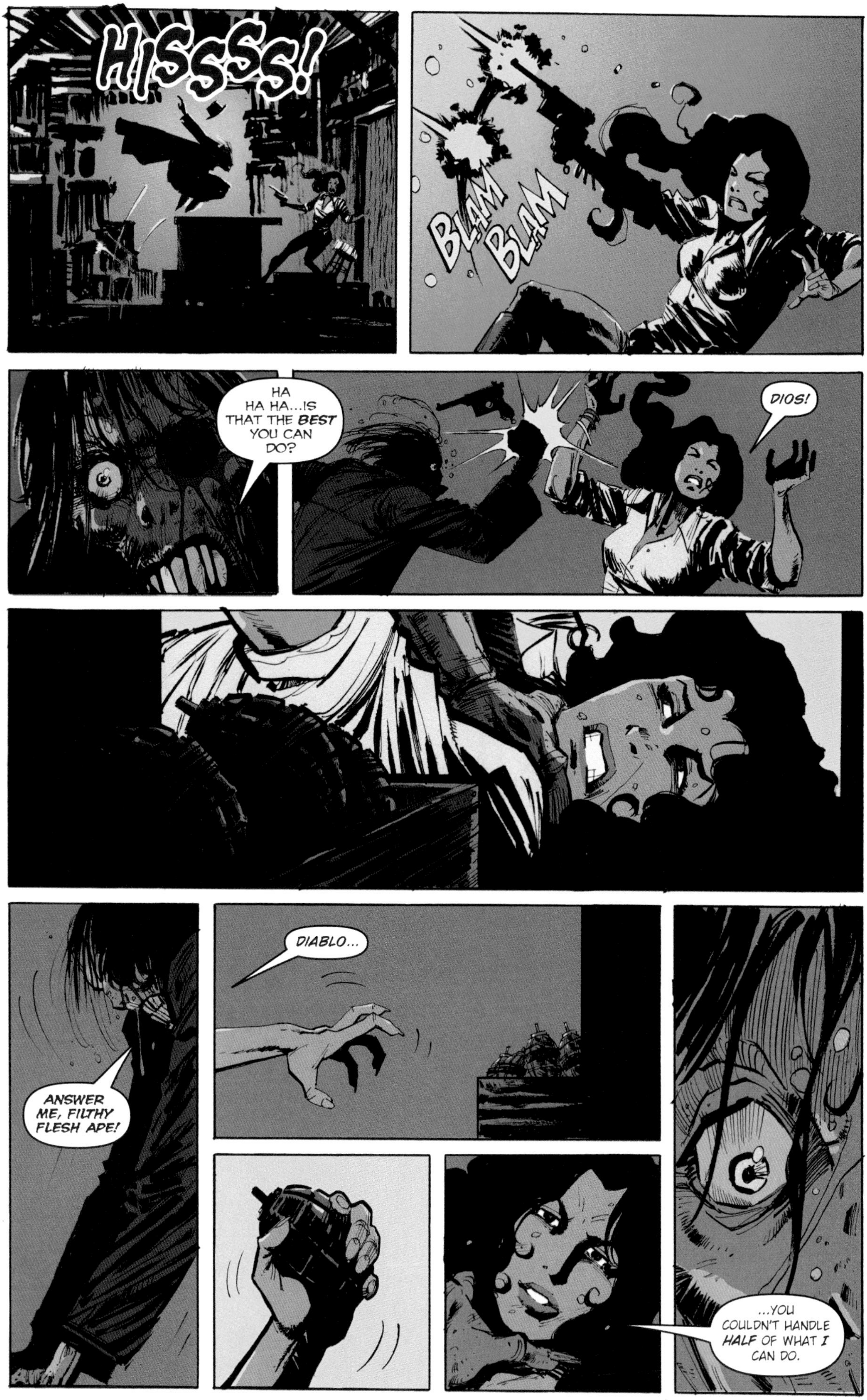
HISSSS!
BLAM BLAM
HA HA HA...IS THAT THE BEST YOU CAN DO?
DIOS!
DIABLO...
ANSWER ME, FILTHY FLESH APE!
...YOU COULDN'T HANDLE HALF OF WHAT I CAN DO.

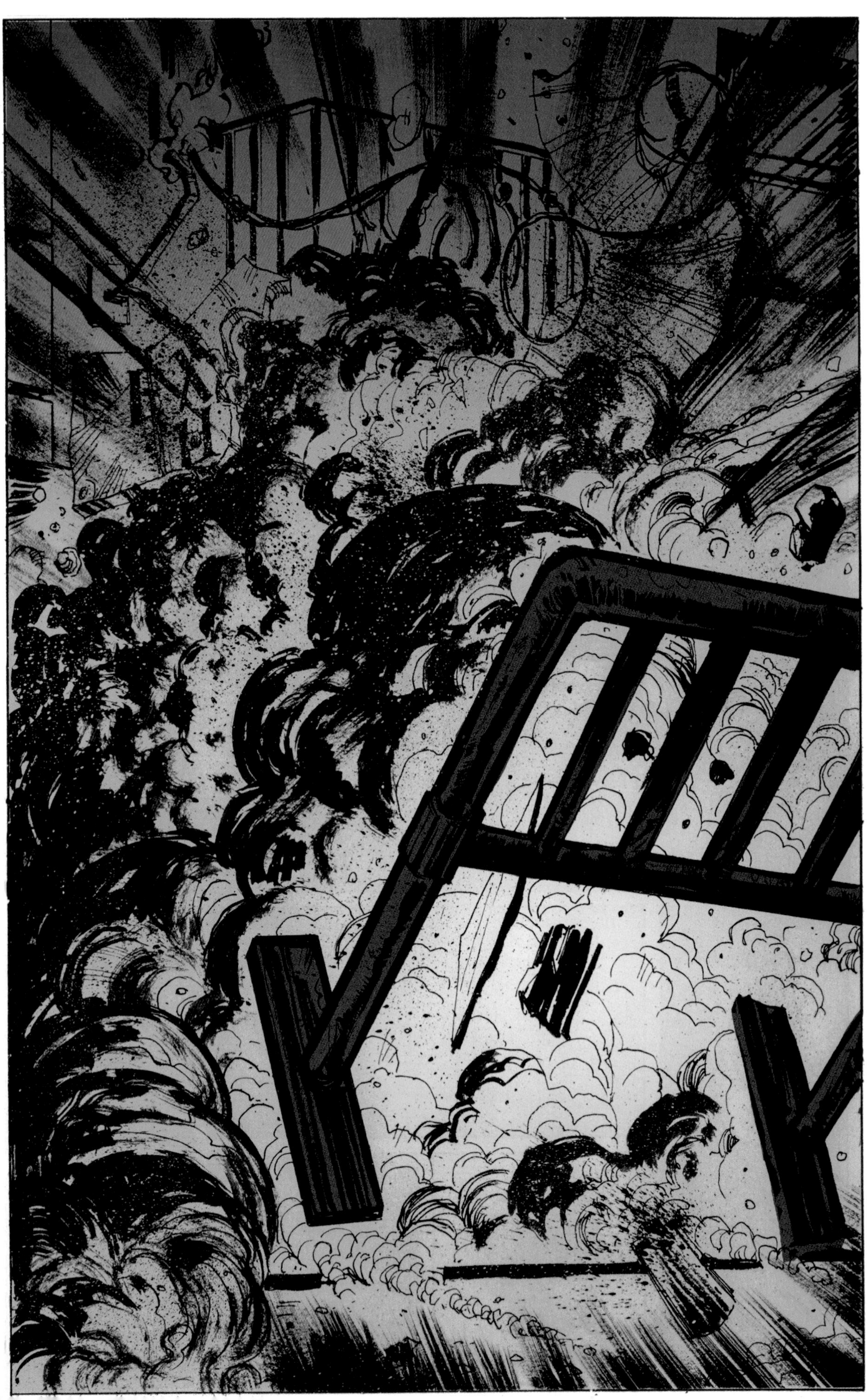

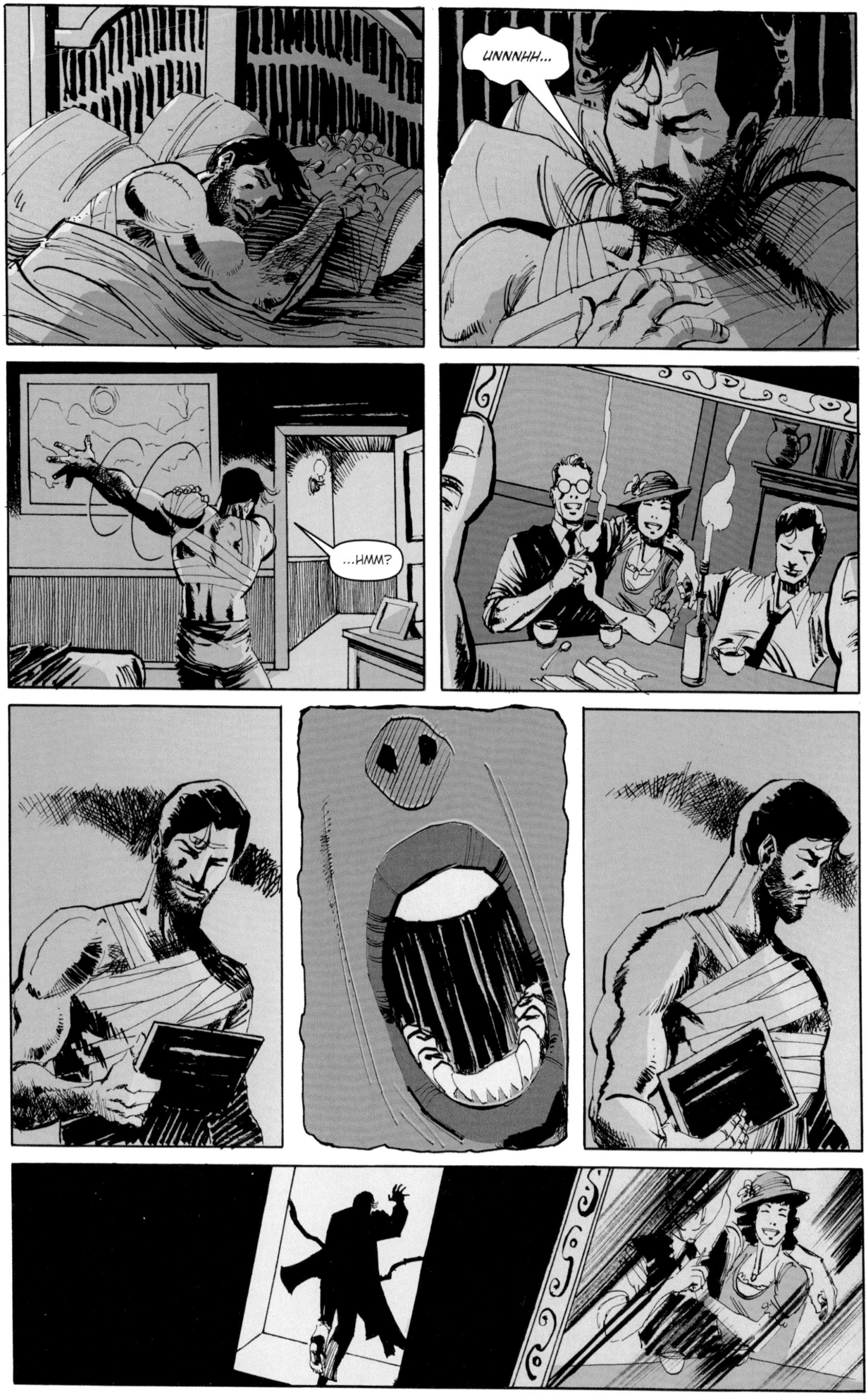
UNNNHH...
...HMM?

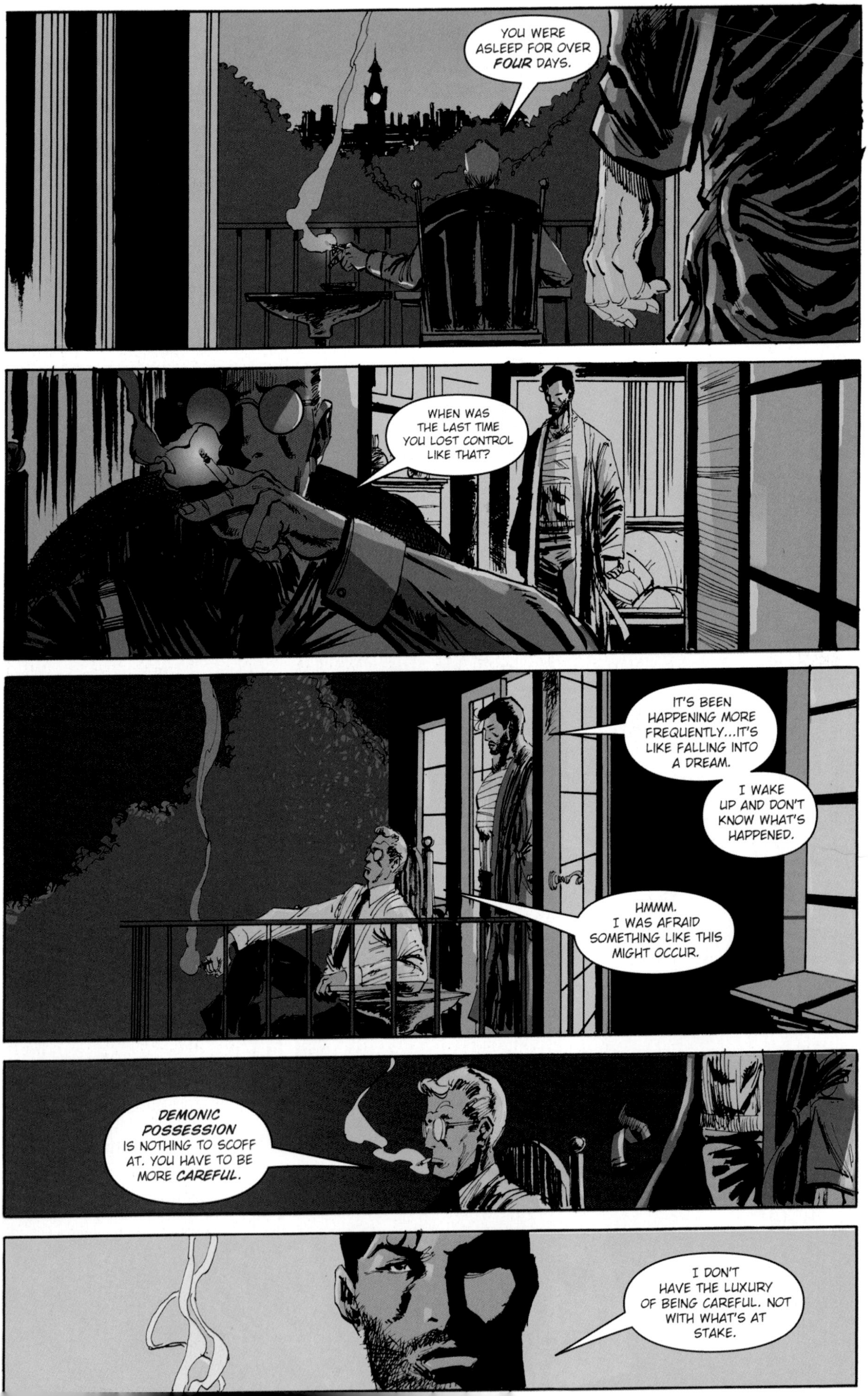
YOU WERE ASLEEP FOR OVER FOUR DAYS.
WHEN WAS THE LAST TIME YOU LOST CONTROL LIKE THAT?
IT'S BEEN HAPPENING MORE FREQUENTLY...IT'S LIKE FALLING INTO A DREAM.
I WAKE UP AND DON'T KNOW WHAT'S HAPPENED.
HMMM. I WAS AFRAID SOMETHING LIKE THIS MIGHT OCCUR.
DEMONIC POSSESSION IS NOTHING TO SCOFF AT. YOU HAVE TO BE MORE CAREFUL.
I DON'T HAVE THE LUXURY OF BEING CAREFUL. NOT WITH WHAT'S AT STAKE.

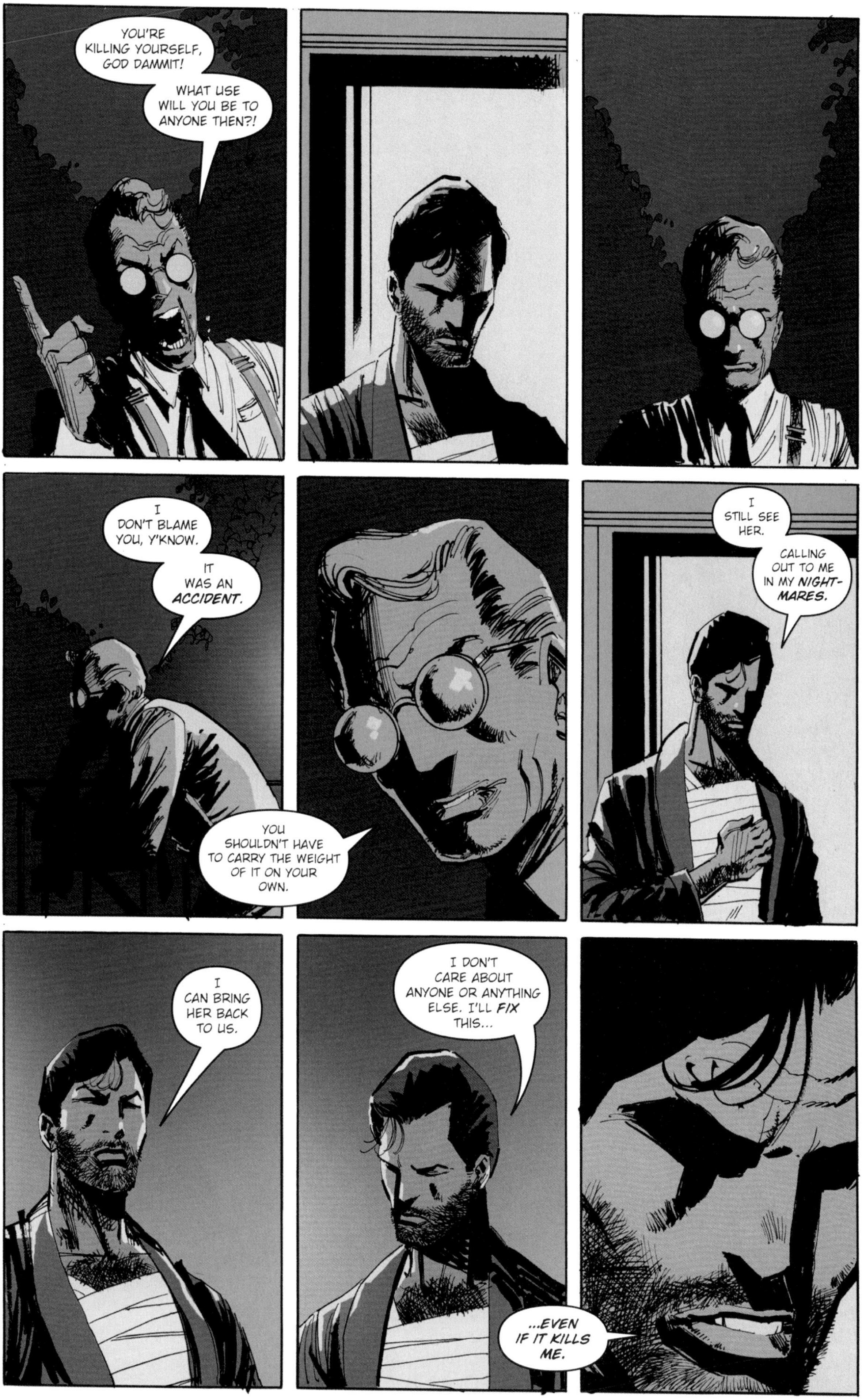
YOU'RE KILLING YOURSELF, GOD DAMMIT!
WHAT USE WILL YOU BE TO ANYONE THEN?!
I DON'T BLAME YOU, Y'KNOW.
IT WAS AN *ACCIDENT*.
YOU SHOULDN'T HAVE TO CARRY THE WEIGHT OF IT ON YOUR OWN.
I STILL SEE HER.
CALLING OUT TO ME IN MY *NIGHT-MARES.*
I CAN BRING HER BACK TO US.
I DON'T CARE ABOUT ANYONE OR ANYTHING ELSE. I'LL *FIX* THIS...
...EVEN IF IT KILLS ME.

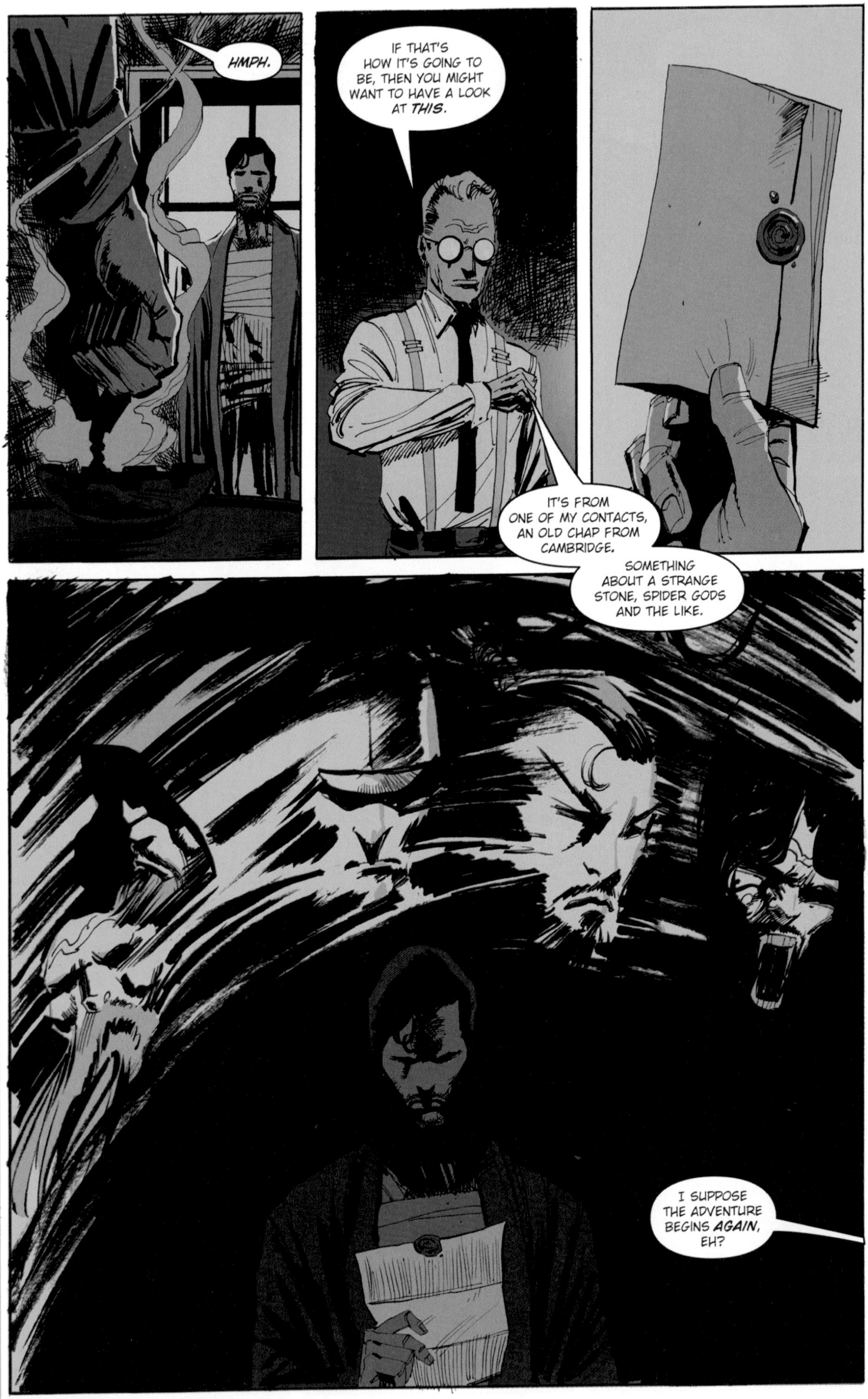
HMPH.
IF THAT'S HOW IT'S GOING TO BE, THEN YOU MIGHT WANT TO HAVE A LOOK AT THIS.
IT'S FROM ONE OF MY CONTACTS, AN OLD CHAP FROM CAMBRIDGE.
SOMETHING ABOUT A STRANGE STONE, SPIDER GODS AND THE LIKE.
I SUPPOSE THE ADVENTURE BEGINS AGAIN, EH?

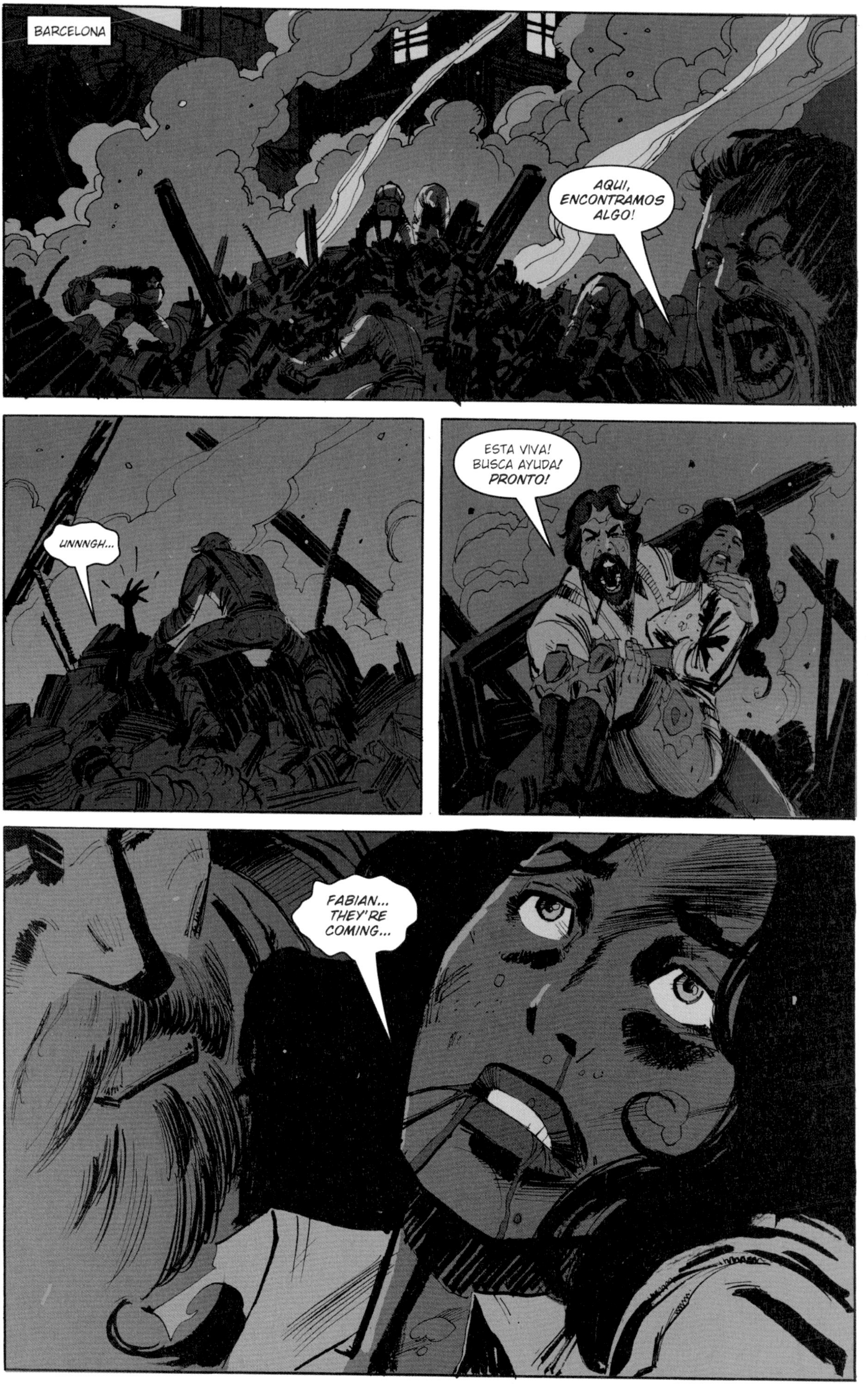
BARCELONA
AQUI, ENCONTRAMOS ALGO!
UNNNGH...
ESTA VIVA! BUSCA AYUDA! PRONTO!
FABIAN... THEY'RE COMING...

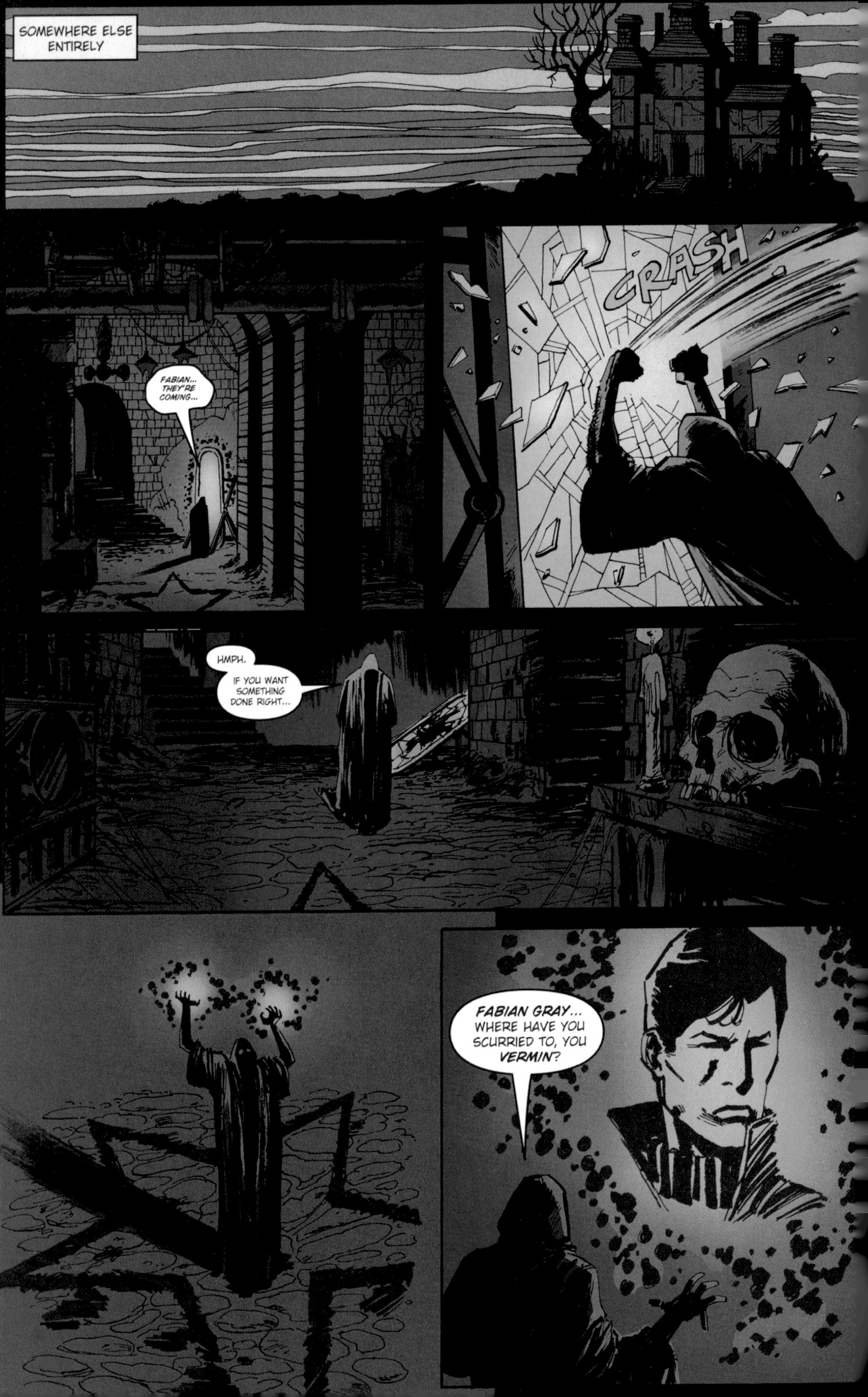
SOMEWHERE ELSE ENTIRELY
FABIAN... THEY'RE COMING...
CRASH
HMPH.
IF YOU WANT SOMETHING DONE RIGHT...
FABIAN GRAY... WHERE HAVE YOU SCURRIED TO, YOU VERMIN?

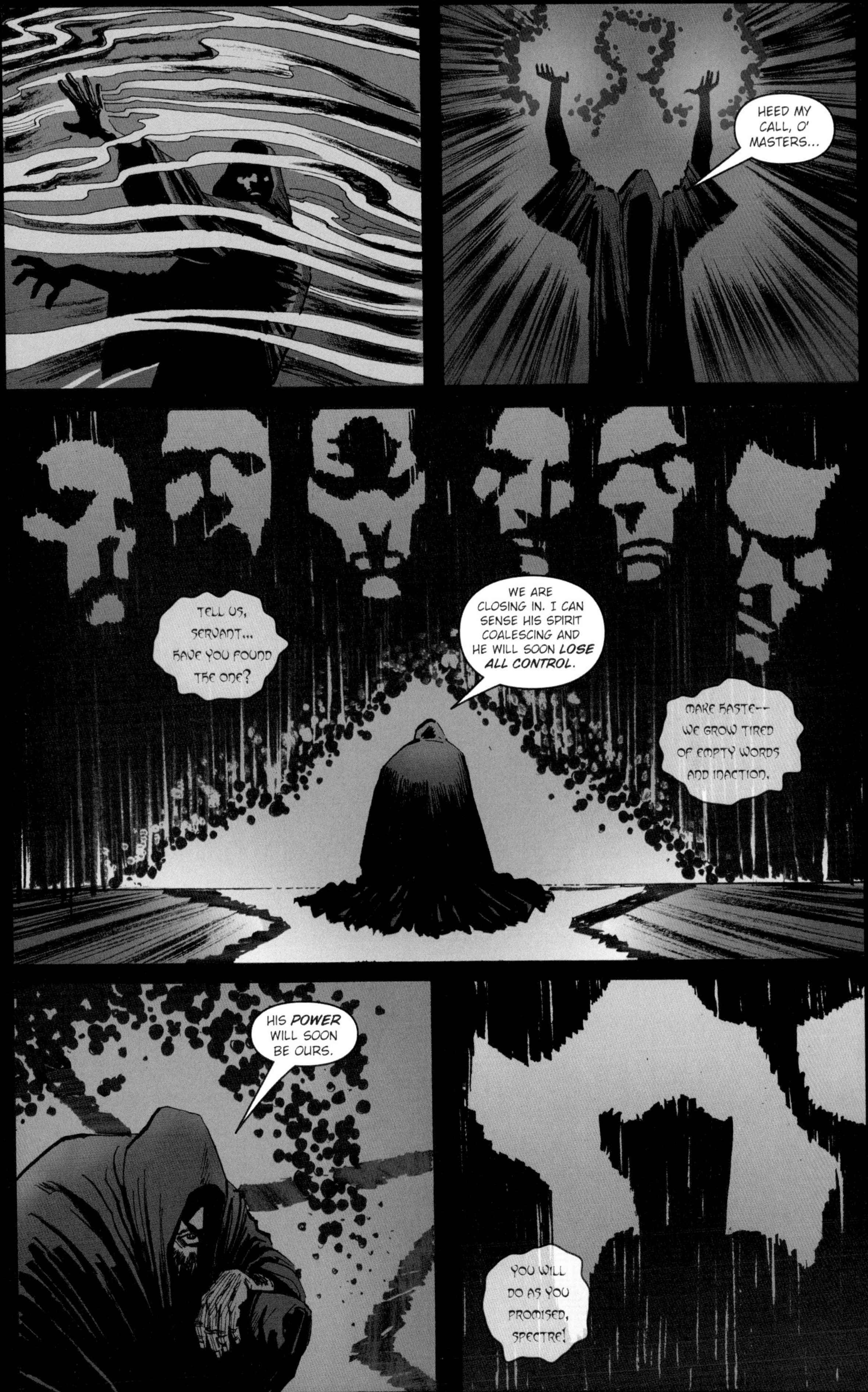
HEED MY CALL, O' MASTERS...
TELL US, SERVANT... HAVE YOU FOUND THE ONE?
WE ARE CLOSING IN. I CAN SENSE HIS SPIRIT COALESCING AND HE WILL SOON **LOSE ALL CONTROL**.
MAKE HASTE-- WE GROW TIRED OF EMPTY WORDS AND INACTION.
HIS **POWER** WILL SOON BE OURS.
YOU WILL DO AS YOU PROMISED, SPECTRE!

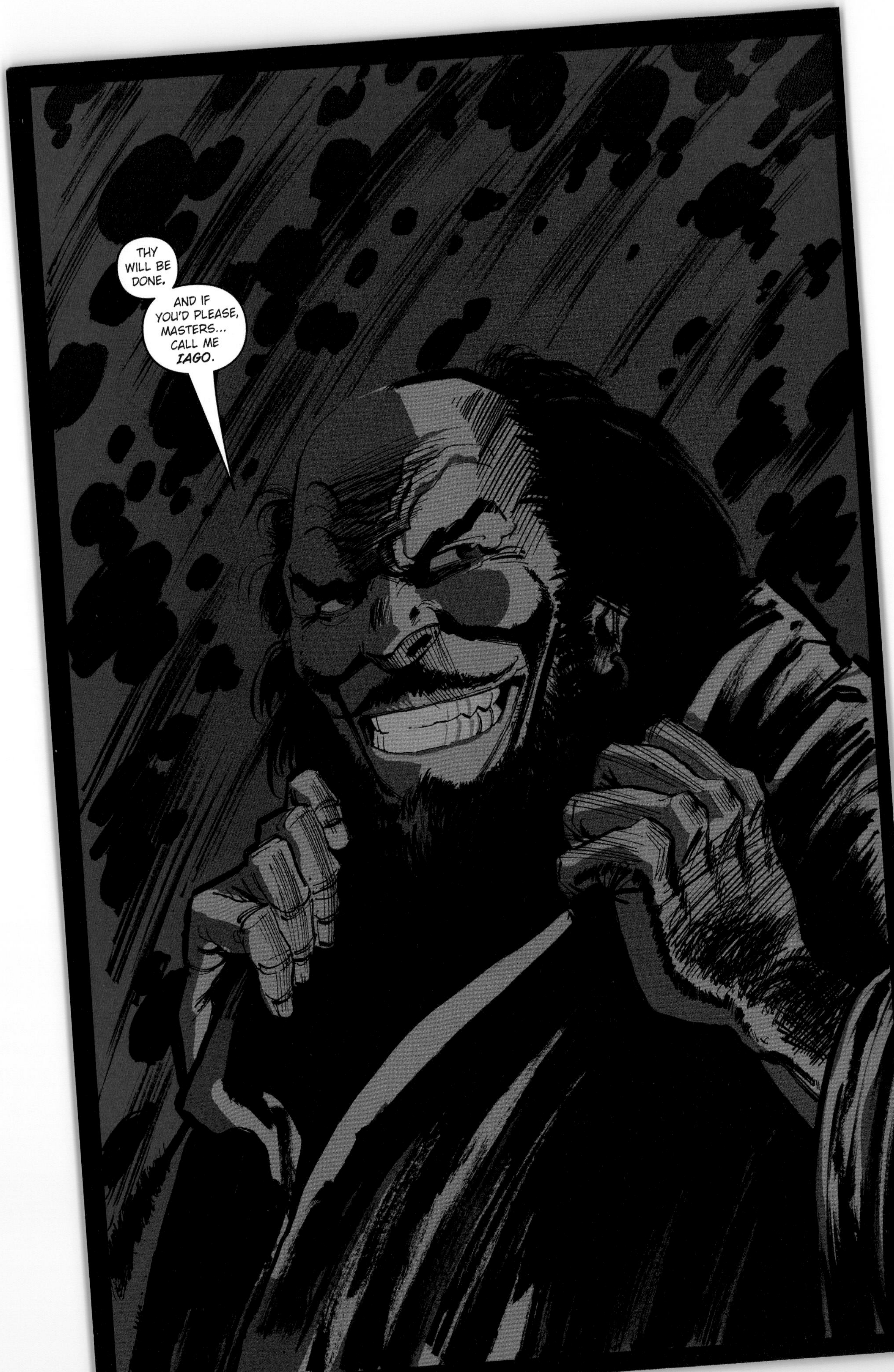
THY WILL BE DONE.
AND IF YOU'D PLEASE, MASTERS... CALL ME IAGO.

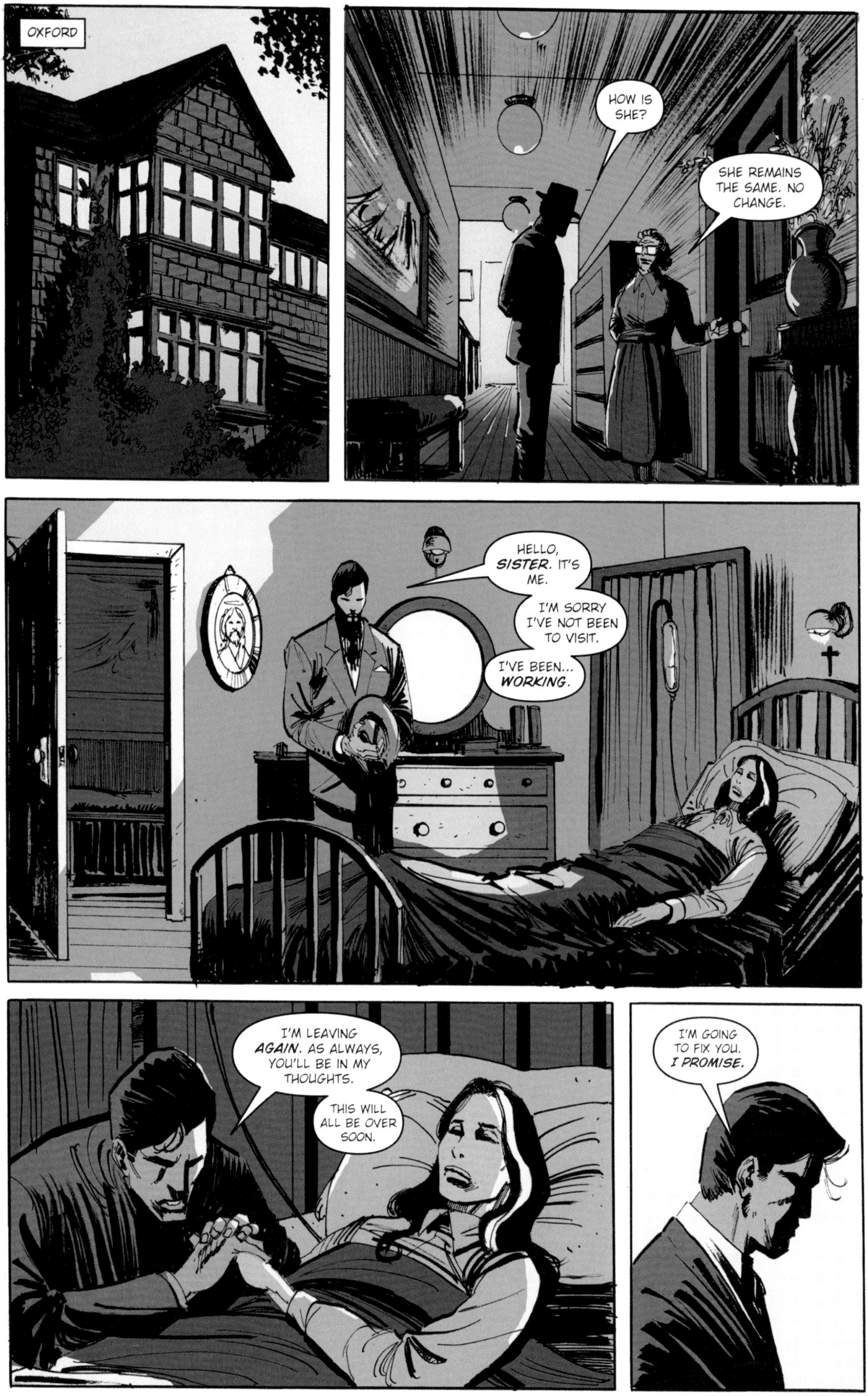
OXFORD
HOW IS SHE?
SHE REMAINS THE SAME. NO CHANGE.
HELLO, SISTER. IT'S ME.
I'M SORRY I'VE NOT BEEN TO VISIT.
I'VE BEEN... WORKING.
I'M LEAVING AGAIN. AS ALWAYS, YOU'LL BE IN MY THOUGHTS.
THIS WILL ALL BE OVER SOON.
I'M GOING TO FIX YOU. I PROMISE.

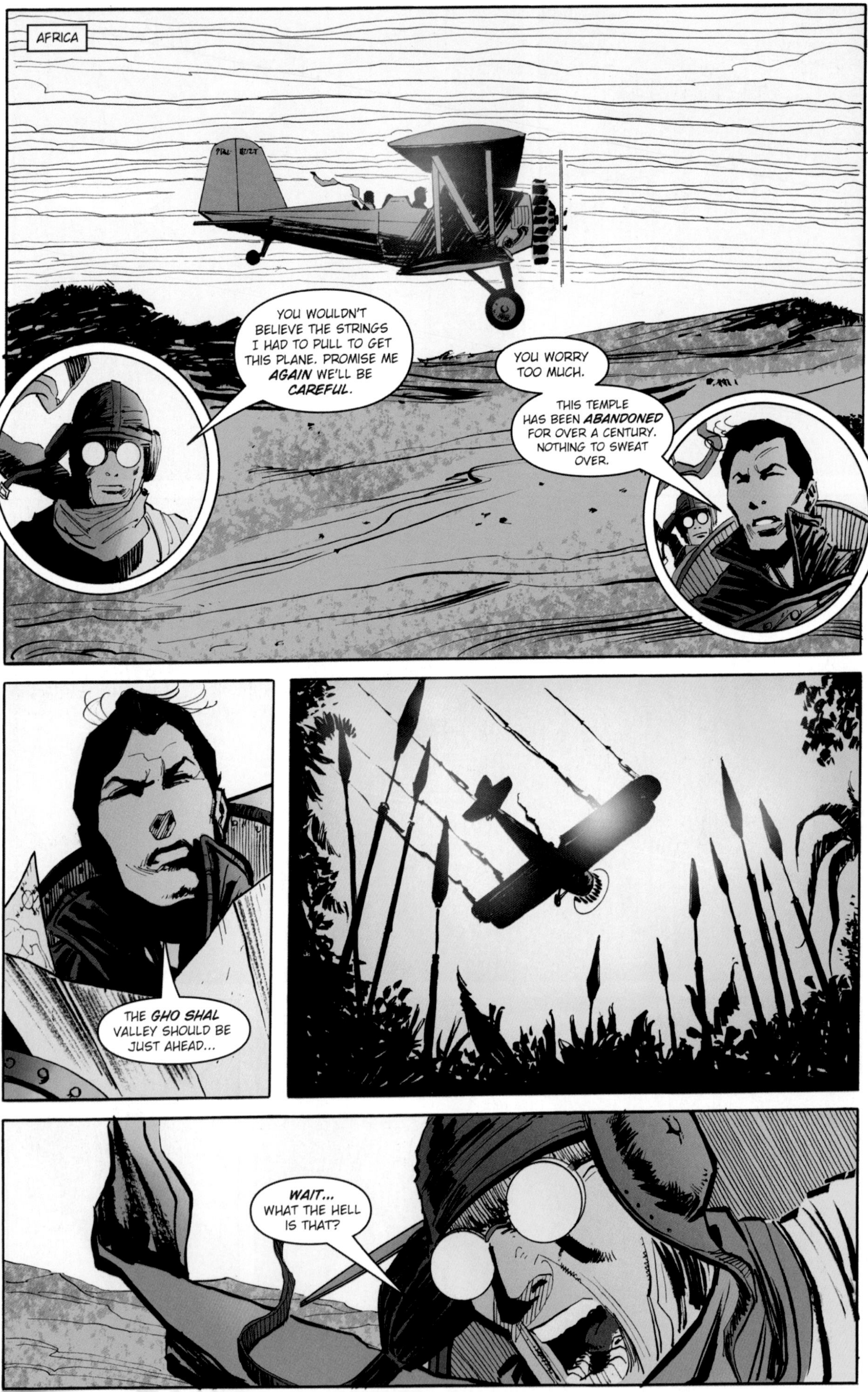
AFRICA
YOU WOULDN'T BELIEVE THE STRINGS I HAD TO PULL TO GET THIS PLANE. PROMISE ME AGAIN WE'LL BE CAREFUL.
YOU WORRY TOO MUCH.
THIS TEMPLE HAS BEEN ABANDONED FOR OVER A CENTURY. NOTHING TO SWEAT OVER.
THE GHO SHAL VALLEY SHOULD BE JUST AHEAD...
WAIT... WHAT THE HELL IS THAT?

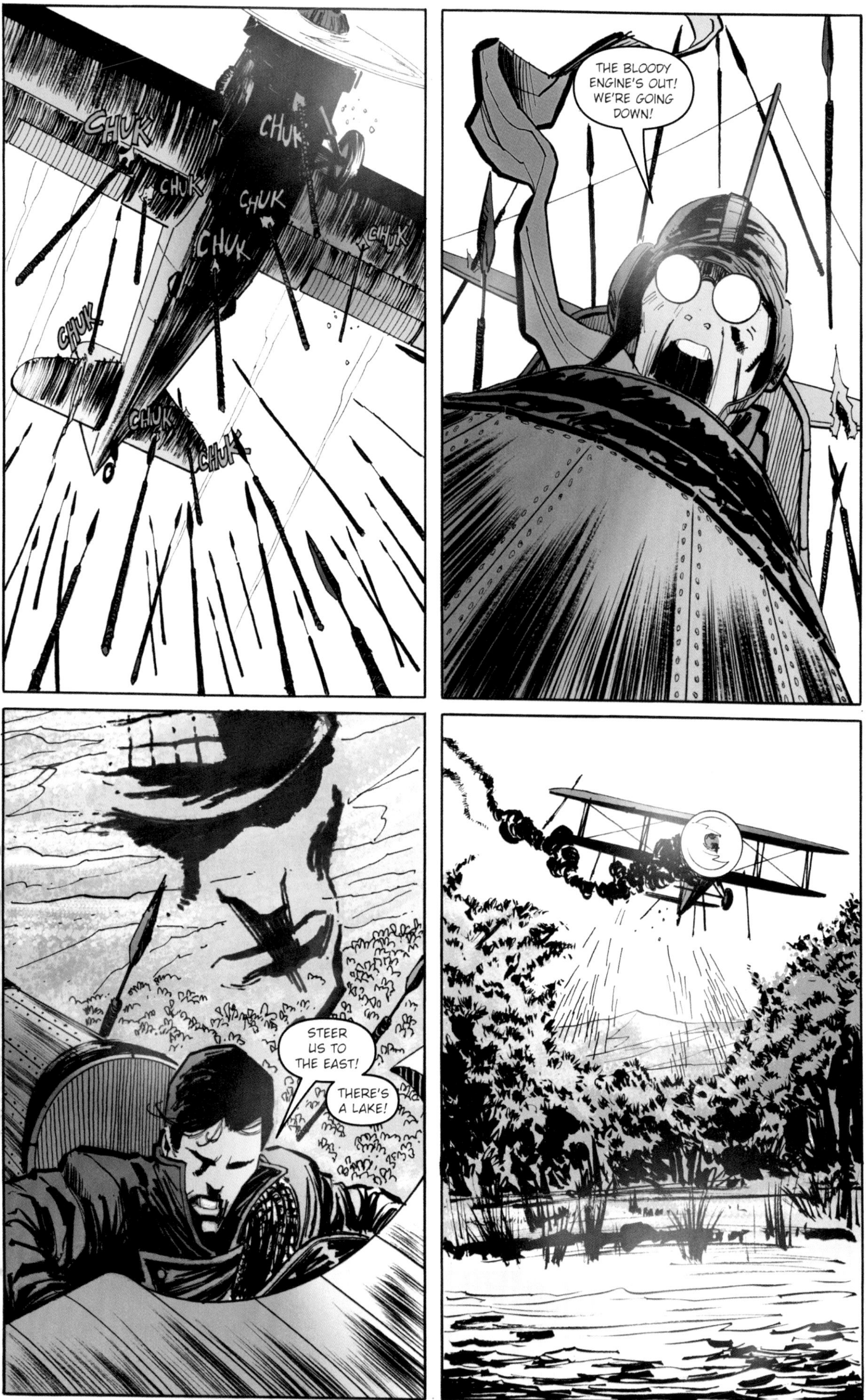
CHUK
CHUK
CHUK
CHUK
CHUK
CHUK
CHUK
CHUK
CHUK
THE BLOODY ENGINE'S OUT! WE'RE GOING DOWN!
STEER US TO THE EAST!
THERE'S A LAKE!

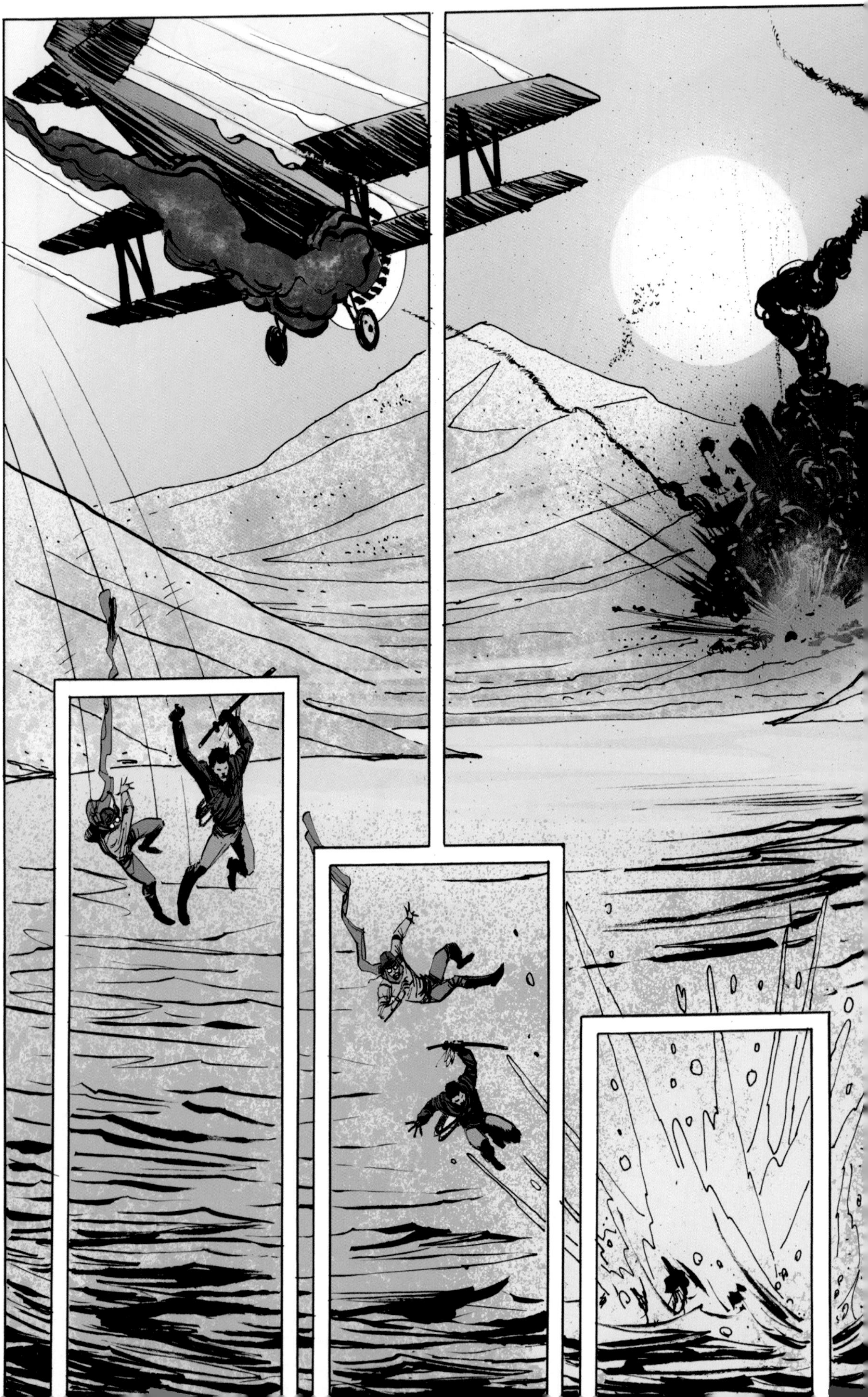

-:GASP!:-

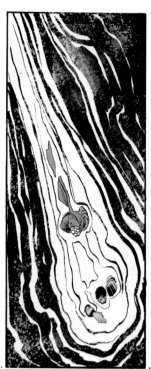

LOOK ALIVE, SEBASTIAN... HERE THEY COME.

M-MAYBE WE CAN TRY SOMETHING A BIT MORE... DIPLOMATIC?

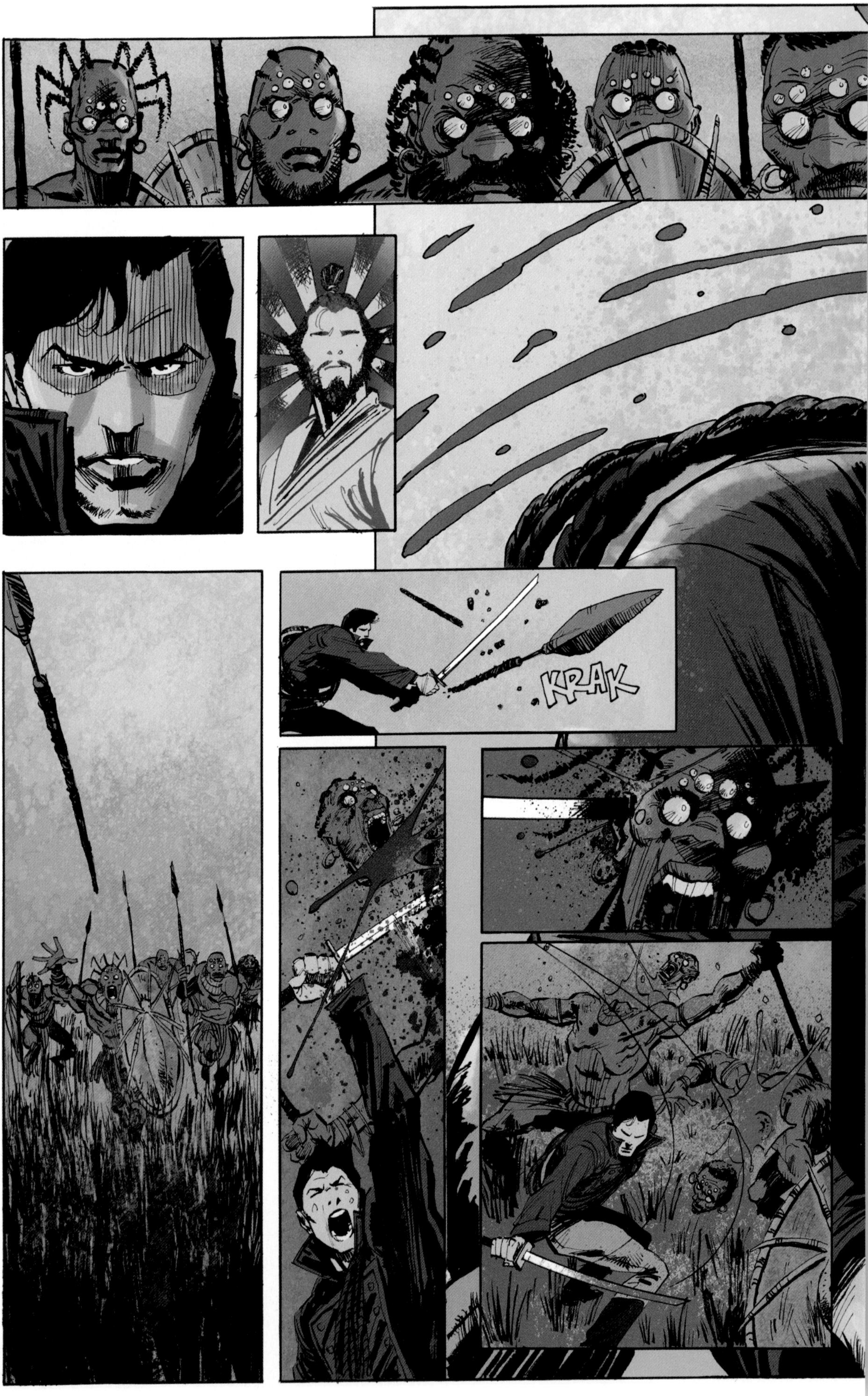
KRAK

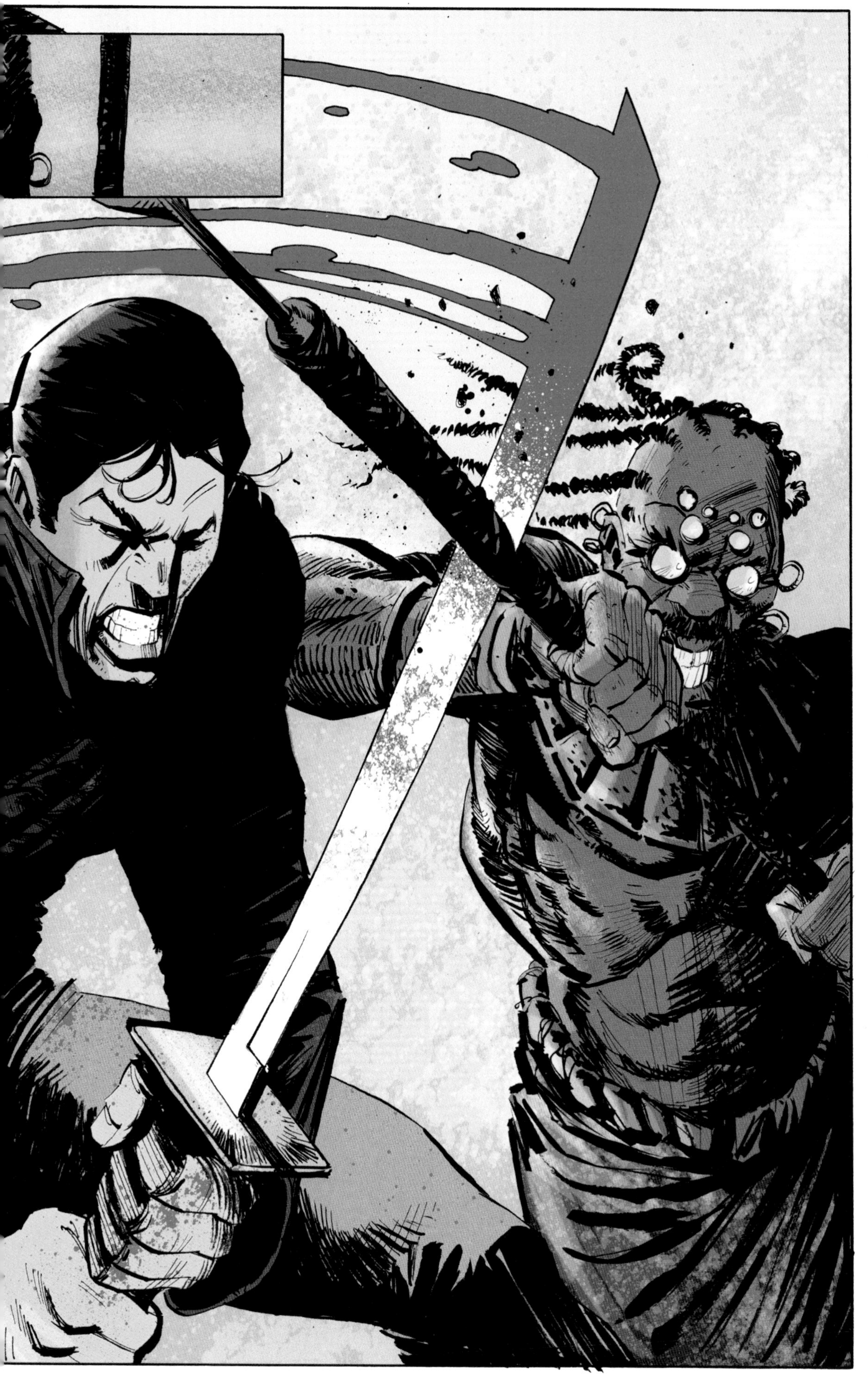

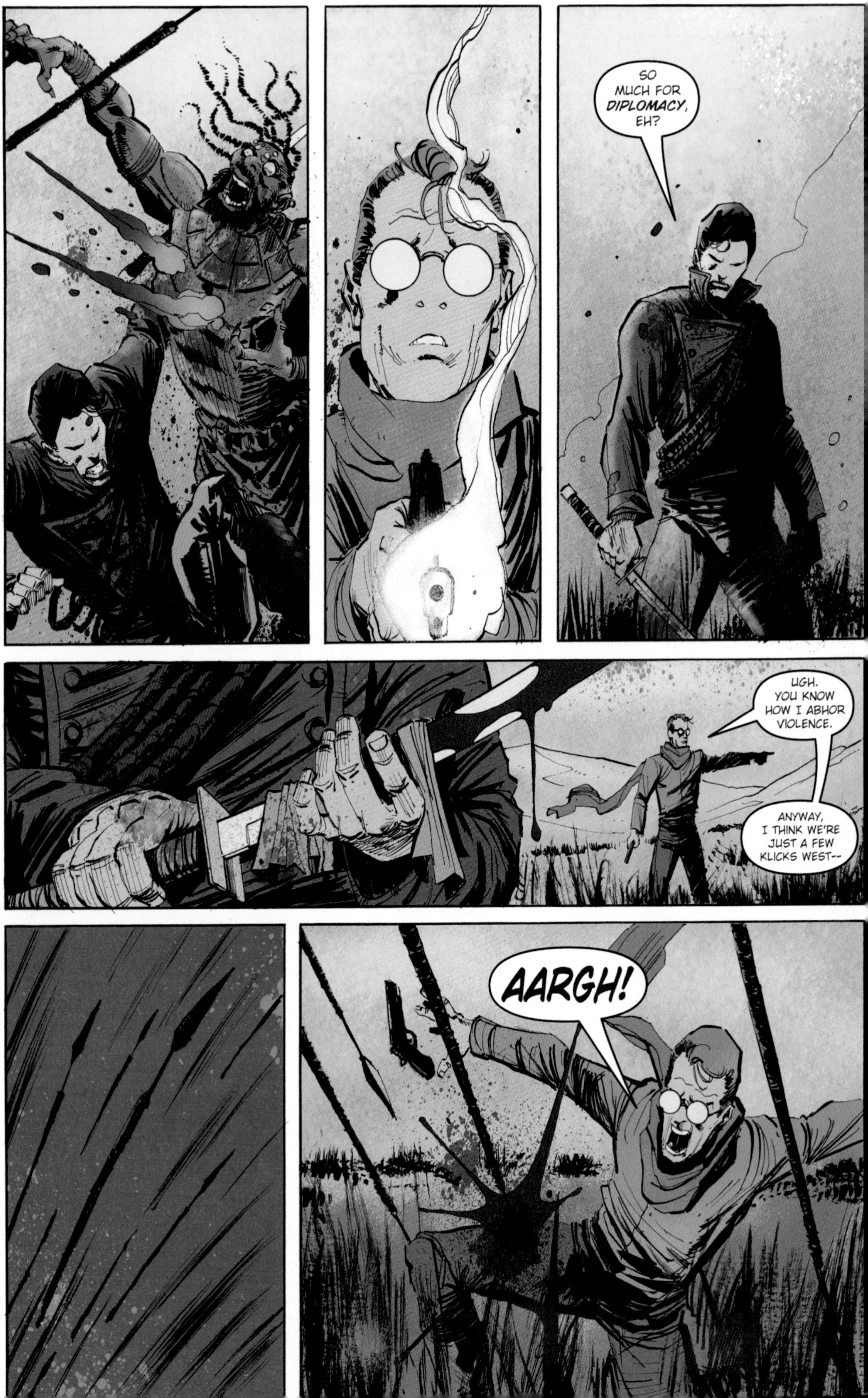
SO MUCH FOR DIPLOMACY, EH?
UGH. YOU KNOW HOW I ABHOR VIOLENCE.
ANYWAY, I THINK WE'RE JUST A FEW KLICKS WEST--
AARGH!

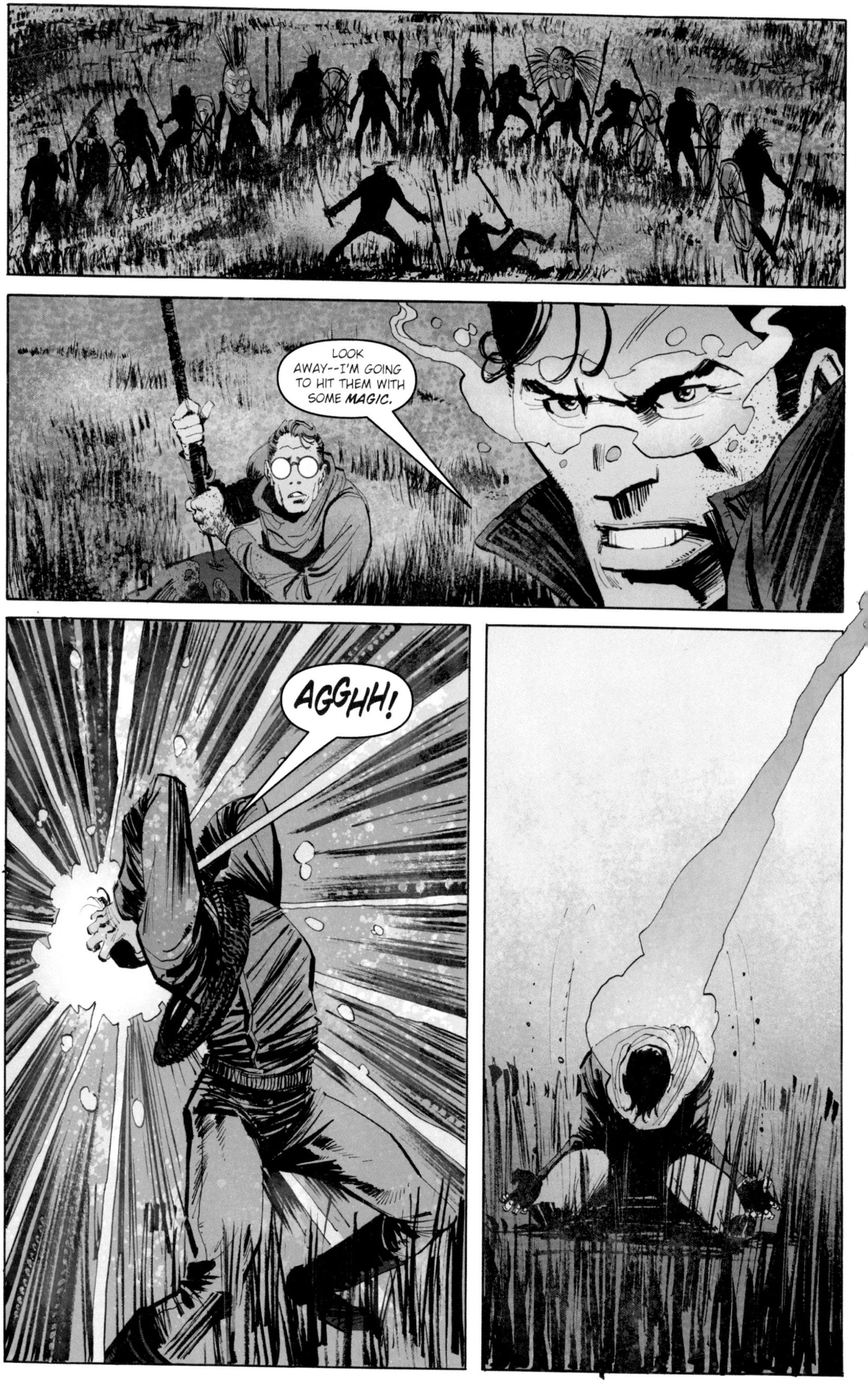
LOOK AWAY--I'M GOING TO HIT THEM WITH SOME *MAGIC.*
AGGHH!

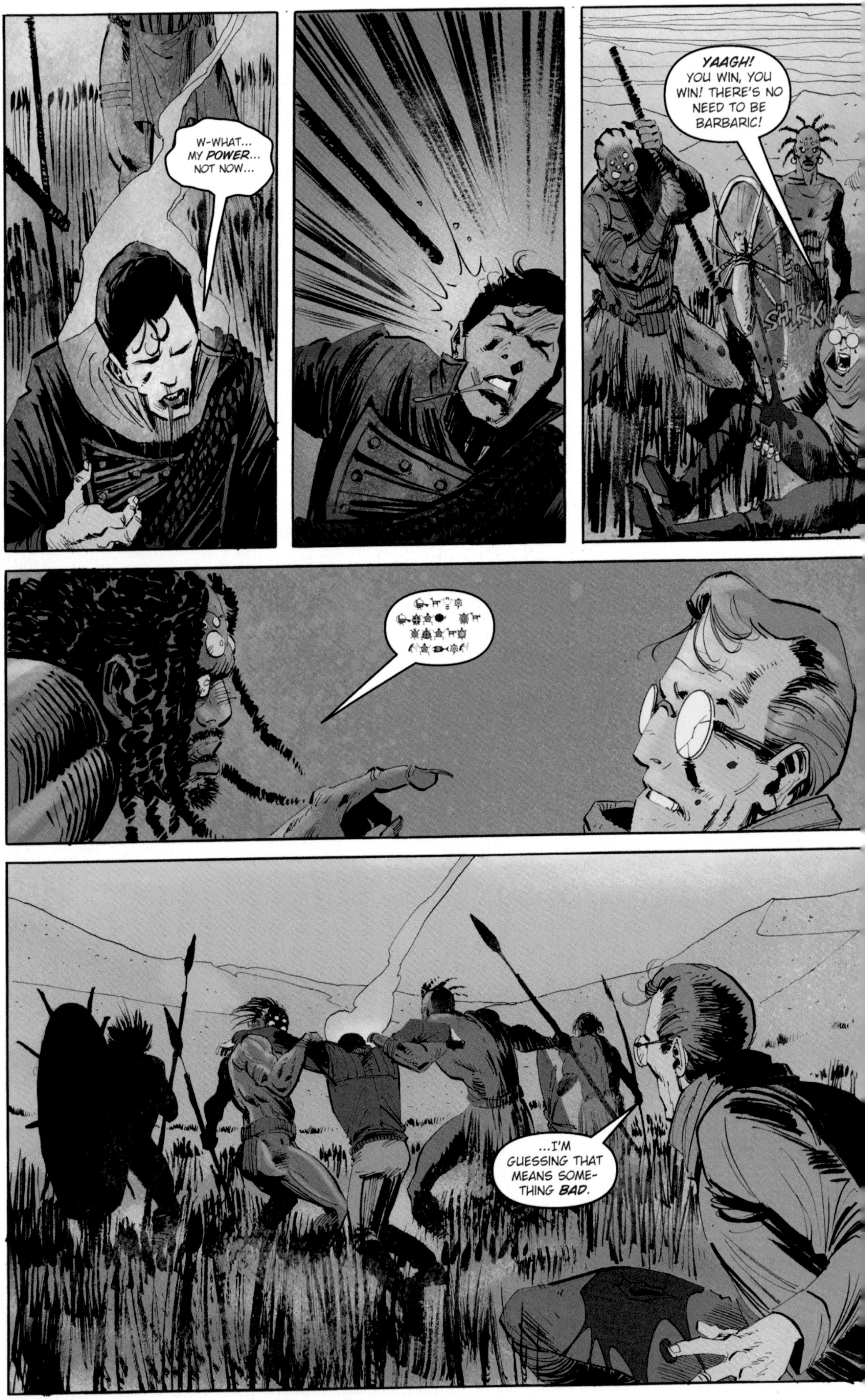
W-WHAT... MY POWER... NOT NOW...
YAAGH! YOU WIN, YOU WIN! THERE'S NO NEED TO BE BARBARIC!
SHRK!
...I'M GUESSING THAT MEANS SOME-THING BAD.

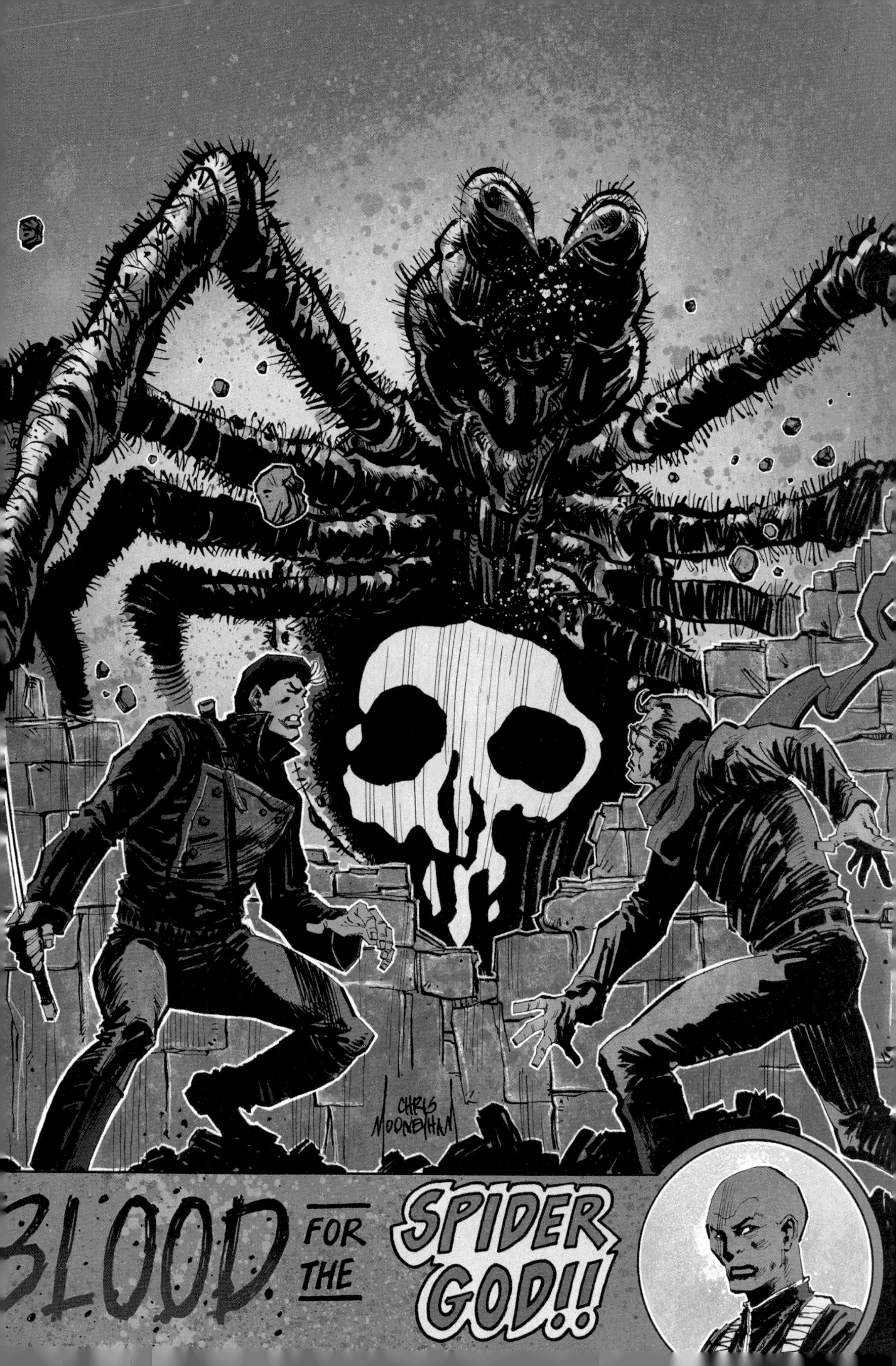
CHRIS MOONEYHAM
BLOOD FOR THE SPIDER GOD!!

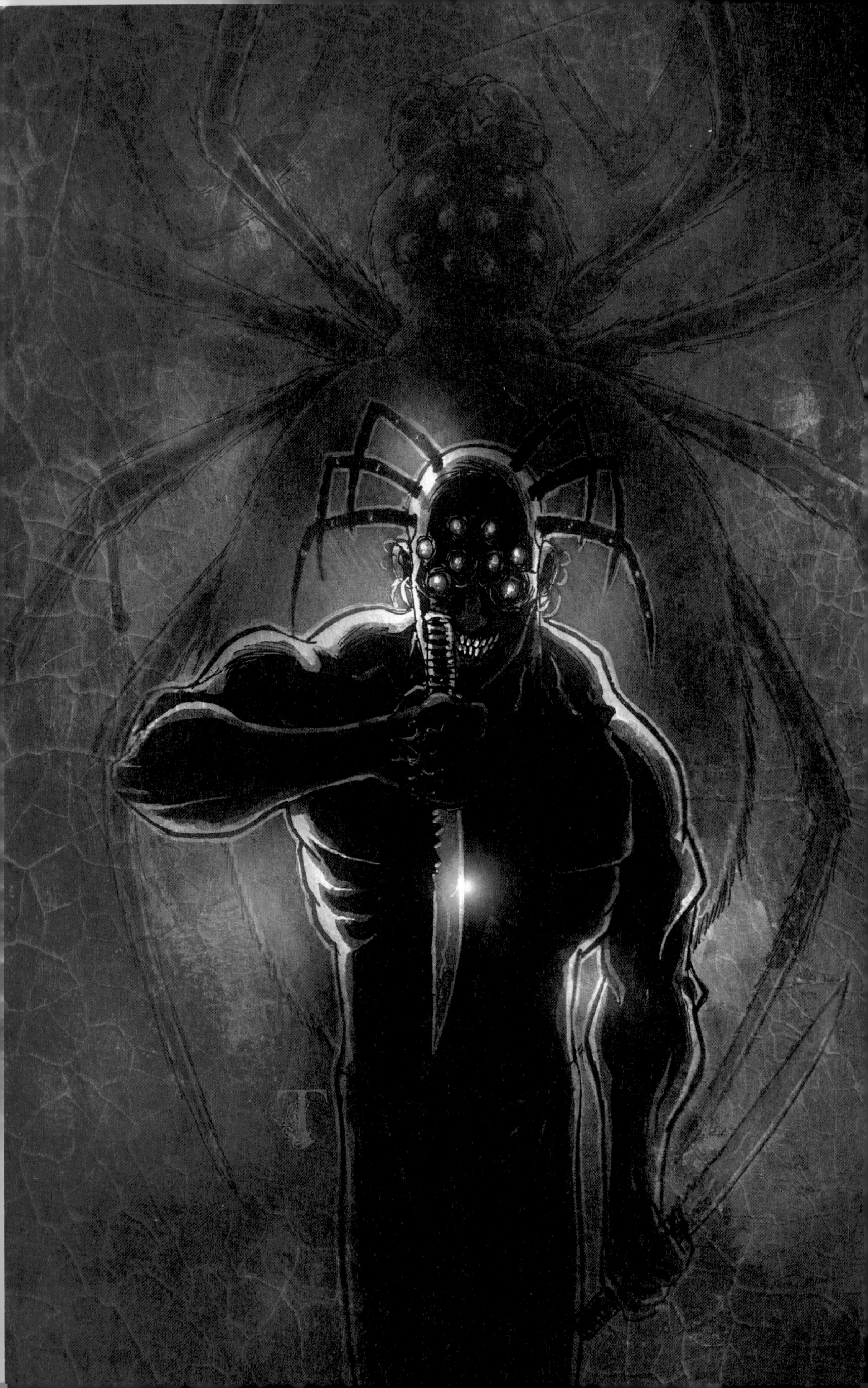

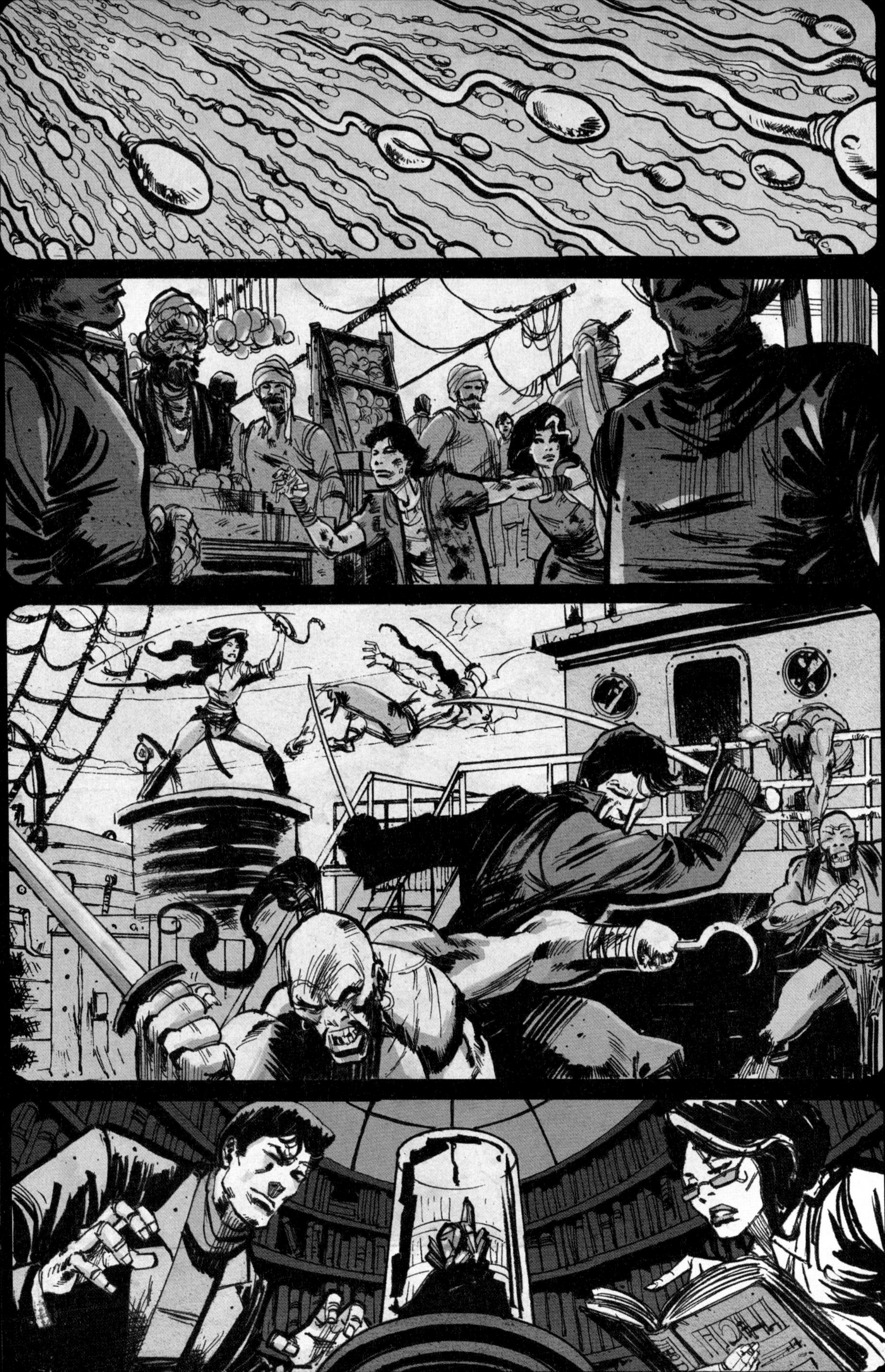

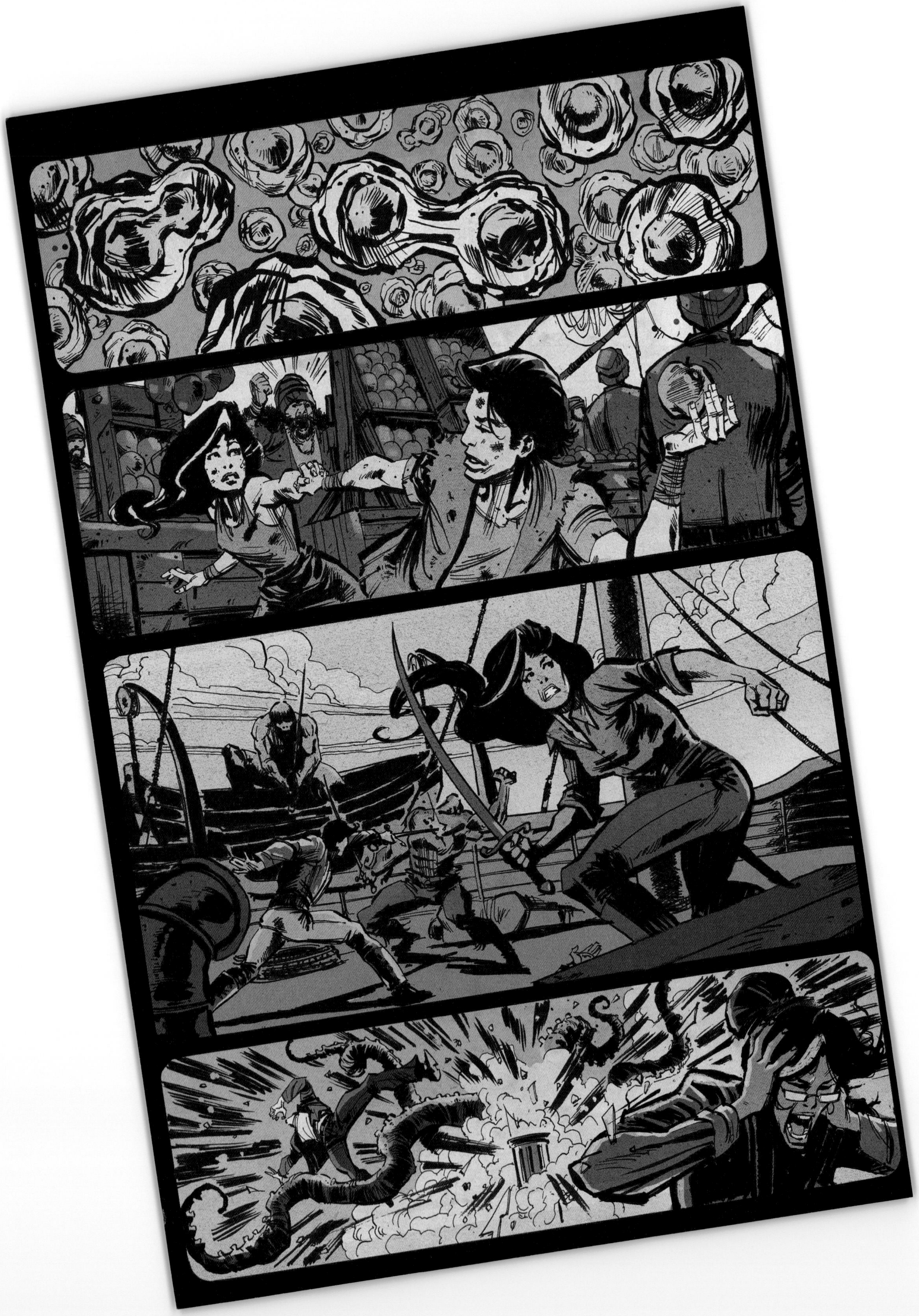

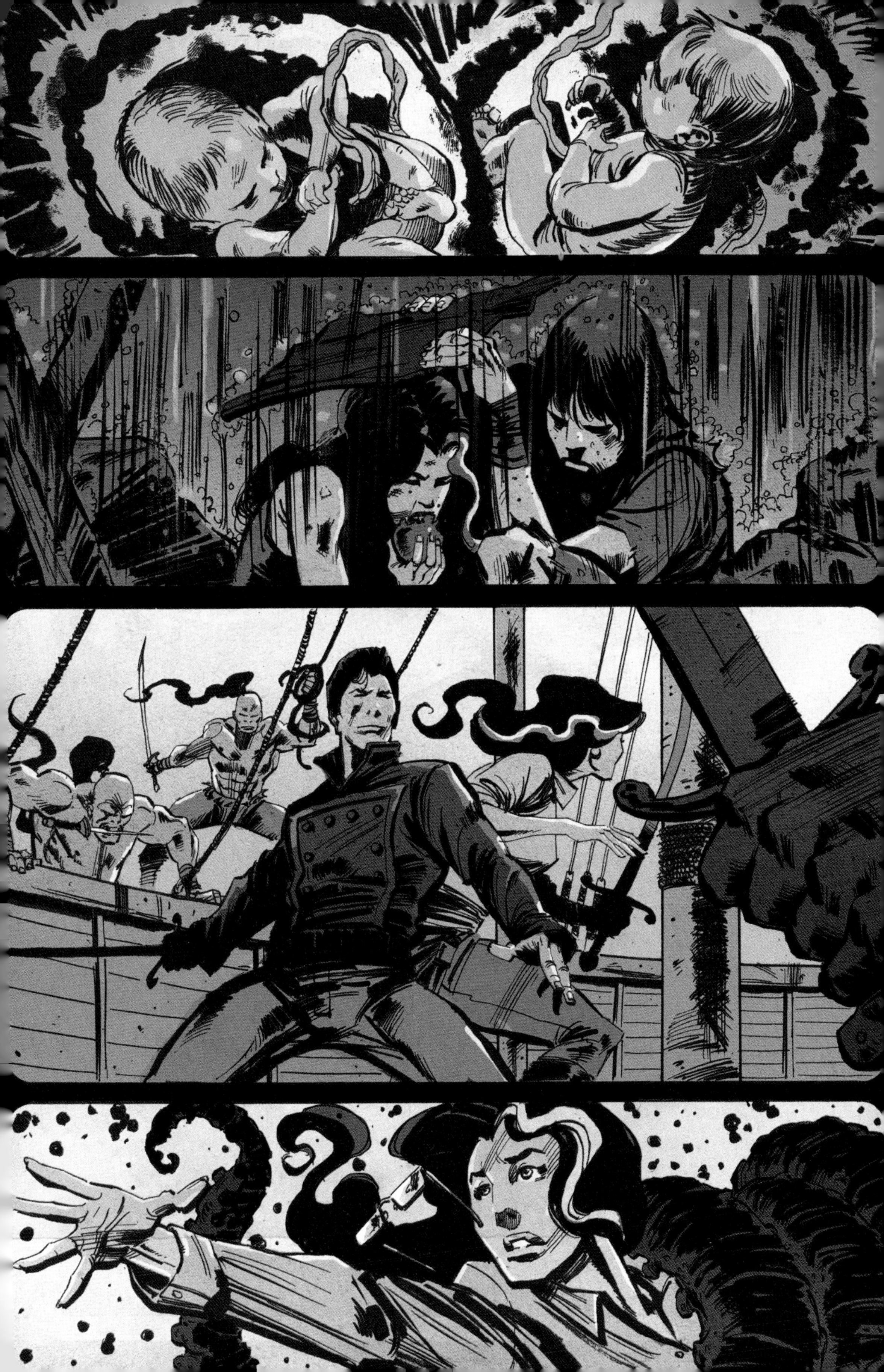

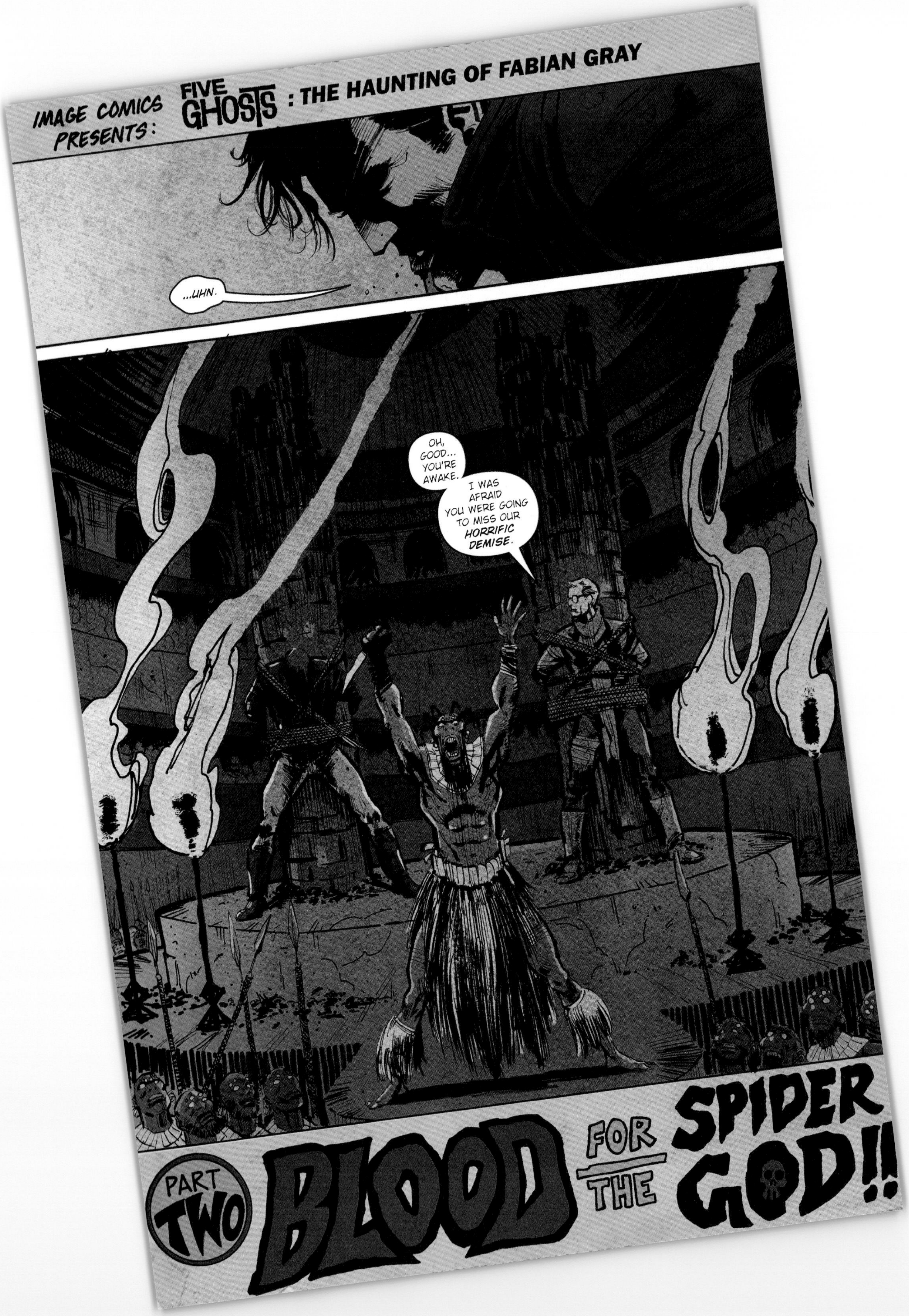
IMAGE COMICS PRESENTS:
FIVE GHOSTS : THE HAUNTING OF FABIAN GRAY
...UHN.
OH, GOOD... YOU'RE AWAKE.
I WAS AFRAID YOU WERE GOING TO MISS OUR HORRIFIC DEMISE.
PART TWO
BLOOD FOR THE SPIDER GOD!!

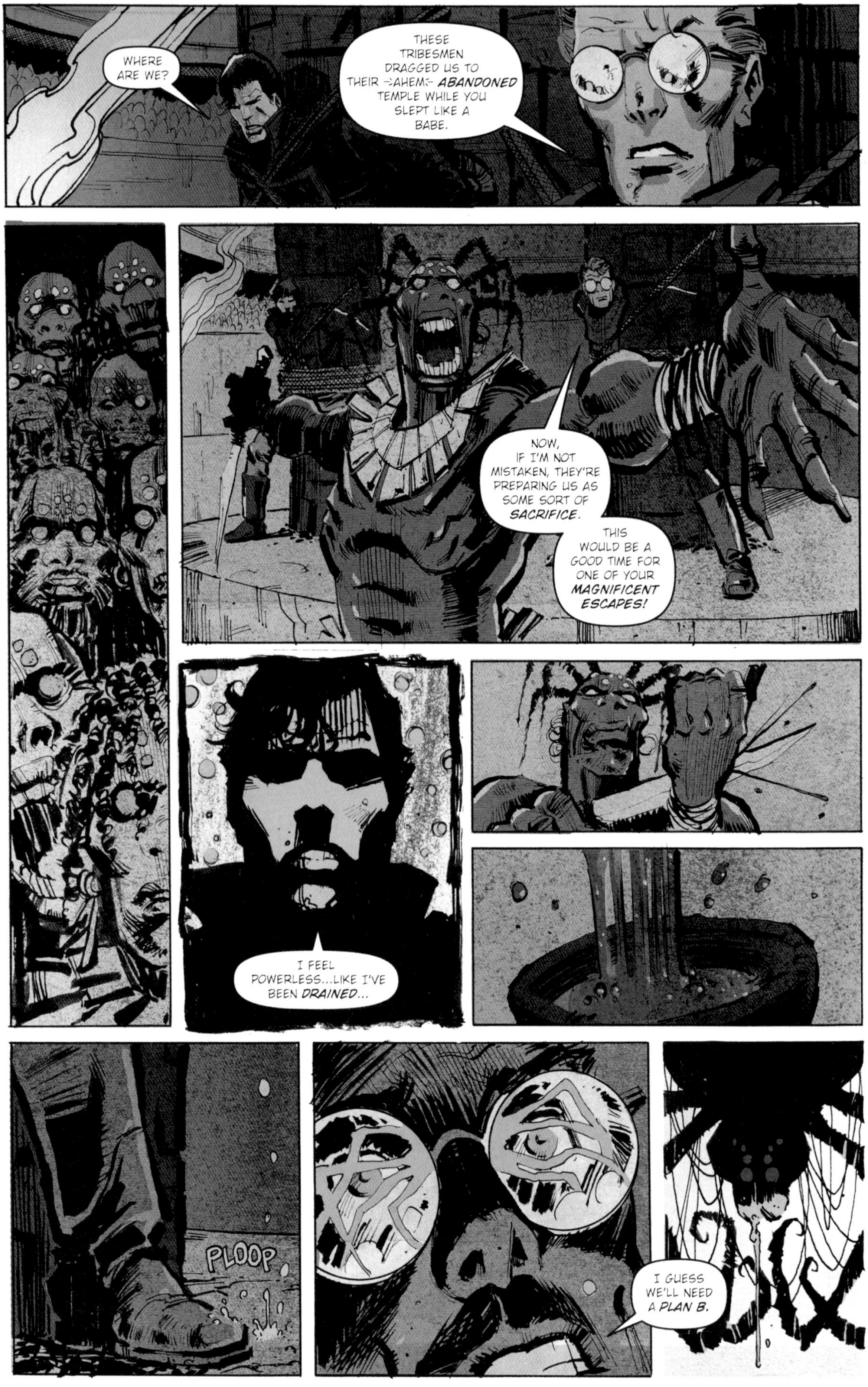
WHERE ARE WE?
THESE TRIBESMEN DRAGGED US TO THEIR --AHEM-- ABANDONED TEMPLE WHILE YOU SLEPT LIKE A BABE.
NOW, IF I'M NOT MISTAKEN, THEY'RE PREPARING US AS SOME SORT OF SACRIFICE.
THIS WOULD BE A GOOD TIME FOR ONE OF YOUR MAGNIFICENT ESCAPES!
I FEEL POWERLESS...LIKE I'VE BEEN DRAINED...
PLOOP
I GUESS WE'LL NEED A PLAN B.

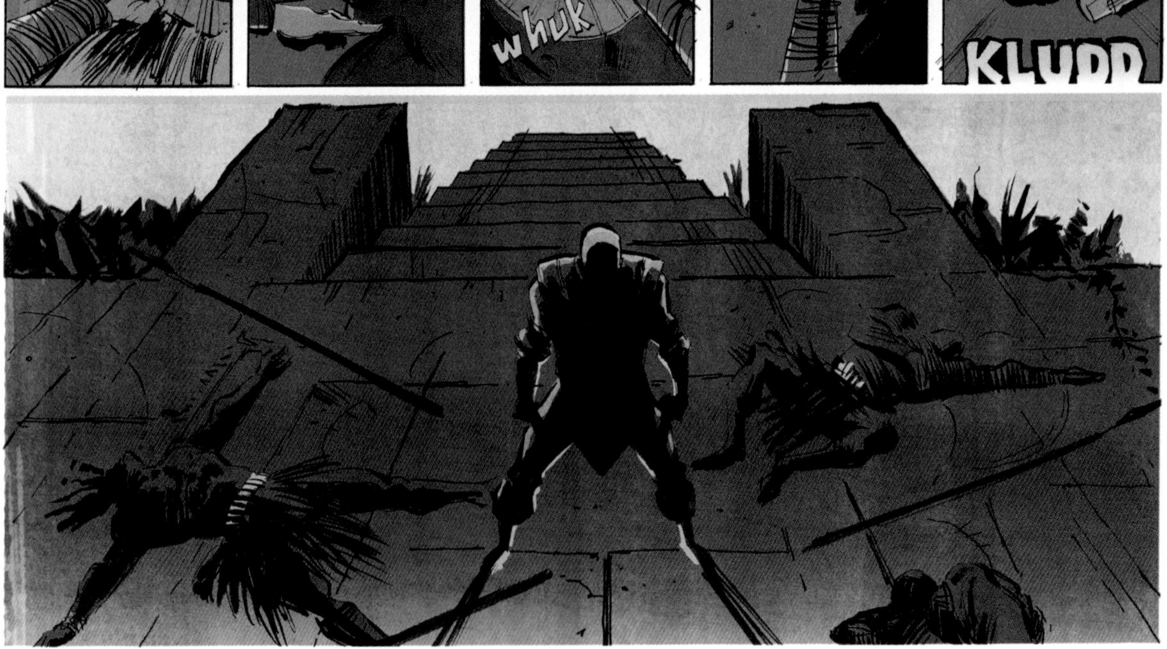
whuk
KLUDD

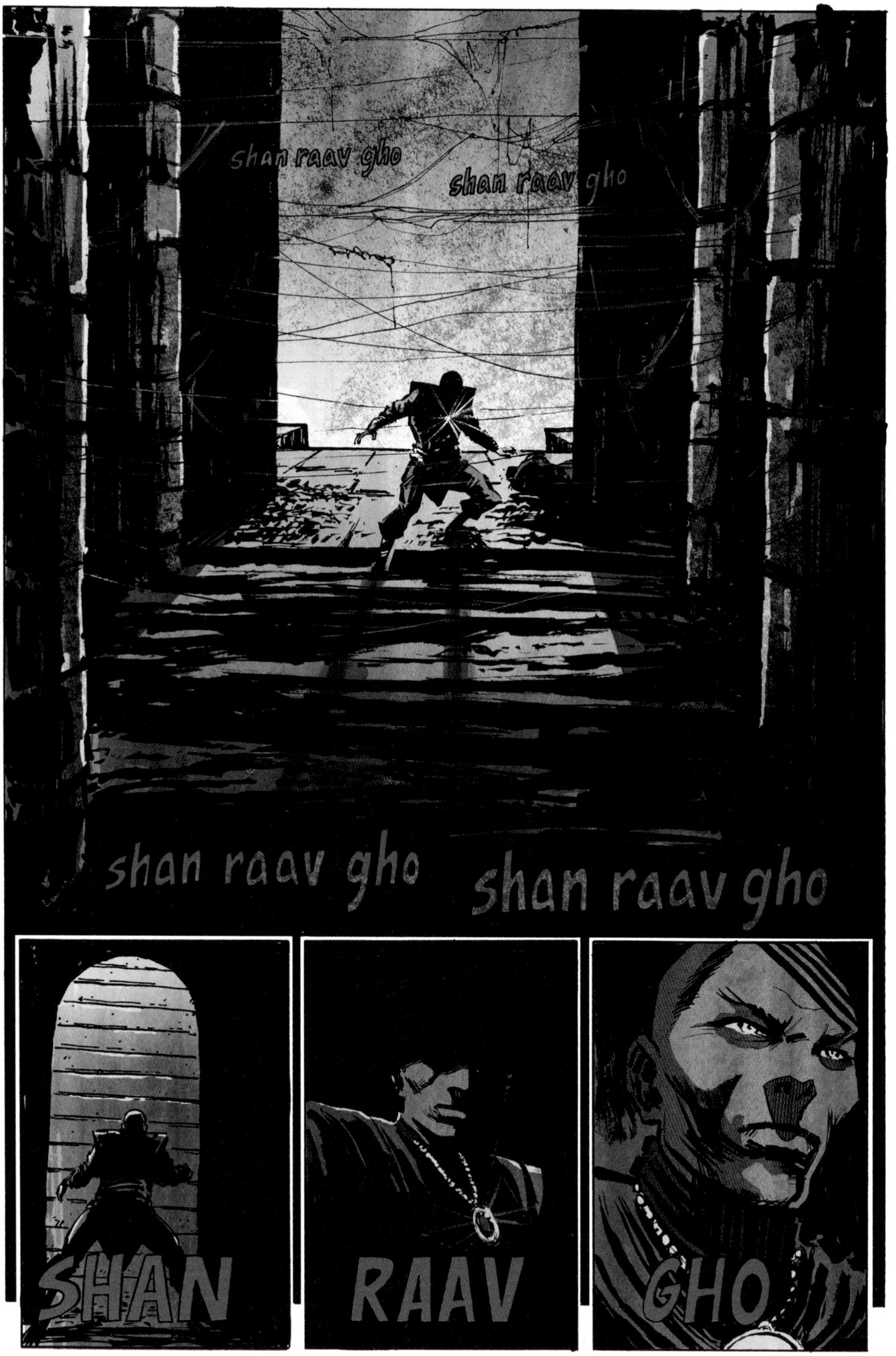
shan raav gho
shan raav gho
shan raav gho
shan raav gho
SHAN
RAAV
GHO

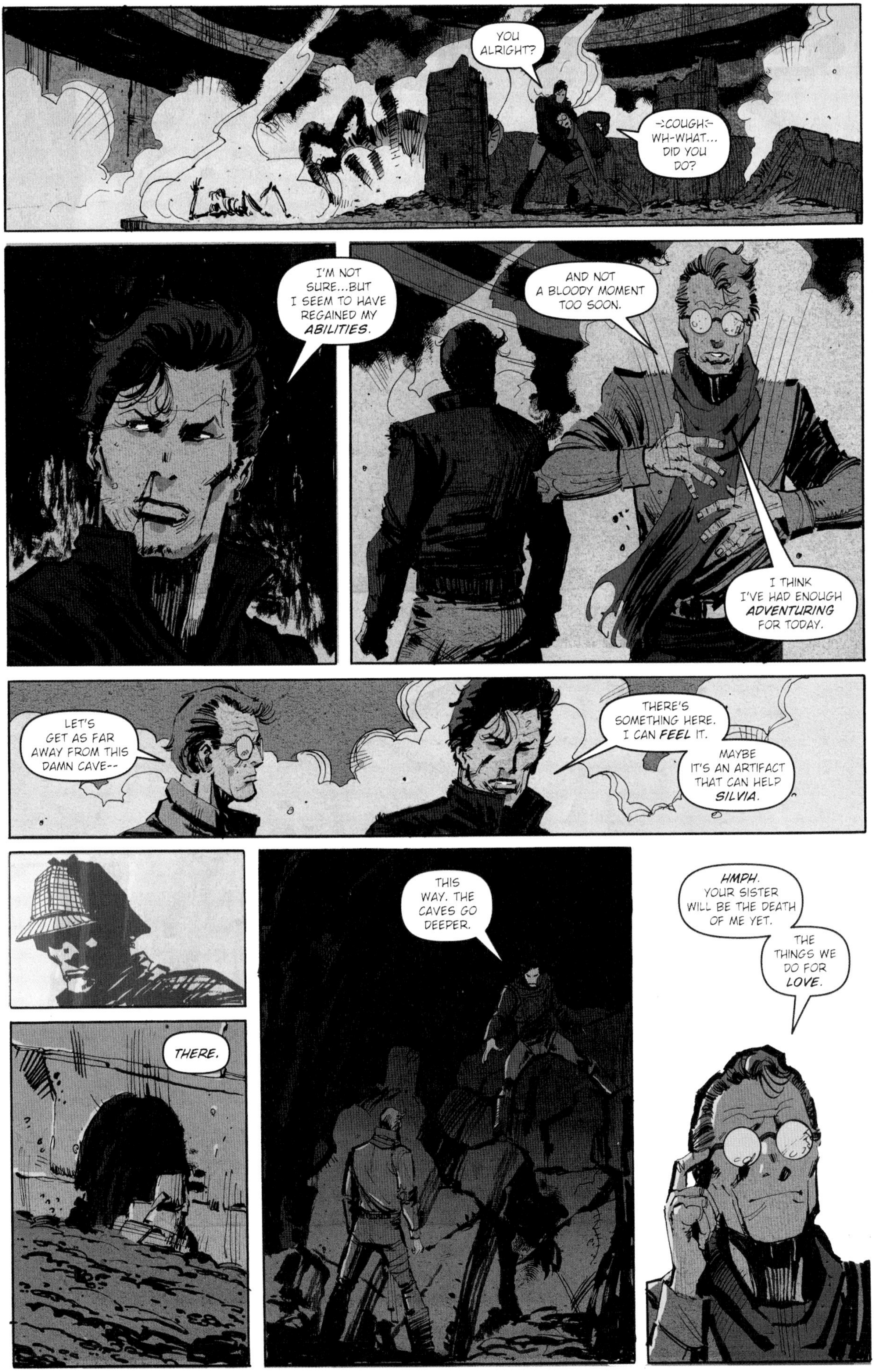
YOU ALRIGHT?
-COUGH- WH-WHAT... DID YOU DO?
I'M NOT SURE...BUT I SEEM TO HAVE REGAINED MY ABILITIES.
AND NOT A BLOODY MOMENT TOO SOON.
I THINK I'VE HAD ENOUGH ADVENTURING FOR TODAY.
LET'S GET AS FAR AWAY FROM THIS DAMN CAVE--
THERE'S SOMETHING HERE. I CAN FEEL IT.
MAYBE IT'S AN ARTIFACT THAT CAN HELP SILVIA.
THERE.
THIS WAY. THE CAVES GO DEEPER.
HMPH. YOUR SISTER WILL BE THE DEATH OF ME YET.
THE THINGS WE DO FOR LOVE.

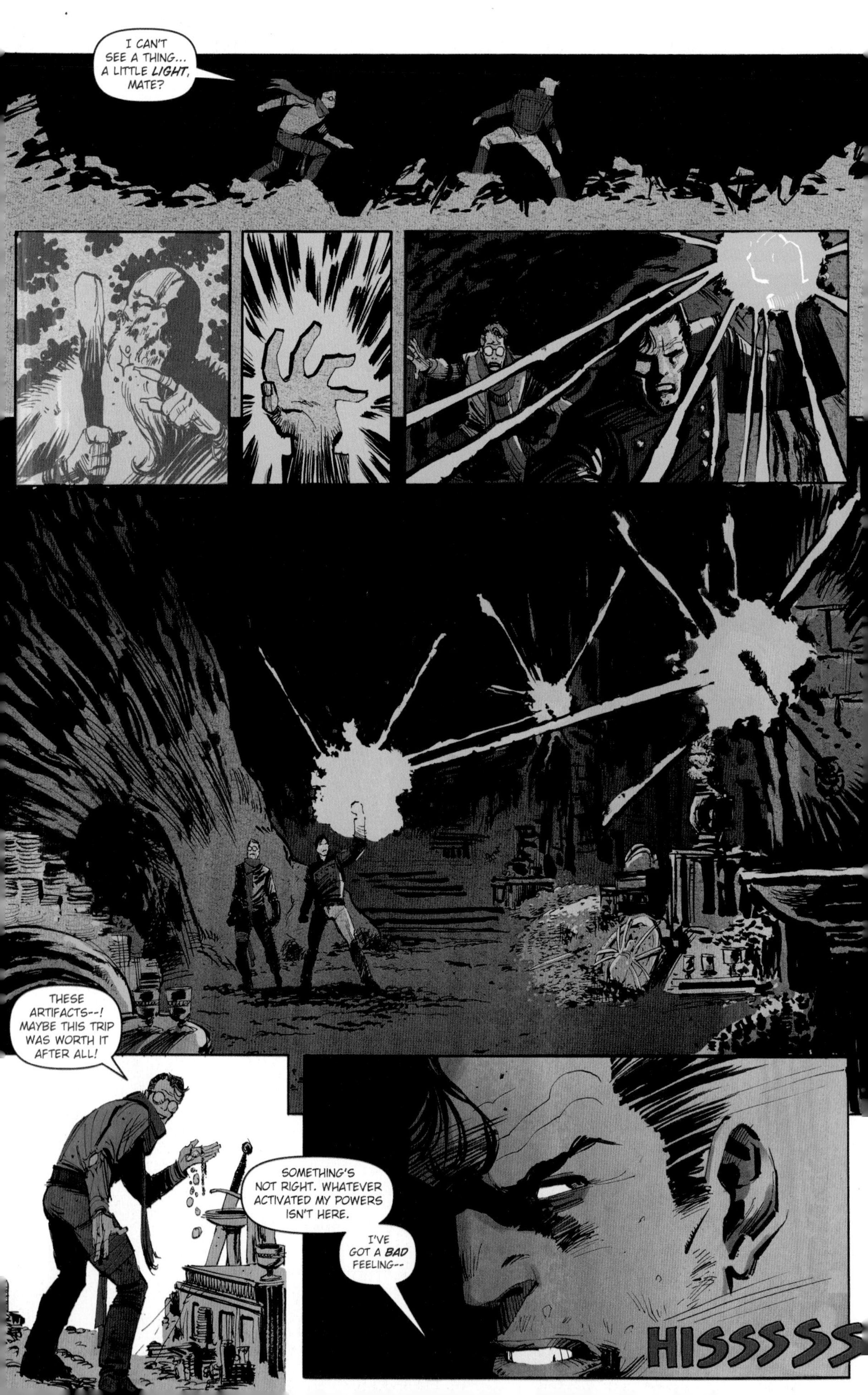
I CAN'T SEE A THING... A LITTLE LIGHT, MATE?
THESE ARTIFACTS--! MAYBE THIS TRIP WAS WORTH IT AFTER ALL!
SOMETHING'S NOT RIGHT. WHATEVER ACTIVATED MY POWERS ISN'T HERE.
I'VE GOT A BAD FEELING--
HISSSSS

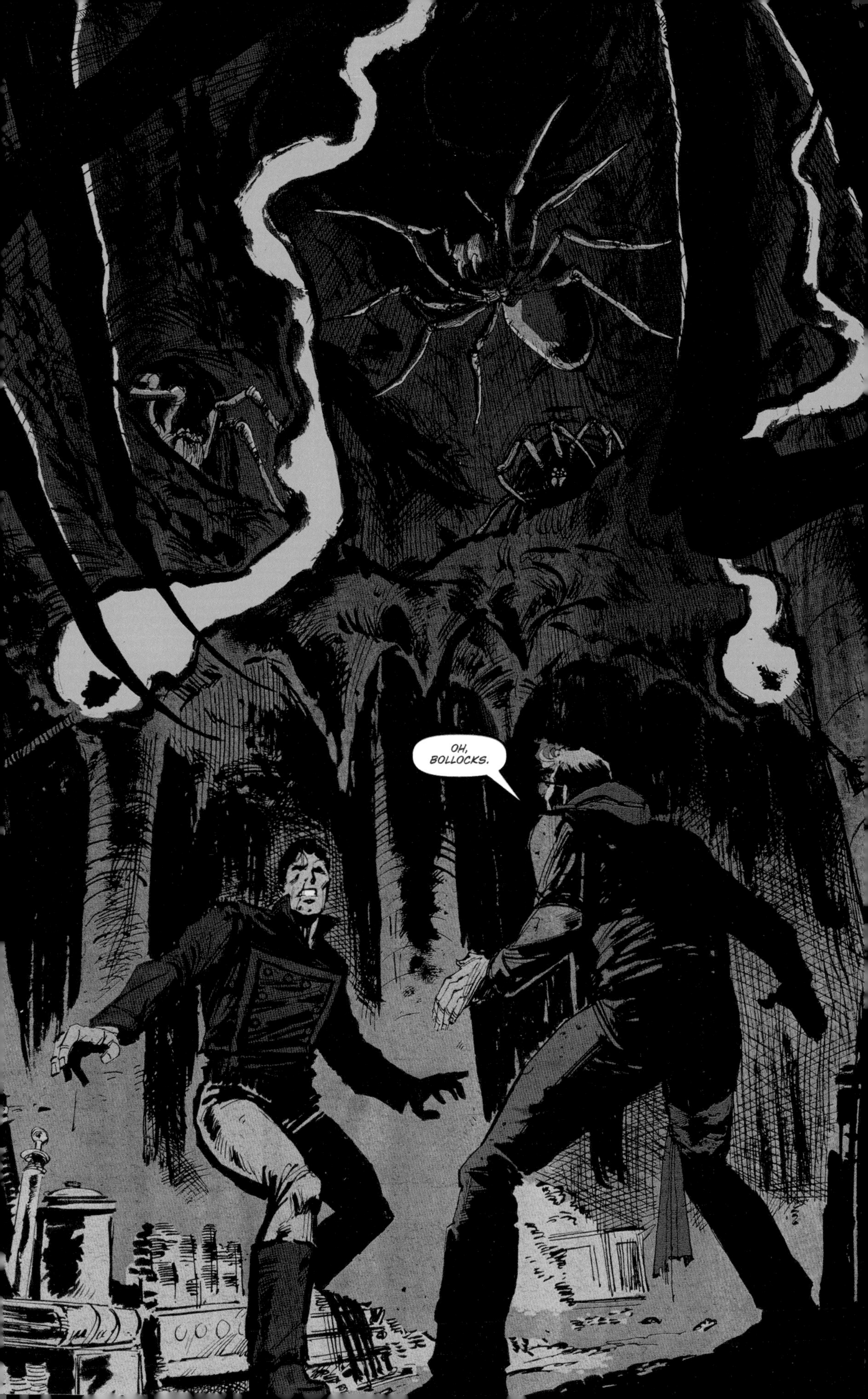
OH, BOLLOCKS.

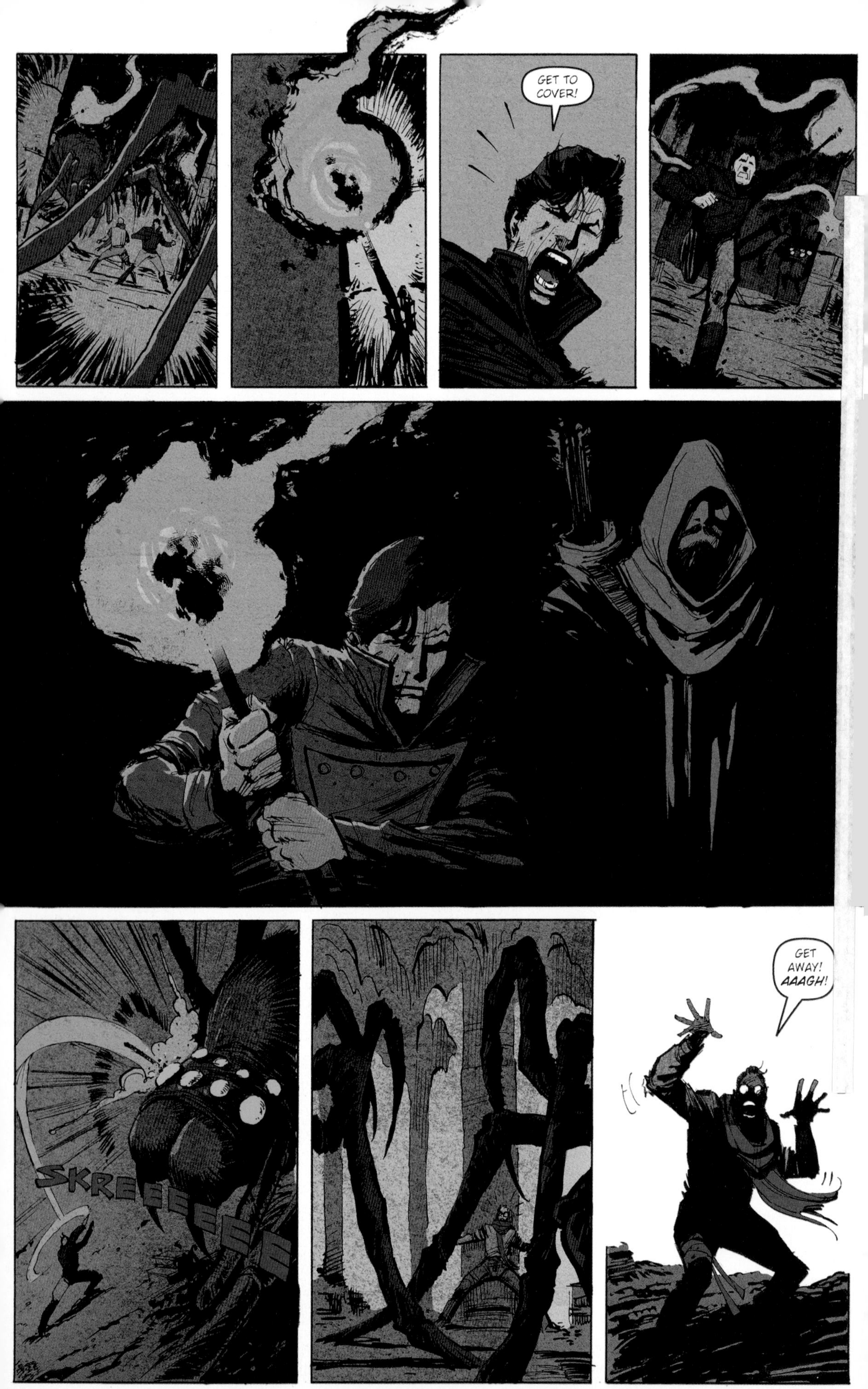
GET TO COVER!
SKREEEEEEE
GET AWAY! AAAGH!

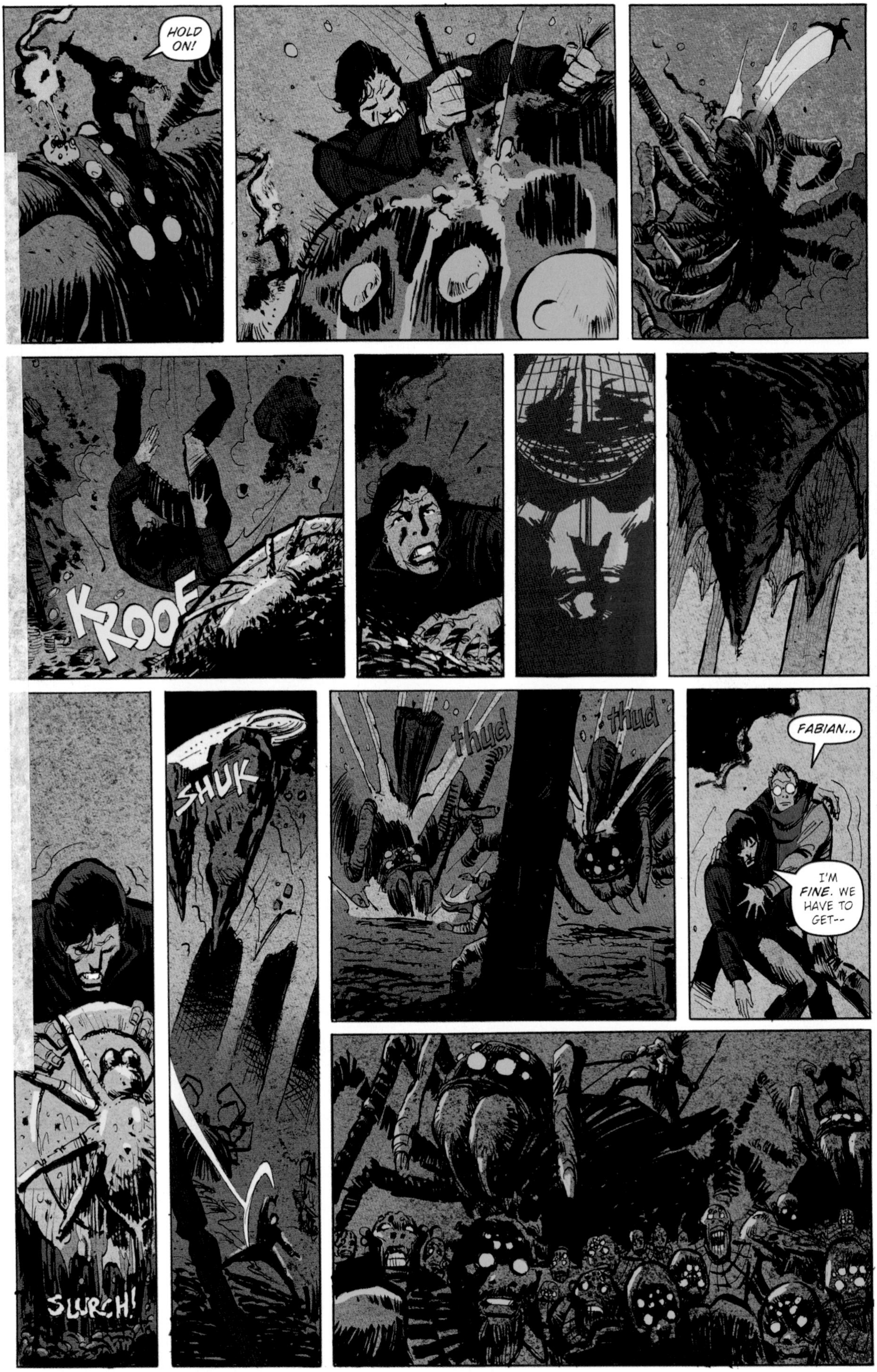
HOLD ON!
KROOF
SLURCH!
SHUK
thud
thud
FABIAN...
I'M FINE. WE HAVE TO GET--

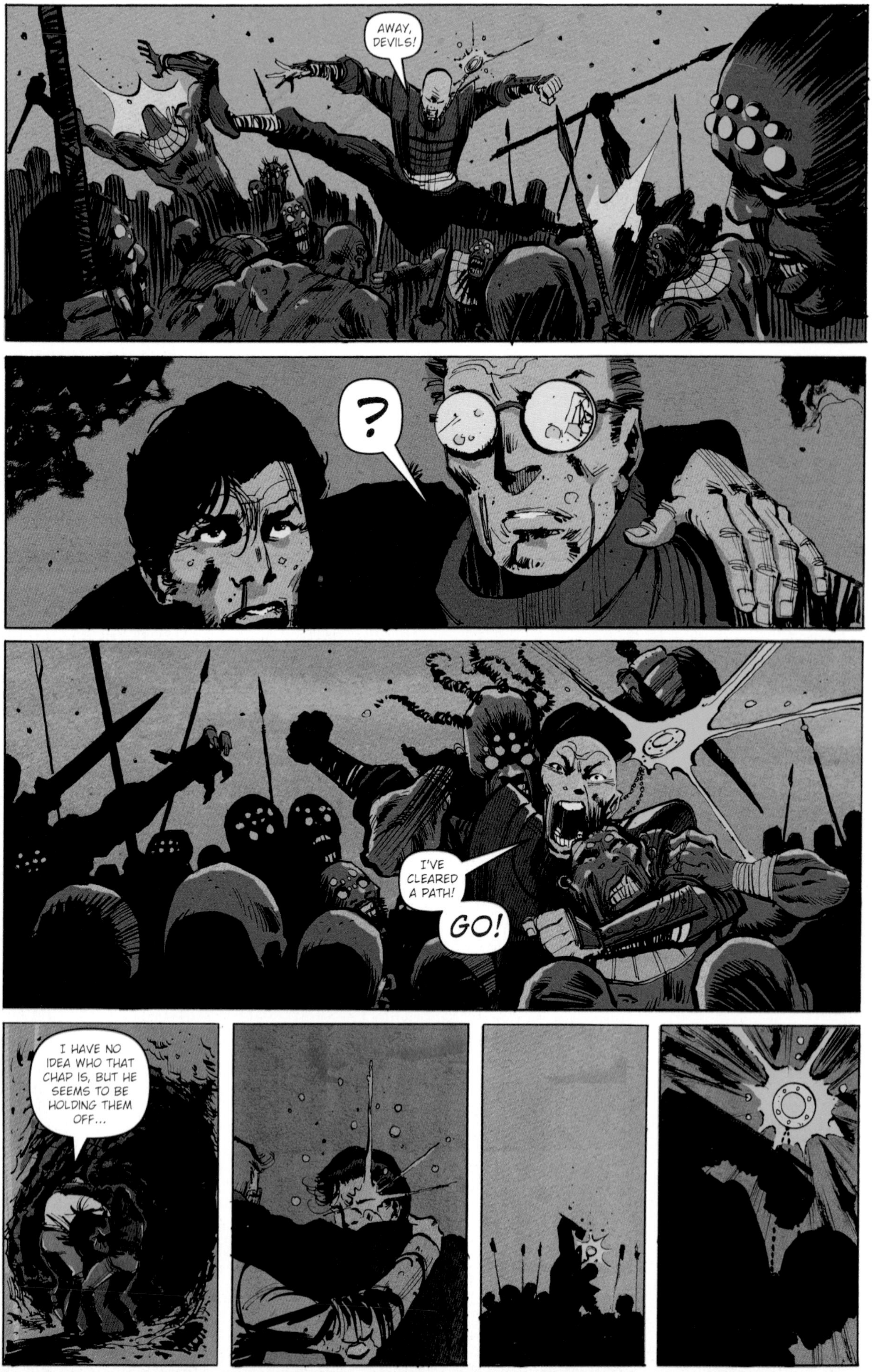
AWAY, DEVILS!
?
I'VE CLEARED A PATH!
GO!
I HAVE NO IDEA WHO THAT CHAP IS, BUT HE SEEMS TO BE HOLDING THEM OFF...

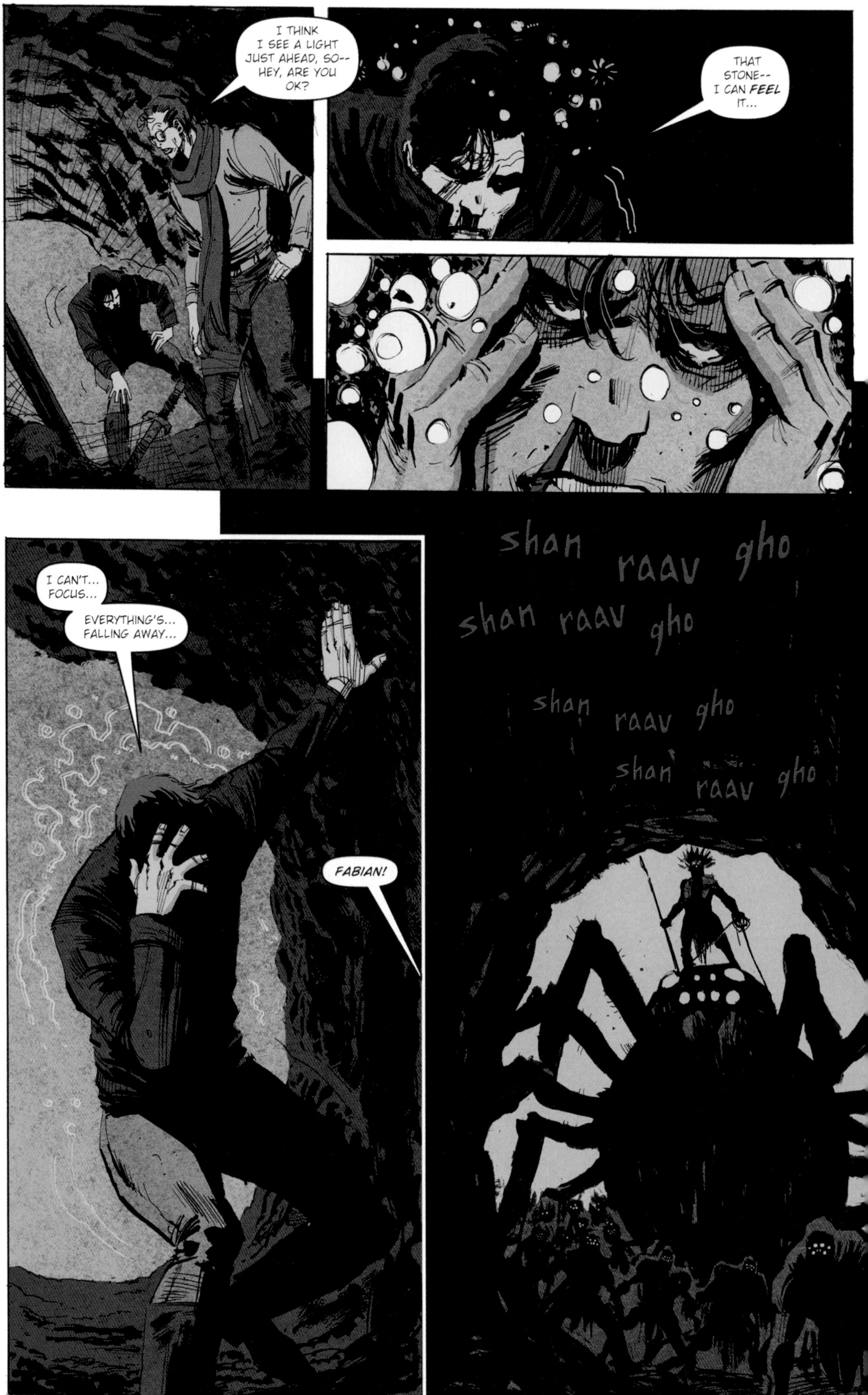

I THINK I SEE A LIGHT JUST AHEAD, SO-- HEY, ARE YOU OK?
THAT STONE-- I CAN FEEL IT...
I CAN'T... FOCUS...
EVERYTHING'S... FALLING AWAY...
FABIAN!
shan raav gho
shan raav gho
shan raav gho
shan raav gho

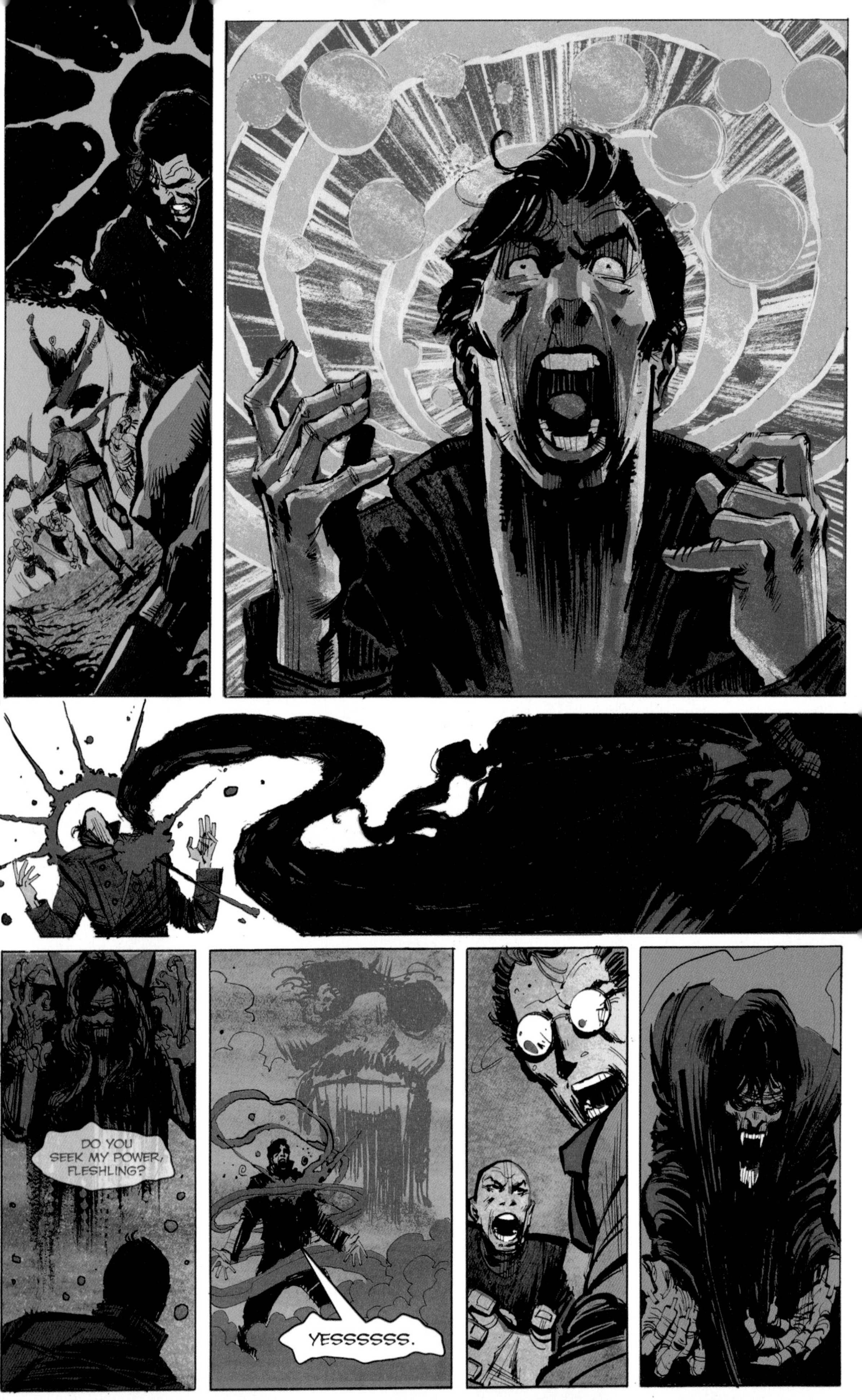
DO YOU SEEK MY POWER, FLESHLING?
YESSSSSS.

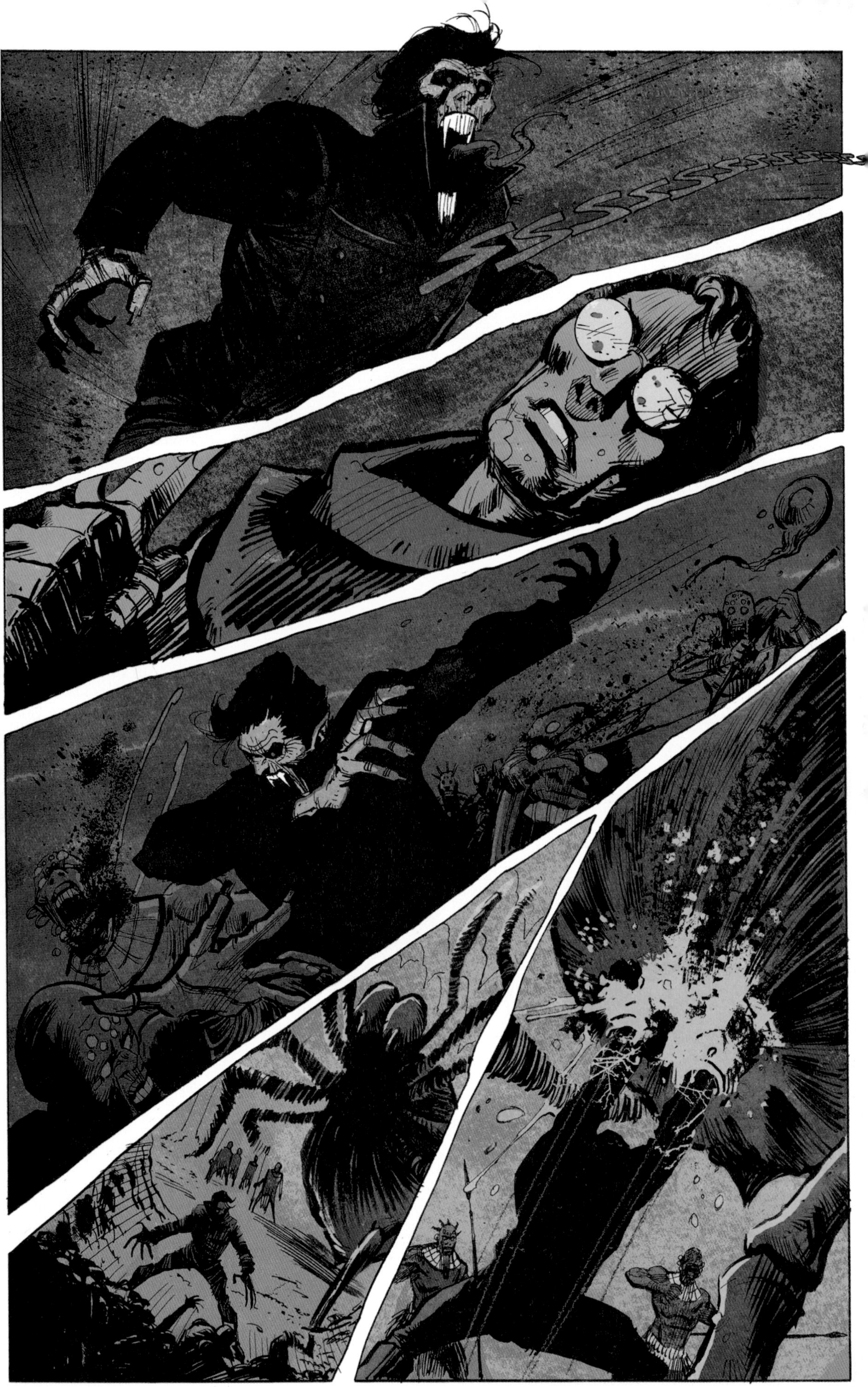
SSSSSSSSSSSSSS

CRASH!

SKRTCH

...FABIAN?

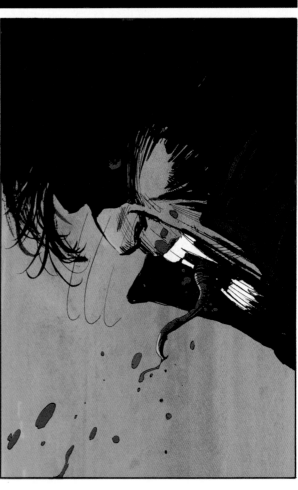

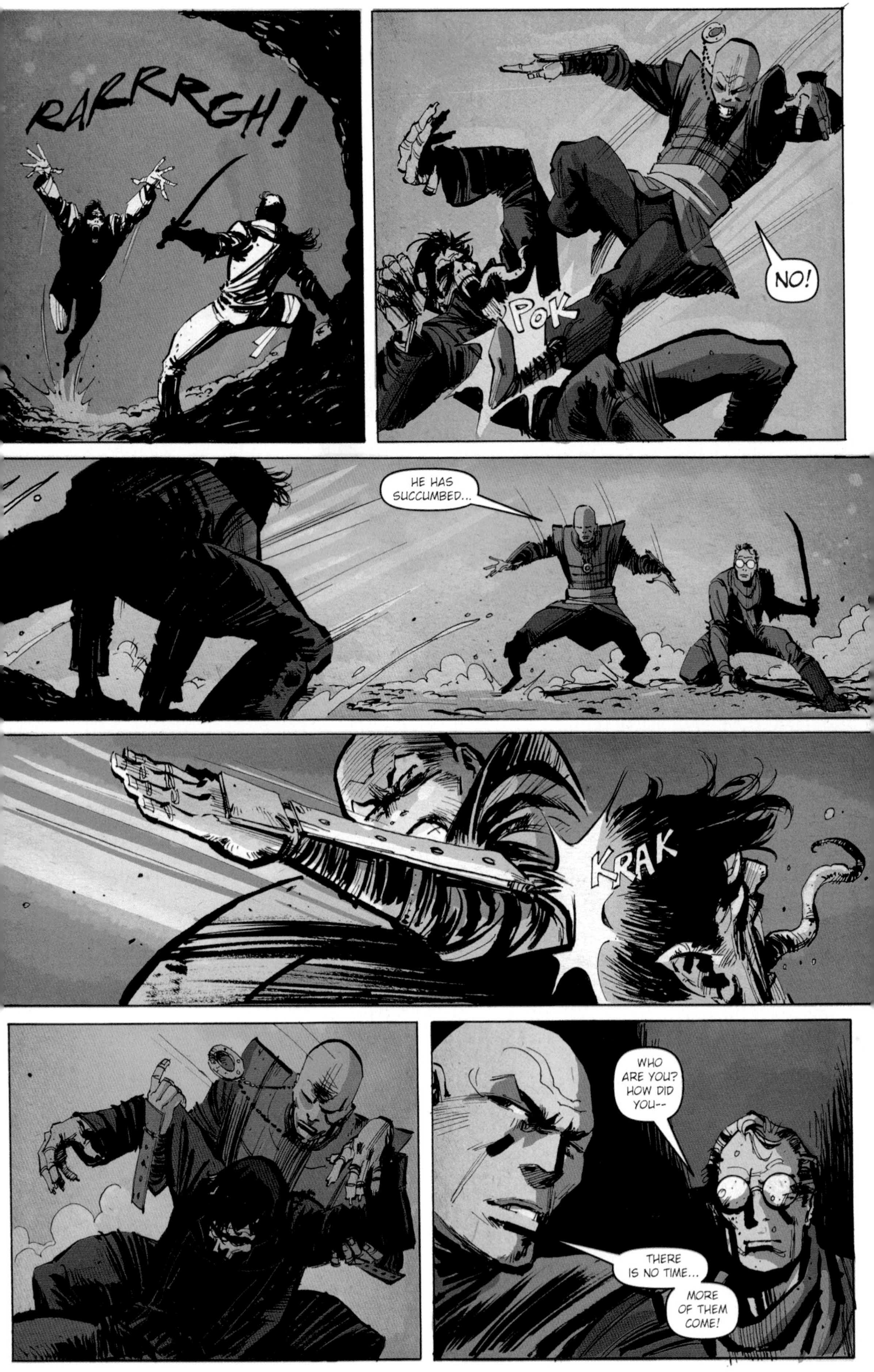
RARRRGH!
NO!
POK
HE HAS SUCCUMBED...
KRAK
WHO ARE YOU? HOW DID YOU--
THERE IS NO TIME...
MORE OF THEM COME!

LISTEN, I'M THANKFUL YOU, UM, *SAVED* US--BUT WHERE ARE WE GOING?

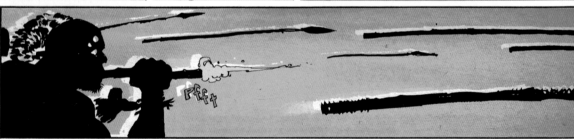

IT'S A DEAD END! WE'RE *DOOMED!*

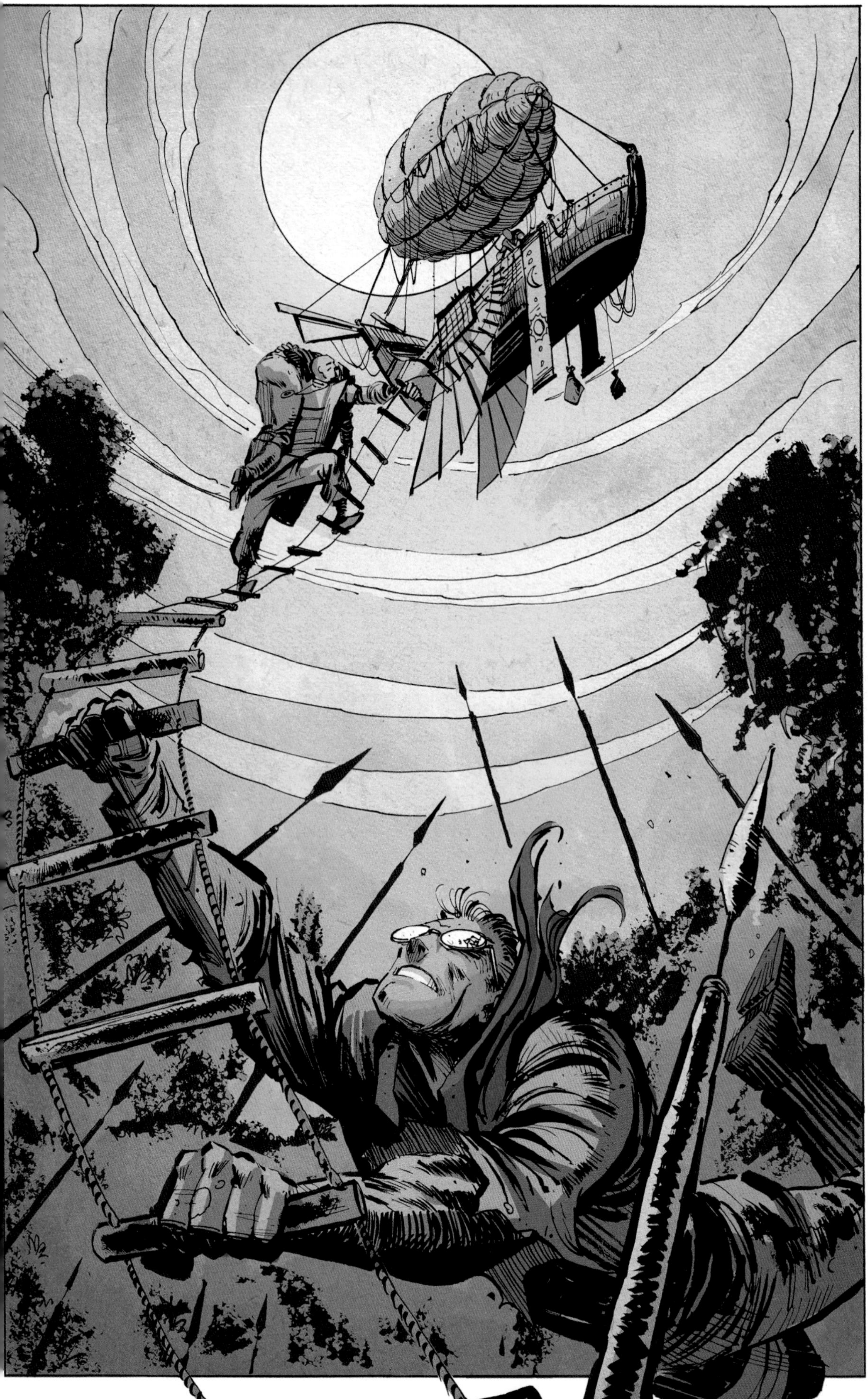

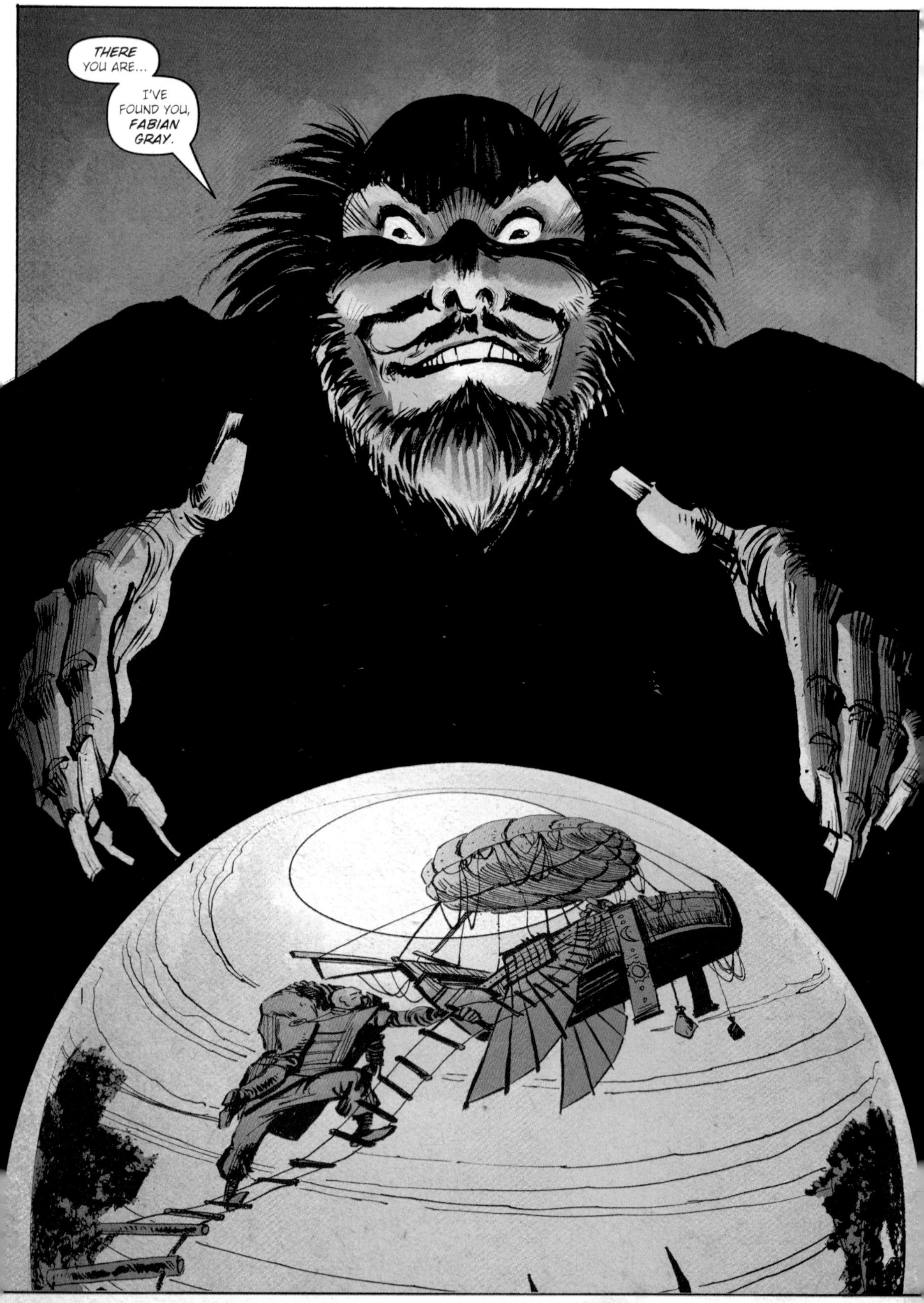
THERE YOU ARE...
I'VE FOUND YOU, FABIAN GRAY.

NEXT ISSUE: THE FORGOTTEN CITY!

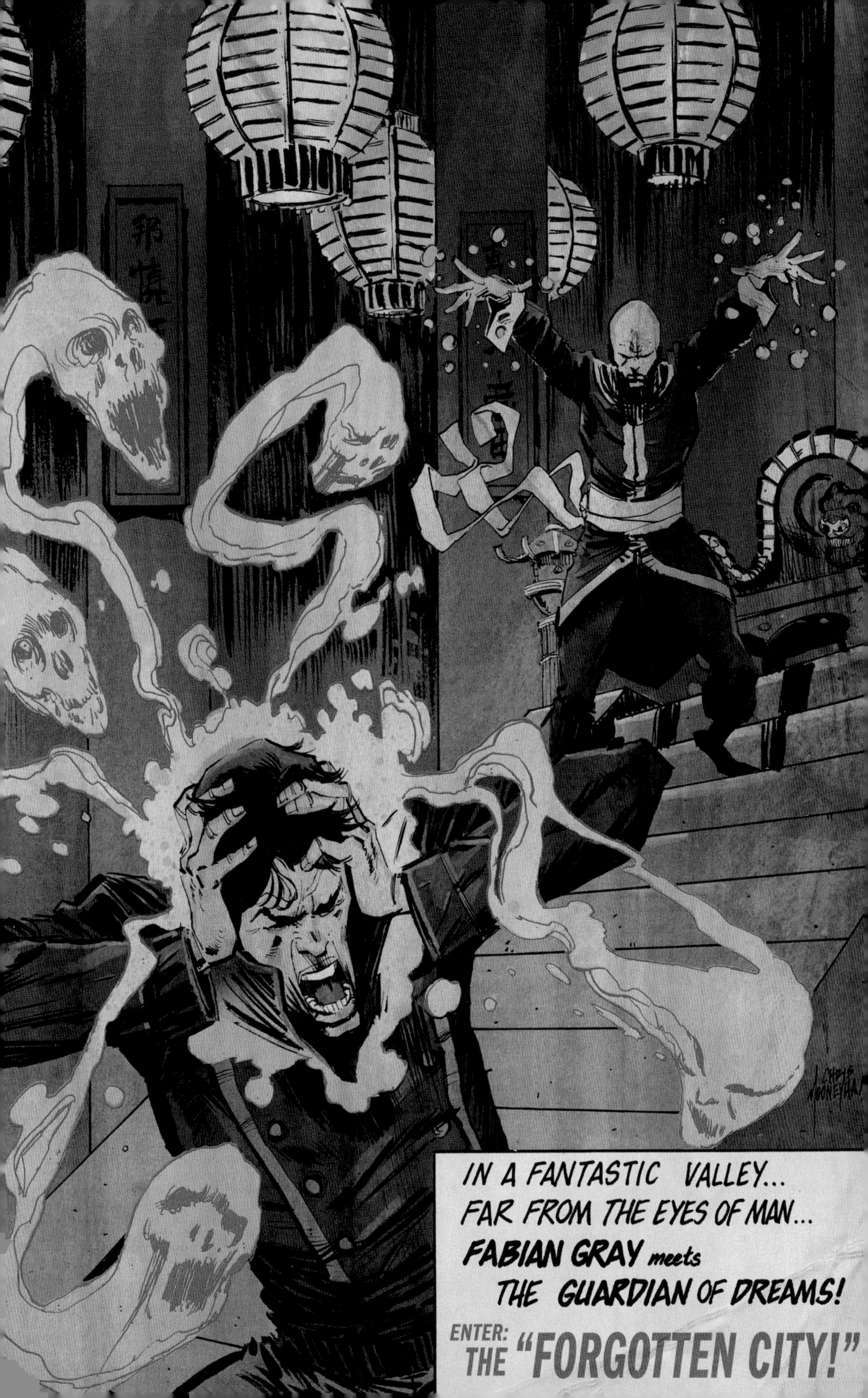
IN A FANTASTIC VALLEY...
FAR FROM THE EYES OF MAN...
FABIAN GRAY meets
THE GUARDIAN OF DREAMS!
ENTER: THE "FORGOTTEN CITY!"

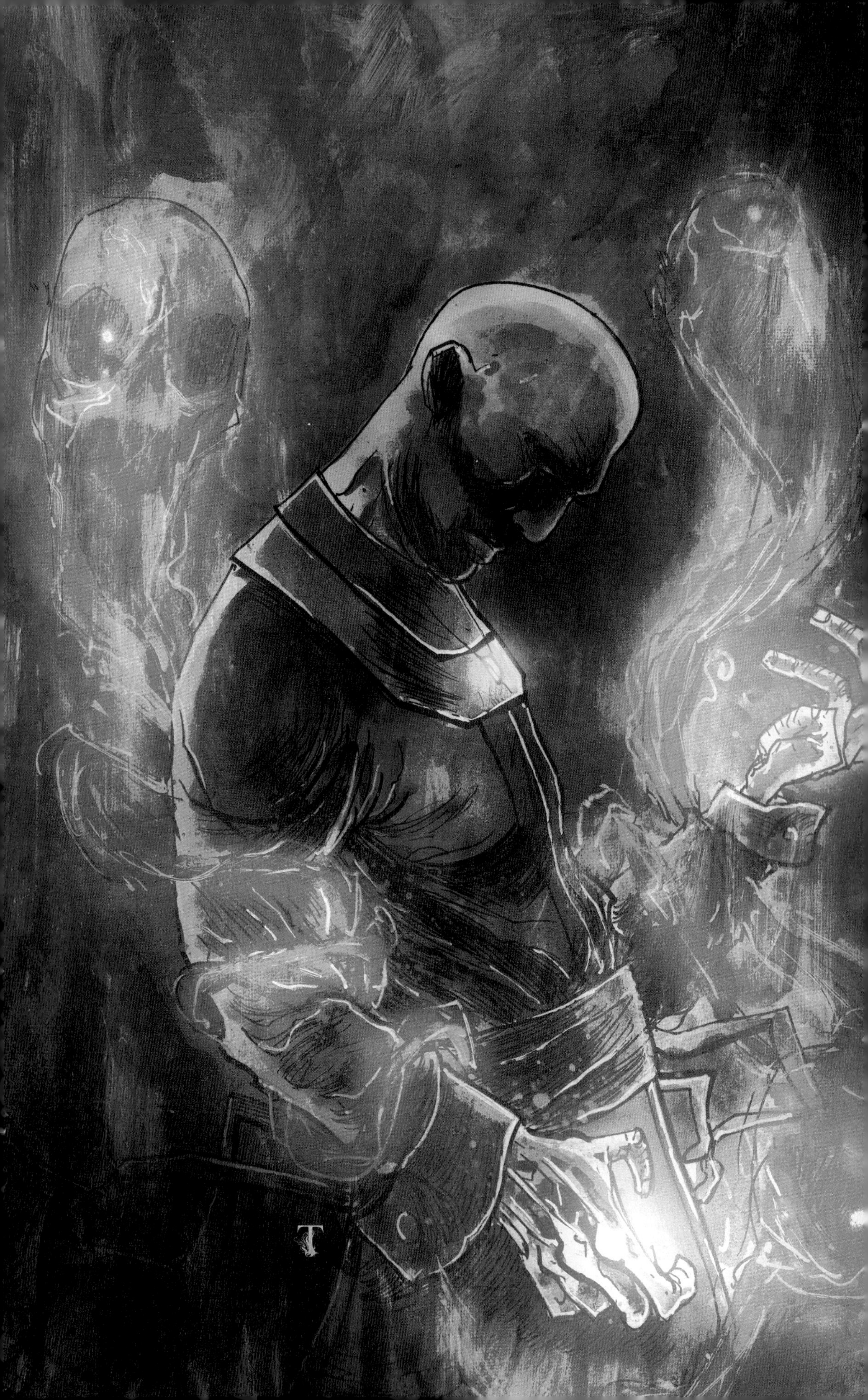

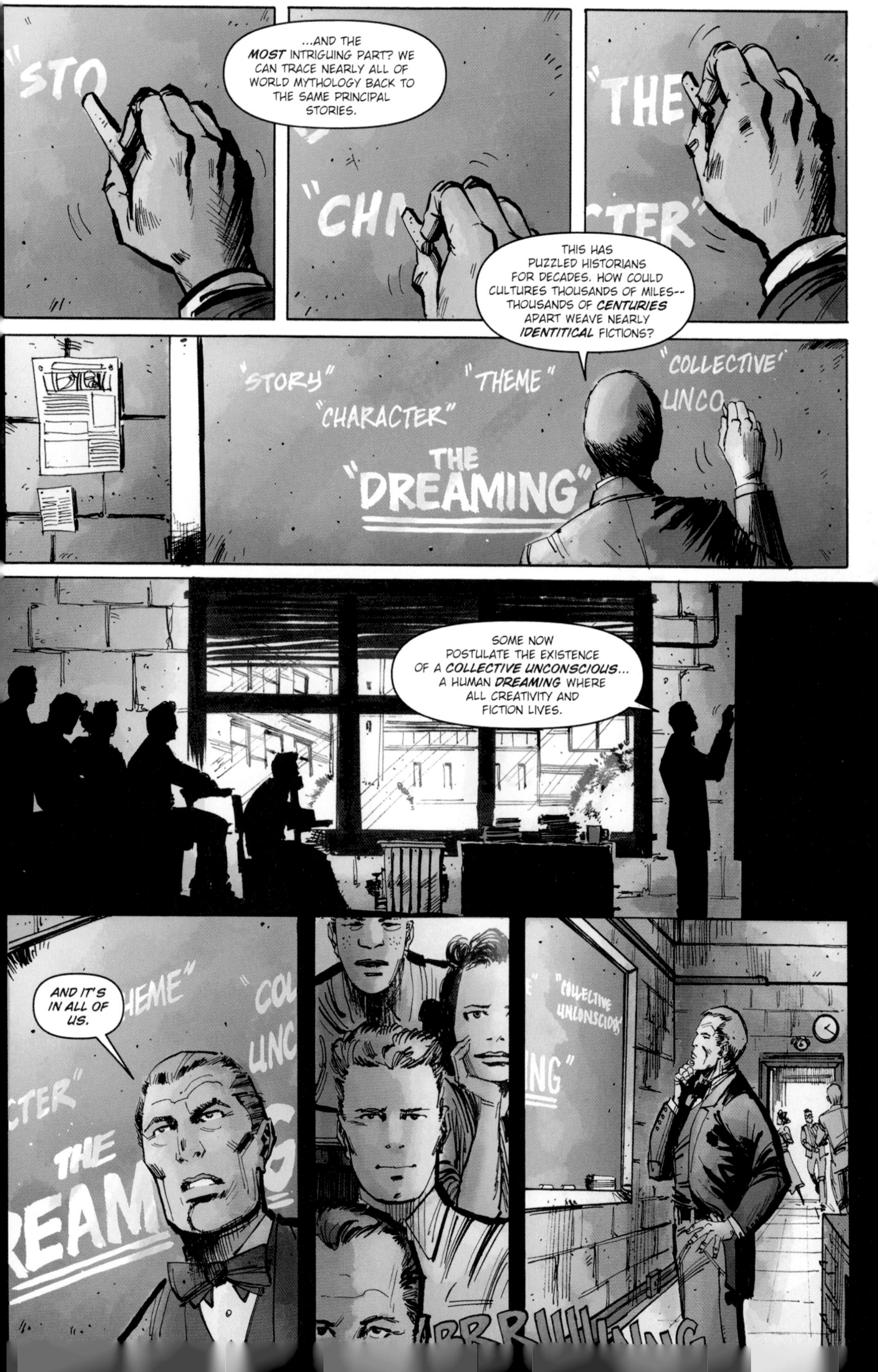
"STO
...AND THE MOST INTRIGUING PART? WE CAN TRACE NEARLY ALL OF WORLD MYTHOLOGY BACK TO THE SAME PRINCIPAL STORIES.
"CH
"THE
TER"
THIS HAS PUZZLED HISTORIANS FOR DECADES. HOW COULD CULTURES THOUSANDS OF MILES-- THOUSANDS OF CENTURIES APART WEAVE NEARLY IDENTITICAL FICTIONS?
"STORY"
"CHARACTER"
"THEME"
"COLLECTIVE"
UNCO
THE "DREAMING"
SOME NOW POSTULATE THE EXISTENCE OF A COLLECTIVE UNCONSCIOUS... A HUMAN DREAMING WHERE ALL CREATIVITY AND FICTION LIVES.
AND IT'S IN ALL OF US.
BRRRIIIIING

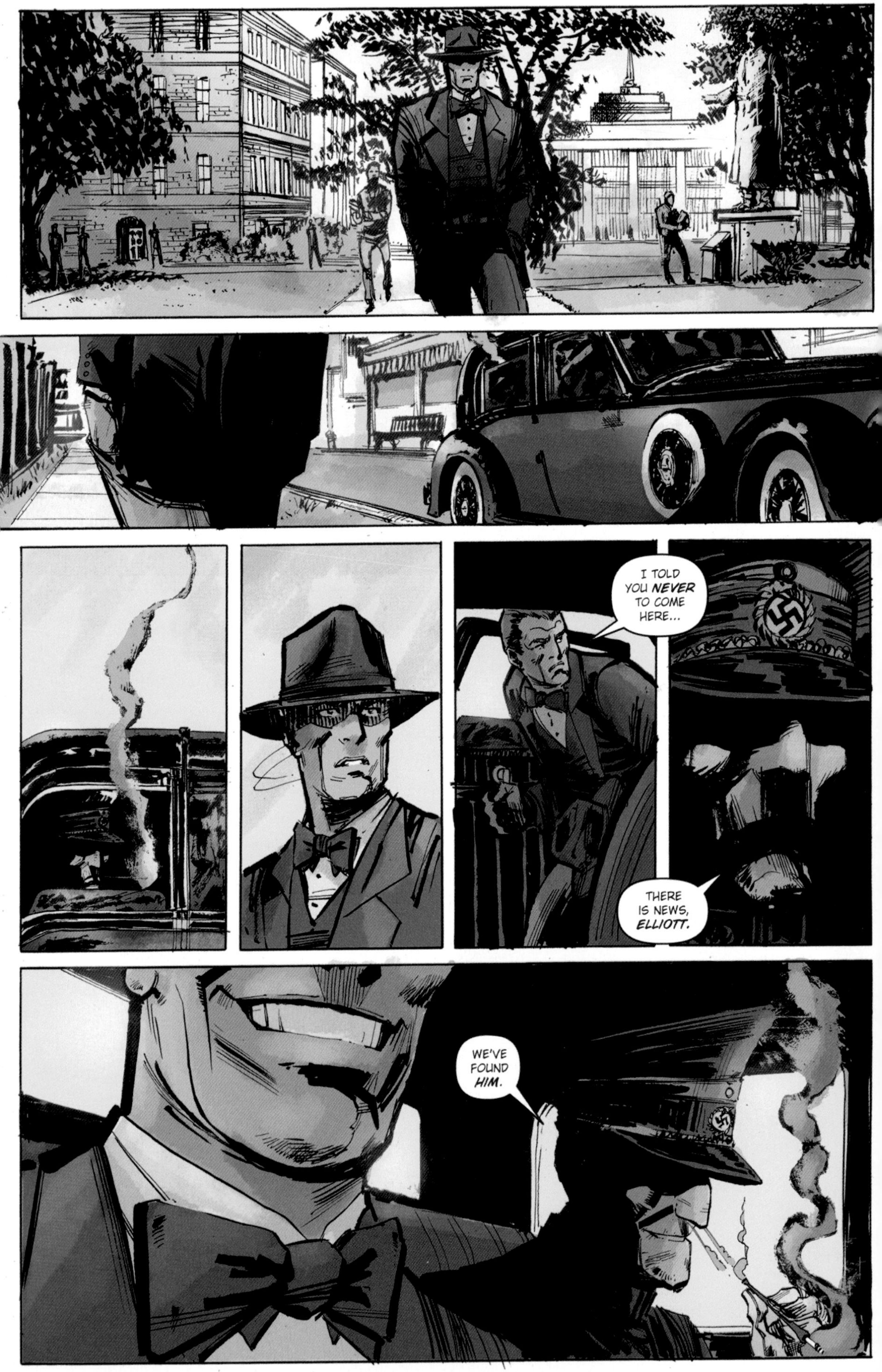
I TOLD YOU **NEVER** TO COME HERE...
THERE IS NEWS, ***ELLIOTT.***
WE'VE FOUND ***HIM***.

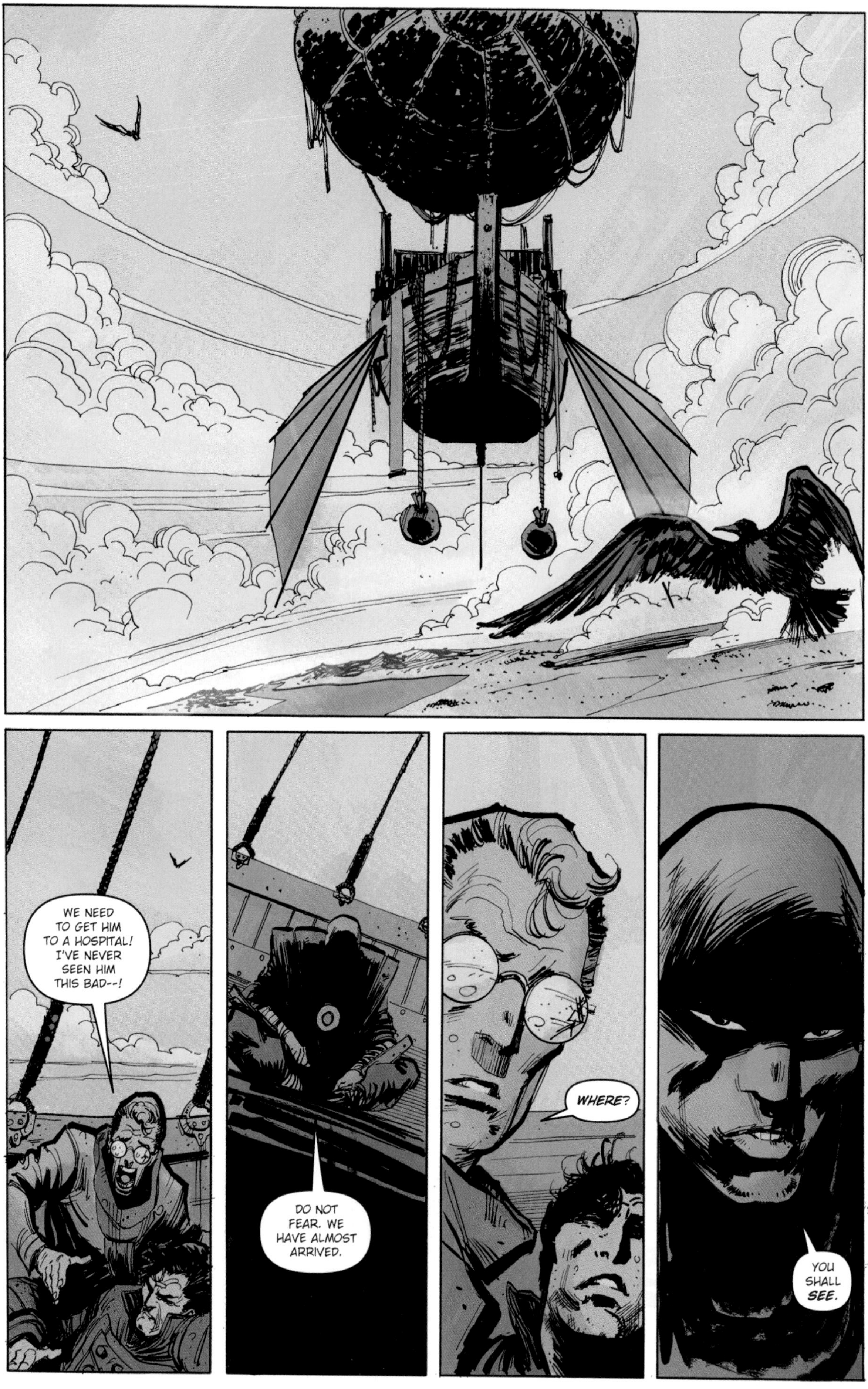
WE NEED TO GET HIM TO A HOSPITAL! I'VE NEVER SEEN HIM THIS BAD--!
DO NOT FEAR. WE HAVE ALMOST ARRIVED.
WHERE?
YOU SHALL SEE.

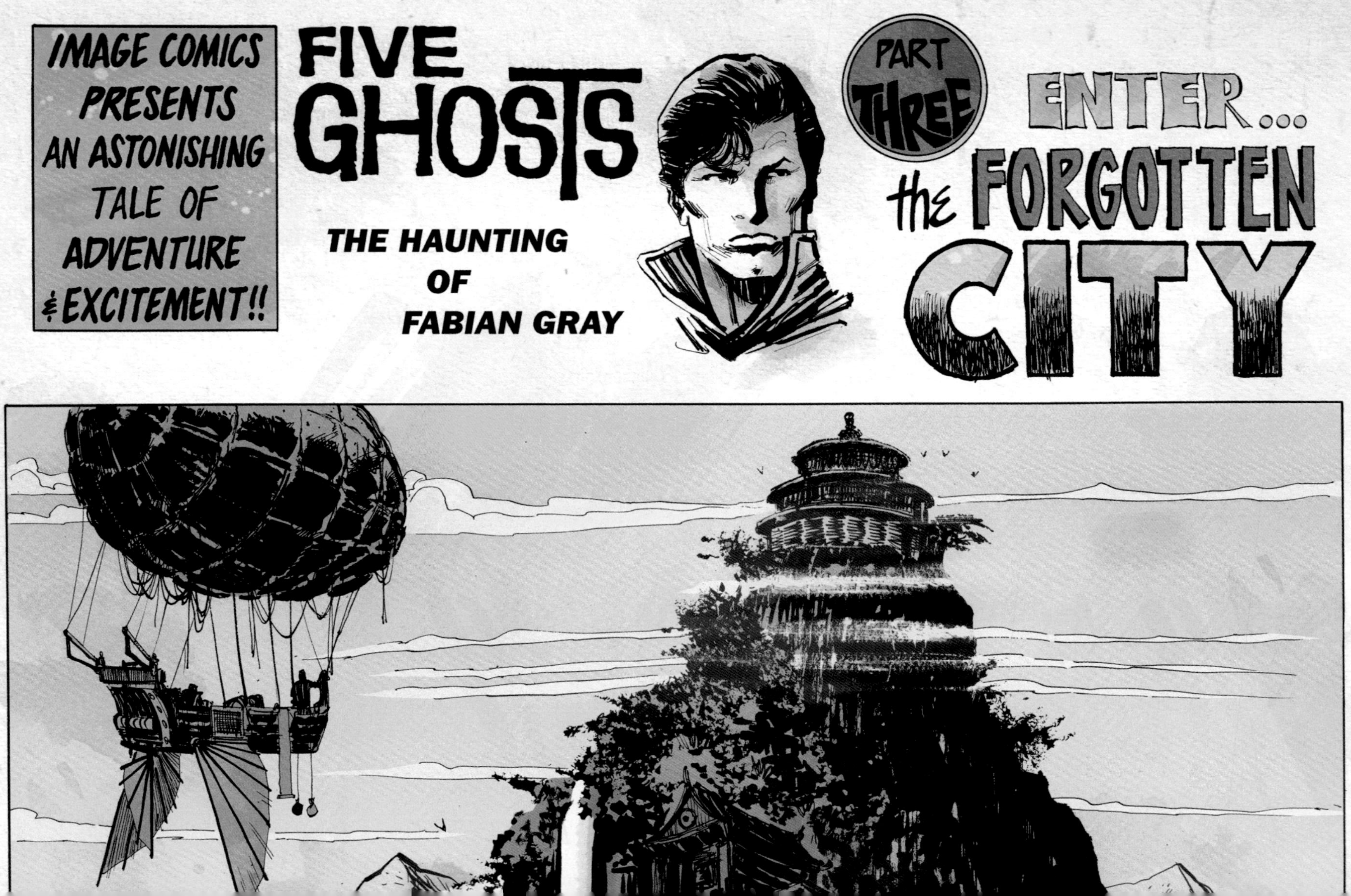
IMAGE COMICS PRESENTS AN ASTONISHING TALE OF ADVENTURE & EXCITEMENT!!
FIVE GHOSTS
THE HAUNTING OF FABIAN GRAY
PART THREE
ENTER... the FORGOTTEN CITY

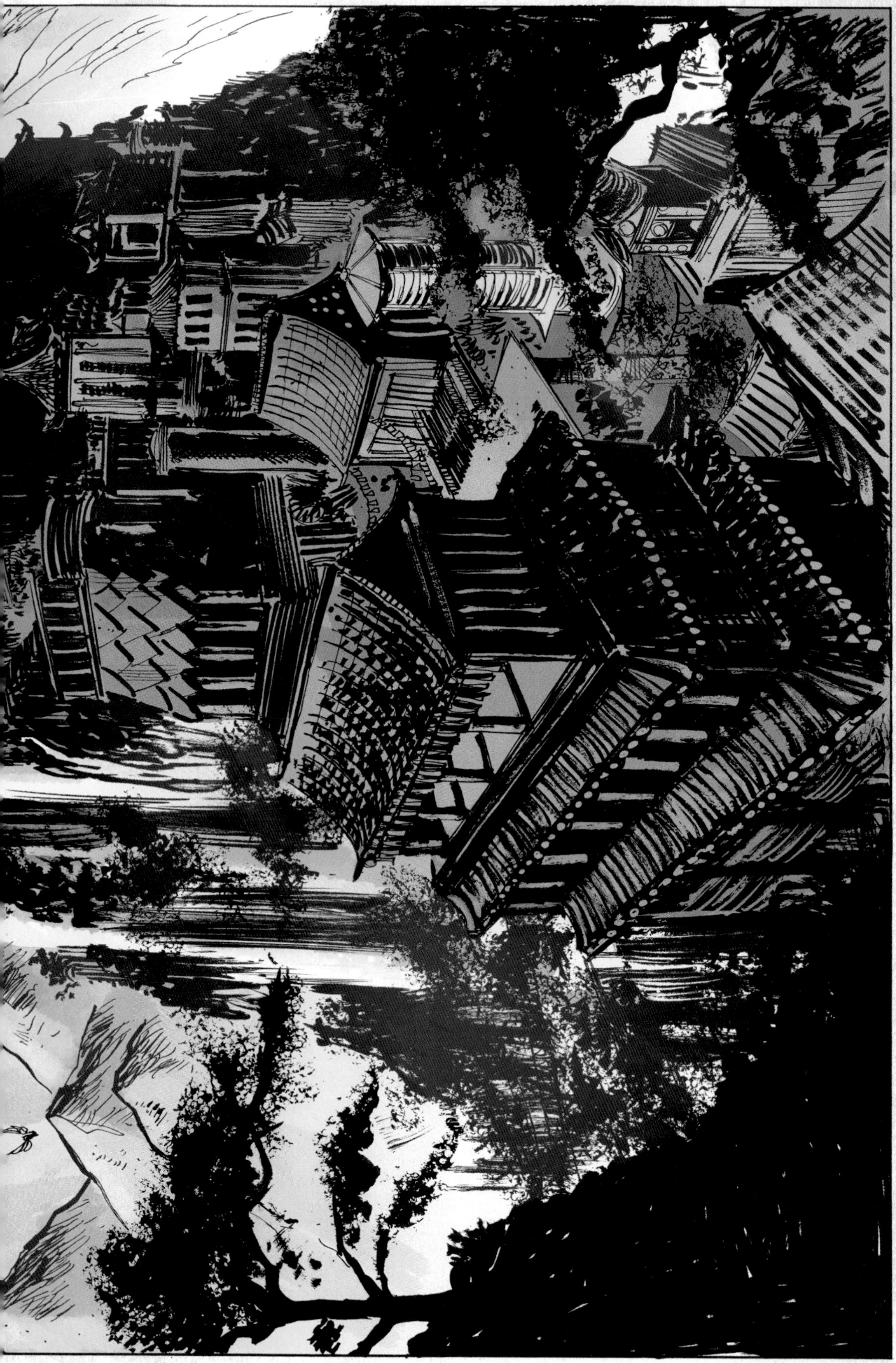

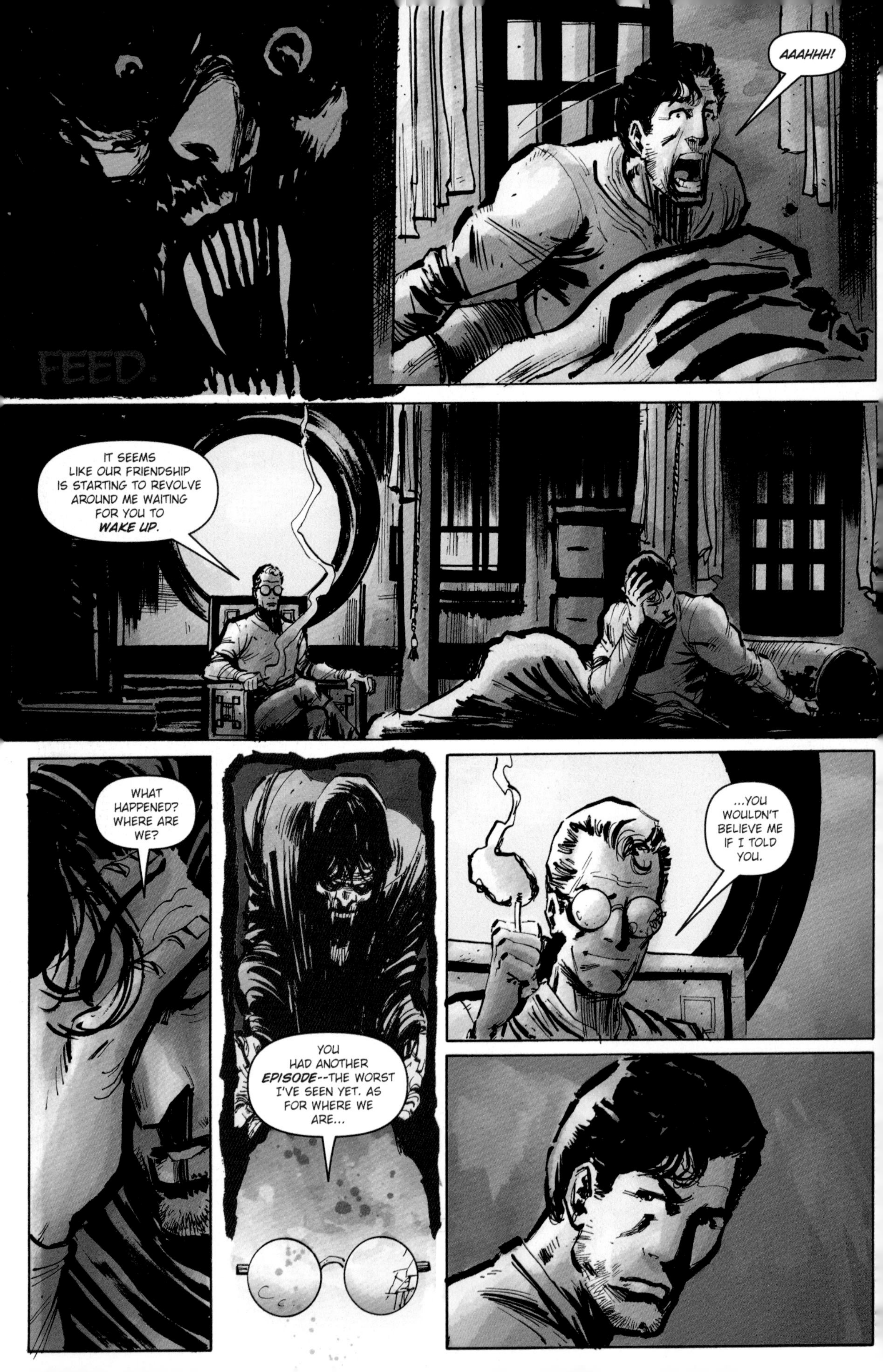
FEED.
AAAHHH!
IT SEEMS LIKE OUR FRIENDSHIP IS STARTING TO REVOLVE AROUND ME WAITING FOR YOU TO *WAKE UP*.
WHAT HAPPENED? WHERE ARE WE?
YOU HAD ANOTHER *EPISODE*--THE WORST I'VE SEEN YET. AS FOR WHERE WE ARE...
...YOU WOULDN'T BELIEVE ME IF I TOLD YOU.

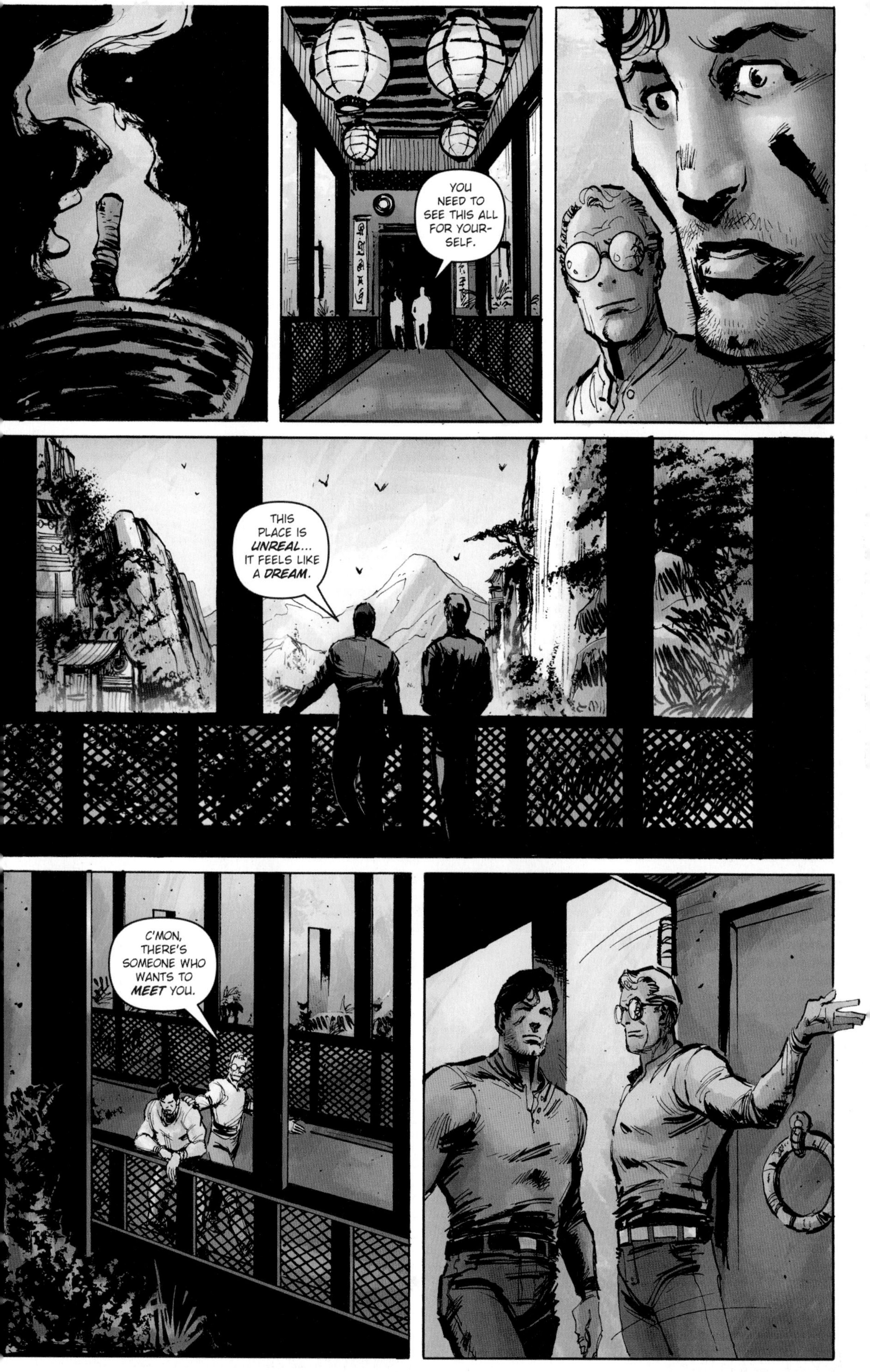
YOU NEED TO SEE THIS ALL FOR YOUR-SELF.
THIS PLACE IS **UNREAL**... IT FEELS LIKE A **DREAM**.
C'MON, THERE'S SOMEONE WHO WANTS TO **MEET** YOU.

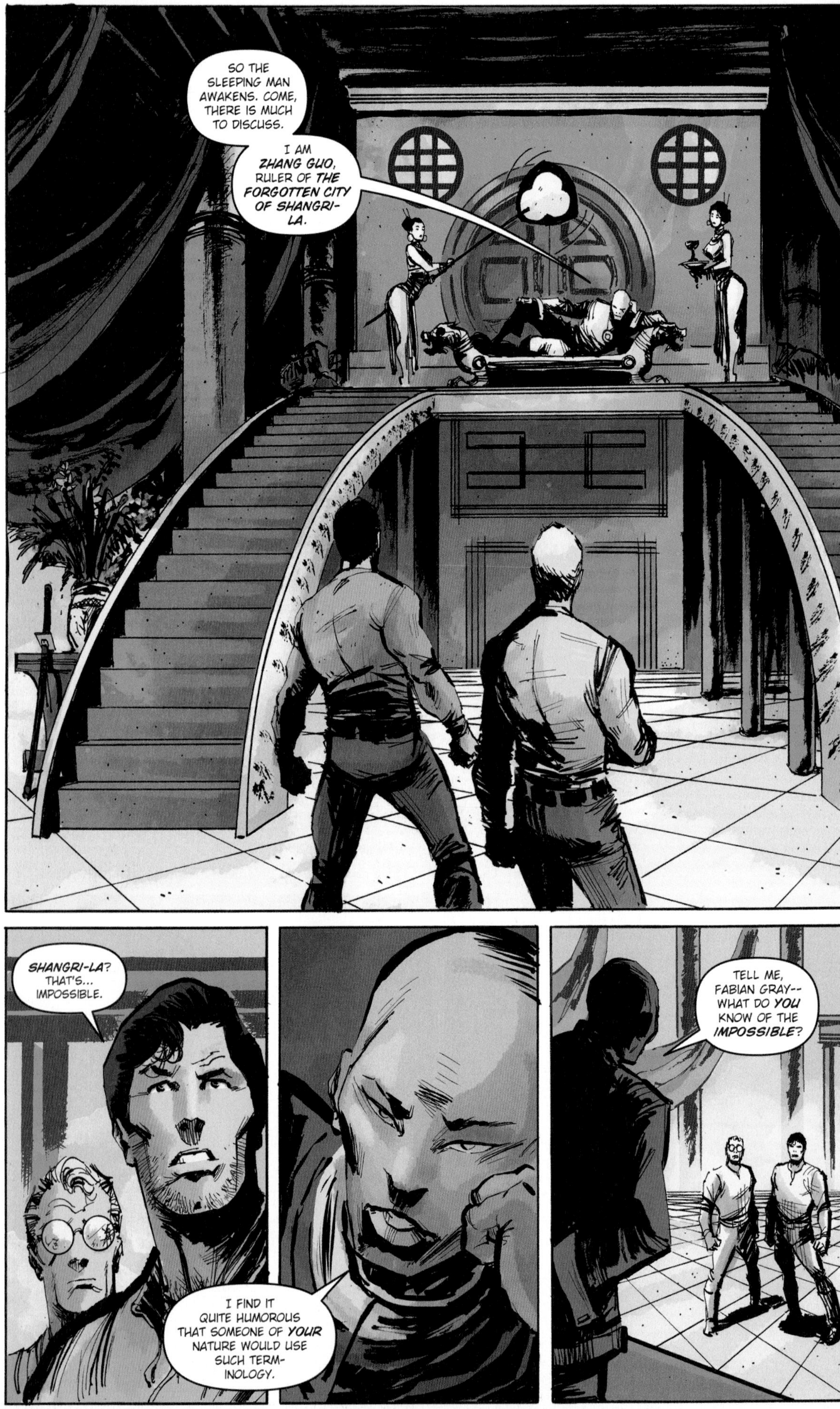
SO THE SLEEPING MAN AWAKENS. COME, THERE IS MUCH TO DISCUSS.
I AM ZHANG GUO, RULER OF THE FORGOTTEN CITY OF SHANGRI-LA.
SHANGRI-LA? THAT'S... IMPOSSIBLE.
I FIND IT QUITE HUMOROUS THAT SOMEONE OF YOUR NATURE WOULD USE SUCH TERM-INOLOGY.
TELL ME, FABIAN GRAY-- WHAT DO YOU KNOW OF THE IMPOSSIBLE?

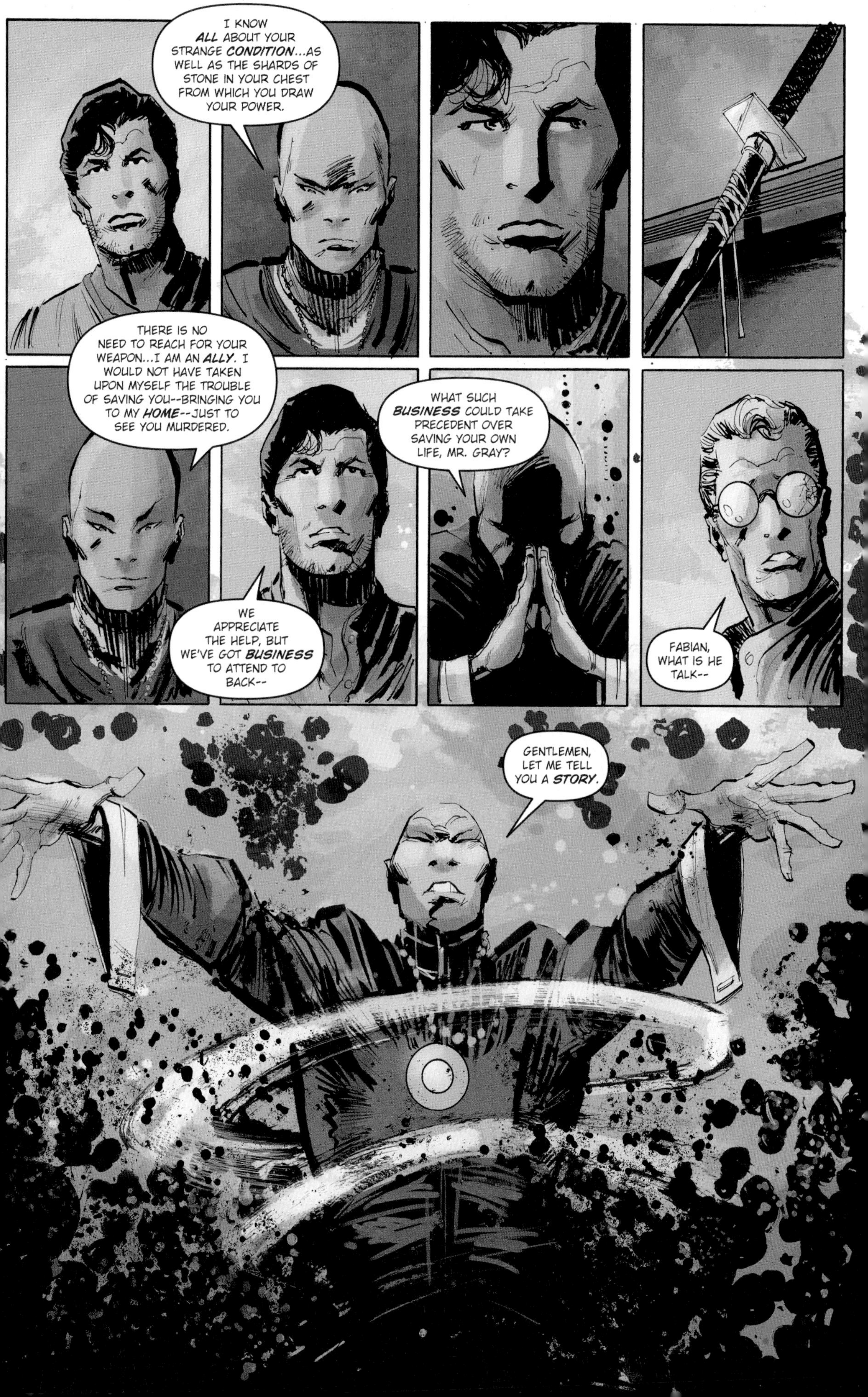
I KNOW ALL ABOUT YOUR STRANGE CONDITION...AS WELL AS THE SHARDS OF STONE IN YOUR CHEST FROM WHICH YOU DRAW YOUR POWER.
THERE IS NO NEED TO REACH FOR YOUR WEAPON...I AM AN ALLY. I WOULD NOT HAVE TAKEN UPON MYSELF THE TROUBLE OF SAVING YOU--BRINGING YOU TO MY HOME--JUST TO SEE YOU MURDERED.
WE APPRECIATE THE HELP, BUT WE'VE GOT BUSINESS TO ATTEND TO BACK--
WHAT SUCH BUSINESS COULD TAKE PRECEDENT OVER SAVING YOUR OWN LIFE, MR. GRAY?
FABIAN, WHAT IS HE TALK--
GENTLEMEN, LET ME TELL YOU A STORY.

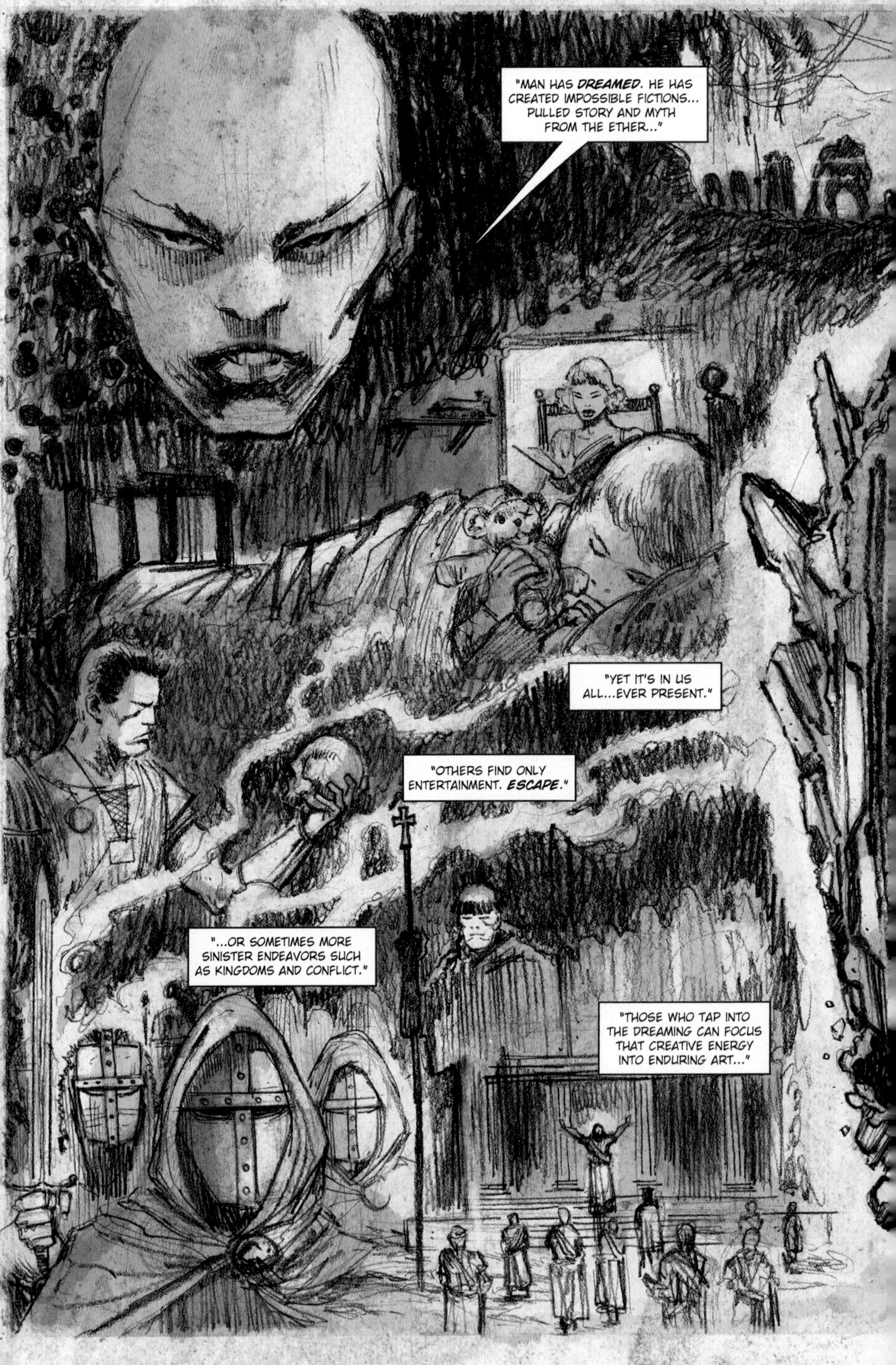
"MAN HAS DREAMED. HE HAS CREATED IMPOSSIBLE FICTIONS... PULLED STORY AND MYTH FROM THE ETHER..."
"YET IT'S IN US ALL...EVER PRESENT."
"OTHERS FIND ONLY ENTERTAINMENT. ESCAPE."
"...OR SOMETIMES MORE SINISTER ENDEAVORS SUCH AS KINGDOMS AND CONFLICT."
"THOSE WHO TAP INTO THE DREAMING CAN FOCUS THAT CREATIVE ENERGY INTO ENDURING ART..."

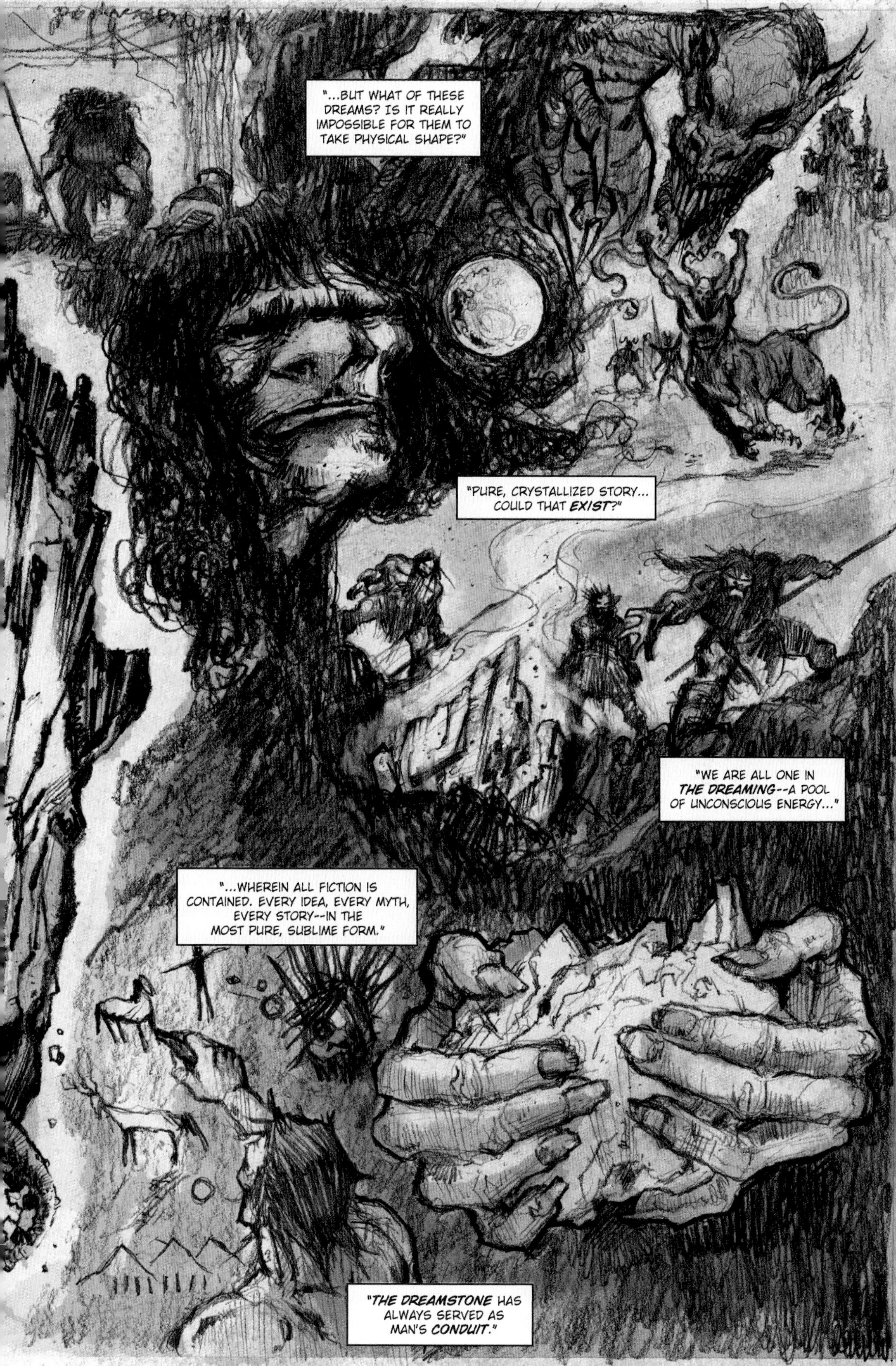
"...BUT WHAT OF THESE DREAMS? IS IT REALLY IMPOSSIBLE FOR THEM TO TAKE PHYSICAL SHAPE?"
"PURE, CRYSTALLIZED STORY... COULD THAT EXIST?"
"WE ARE ALL ONE IN THE DREAMING--A POOL OF UNCONSCIOUS ENERGY..."
"...WHEREIN ALL FICTION IS CONTAINED. EVERY IDEA, EVERY MYTH, EVERY STORY--IN THE MOST PURE, SUBLIME FORM."
"THE DREAMSTONE HAS ALWAYS SERVED AS MAN'S CONDUIT."

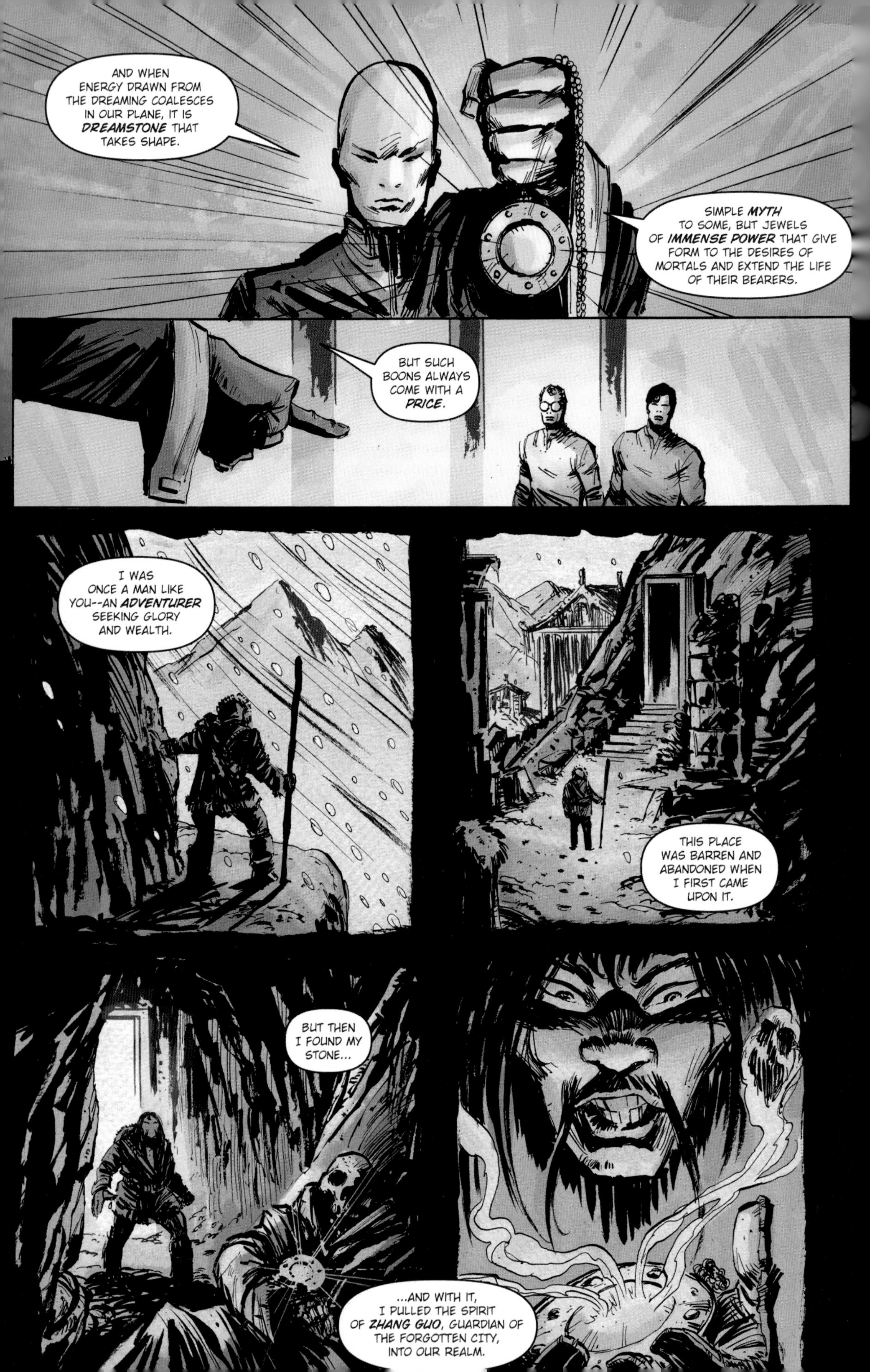
AND WHEN ENERGY DRAWN FROM THE DREAMING COALESCES IN OUR PLANE, IT IS *DREAMSTONE* THAT TAKES SHAPE.
SIMPLE *MYTH* TO SOME, BUT JEWELS OF *IMMENSE POWER* THAT GIVE FORM TO THE DESIRES OF MORTALS AND EXTEND THE LIFE OF THEIR BEARERS.
BUT SUCH BOONS ALWAYS COME WITH A *PRICE*.
I WAS ONCE A MAN LIKE YOU--AN *ADVENTURER* SEEKING GLORY AND WEALTH.
THIS PLACE WAS BARREN AND ABANDONED WHEN I FIRST CAME UPON IT.
BUT THEN I FOUND MY STONE...
...AND WITH IT, I PULLED THE SPIRIT OF *ZHANG GUO*, GUARDIAN OF THE FORGOTTEN CITY, INTO OUR REALM.

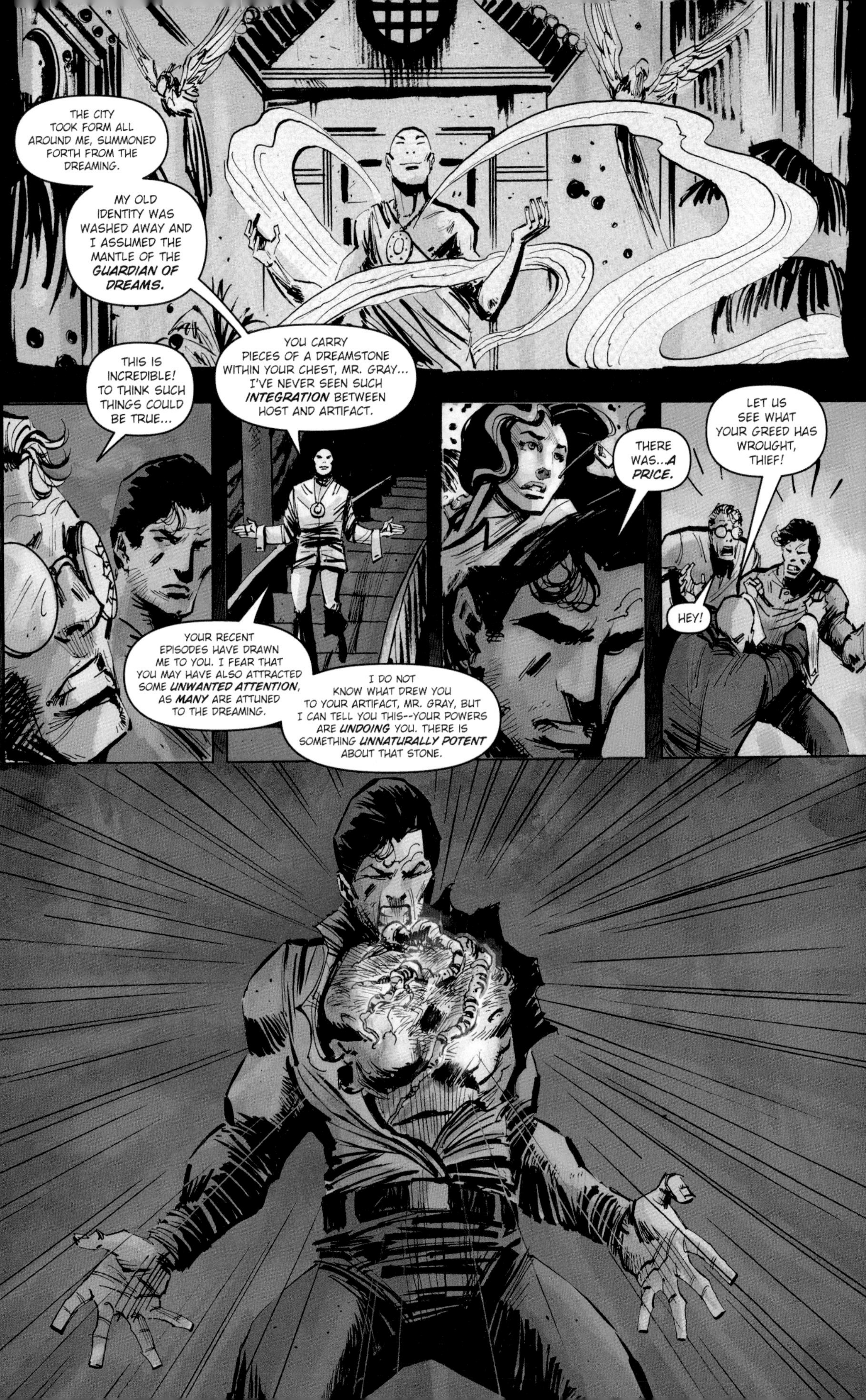
THE CITY TOOK FORM ALL AROUND ME, SUMMONED FORTH FROM THE DREAMING.
MY OLD IDENTITY WAS WASHED AWAY AND I ASSUMED THE MANTLE OF THE GUARDIAN OF DREAMS.
THIS IS INCREDIBLE! TO THINK SUCH THINGS COULD BE TRUE...
YOU CARRY PIECES OF A DREAMSTONE WITHIN YOUR CHEST, MR. GRAY... I'VE NEVER SEEN SUCH INTEGRATION BETWEEN HOST AND ARTIFACT.
YOUR RECENT EPISODES HAVE DRAWN ME TO YOU. I FEAR THAT YOU MAY HAVE ALSO ATTRACTED SOME UNWANTED ATTENTION, AS MANY ARE ATTUNED TO THE DREAMING.
THERE WAS...A PRICE.
I DO NOT KNOW WHAT DREW YOU TO YOUR ARTIFACT, MR. GRAY, BUT I CAN TELL YOU THIS--YOUR POWERS ARE UNDOING YOU. THERE IS SOMETHING UNNATURALLY POTENT ABOUT THAT STONE.
LET US SEE WHAT YOUR GREED HAS WROUGHT, THIEF!
HEY!

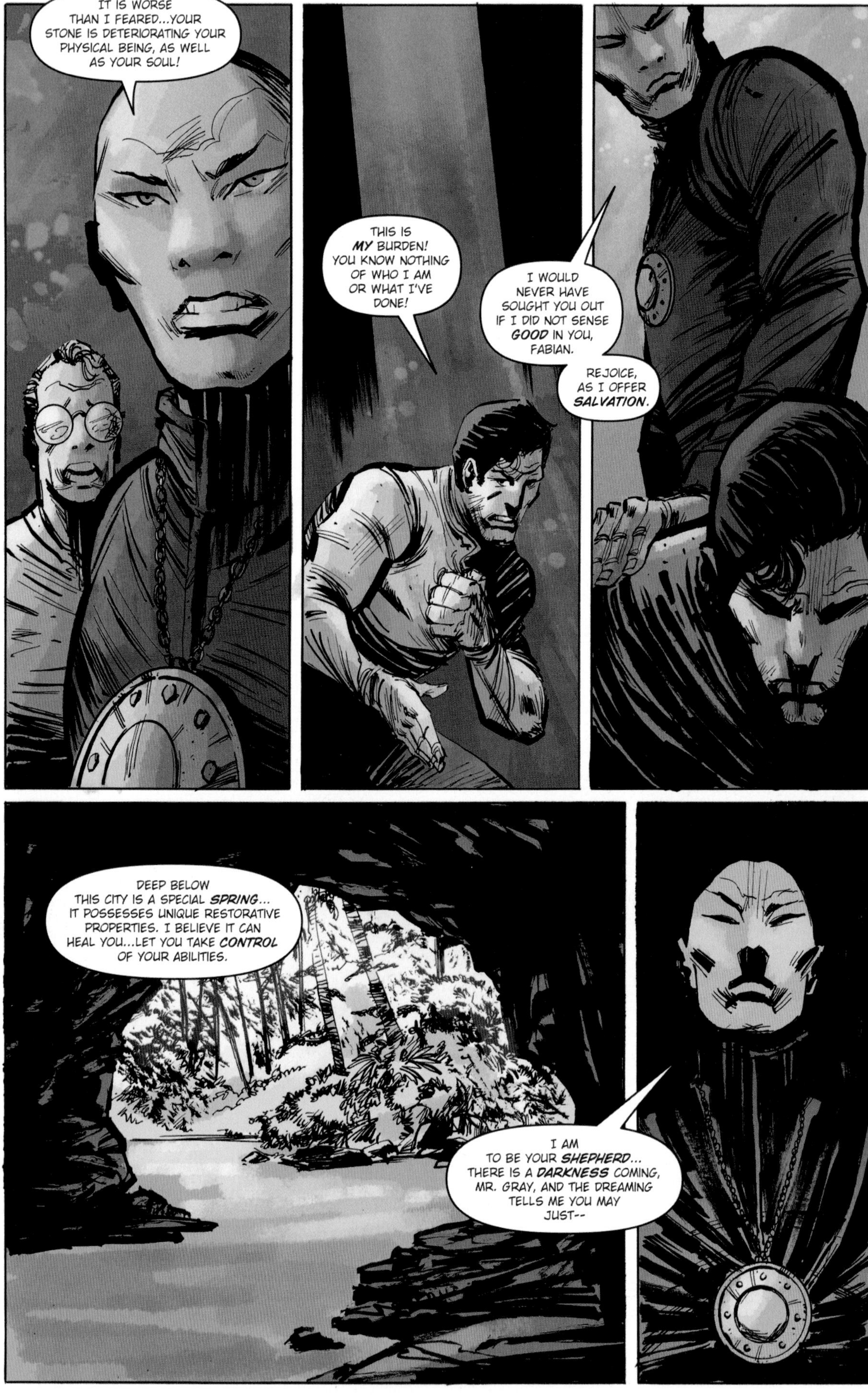
IT IS WORSE THAN I FEARED...YOUR STONE IS DETERIORATING YOUR PHYSICAL BEING, AS WELL AS YOUR SOUL!
THIS IS MY BURDEN! YOU KNOW NOTHING OF WHO I AM OR WHAT I'VE DONE!
I WOULD NEVER HAVE SOUGHT YOU OUT IF I DID NOT SENSE GOOD IN YOU, FABIAN.
REJOICE, AS I OFFER SALVATION.
DEEP BELOW THIS CITY IS A SPECIAL SPRING... IT POSSESSES UNIQUE RESTORATIVE PROPERTIES. I BELIEVE IT CAN HEAL YOU...LET YOU TAKE CONTROL OF YOUR ABILITIES.
I AM TO BE YOUR SHEPHERD... THERE IS A DARKNESS COMING, MR. GRAY, AND THE DREAMING TELLS ME YOU MAY JUST--

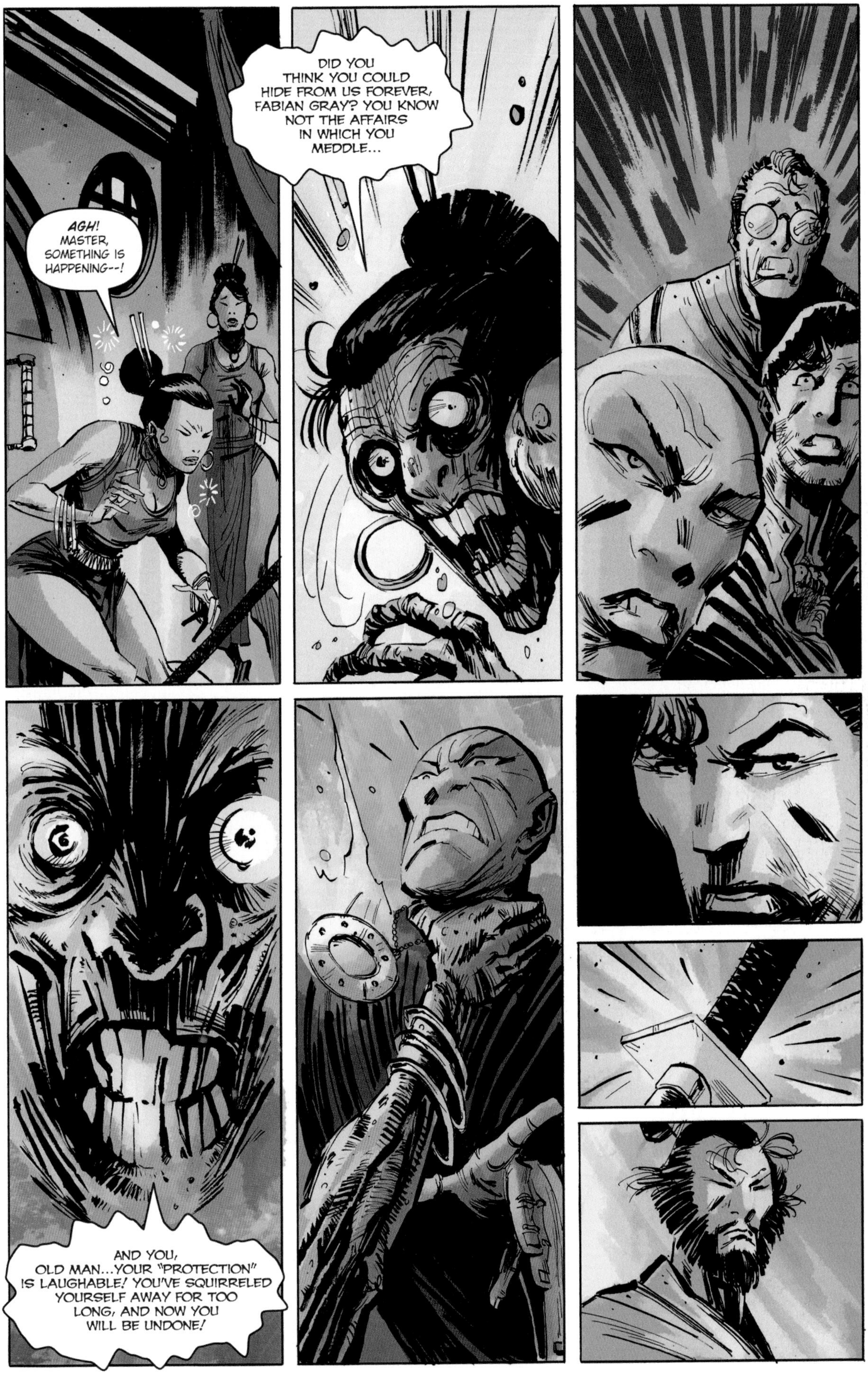
AGH! MASTER, SOMETHING IS HAPPENING--!
DID YOU THINK YOU COULD HIDE FROM US FOREVER, FABIAN GRAY? YOU KNOW NOT THE AFFAIRS IN WHICH YOU MEDDLE...
AND YOU, OLD MAN...YOUR "PROTECTION" IS LAUGHABLE! YOU'VE SQUIRRELED YOURSELF AWAY FOR TOO LONG, AND NOW YOU WILL BE UNDONE!

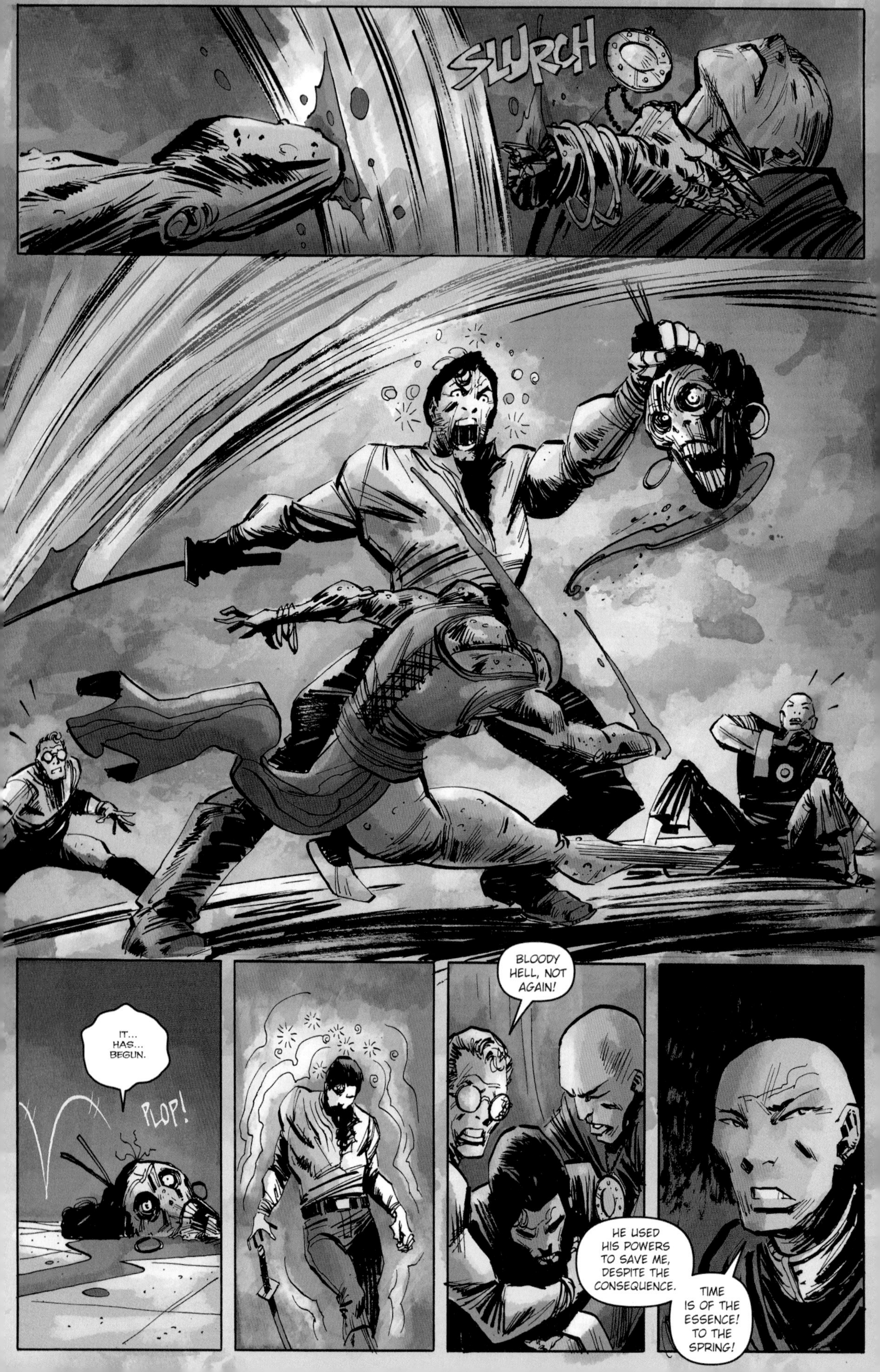
SLURCH
IT... HAS... BEGUN.
PLOP!
BLOODY HELL, NOT AGAIN!
HE USED HIS POWERS TO SAVE ME, DESPITE THE CONSEQUENCE.
TIME IS OF THE ESSENCE! TO THE SPRING!

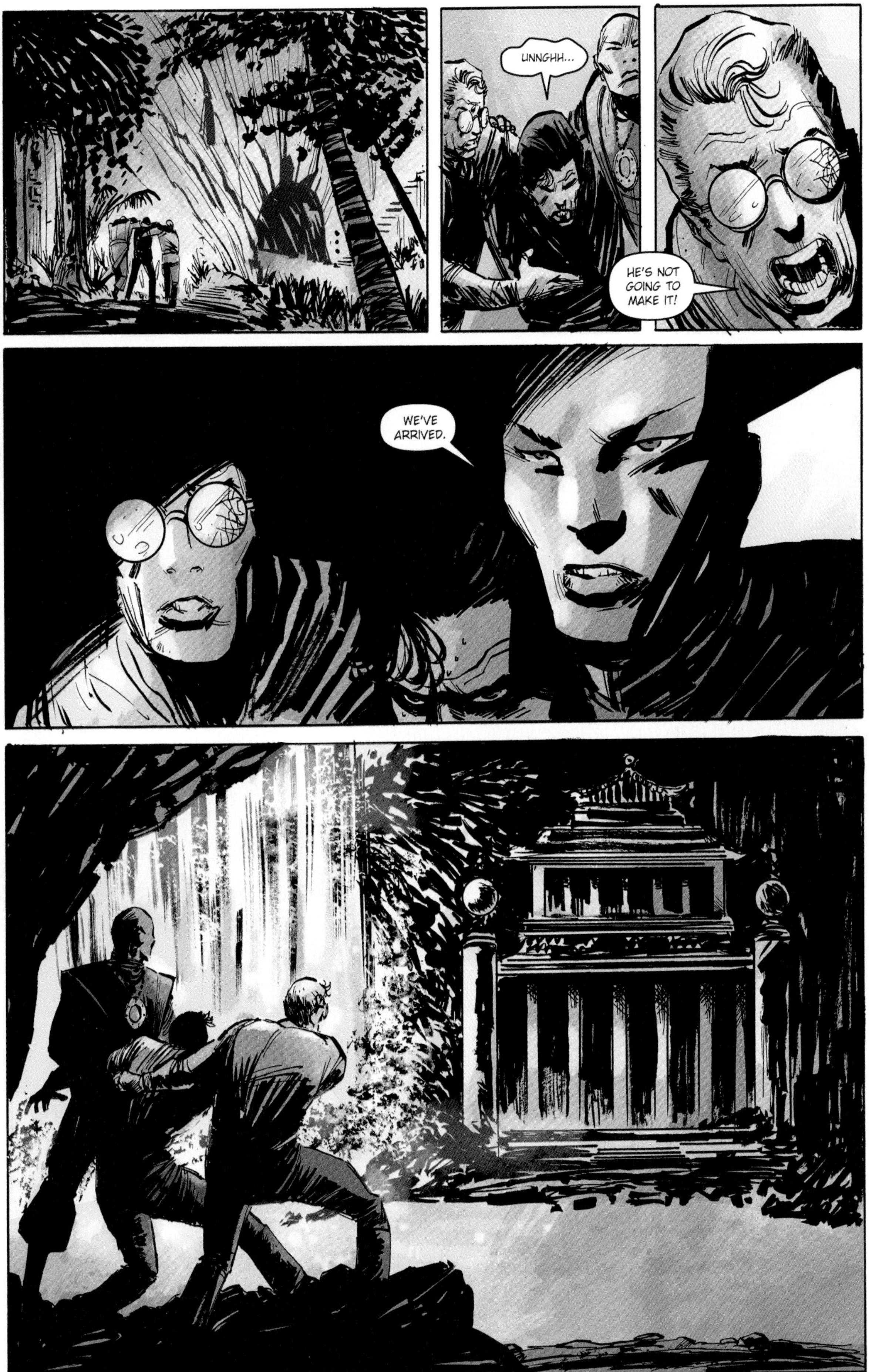
UNNGHH...
HE'S NOT GOING TO MAKE IT!
WE'VE ARRIVED.

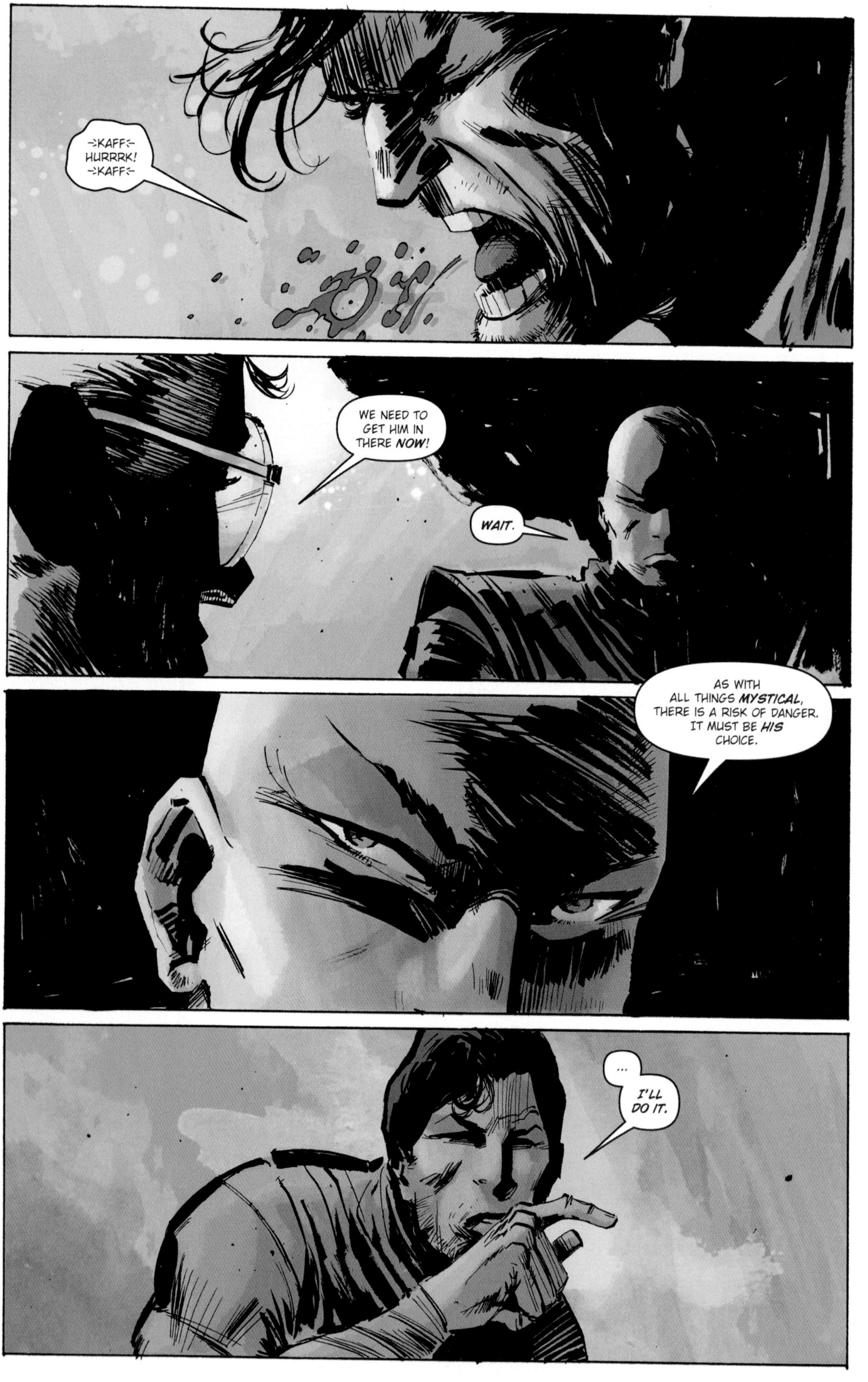
-KAFF- HURRRK! -KAFF-
WE NEED TO GET HIM IN THERE NOW!
WAIT.
AS WITH ALL THINGS MYSTICAL, THERE IS A RISK OF DANGER. IT MUST BE HIS CHOICE.
...
I'LL DO IT.

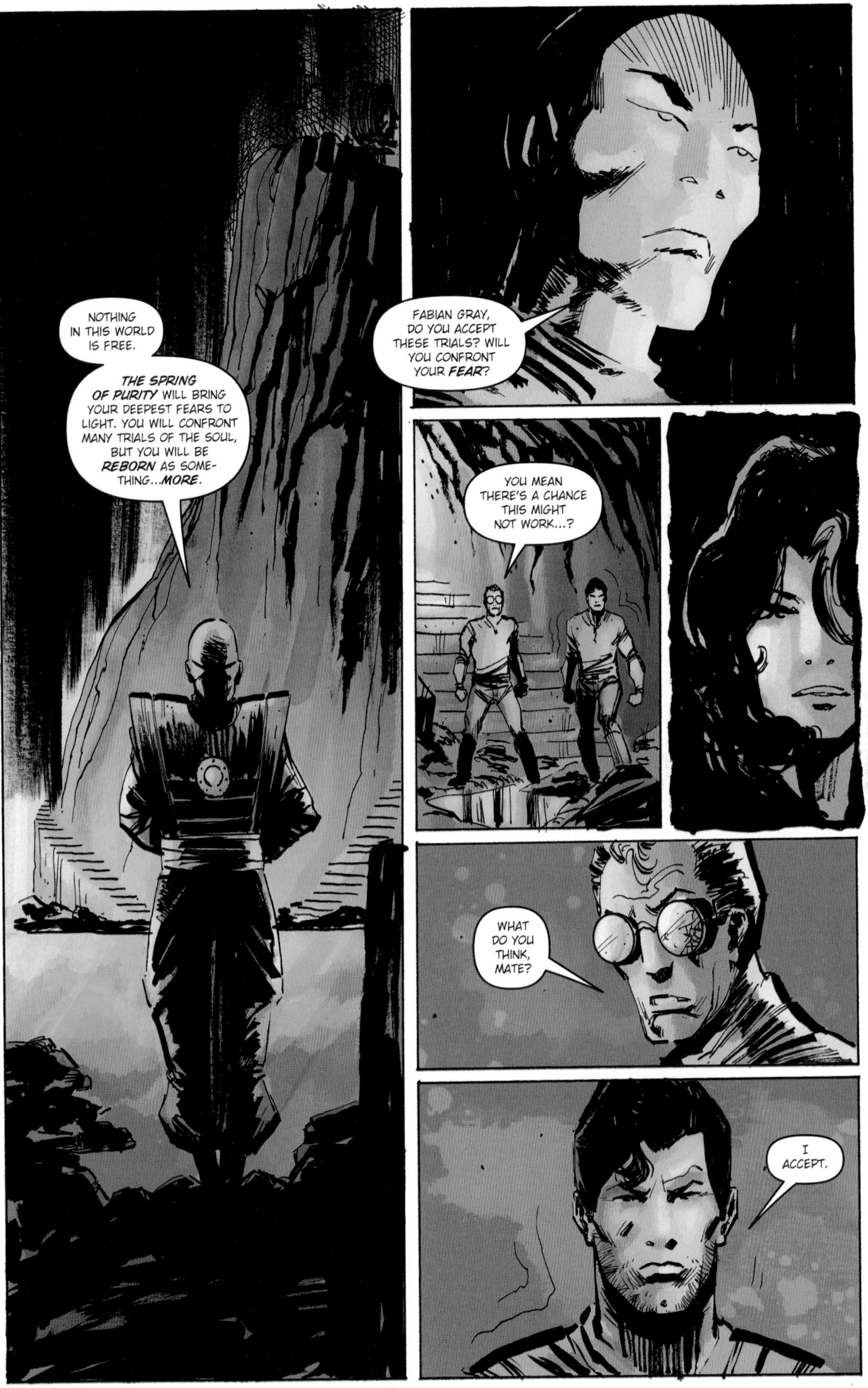
NOTHING IN THIS WORLD IS FREE.
THE SPRING OF PURITY WILL BRING YOUR DEEPEST FEARS TO LIGHT. YOU WILL CONFRONT MANY TRIALS OF THE SOUL, BUT YOU WILL BE REBORN AS SOMETHING...MORE.
FABIAN GRAY, DO YOU ACCEPT THESE TRIALS? WILL YOU CONFRONT YOUR FEAR?
YOU MEAN THERE'S A CHANCE THIS MIGHT NOT WORK...?
WHAT DO YOU THINK, MATE?
I ACCEPT.

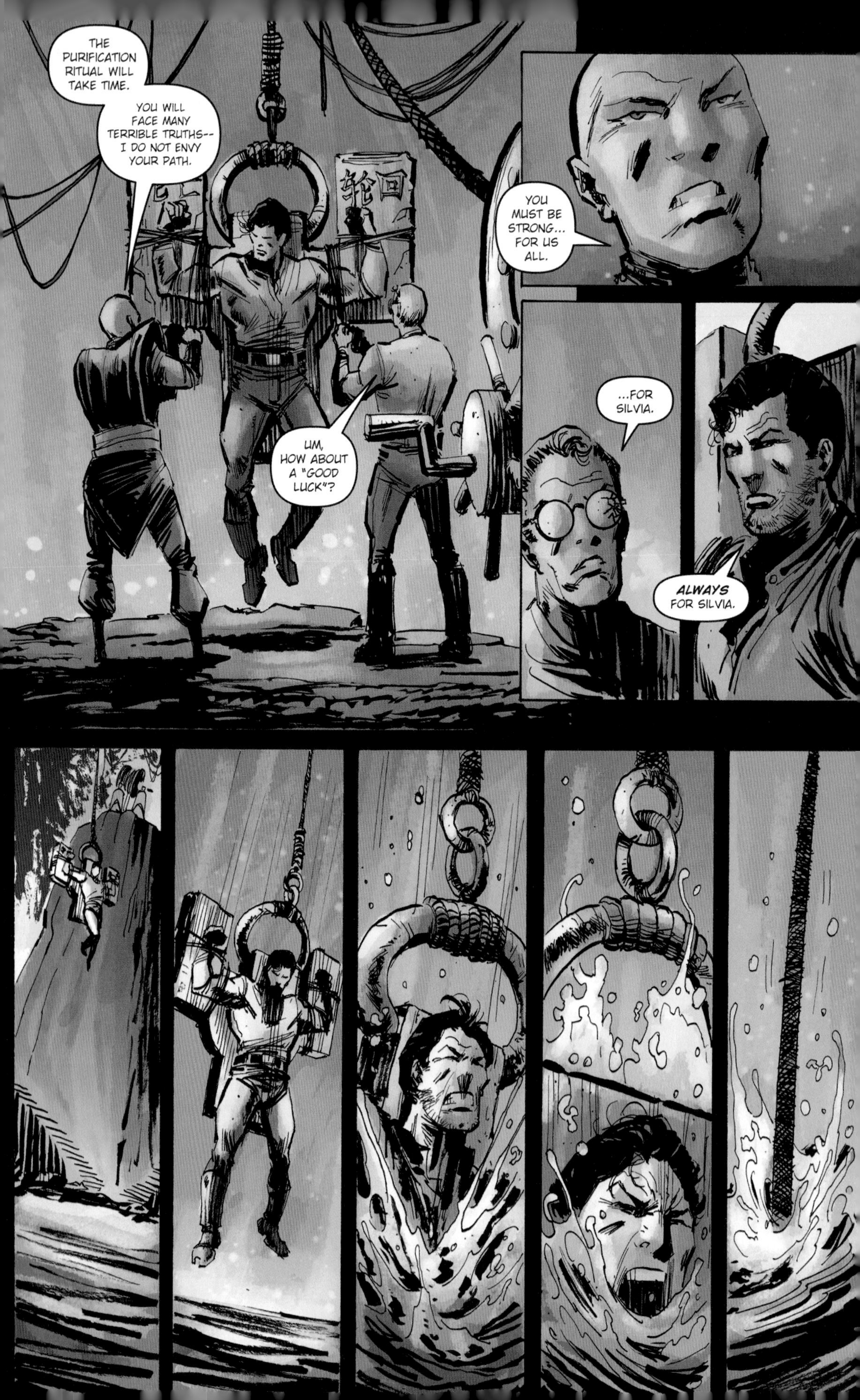
THE PURIFICATION RITUAL WILL TAKE TIME.
YOU WILL FACE MANY TERRIBLE TRUTHS-- I DO NOT ENVY YOUR PATH.
UM, HOW ABOUT A "GOOD LUCK"?
YOU MUST BE STRONG... FOR US ALL.
...FOR SILVIA.
ALWAYS FOR SILVIA.

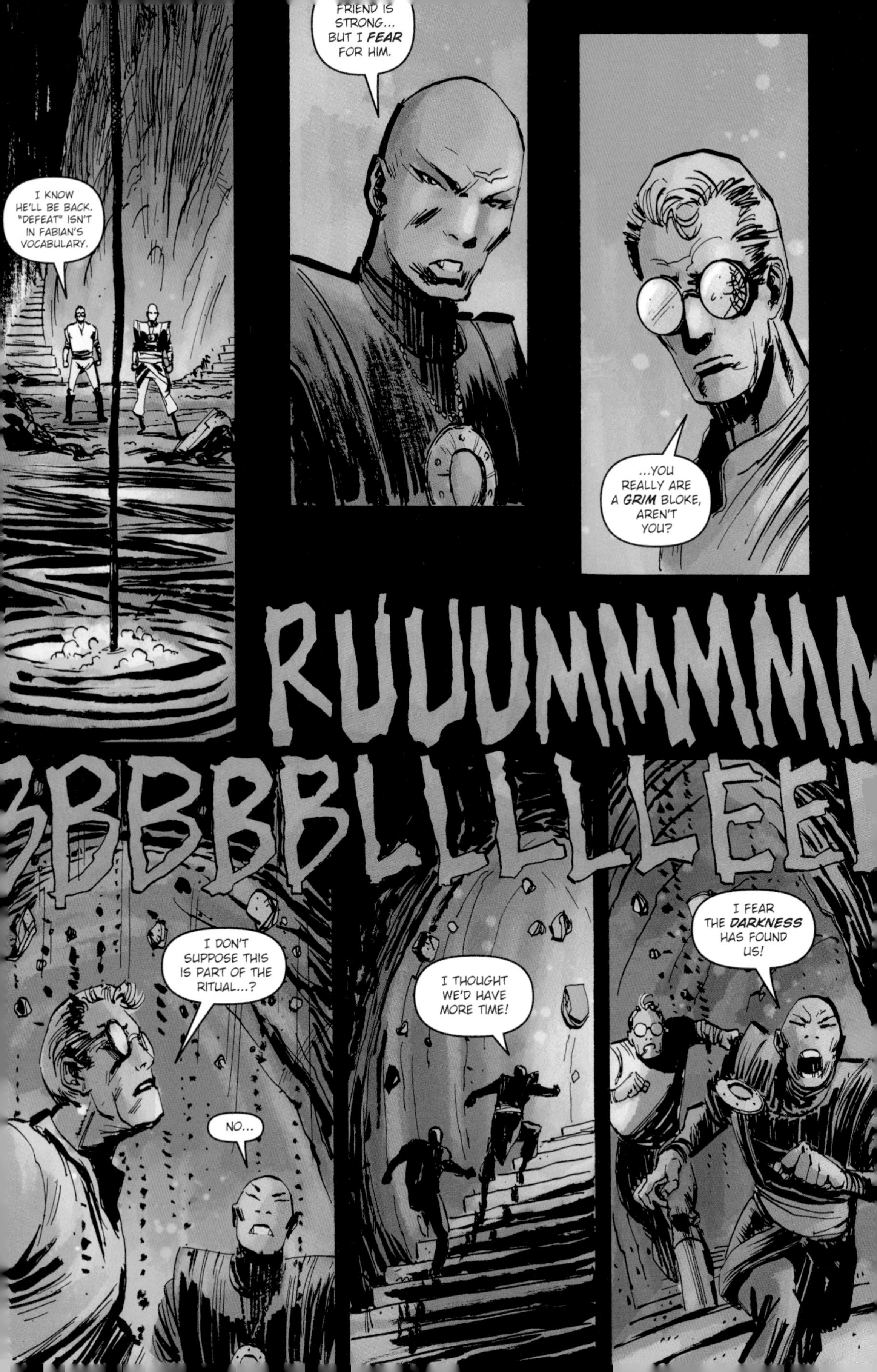

I KNOW HE'LL BE BACK. "DEFEAT" ISN'T IN FABIAN'S VOCABULARY.
FRIEND IS STRONG... BUT I *FEAR* FOR HIM.
...YOU REALLY ARE A *GRIM* BLOKE, AREN'T YOU?
RUUUMMMMM
BBBBLLLLLEE
I DON'T SUPPOSE THIS IS PART OF THE RITUAL...?
NO...
I THOUGHT WE'D HAVE MORE TIME!
I FEAR THE *DARKNESS* HAS FOUND US!

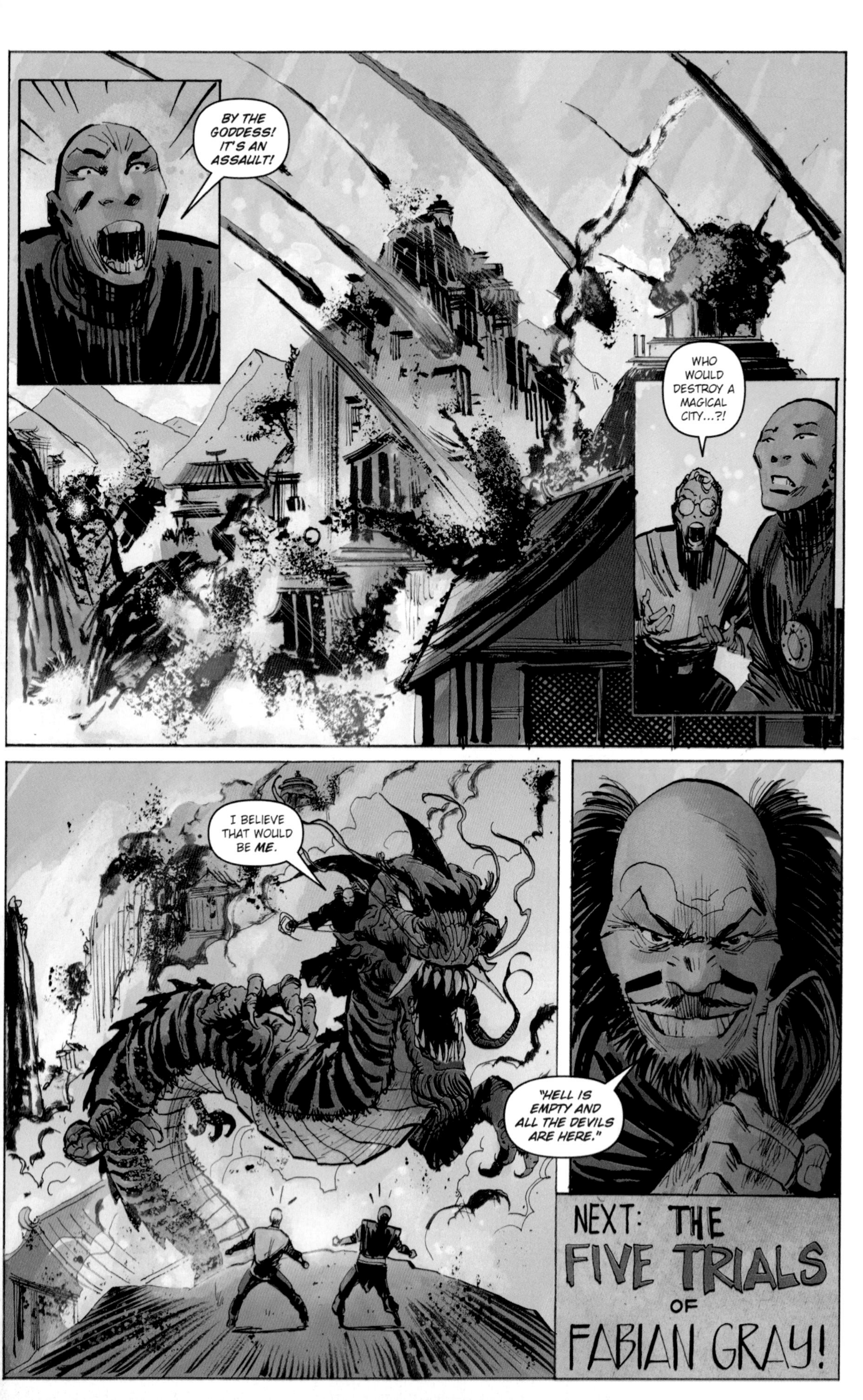

BY THE GODDESS! IT'S AN ASSAULT!
WHO WOULD DESTROY A MAGICAL CITY...?!
I BELIEVE THAT WOULD BE *ME*.
"HELL IS EMPTY AND ALL THE DEVILS ARE HERE."
NEXT: THE FIVE TRIALS OF FABIAN GRAY!

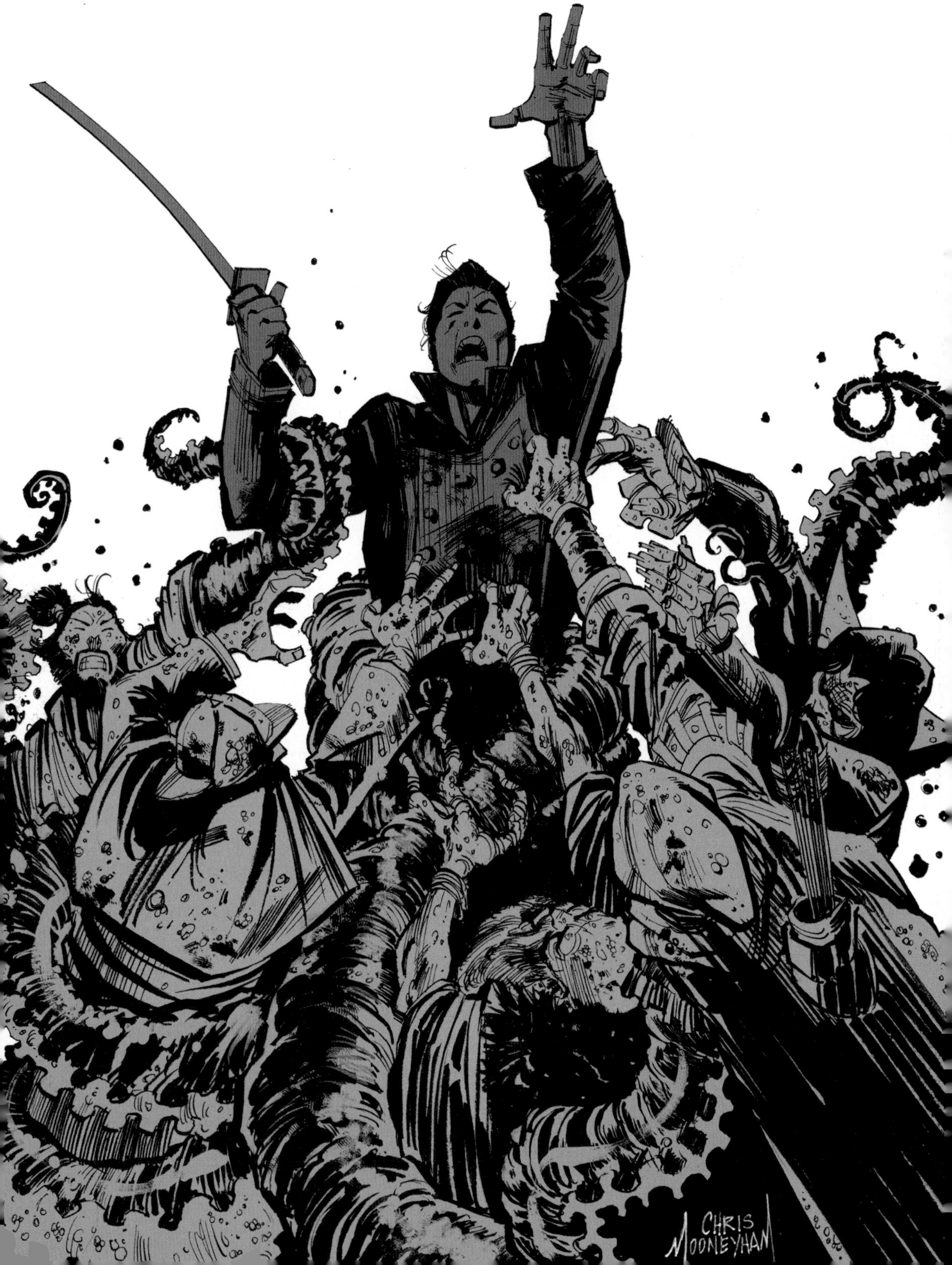
CHRIS MOONEYHAM

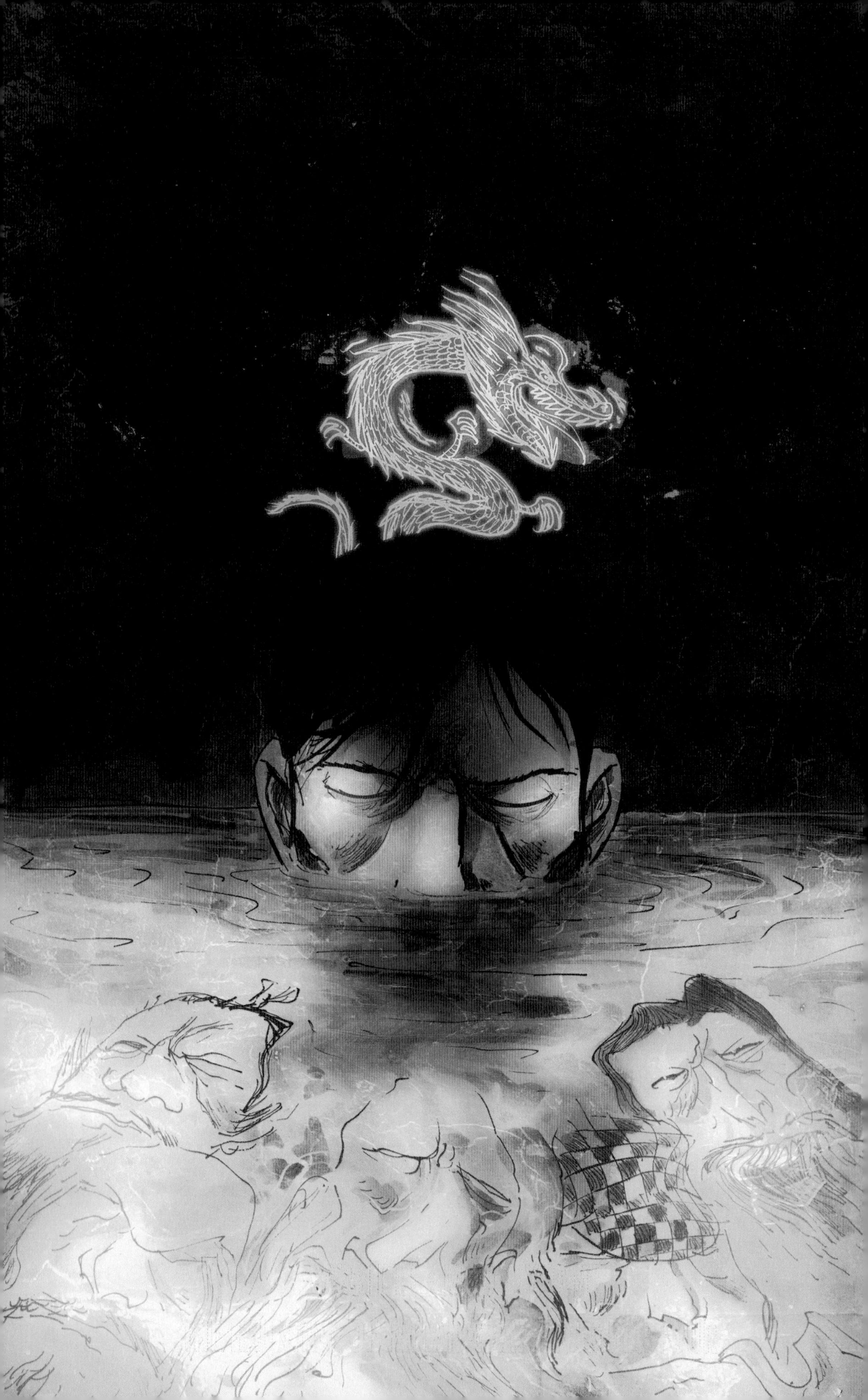

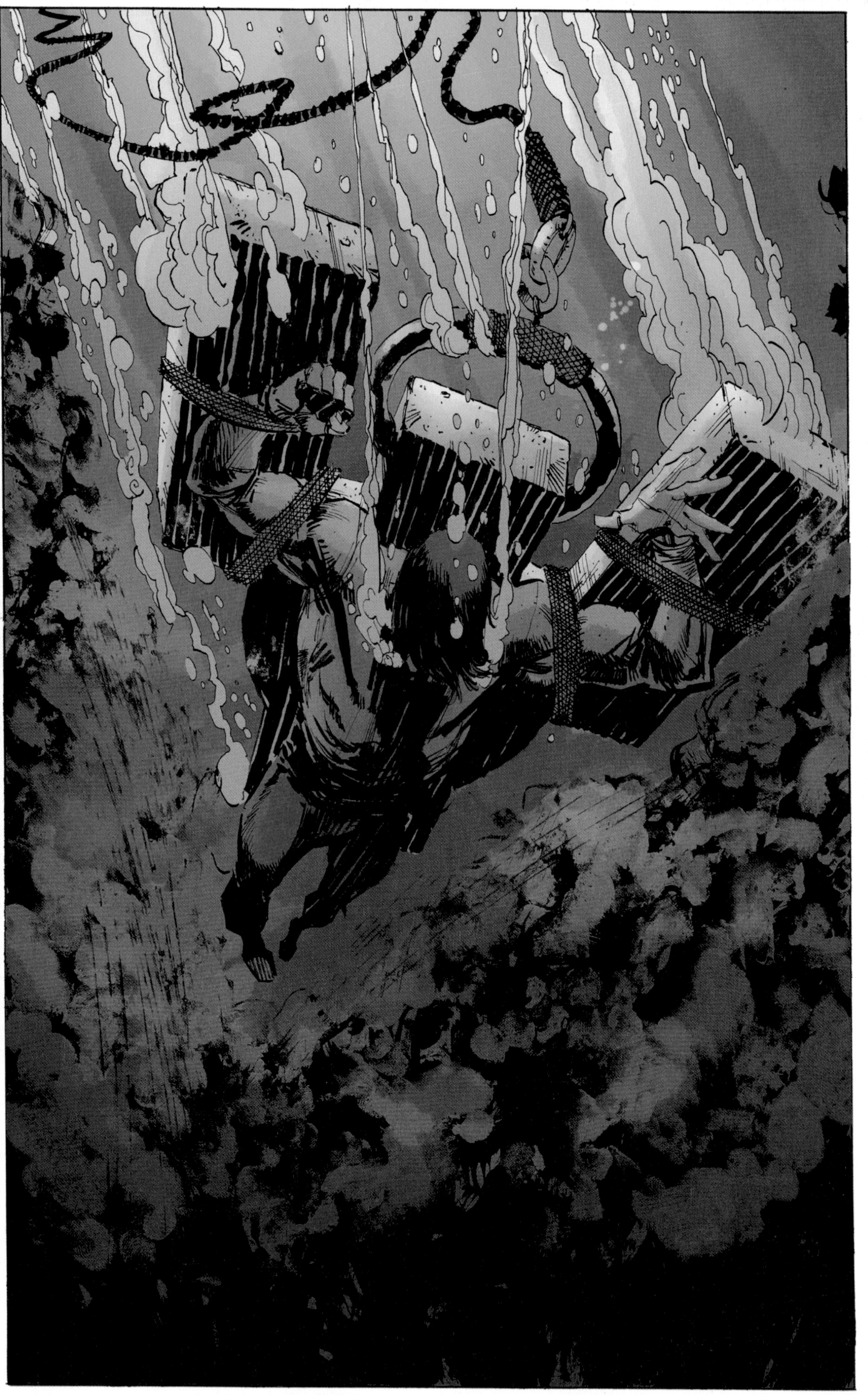

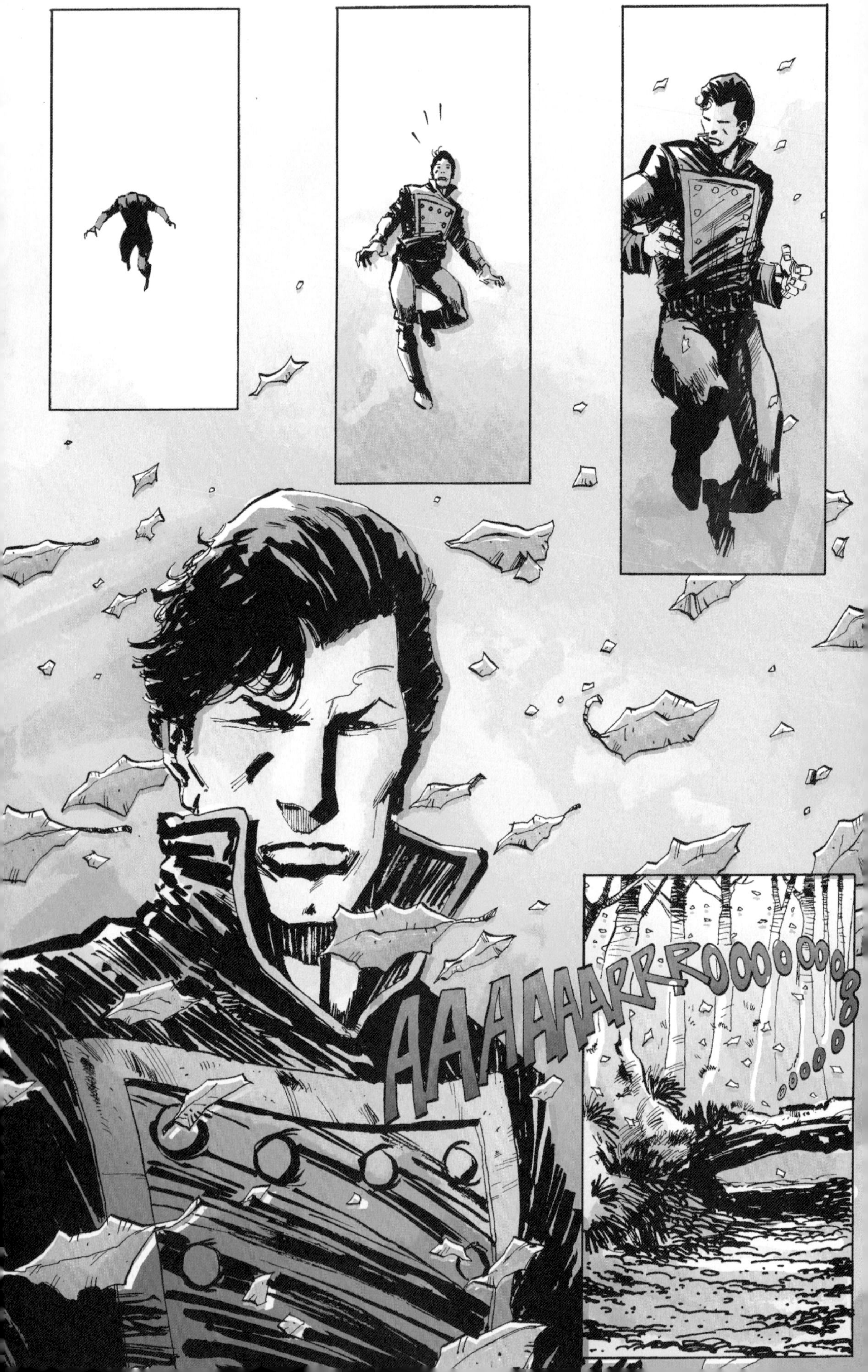
AAAAAARRROOOOOOOOOOOO

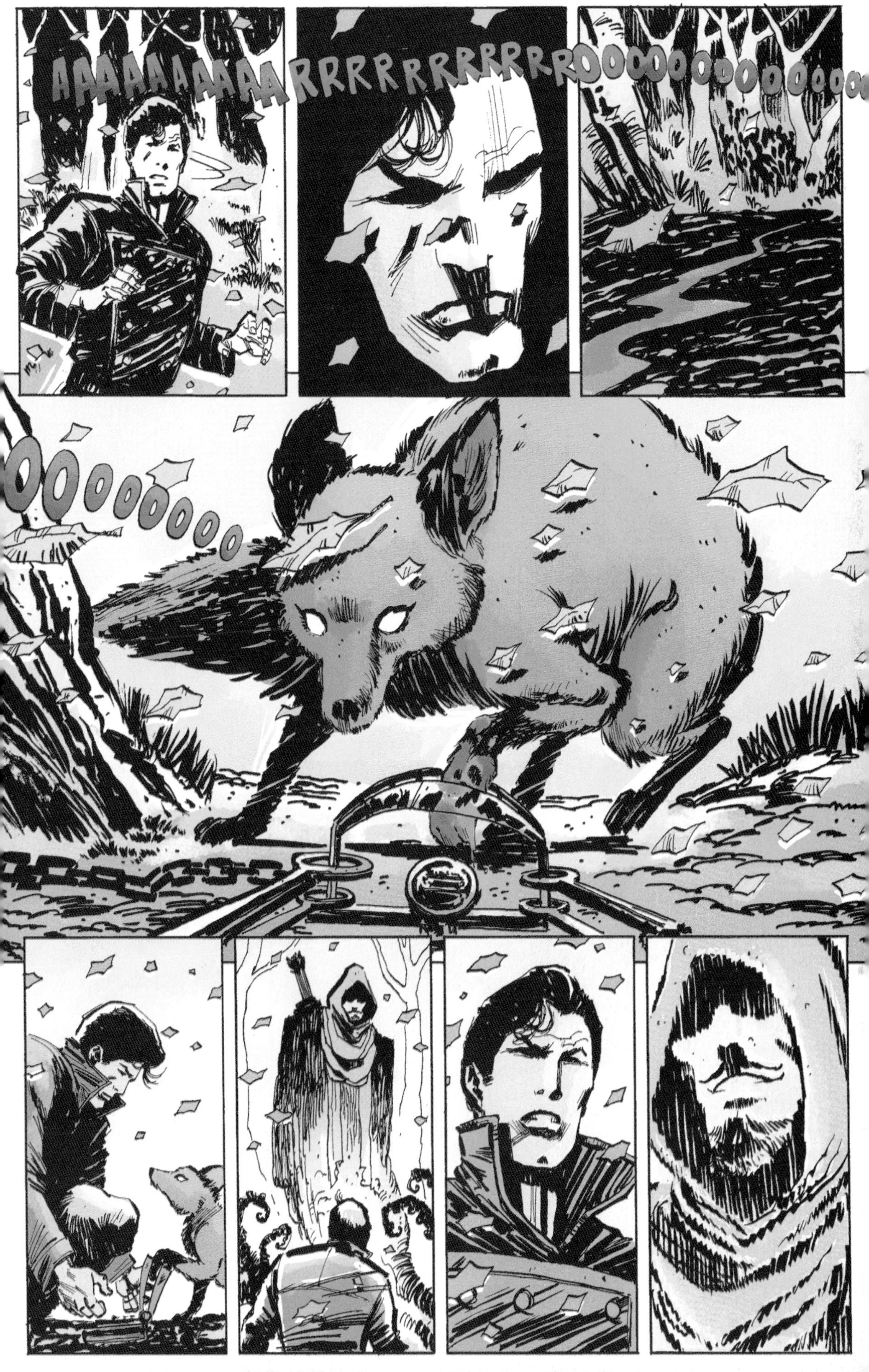
AAAAAAAAAARRRRRRRRRROOOOOOOOOOOOOO
OOOOOOOOO

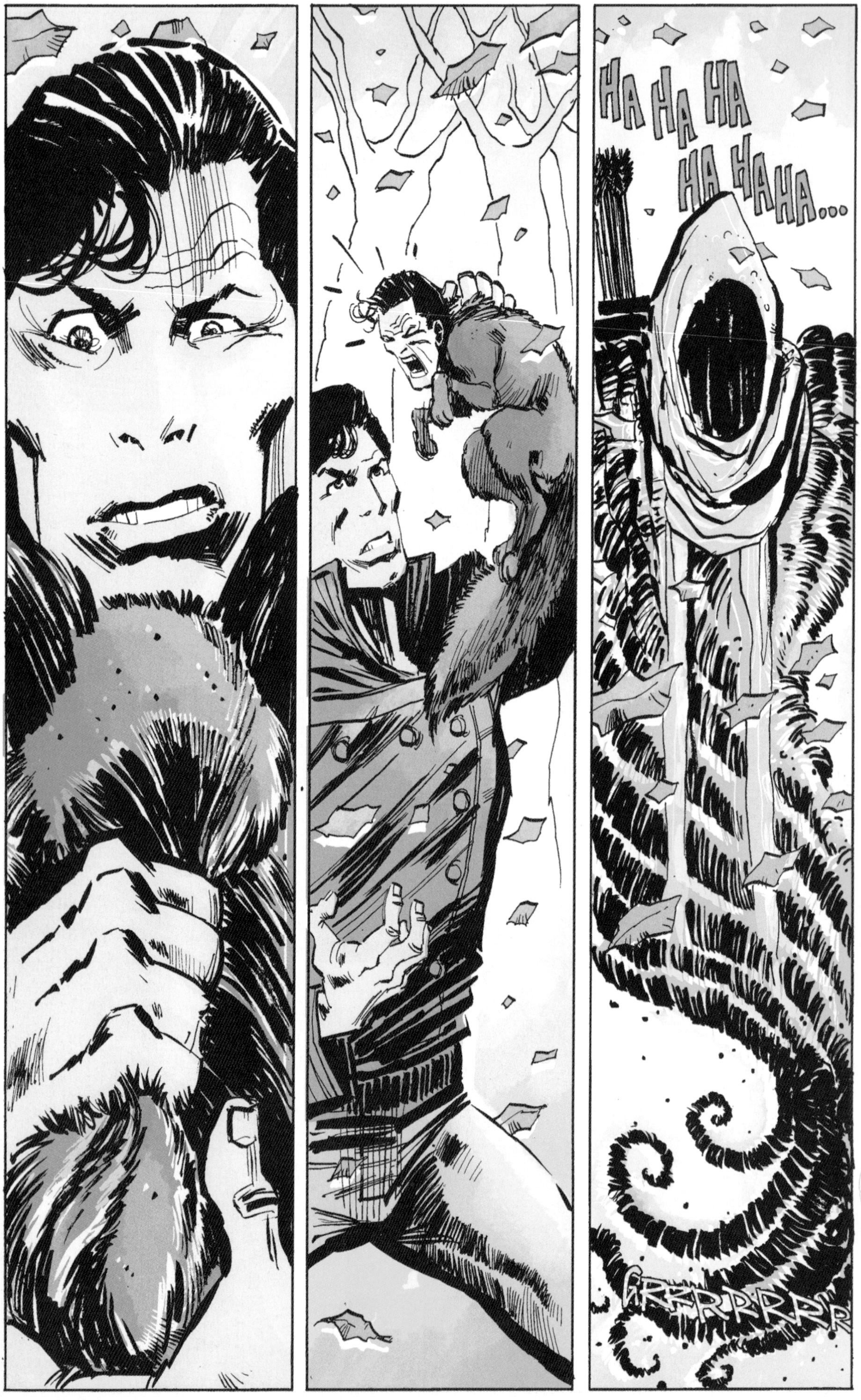
HA HA HA
HA HAHA...
GRRRRRRRR

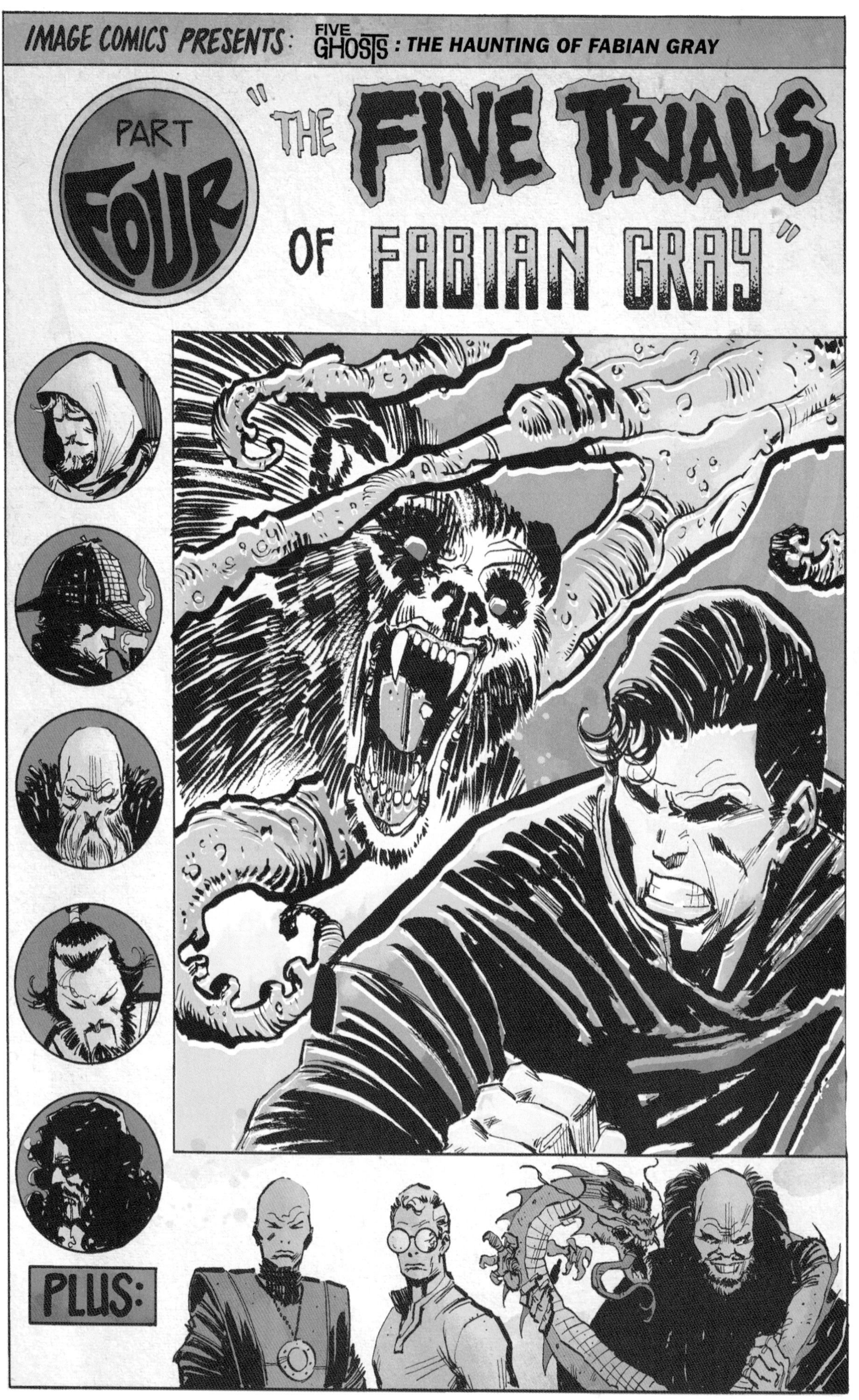
IMAGE COMICS PRESENTS: FIVE GHOSTS : THE HAUNTING OF FABIAN GRAY
PART FOUR
"THE FIVE TRIALS OF FABIAN GRAY"
PLUS:

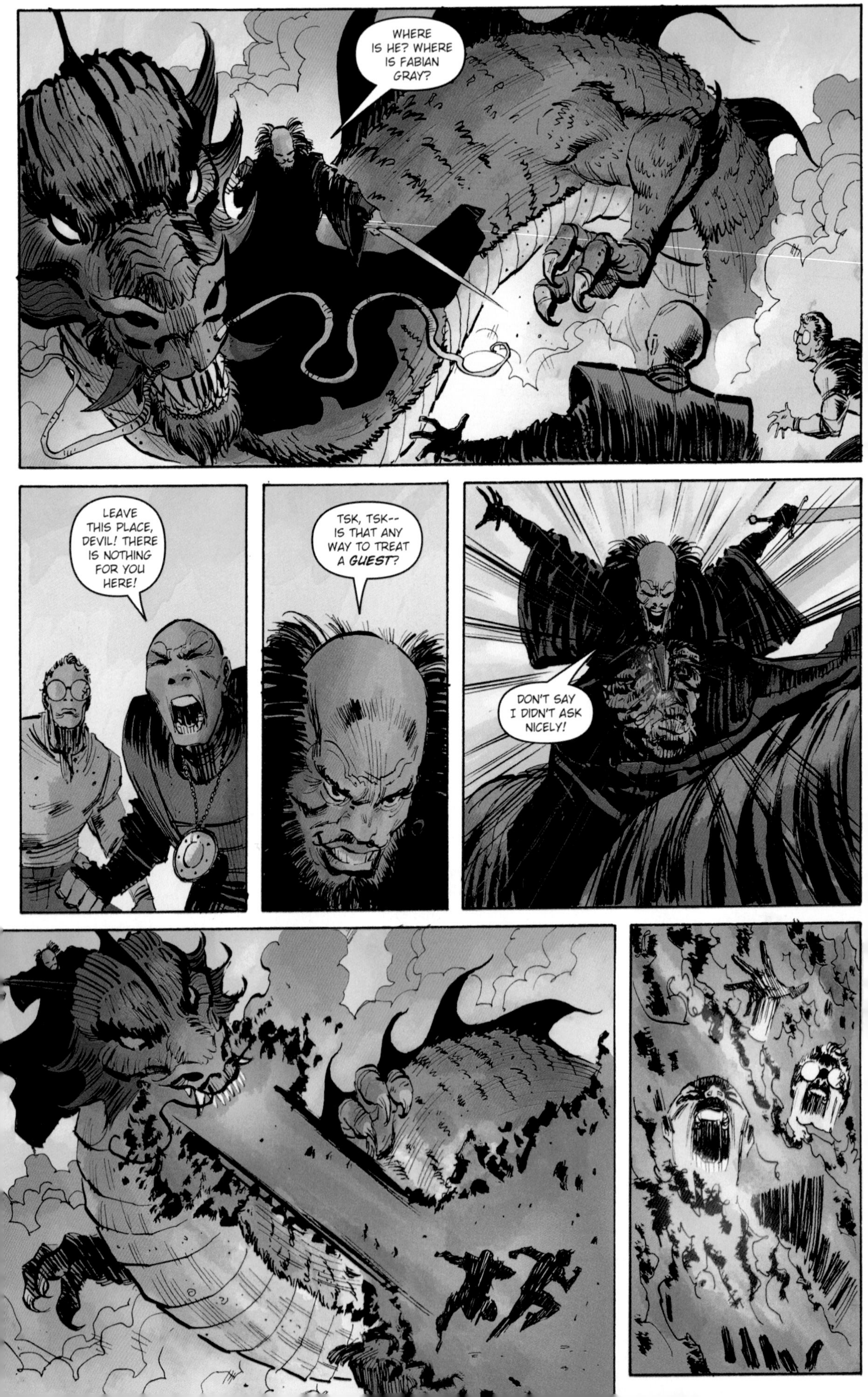
WHERE IS HE? WHERE IS FABIAN GRAY?
LEAVE THIS PLACE, DEVIL! THERE IS NOTHING FOR YOU HERE!
TSK, TSK-- IS THAT ANY WAY TO TREAT A GUEST?
DON'T SAY I DIDN'T ASK NICELY!

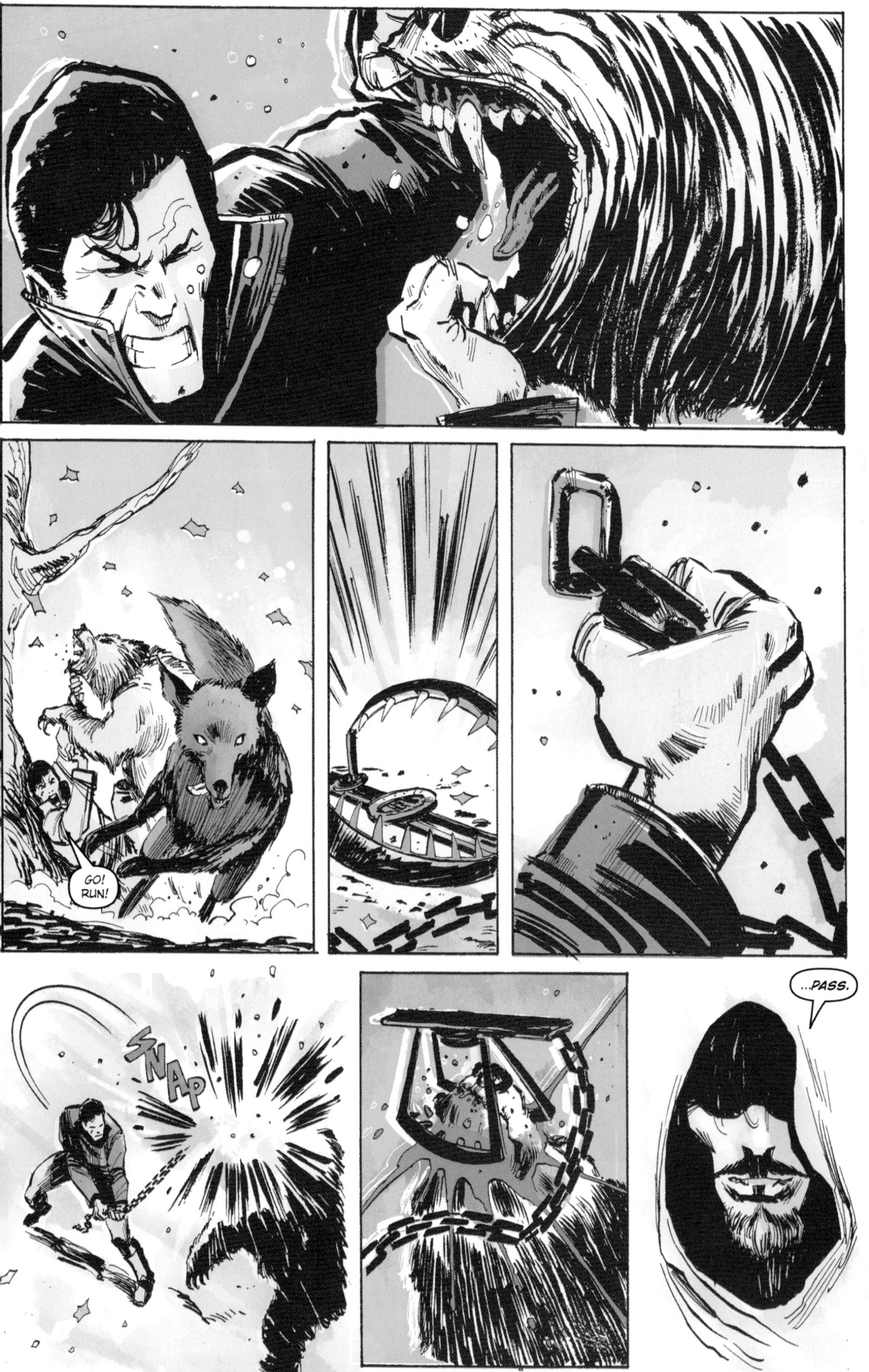
GO! RUN!
SNAP
...PASS.

...HUH?

I'M SOMEWHERE ELSE...

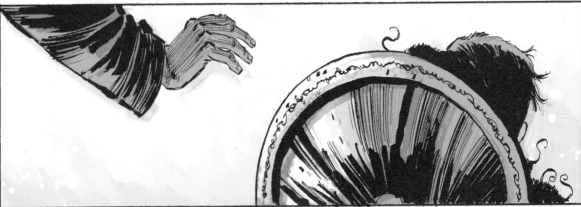

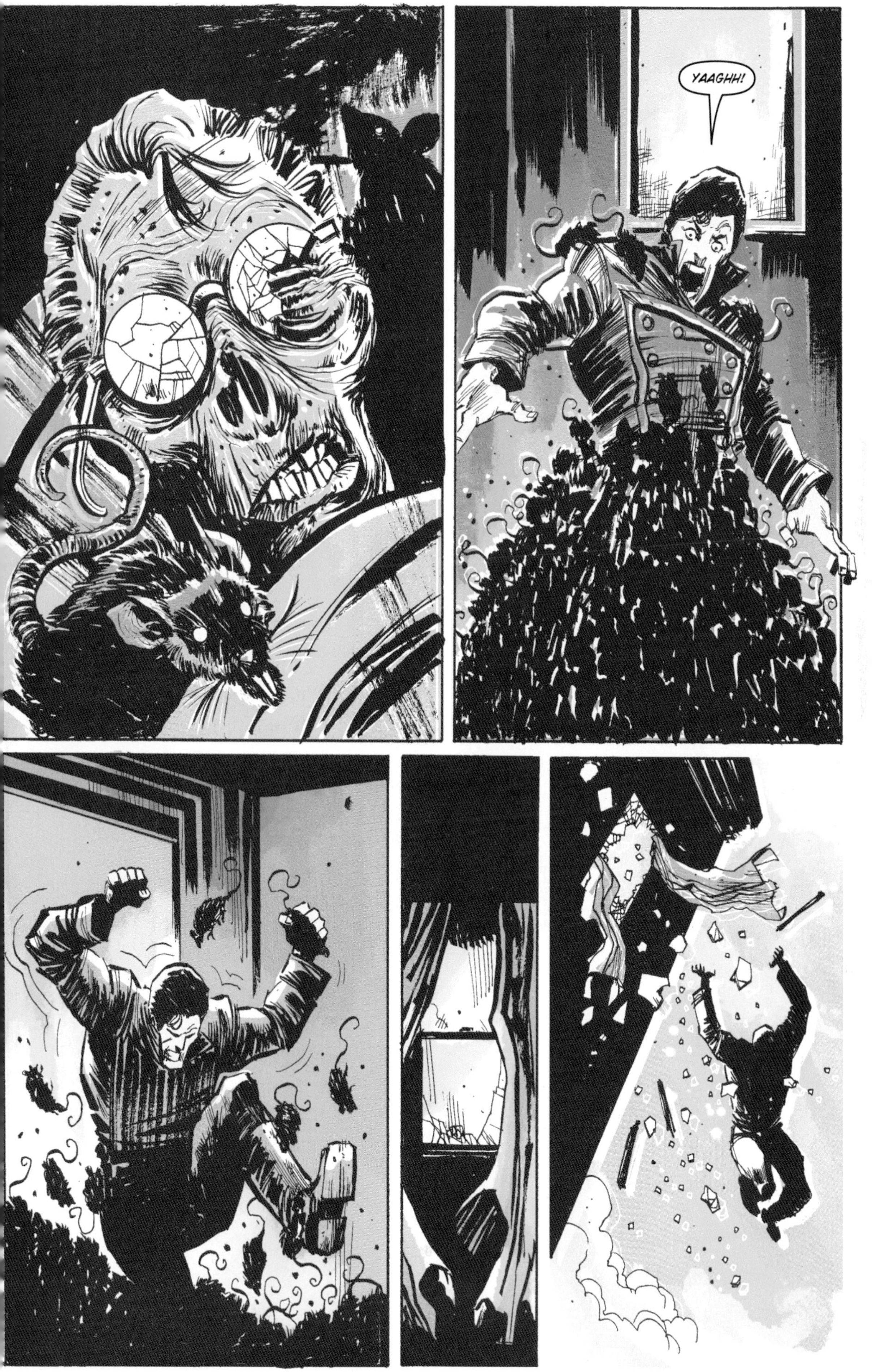
YAAGHH!

THIS...IS SOME KIND OF *NIGHTMARE*...

HUH?

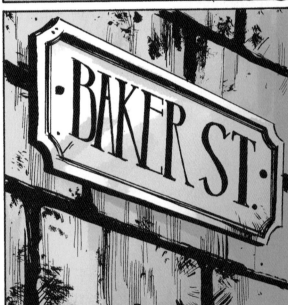

NO, NOT A NIGHTMARE... IT'S A *TEST*.

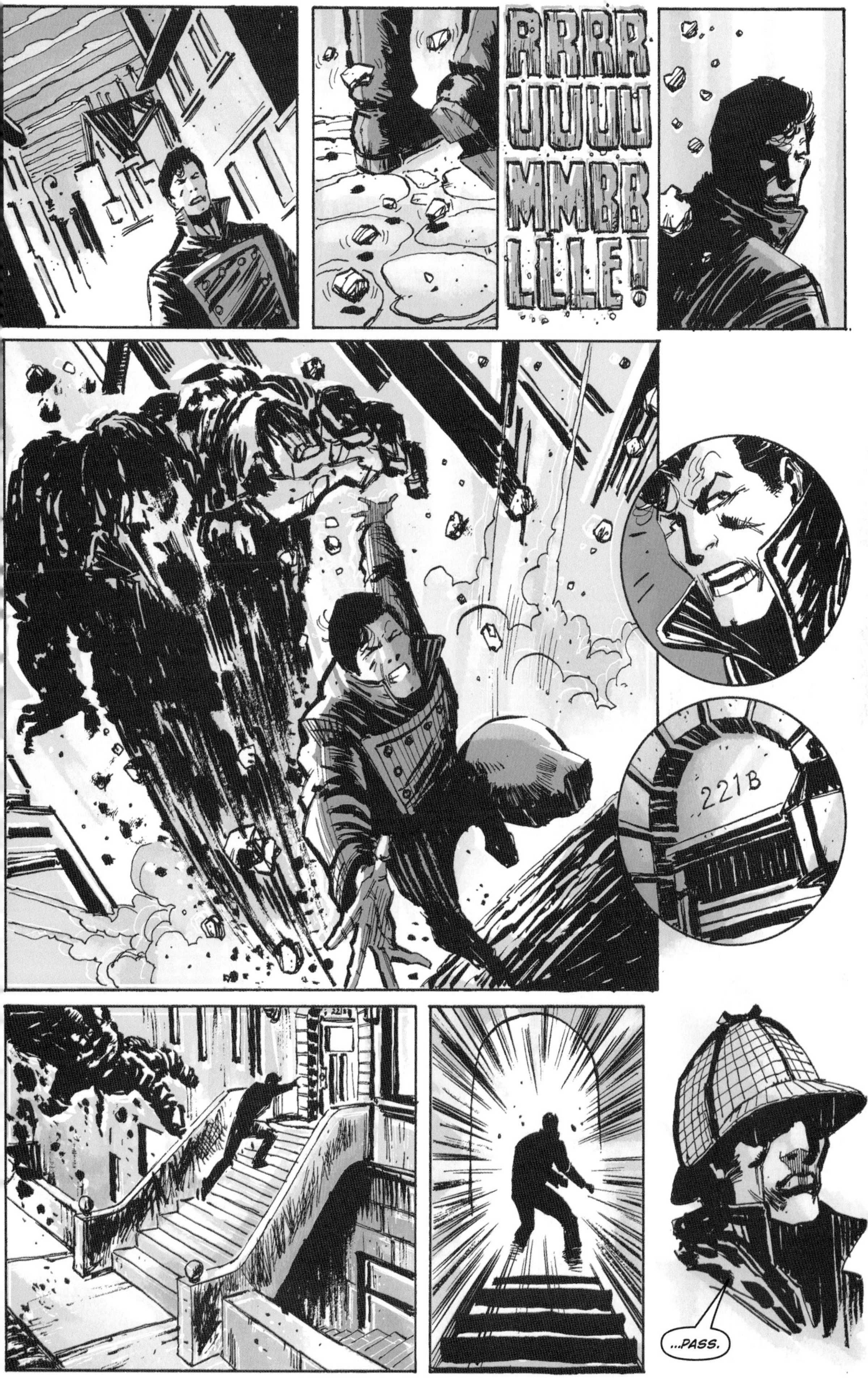
RRRRUUUUMMBBLLLE!
221B
...PASS.

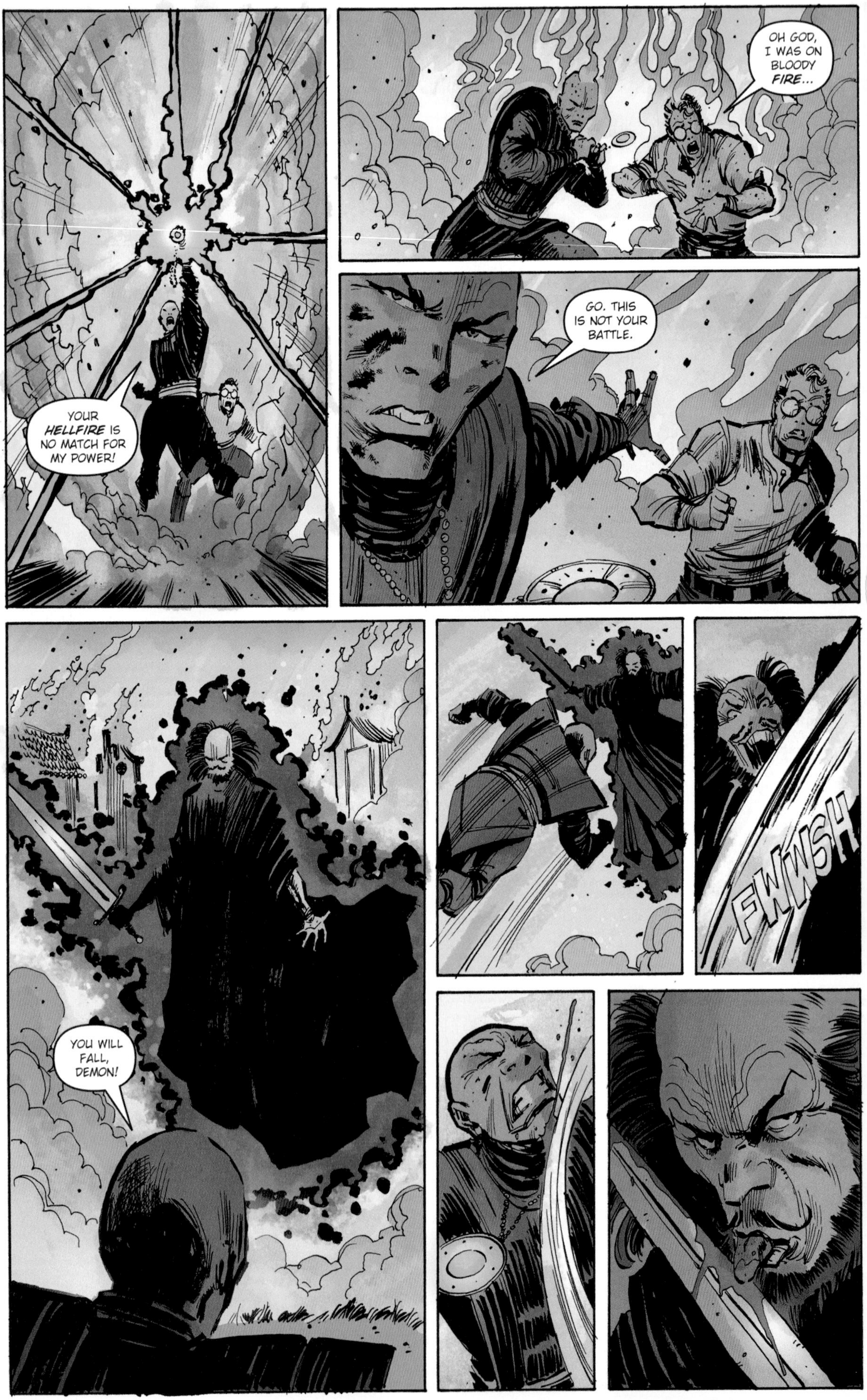
YOUR HELLFIRE IS NO MATCH FOR MY POWER!
OH GOD, I WAS ON BLOODY FIRE...
GO. THIS IS NOT YOUR BATTLE.
YOU WILL FALL, DEMON!
FWWSH

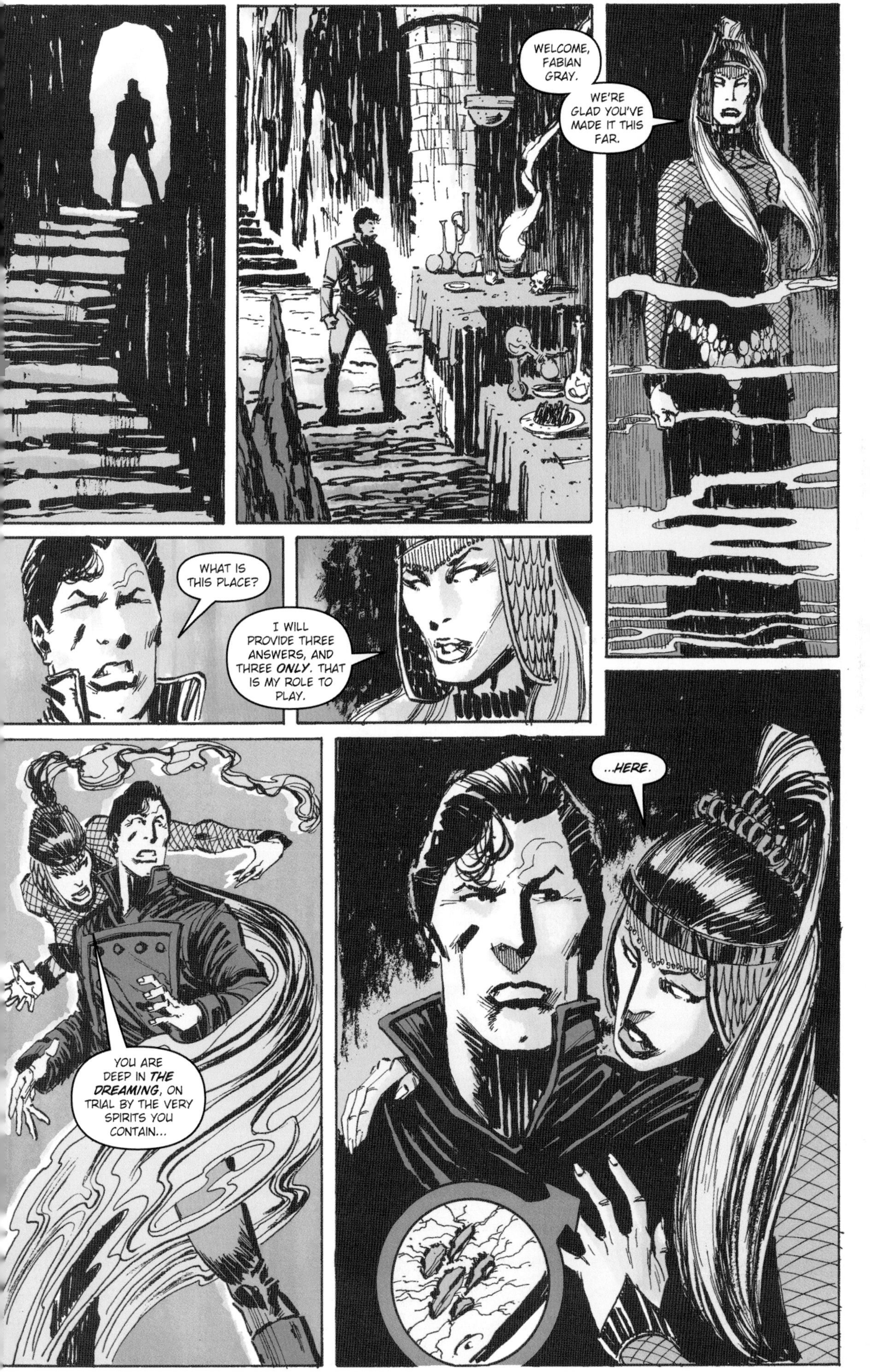
WELCOME, FABIAN GRAY.
WE'RE GLAD YOU'VE MADE IT THIS FAR.
WHAT IS THIS PLACE?
I WILL PROVIDE THREE ANSWERS, AND THREE **ONLY**. THAT IS MY ROLE TO PLAY.
YOU ARE DEEP IN **THE DREAMING**, ON TRIAL BY THE VERY SPIRITS YOU CONTAIN...
...**HERE**.

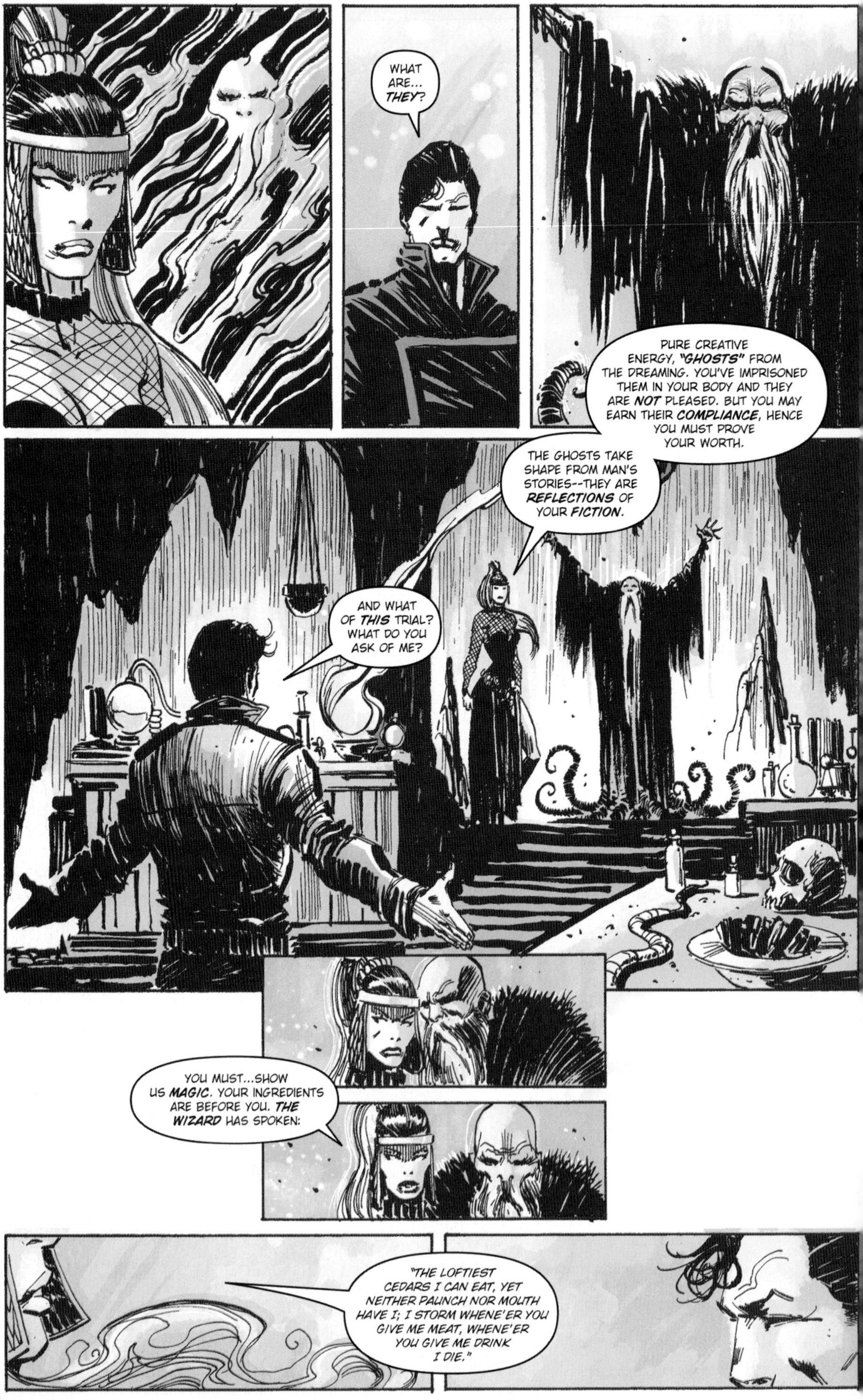
WHAT ARE... THEY?
PURE CREATIVE ENERGY, "GHOSTS" FROM THE DREAMING. YOU'VE IMPRISONED THEM IN YOUR BODY AND THEY ARE NOT PLEASED. BUT YOU MAY EARN THEIR COMPLIANCE, HENCE YOU MUST PROVE YOUR WORTH.
THE GHOSTS TAKE SHAPE FROM MAN'S STORIES--THEY ARE REFLECTIONS OF YOUR FICTION.
AND WHAT OF THIS TRIAL? WHAT DO YOU ASK OF ME?
YOU MUST...SHOW US MAGIC. YOUR INGREDIENTS ARE BEFORE YOU. THE WIZARD HAS SPOKEN:
"THE LOFTIEST CEDARS I CAN EAT, YET NEITHER PAUNCH NOR MOUTH HAVE I; I STORM WHENE'ER YOU GIVE ME MEAT, WHENE'ER YOU GIVE ME DRINK I DIE."

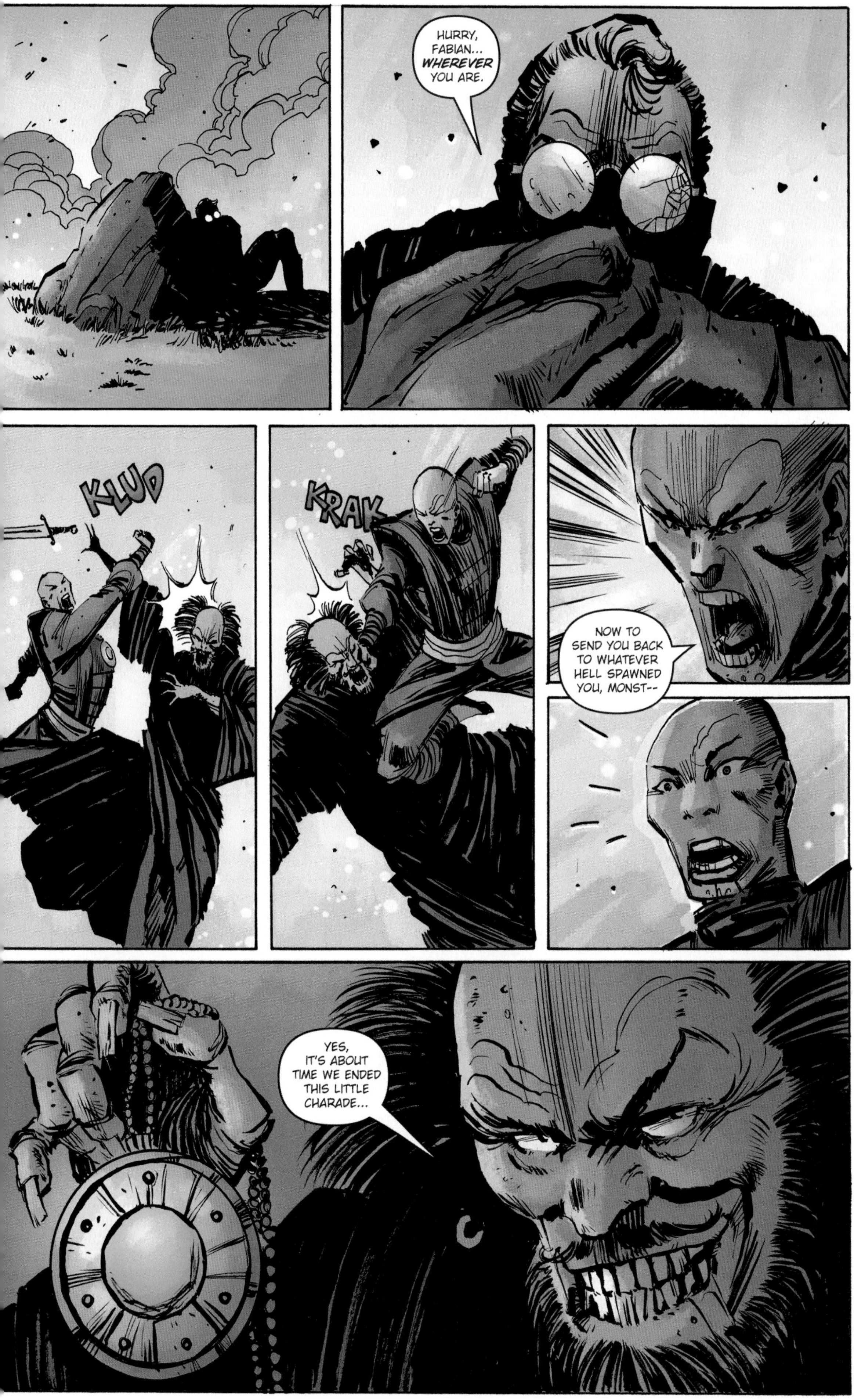
HURRY, FABIAN... *WHEREVER* YOU ARE.
KLUD
KRAK
NOW TO SEND YOU BACK TO WHATEVER HELL SPAWNED YOU, MONST--
YES, IT'S ABOUT TIME WE ENDED THIS LITTLE CHARADE...

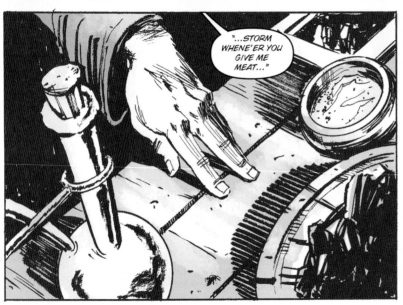

"...STORM WHENE'ER YOU GIVE ME MEAT..."

DAMN THIS POINTLESS RIDDLE!

MAYBE I *DESERVE* TO WANDER LOST IN A DREAM FOREVER...IT'S MY FAULT--SILVIA, I'M SORRY...

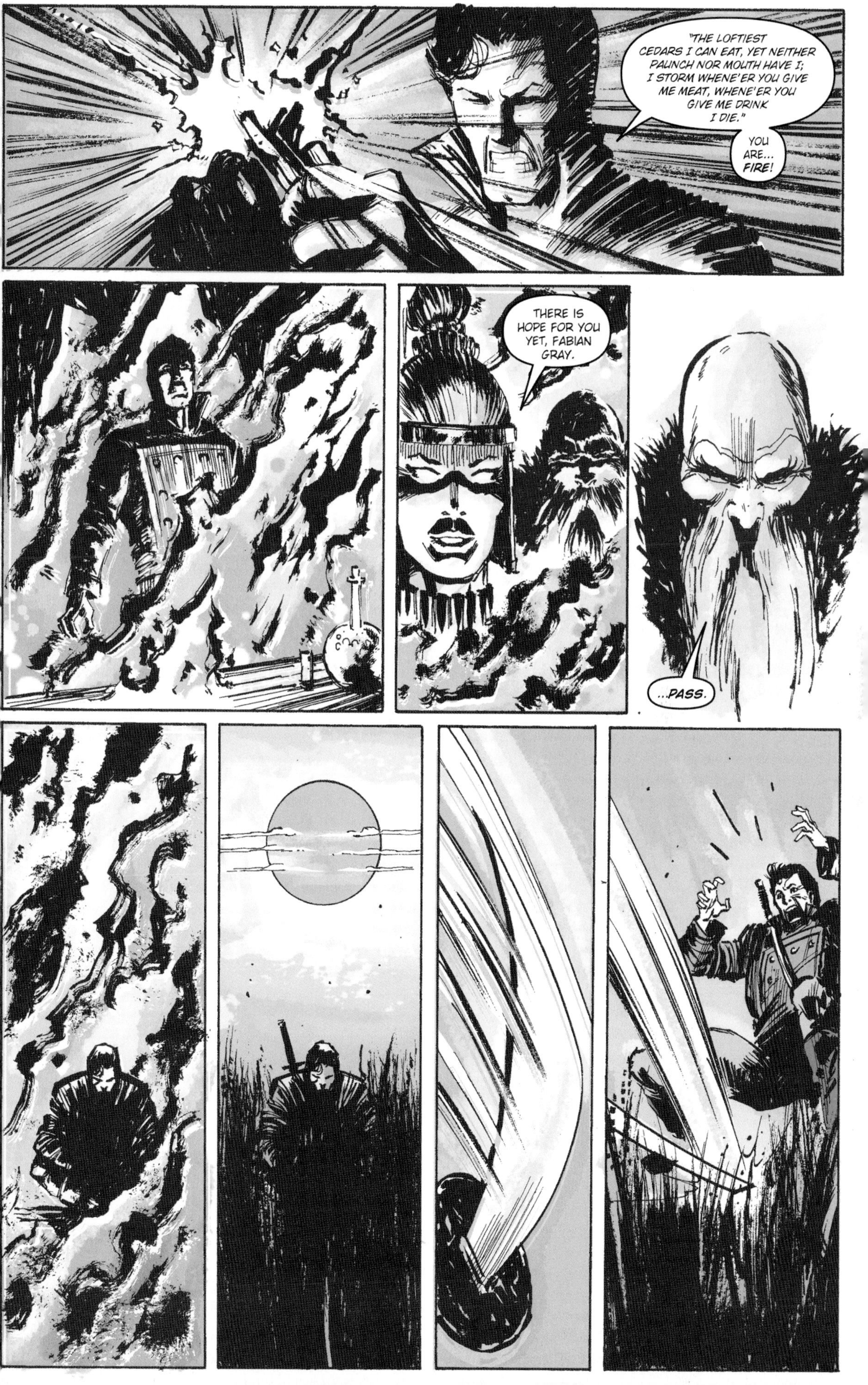
"THE LOFTIEST CEDARS I CAN EAT, YET NEITHER PAUNCH NOR MOUTH HAVE I; I STORM WHENE'ER YOU GIVE ME MEAT, WHENE'ER YOU GIVE ME DRINK I DIE."
YOU ARE... FIRE!
THERE IS HOPE FOR YOU YET, FABIAN GRAY.
...PASS.

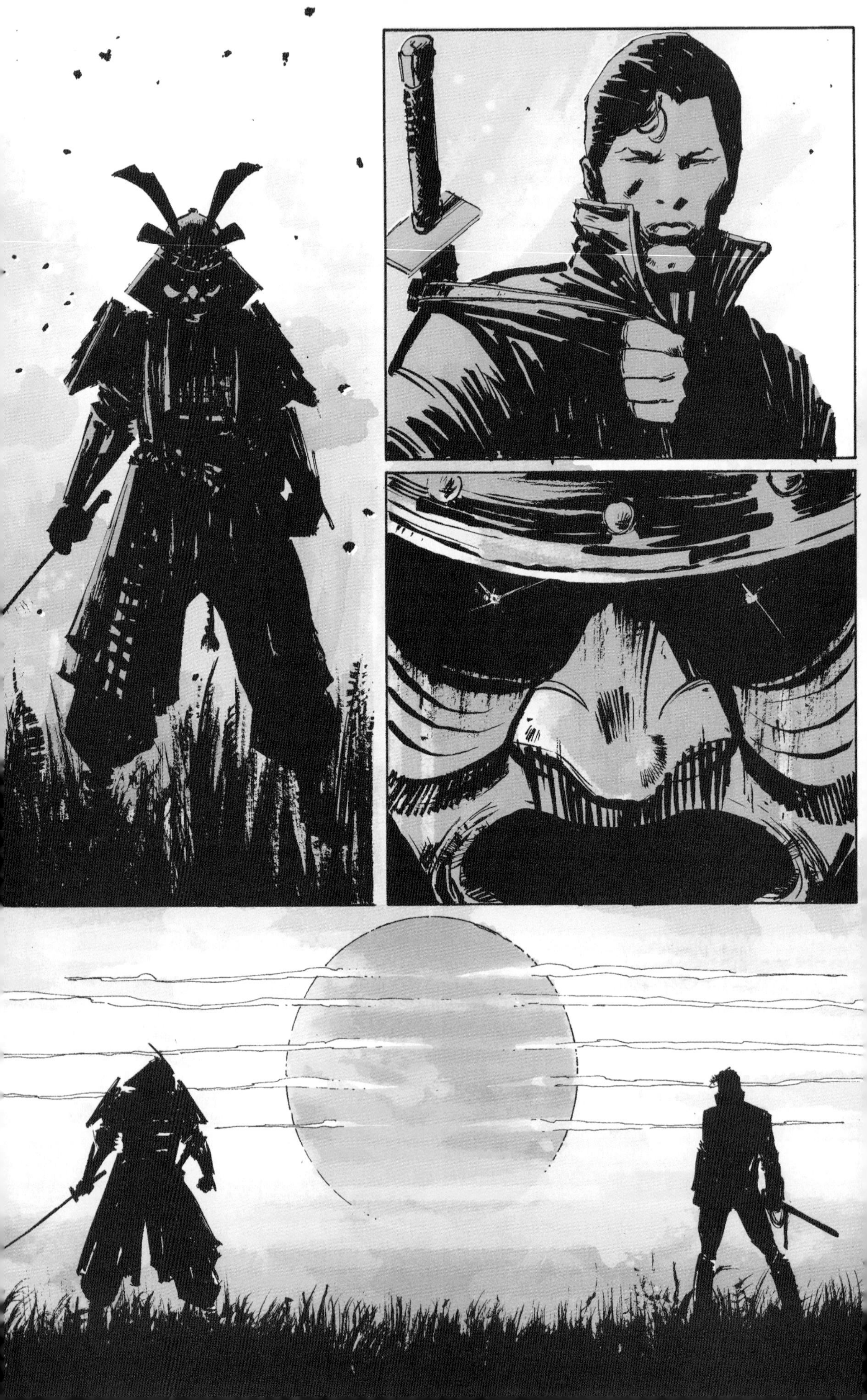

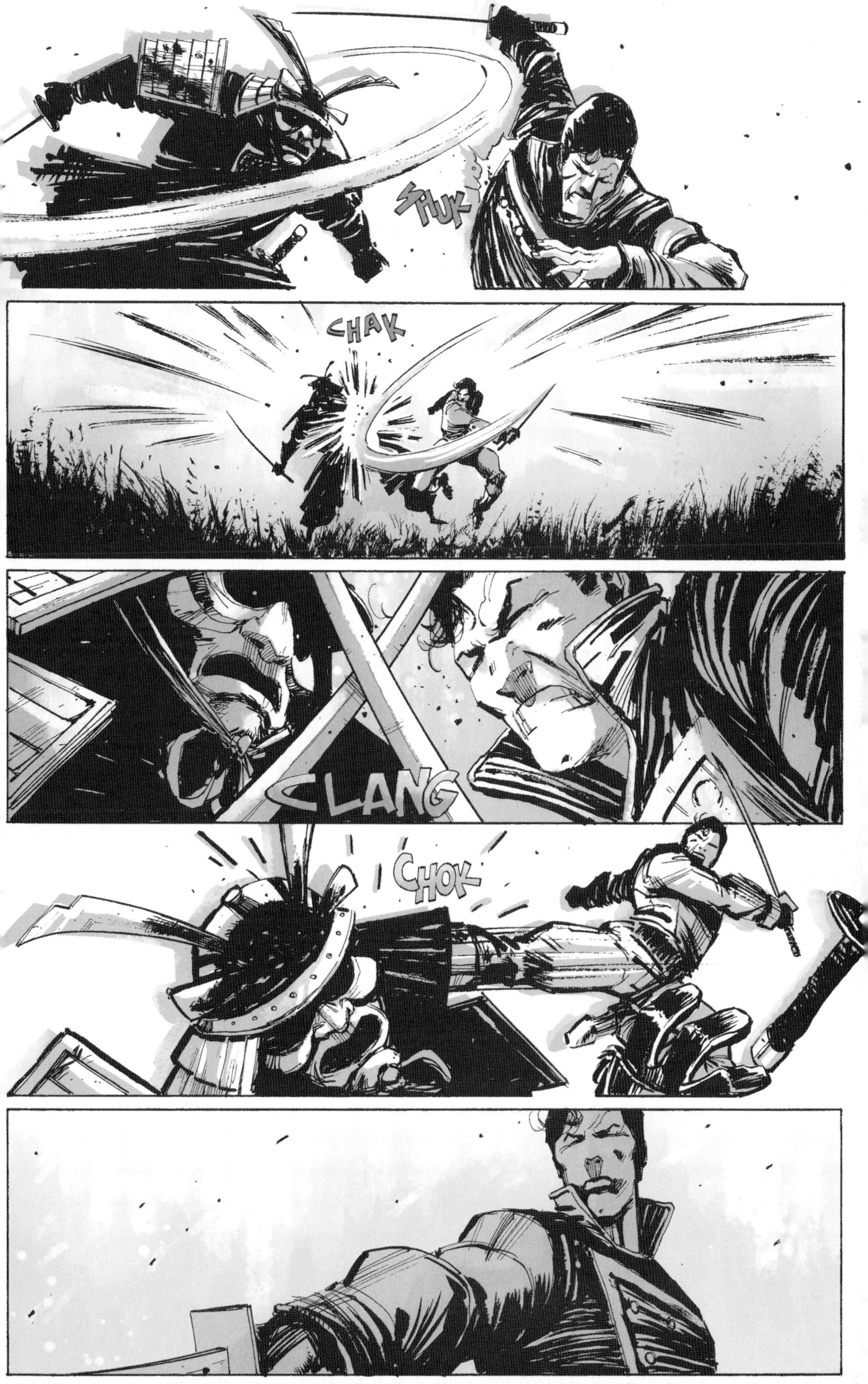
SHUK
CHAK
CLANG
CHOK

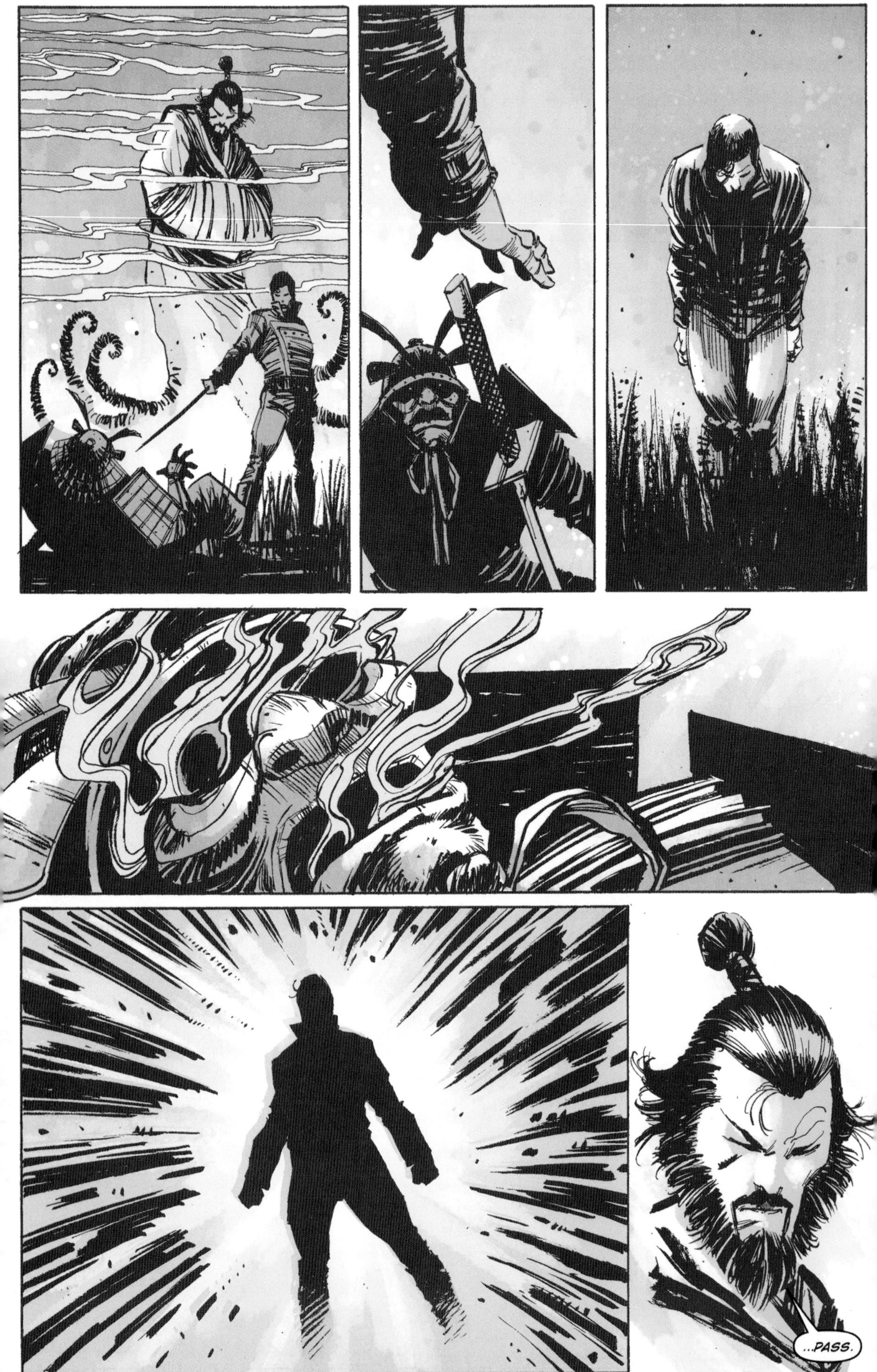
...PASS.

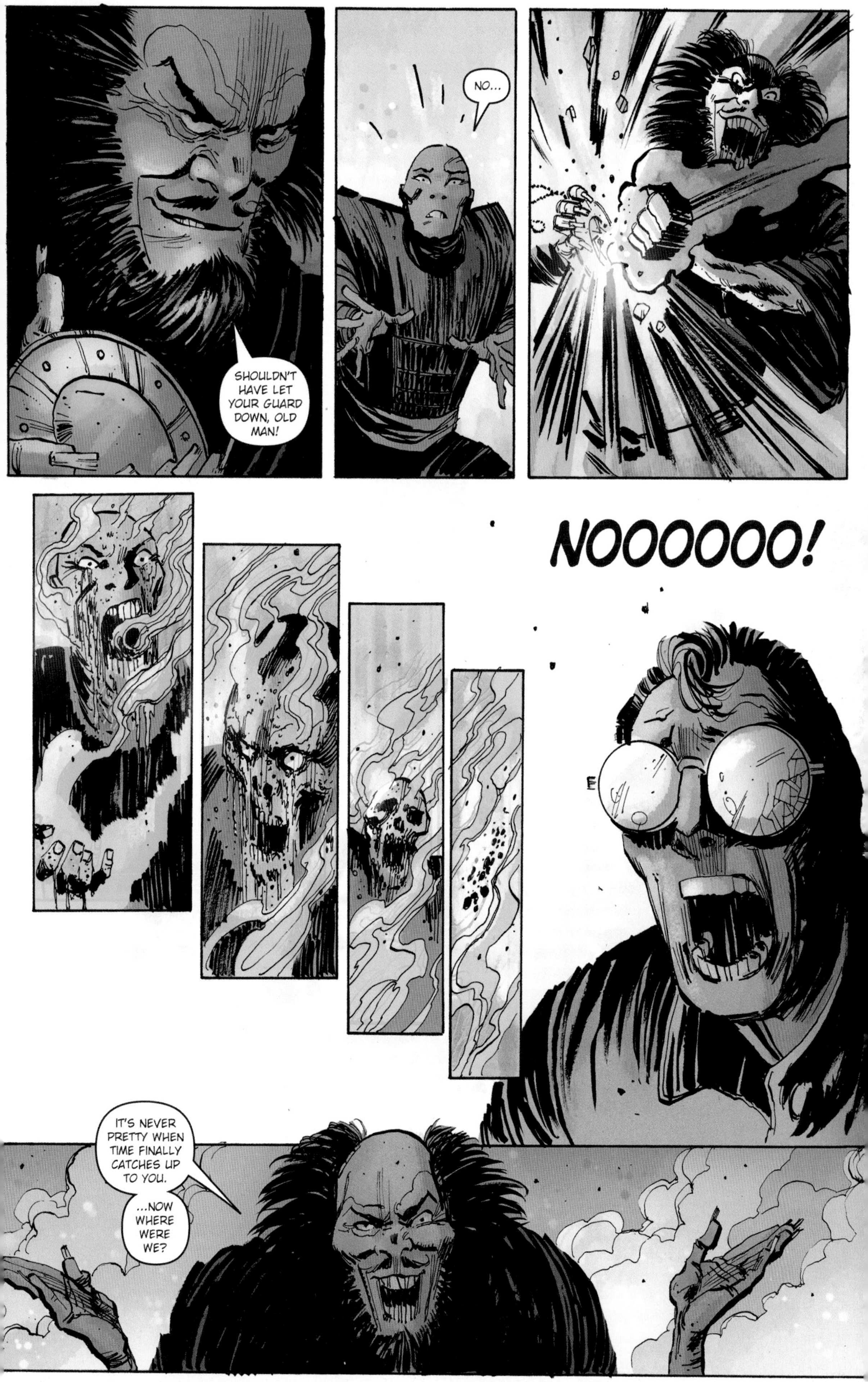
SHOULDN'T HAVE LET YOUR GUARD DOWN, OLD MAN!
NO...
NOOOOOO!
IT'S NEVER PRETTY WHEN TIME FINALLY CATCHES UP TO YOU.
...NOW WHERE WERE WE?

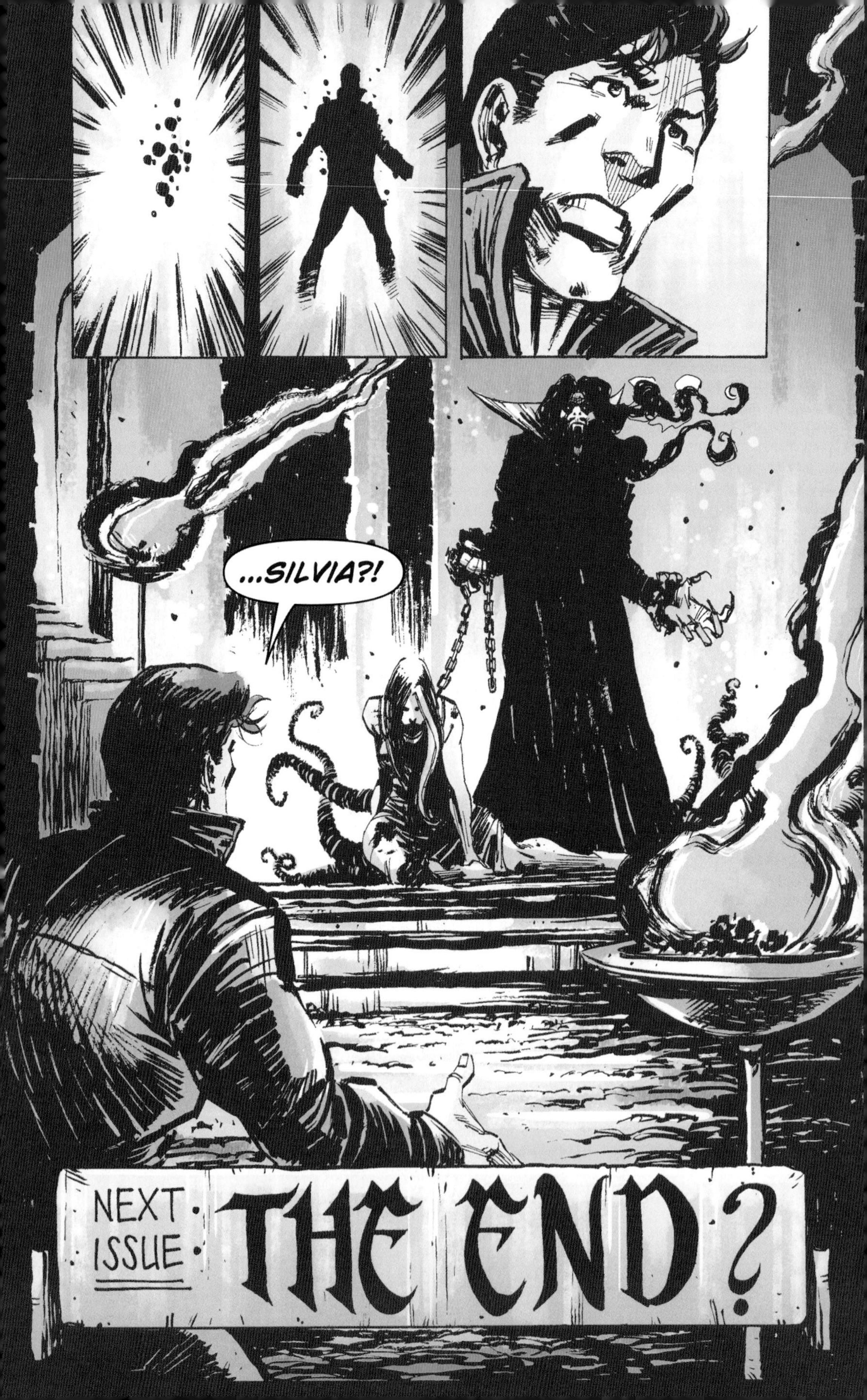
...SILVIA?!
NEXT ISSUE
THE END?

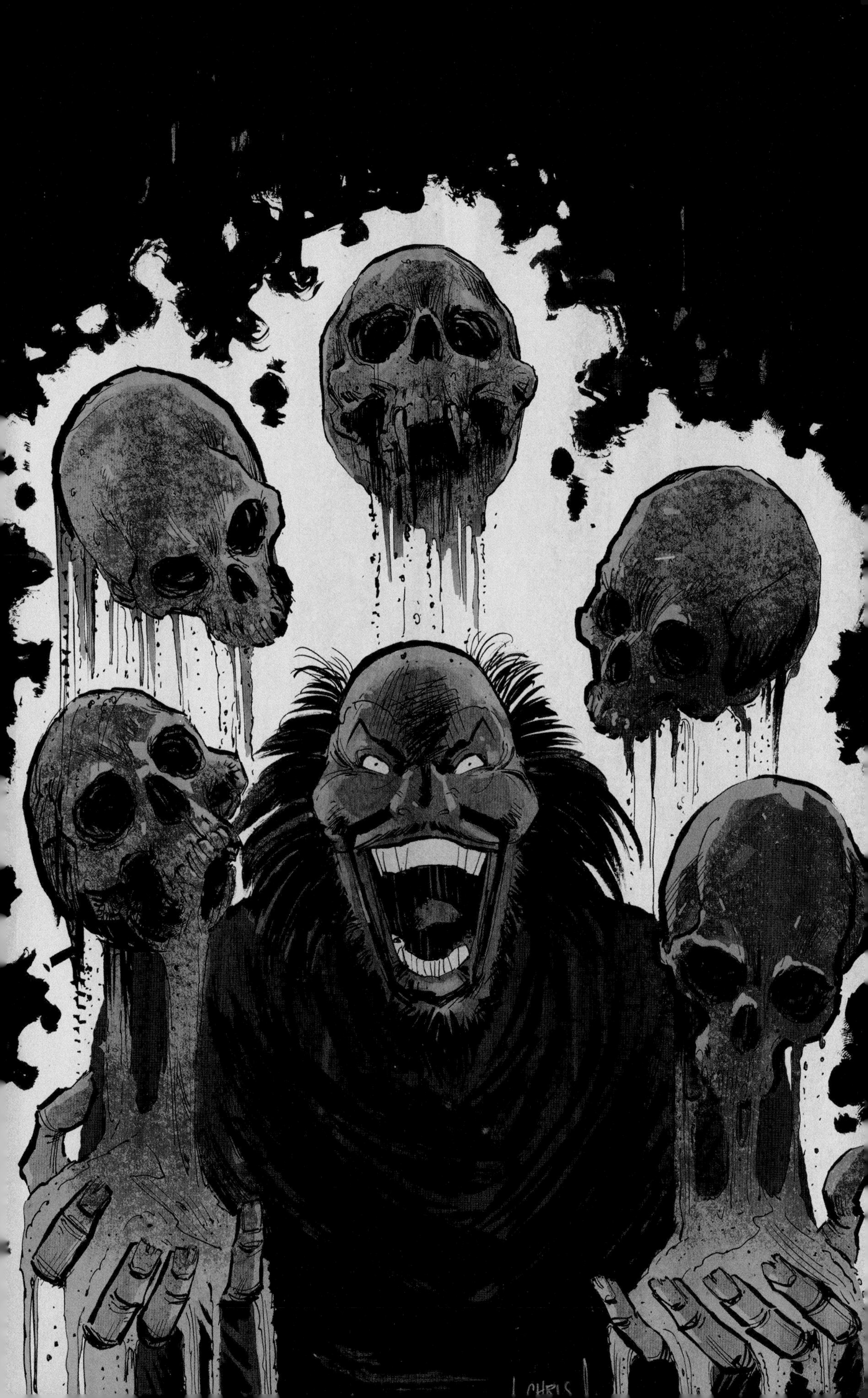

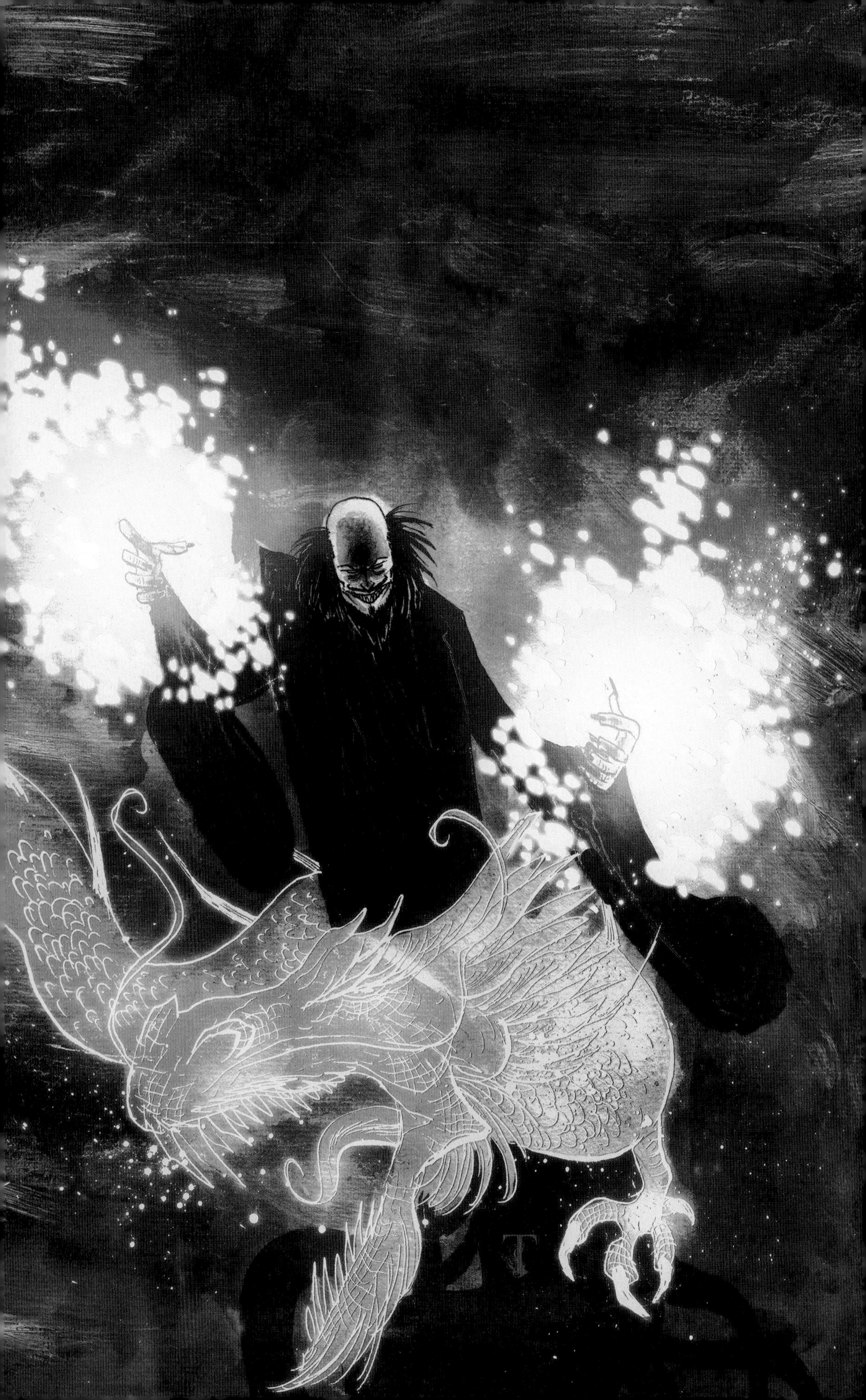

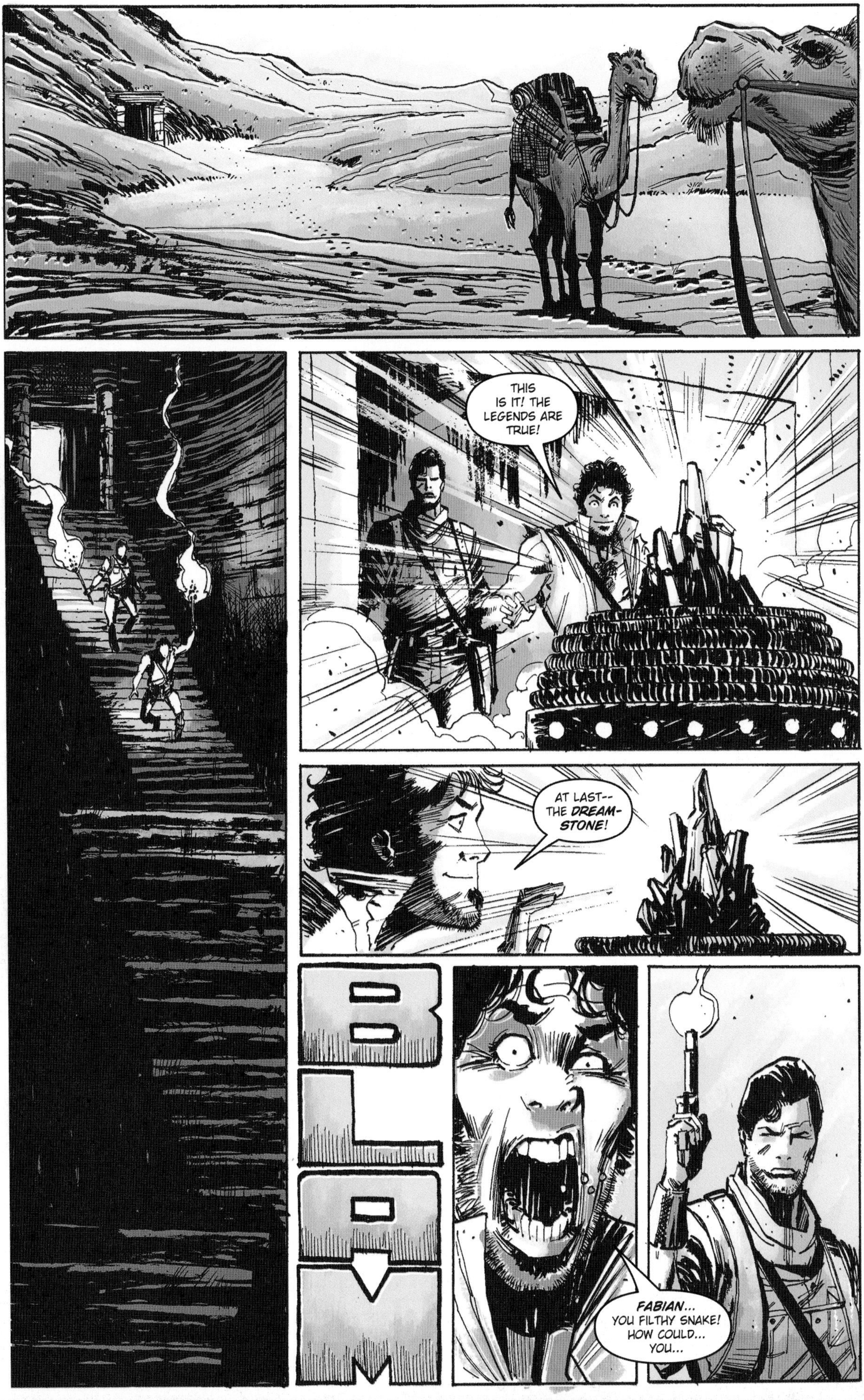

THIS IS IT! THE LEGENDS ARE TRUE!
AT LAST-- THE *DREAM-STONE!*
BLAM
FABIAN... YOU FILTHY SNAKE! HOW COULD... YOU...

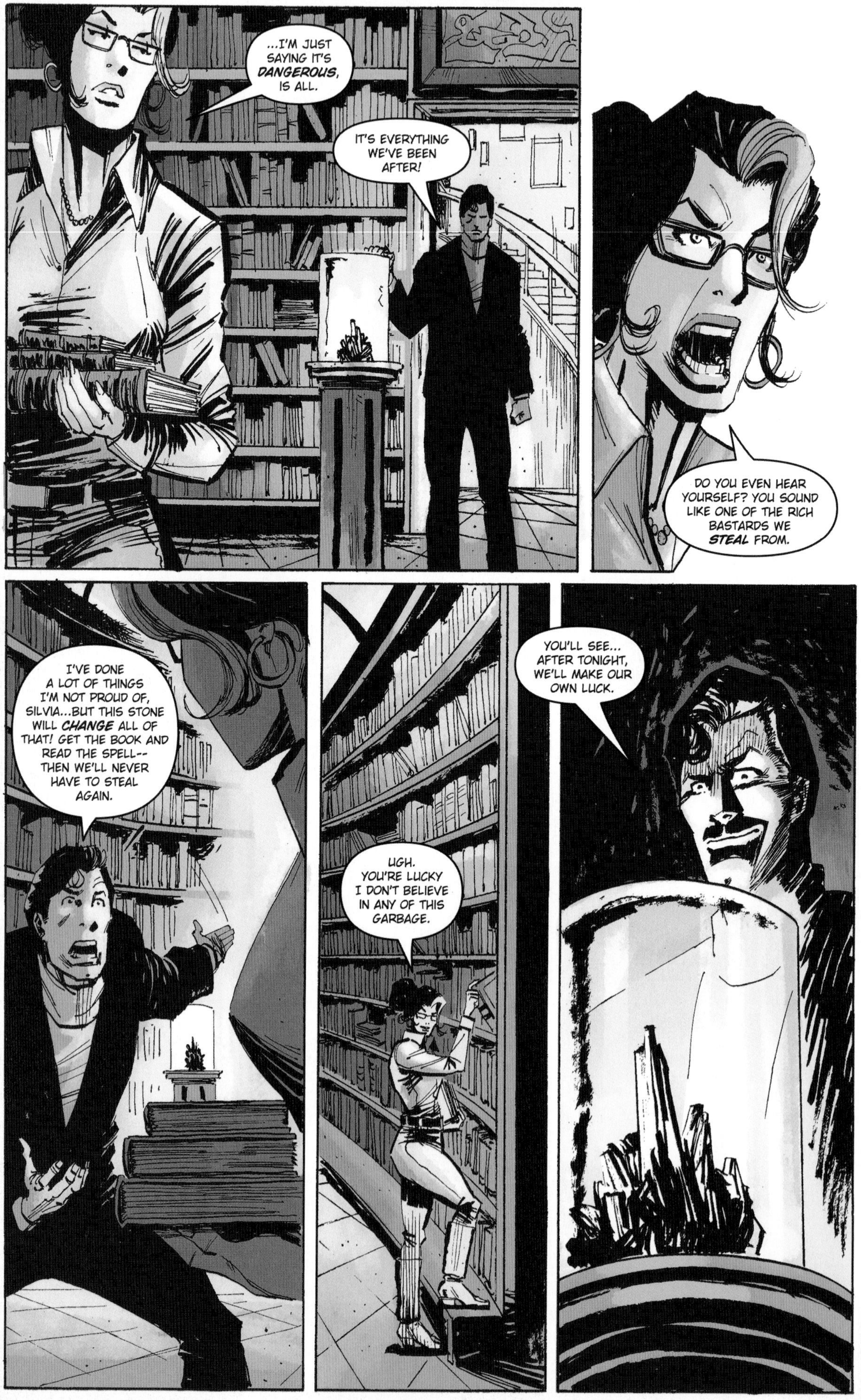
...I'M JUST SAYING IT'S *DANGEROUS*, IS ALL.
IT'S EVERYTHING WE'VE BEEN AFTER!
DO YOU EVEN HEAR YOURSELF? YOU SOUND LIKE ONE OF THE RICH BASTARDS WE *STEAL* FROM.
I'VE DONE A LOT OF THINGS I'M NOT PROUD OF, SILVIA...BUT THIS STONE WILL *CHANGE* ALL OF THAT! GET THE BOOK AND READ THE SPELL-- THEN WE'LL NEVER HAVE TO STEAL AGAIN.
UGH. YOU'RE LUCKY I DON'T BELIEVE IN ANY OF THIS GARBAGE.
YOU'LL SEE... AFTER TONIGHT, WE'LL MAKE OUR OWN LUCK.

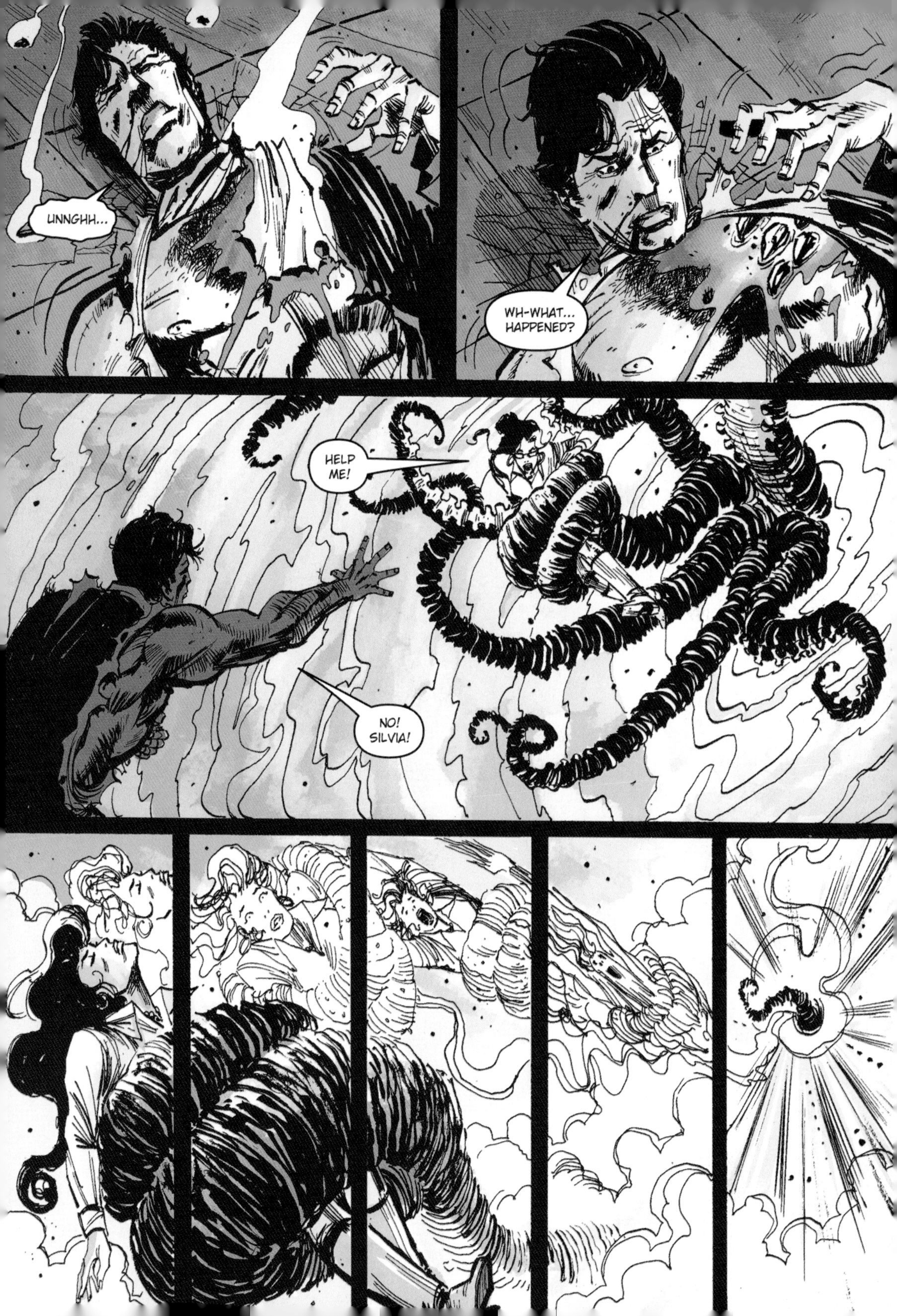
UNNGHH...
WH-WHAT... HAPPENED?
HELP ME!
NO! SILVIA!

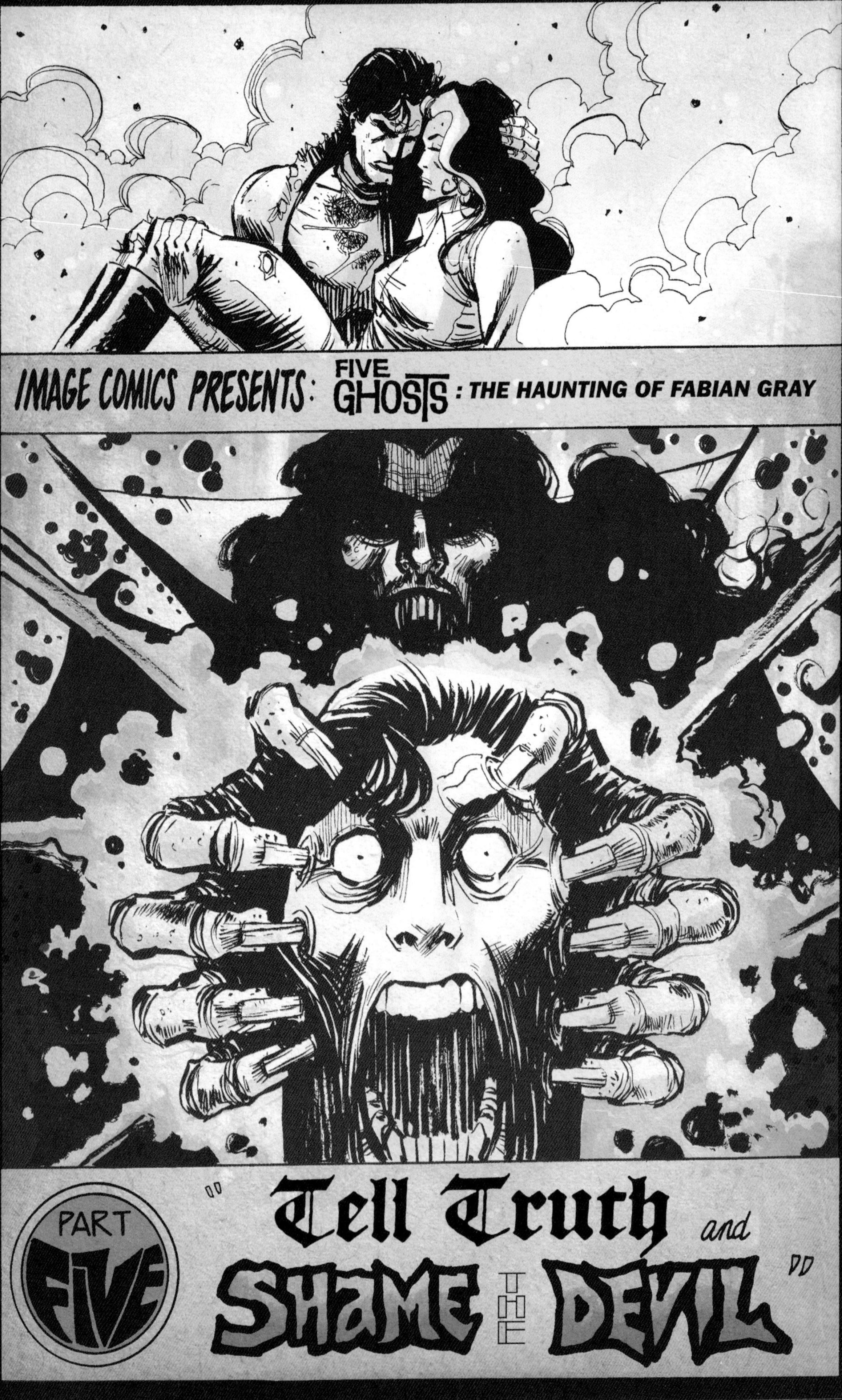
IMAGE COMICS PRESENTS: FIVE GHOSTS : THE HAUNTING OF FABIAN GRAY
PART FIVE
"Tell Truth and SHAME THE DEVIL"

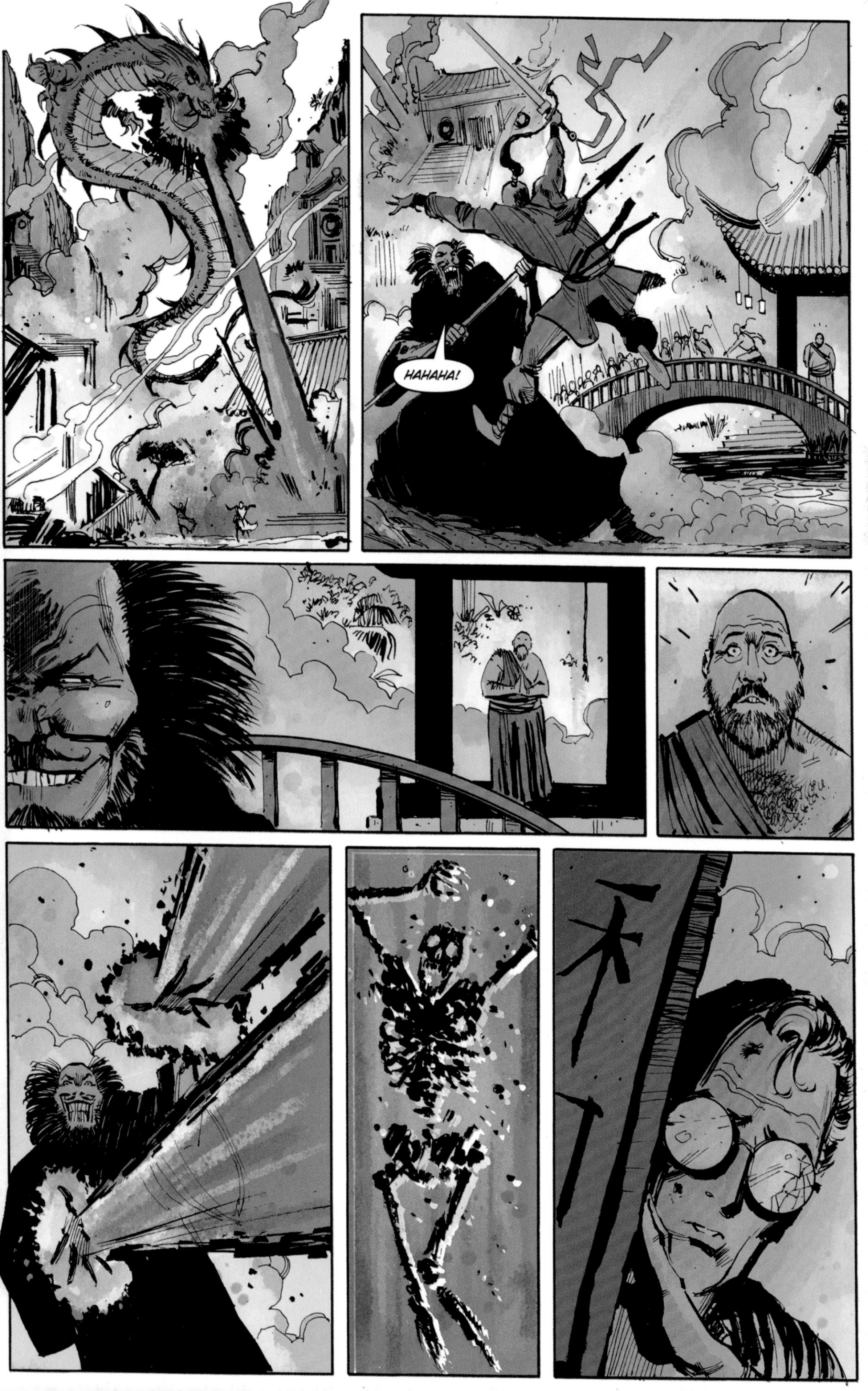
HAHAHA!

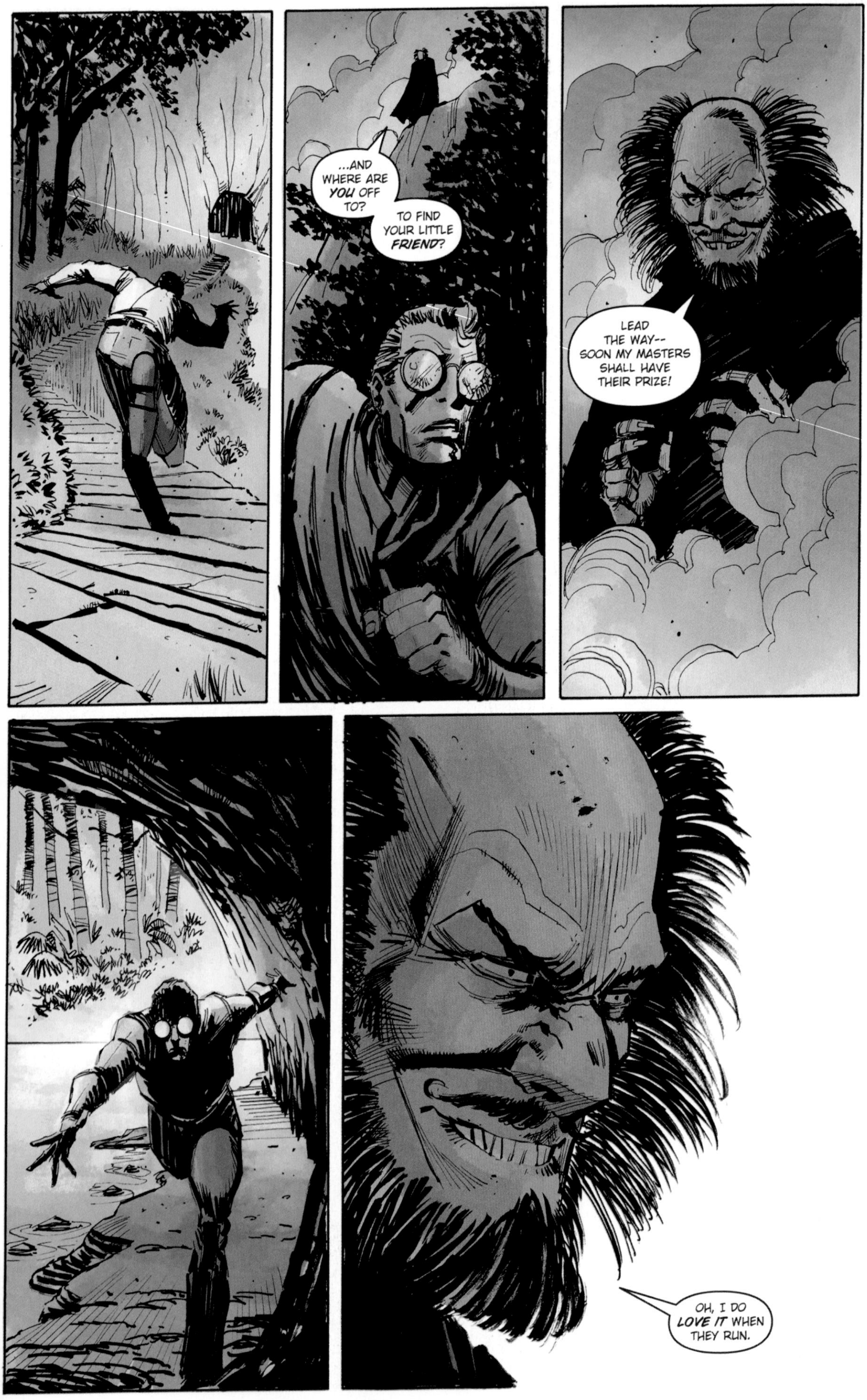
...AND WHERE ARE YOU OFF TO?
TO FIND YOUR LITTLE FRIEND?
LEAD THE WAY-- SOON MY MASTERS SHALL HAVE THEIR PRIZE!
OH, I DO LOVE IT WHEN THEY RUN.

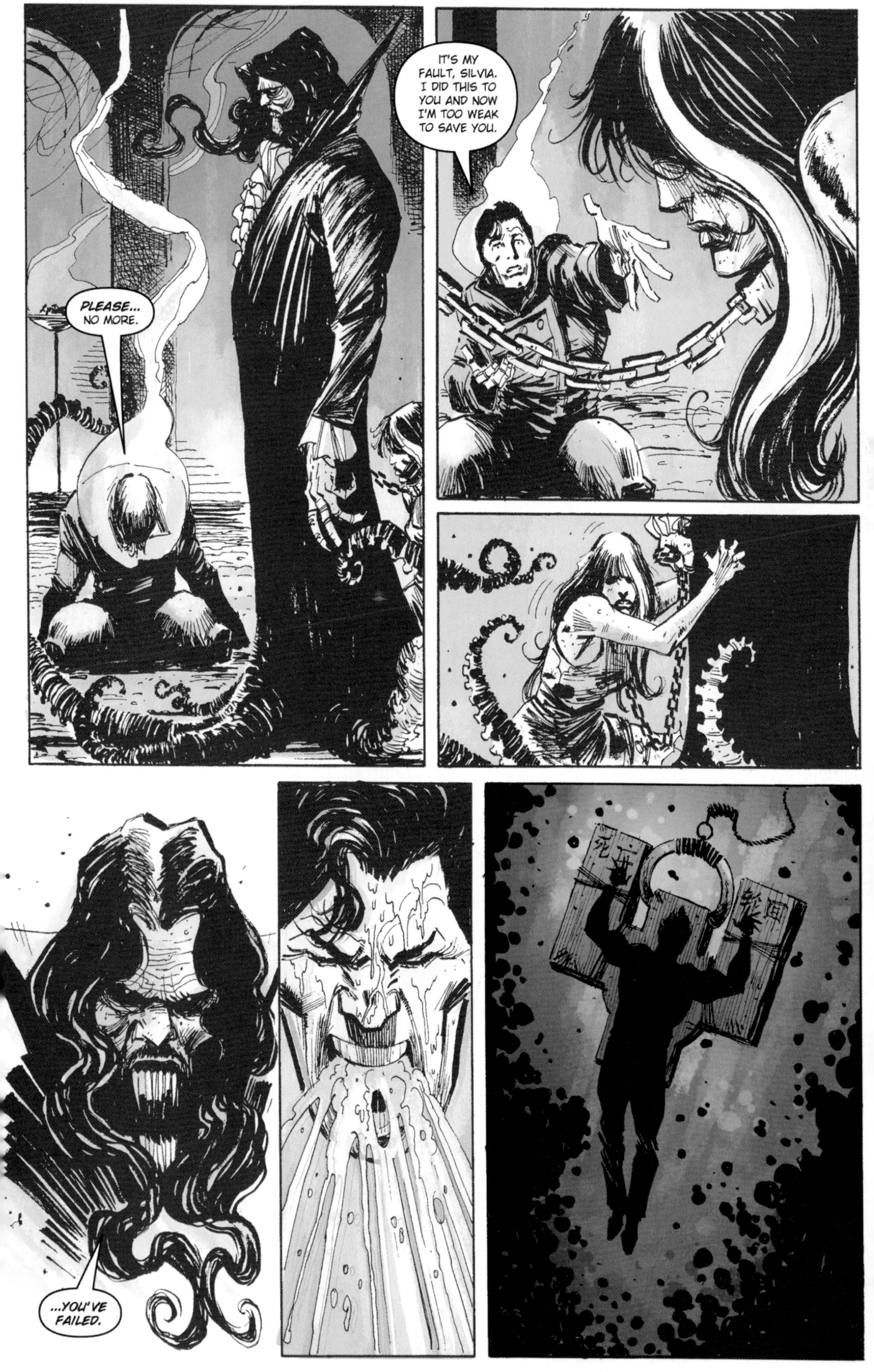
PLEASE... NO MORE.
IT'S MY FAULT, SILVIA. I DID THIS TO YOU AND NOW I'M TOO WEAK TO SAVE YOU.
...YOU'VE FAILED.

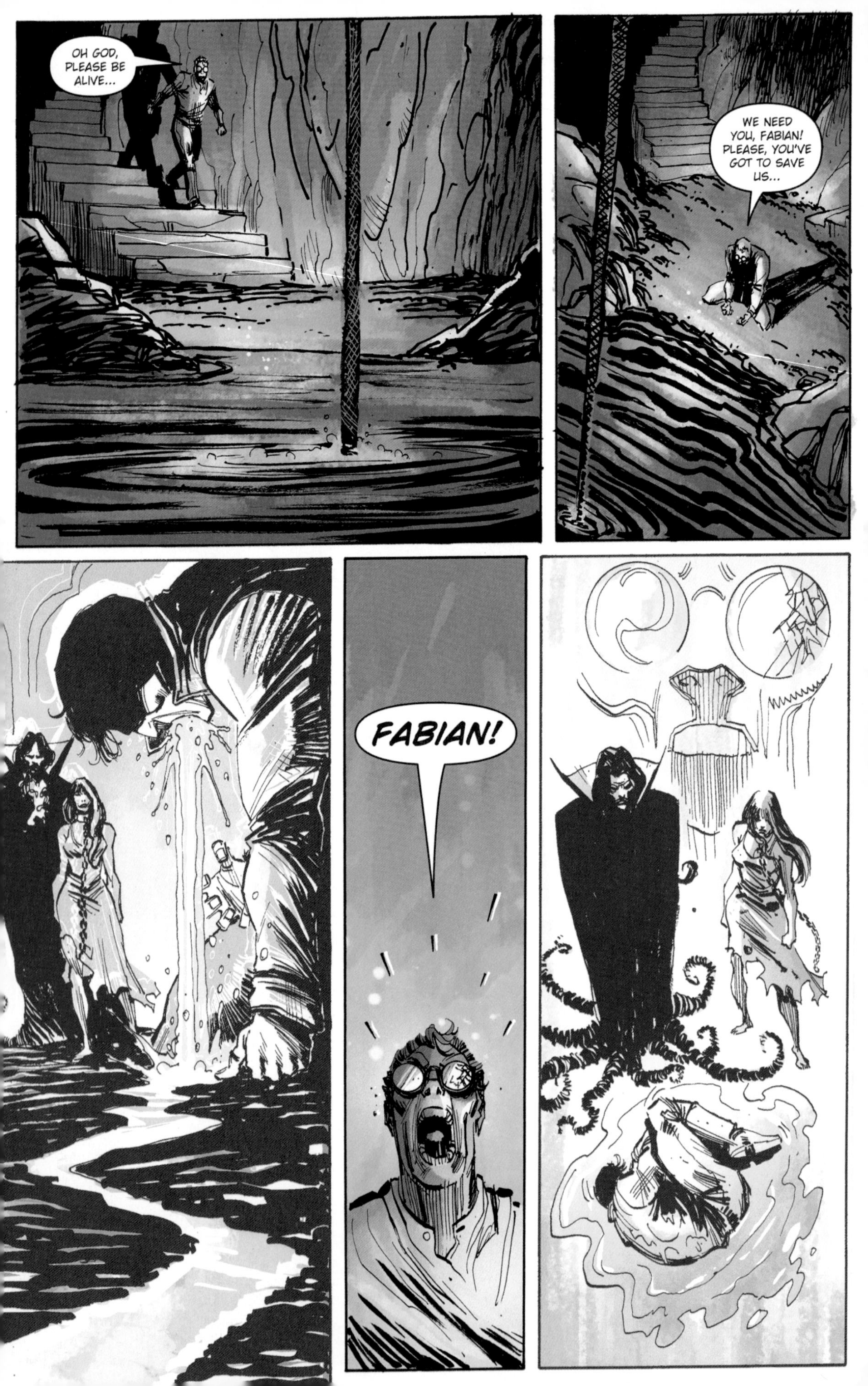
OH GOD, PLEASE BE ALIVE...
WE NEED YOU, FABIAN! PLEASE, YOU'VE GOT TO SAVE US...
FABIAN!

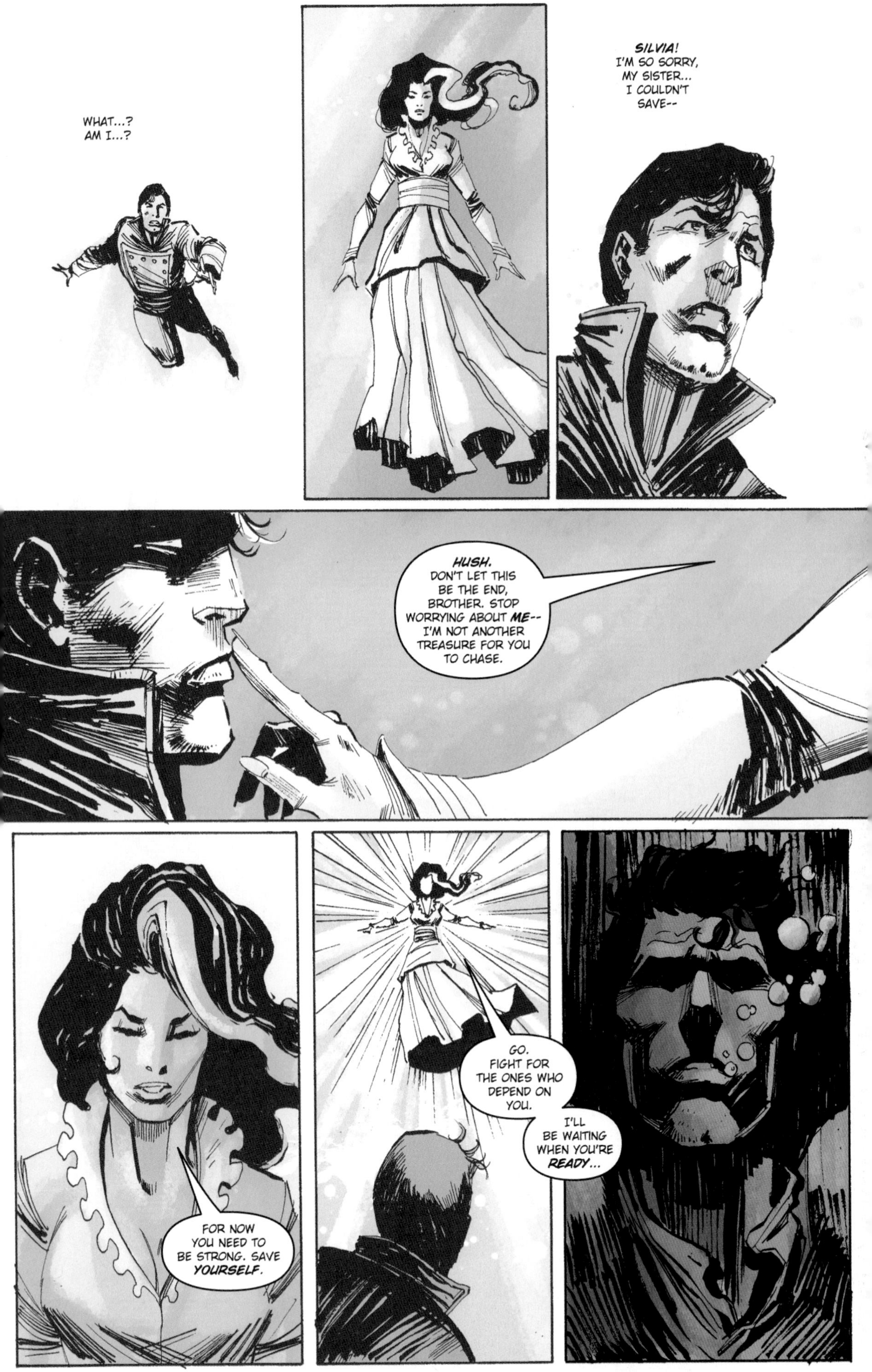
WHAT...? AM I...?
SILVIA! I'M SO SORRY, MY SISTER... I COULDN'T SAVE--
HUSH. DON'T LET THIS BE THE END, BROTHER. STOP WORRYING ABOUT ME-- I'M NOT ANOTHER TREASURE FOR YOU TO CHASE.
FOR NOW YOU NEED TO BE STRONG. SAVE YOURSELF.
GO. FIGHT FOR THE ONES WHO DEPEND ON YOU.
I'LL BE WAITING WHEN YOU'RE READY...

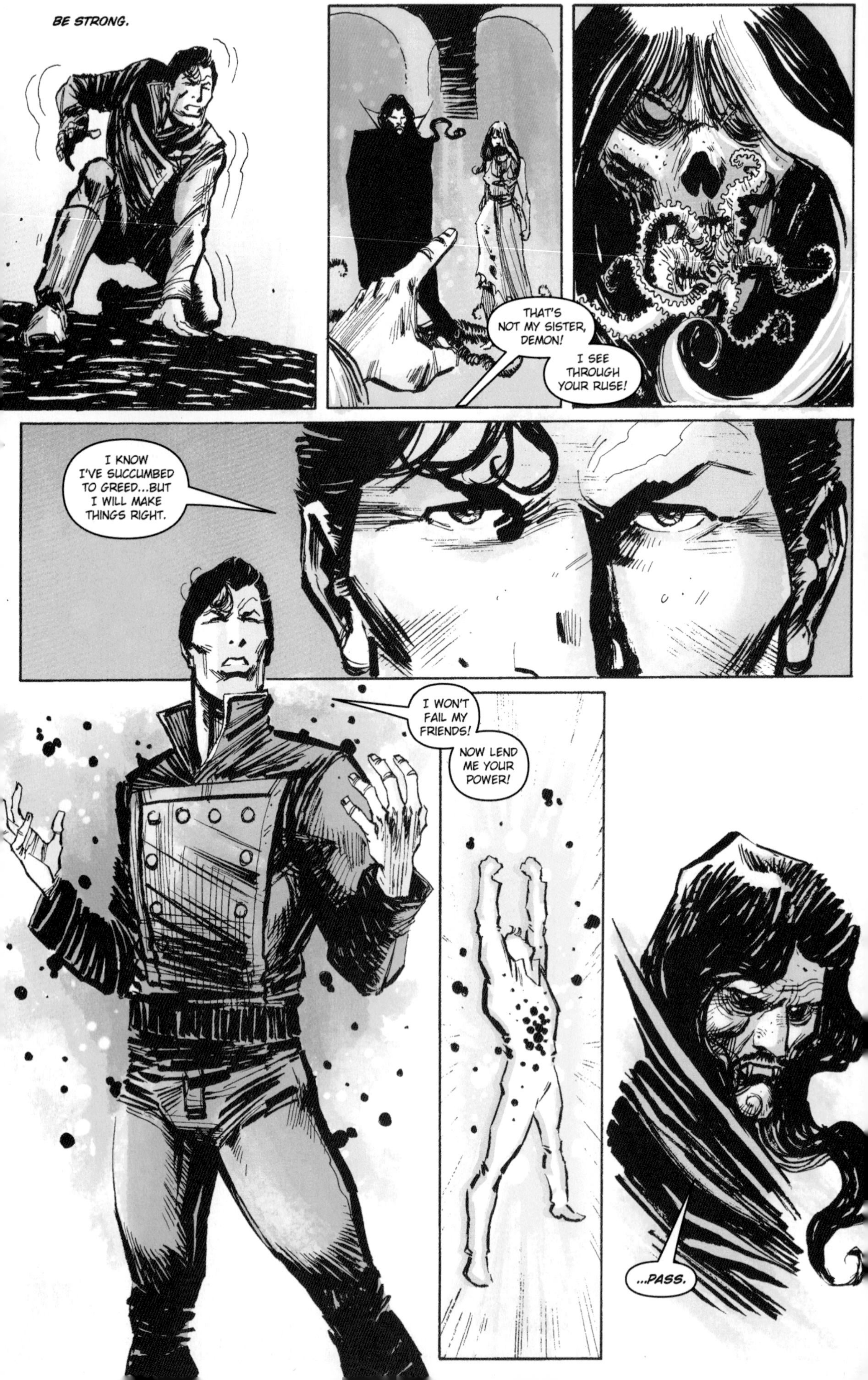
BE STRONG.
THAT'S NOT MY SISTER, DEMON!
I SEE THROUGH YOUR RUSE!
I KNOW I'VE SUCCUMBED TO GREED...BUT I WILL MAKE THINGS RIGHT.
I WON'T FAIL MY FRIENDS!
NOW LEND ME YOUR POWER!
...PASS.

PLATE No. 2

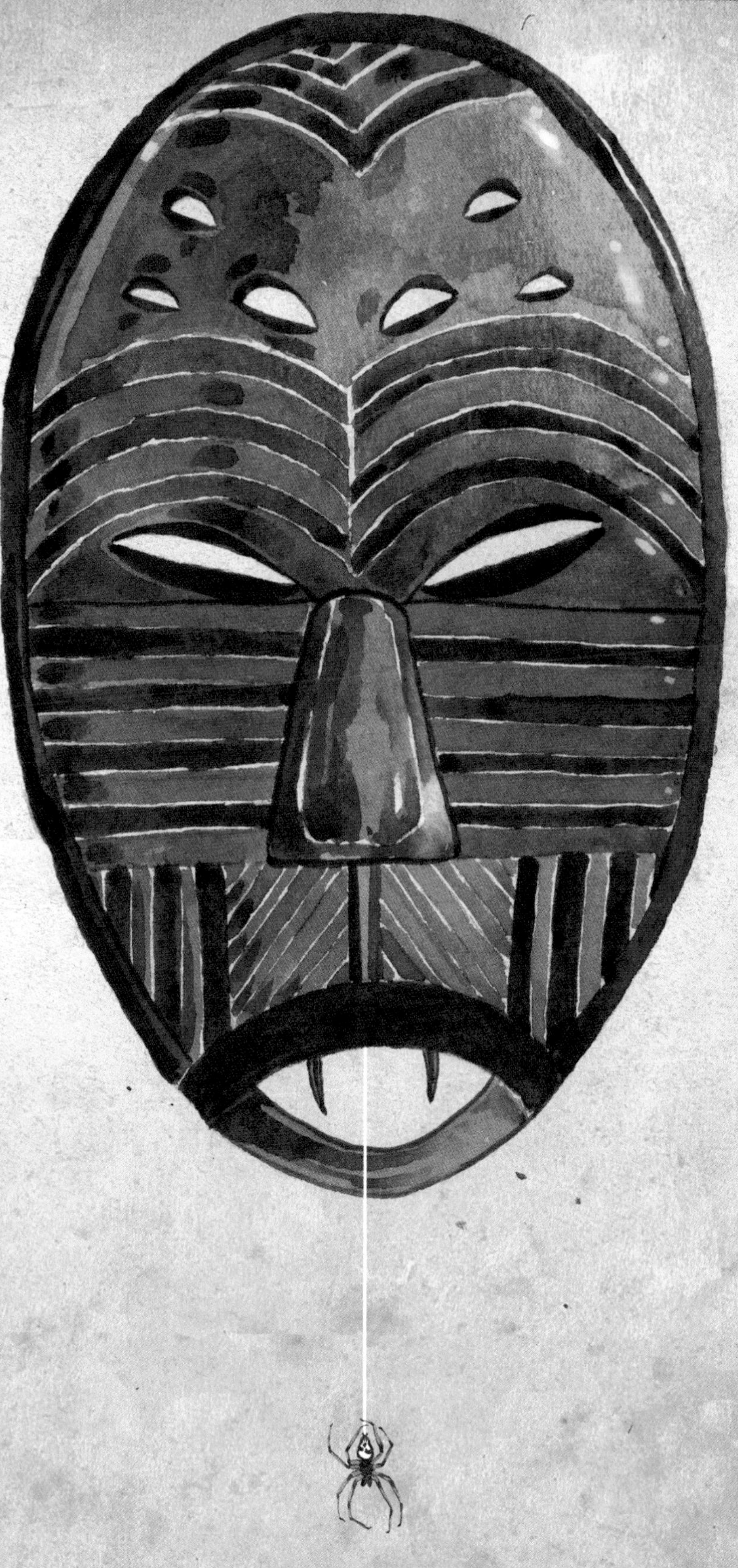

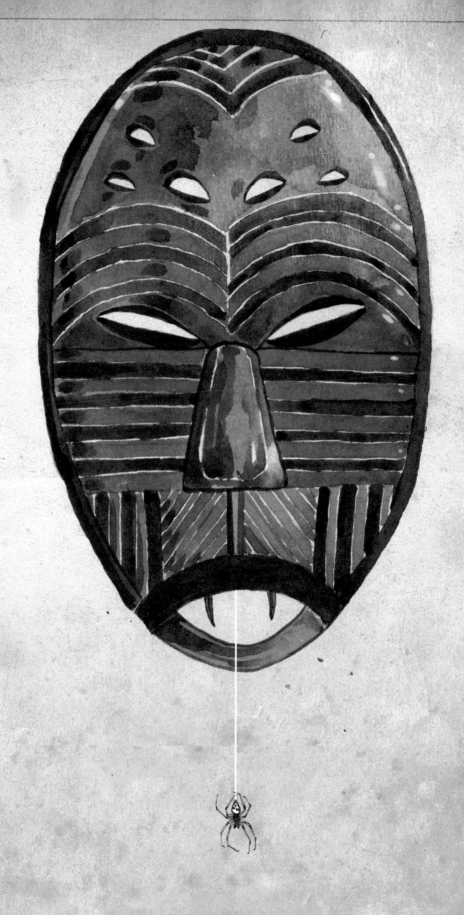

S.M. Vidaurri

FRANK J. BARBIERE IS A WRITER FROM BROOKLYN. HE IS A FORMER ENGLISH TEACHER AND A GRADUATE OF RUTGERS UNIVERSITY & THE GRADUATE SCHOOL OF EDUCATION. HIS WORK HAS BEEN FEATURED IN THE PAGES OF ***DARK HORSE PRESENTS*** AND HE IS CURRENTLY WRITING ***BLACKOUT*** AND ***THE WHITE SUITS*** FOR ***DARK HORSE COMICS***.

HTTP://WWW.ATLASINCOGNITA.COM
@ATLASINCOGNITA

CHRIS MOONEYHAM GRADUATED FROM THE JOE KUBERT SCHOOL OF CARTOON AND GRAPHIC ART IN 2010. HE LIVES IN WISCONSIN AND READS COMICS. THE END.

HTTP://MOONEYHAM.TUMBLR.COM
@CTMOONEYHAM

FIVE GHOSTS CREATED BY BARBIERE & MOONEYHAM
AN ATLAS INCOGNITA PRODUCTION